THE BOOTLEGGER

AN ISAAC BELL ADVENTURE

THE BOOTLEGGER

CLIVE CUSSLER
AND JUSTIN SCOTT

LARGE PRINT PRESS
A part of Gale, Cengage Learning

GALE
CENGAGE Learning·

Farmington Hills, Mich • San Francisco • New York • Waterville, Maine
Meriden, Conn • Mason, Ohio • Chicago

GALE
CENGAGE Learning

Copyright © 2014 by Sandecker, RLLLP.
Interior illustrations by Roland Dahlquist.
Large Print Press, a part of Gale, Cengage Learning.

LIBRARY OF CONGRESS CATALOGING-IN-PUBLICATION DATA

Cussler, Clive.
    The bootlegger : an Isaac Bell adventure / by Clive Cussler and Justin Scott. — Large print edition.
    pages ; cm. (Wheeler publishing large print hardcover)
    ISBN 978-1-4104-6403-3 (hardcover) — ISBN 1-4104-6403-2 (hardcover)
    1. Bell, Isaac (Fictitious character)—Fiction. 2. Private investigators—Fiction. 3. Prohibition—Fiction. 4. Large type books. I. Scott, Justin. II. Title.
PS3553.U75B66 2014b
813'.54—dc23   2014001020

ISBN 13: 978-1-59413-836-2 (pbk.)
ISBN 10: 1-59413-836-2 (pbk.)

Published in 2015 by arrangement with G. P. Putnam's Sons, a member of Penguin Group (USA) LLC, a Penguin Random House Company

For Janet

■ ■ ■ ■

Book One:
Rum Row

1921

■ ■ ■ ■

Bell Disguised as a Bootlegger

1

Two men in expensive clothes, a bootlegger and his bodyguard, dangled a bellboy upside down from the Hotel Gotham's parapet.

The bodyguard held him by his ankles, nineteen stories above 55th Street. It was night. No one saw, and the boy's screams were drowned out by the Fifth Avenue buses, the El thundering up Sixth, and trolley bells clanging on Madison.

The bootlegger shouted down at him, "Every bellhop in the hotel sells my booze! Whatsamatter with you?"

Church spires and mansion turrets reached for him like teeth.

"Last chance, sonny."

A tall man in a summer suit glided silently across the roof. He drew a Browning automatic from his coat and a throwing knife from his boot. He mounted the parapet and pressed the pistol to the bodyguard's temple.

"Hold tight."

The bodyguard froze. The bootlegger shrank from the blade pricking his throat.

"Who the —"

"Isaac Bell. Van Dorn Agency. Sling him in on the count of two."

"If you shoot, we drop him."

"You'll have holes in your heads before he passes the eighteenth floor . . . On my count: One! Pull him up. Two! Swing him over the edge . . . Lay him on the roof — Are you O.K., son?"

The bellboy had tears in his eyes. He nodded, head bobbing like a puppet.

"Go downstairs," Isaac Bell told him, sliding his knife back in his boot and shifting the automatic to his left hand. "Tell your boss Chief Investigator Bell said to give you the week off and a fifty-dollar bonus for standing up to bootleggers."

The bodyguard chose his moment well. When the tall detective reached down to help the boy stand, he swung a heavy, ring-studded fist. Skillfully thrown with the full power of a big man's muscle behind it, it was blocked before it traveled four inches.

A bone-cracking counterpunch staggered him. His knees buckled and he collapsed on the tar. The bootlegger shot empty hands into the sky. "O.K., O.K."

10

■ ■ ■ ■

The Van Dorn Detective Agency — an operation with field offices in every city in the country and many abroad — maintained warm relations with the police. But Isaac Bell spotted trouble when he walked into the 54th Street precinct house.

The desk sergeant couldn't meet his eye.

Bell reached across the high desk to shake his hand anyway. This particular sergeant's father, retired roundsman Paddy O'Riordan, augmented his pension as a part-time night watchman for Van Dorn Protective Services.

"How's your dad?"

Paddy was doing fine.

"Any chance of interviewing the bootlegger we caught at the Gotham?"

"The big guy's at the hospital getting his jaw wired."

"I want the little one, the boss."

"Surety company paid his bond."

Bell was incensed. "*Bail?* For attempted murder?"

"They expect the protection they pay for," said Sergeant O'Riordan, poker-faced. "What I would do next time, Mr. Bell, instead of calling us, throw them in the river."

Bell watched for the cop's reaction when he replied, "I reckoned Coasties would fish them out."

O'Riordan agreed with a world-weary "Yeah," confirming the rumors that even some officers of the United States Coast Guard — the arm of the Treasury Department charged with enforcing Prohibition at sea — were in the bootleggers' pockets.

Starting this afternoon, thought Bell, the Van Dorns would put a stop to that.

One big hand firm on the throttle of his S-1 Flying Yacht, the other on the wheel, Isaac Bell began racing down the East River for take-off speed. He dodged a railcar float and steered into a rapidly narrowing slot between a tugboat pushing a fleet of coal barges and another towing a bright red barge of dynamite. Joseph Van Dorn, the burly, scarlet-whiskered founder of the detective agency, sat beside him in the open cockpit, lost in thought.

The Greenpoint ferry surged out of the 23rd Street Terminal straight in their path. The sight of the slab-sided vessel, suddenly enormous in their windshield, made Joseph Van Dorn sit up straight. A brave and cool-headed man, he asked, "Do we have time to stop?"

Bell shoved his throttle wide open.

The Liberty engine mounted behind them on the wing thundered.

He hauled hard on the wheel.

The Loening S-1 held speed and altitude records but was notoriously slow to respond to the controls. Bell had replaced its stick and pedals with a combined steering and elevating Blériot wheel, in hopes of making it nimbler.

Passengers on the Greenpoint ferry backed from the rail.

Bell gave the wheel one last firm tug.

The Flying Yacht lunged off the water and cleared the ferry with a foot to spare.

"There ought to be a law against flying like you," said Van Dorn.

Bell flew under the Williamsburg Bridge and between the spotting masts of a battleship docked at the Navy Yard. "Sorry to distract you from your dire thoughts."

"You'll distract us both to kingdom come."

Bell headed across leaf-green Brooklyn at one hundred twenty miles an hour.

Van Dorn resumed pondering how to deal with misfortune.

The World War had upended his agency. Some of his best detectives had been killed fighting in the trenches. Others died shockingly young in the influenza epidemic. A post-war recession in the business world was bankrupting clients. And only yesterday, Isaac Bell had discovered that bootleggers, who were getting rich quick off Prohibition by bribing cops and politicians, had corrupted two of his best house detectives at the Hotel Gotham.

Bell climbed to three thousand feet before they reached the Rockaways. Where the white sand beach slid into the ocean like a flaying knife, he turned and headed east above the string of barrier islands that sheltered Long Island from the raw fury of the Atlantic. A booze smugglers' paradise of hidden bays and marshes, inlets, creeks and canals stretched in the lee of those islands as far as he could see.

Thirty miles from New York, he banked the plane out over the steel-blue ocean and began to descend.

"Can I come in the launch, Chief?"

Seaman Third Class Asa Somers, the youngest sailor on the Coast Guard cutter CG-9, was beside himself. He had finally made it to sea, patrolling the Fire Island coast for rumrunners on a ship with a cannon and machine guns. Now the fastest flying boat in the world — a high-wing pusher monoplane — was looping down from the sky. And if the roar of its four-hundred-horsepower Liberty motor wasn't thrilling enough, it was bringing a famous crime fighter he'd read about in *Boys' Life* and the *Police Gazette* — Mr. Joseph Van Dorn, whose army of private detectives vowed: "We never give up! Never!"

"What's got you all stirred up?" growled the white-haired chief petty officer.

"I want to meet Mr. Van Dorn when he lands."

"He ain't gonna land."

"Why not?"

"Open your eyes, boy. See that swell? Four-foot seas'll kick that flying boat ass over teakettle."

"Maybe he'll give it a whirl," Somers said, with little hope. *Flight Magazine* praised the S-1's speed a lot more than its handling.

"If he does," said the chief, "you can come in the launch to pick up the bodies."

Up on the flying bridge, CG-9's skipper expressed the same opinion.

"Stand by with grappling hooks."

The flying boat circled lower. When it whipped past, skimming wave tops, Somers recognized Van Dorn, who was seated beside the pilot in the glass-surrounded, open-roofed cockpit, by his red whiskers

15

bristling in the slipstream.

The roar of the big twelve-cylinder engine faded to a whisper.

"Lunatic," growled the chief.

But young Somers watched the Air Yacht's ailerons. The wing flaps fluttered up and down almost faster than the eye could see as the pilot fought to keep her on an even keel. Back in her tail unit, the horizontal stabilizer bit the air, and down she came, steady as a locomotive on rails. Her long V-shaped hull touched the water, flaring a vapor-thin wake. Her wing floats skimmed the swell, and she settled lightly.

"Somers! Man the bow line."

The boy leaped into the launch and they motored across the hundred yards that separated the cutter and the flying boat. The huge four-bladed propeller behind the wing stopped spinning, and the pilot, who had made an almost impossible landing look easy, climbed down from the cockpit onto the running board that extended around the front of the rocking hull. He was a tall, lean, fair-haired man with a no-nonsense expression on his handsome face. His golden hair and thick mustache were impeccably groomed. His tailored suit and the broad-brimmed hat pulled tight on his head were both white.

16

Somers dropped the bow line.

"What in blazes are you doing?" bellowed the chief.

"I bet that's Isaac Bell!"

"I don't care if it's Mary Pickford! Don't foul that line!"

The boy re-coiled the line, his gaze locked on the pilot. It had to be him. Bell's picture was never in a magazine. But reports on Van Dorn always mentioned his chief investigator's white suit and it suddenly struck Somers that the camera-shy detective could go incognito in a flash simply by changing his clothes.

"Heave a line, son!" he called. "Come on, you can do it — on the jump!"

Somers remembered to let the coil reel out of his palm as the chief had taught him. To his eternal gratitude the rope fell into Bell's big hand.

"Good shot." He pulled the plane and the boat together.

Somers asked, "Are you Isaac Bell, sir?"

"I'm his butler. Mum's the word — Bell is still passed out in a speakeasy. Now, let's get Mr. Van Dorn into your boat without dropping him in the drink. Ready?"

Bell reached to help Van Dorn, a heavily built man in his fifties with a prominent roman nose and hooded eyes. Van Dorn ignored Bell's hand. Bell seized his elbow and guided him toward Somers with a conspiratorial grin.

"Hang on tight, son, he's not as spry as he looks."

Behind his grin, Bell's blue eyes were cool and alert. He watched carefully as the older man stepped between the bouncing craft, and he relaxed only after Somers had him safely aboard.

"What's your name, sailor?" asked Van Dorn in a voice that had the faintest lilt of an Irish accent.

"Seaman Third Class Asa Somers, sir."

"Lied about your age?"

"How did you know?" Somers whispered.

"I worked that dodge to join the Marines." He shot a thumbs-up toward the stern. "All aboard, Chief. Back to the ship."

"Aye, sir."

The boat wheeled away from the seaplane.

Van Dorn called to Bell, "Watch yourself at the Gotham. Don't forget, those shameless SOBs have fifty pounds on you."

If a mountain lion could smile, thought Asa Somers, it would smile like Isaac Bell when he answered, "Forget? Never."

Joseph Van Dorn cast a skeptical eye on CG-9, a surplus submarine chaser the U.S.

Navy had palmed off on the Coast Guard for Prohibition patrol. With a crow's nest above a flying bridge, six-cylinder gasoline engines driving triple screws, and a three-inch Poole gun mounted on the foredeck, she had been built to spot, chase, and sink slow-moving German U-boats — not fast rumrunners.

She'd been worked hard in the war and scantly maintained since. The drone of pumps told him that her wooden hull had worked open many a leak. Her motor valves were chattering, even at half speed. She would still pack a punch with the Poole gun and a brace of .30-06 Lewis machine guns on the bridge wings. But even if she somehow managed to get in range of a rumrunner, who was trained to fire them?

Her middle-aged skipper was pouch-eyed and red-nosed. Her aged chief petty officer looked like a Spanish-American War vet. And the crew — with the exception of young Somers, who had scrambled eagerly up the mast to the lookout perch in the crow's nest as soon as they shipped the launch — were pretty much the quality Van Dorn expected of recruits paid twenty-one dollars a month.

The skipper greeted him warily.

Van Dorn disarmed him with the amiable

smile that had sent many a criminal to the penitentiary wondering why he had allowed this jovial gent close enough to clamp a steely hand on the scruff of his neck. A twinkle in the eye and a warm chortle in the voice fostered the notion of an easygoing fellow.

"I suppose your commandant told you the Treasury Department hired my detective agency to recommend how better to combat the illegal liquor traffic. But I bet scuttlebutt says we're investigating who's in cahoots with the bootleggers — pocketing bribes to look the other way."

"They don't have to bribe us. They outrun us, and they outnumber us. Or someone — I'm not saying who 'cause I don't know who — tips them where we're patrolling. Or they radio false distress calls; we're supposed to save lives, so we steam to the rescue, leaving our station wide open. If we happen to catch 'em, the courts turn 'em loose and they buy their speedboats back at government auction."

Van Dorn took a fresh look at the skipper. Maybe his nose was red from a head cold. Drinking man or not, he sounded genuinely indignant and fed up. Who could blame him?

In the year since Prohibition — the banning of the sale of alcohol by the Eighteenth Amendment to the Constitution and the Volstead Act — it seemed half the country had agreed to break the law. Millions of people would pay handsomely for a drink. Short of striking oil or gold in your backyard, there was no way to get rich quicker than to sell hooch. All you needed was a boat you could run a few miles offshore to a rum fleet of foreign-registered freighters and schooners anchored beyond the law in international waters. The newspapers had made a hero of Bill McCoy, captain of a schooner registered in the British Bahama Islands. He had come up with the scheme for circumventing the law, which made enforcing Prohibition a mug's game.

"Like the song says" — Van Dorn recited a lyric from Irving Berlin's latest hit — " 'You cannot make your shimmy shake on tea.' How fast are the taxis?"

While fishermen and yacht owners sailed out to the rum fleet to buy a few bottles, big business was conducted by "taxis" or "contact boats" — high-powered, shallow-draft vessels in which professional rumrunners smuggled hundreds of cases ashore to bootleggers who paid top dollar.

"They build 'em faster every day."

Van Dorn shook his head, feigning dismay.

Isaac Bell had already convinced him to recommend flying-boat patrols, though God knows who would pay for them. Congress banned booze but failed to cough up money for enforcement.

"Taxi!"

All eyes shot to the crow's nest.

Joseph Van Dorn whipped a pair of binoculars from his voluminous overcoat and focused in the direction Asa Somers was pointing his telescope. Low in the water and painted as gray as the sea and the sky, the rum boat was barely visible at a thousand yards.

"Full speed!" ordered the skipper, and bounded up the ladder to the flying bridge atop the wheelhouse. Van Dorn climbed heavily after him.

The engines ground harder. Valves stormed louder. The subchaser dug her stern in and boiled a white wake. "Fifteen knots," said the skipper.

Subchasers had been built to do eighteen, but the oily blue smoke spewing from her exhaust ports told Van Dorn her worn engines were pushing their limits. Their quarry was overloaded, with its gunnels almost submerged, but it was churning along at seventeen or eighteen knots and growing fainter in the distance.

"Gunner! Put a shot across his bow."

The Poole gun barked, shaking the deck. It was not apparent through Van Dorn's powerful glasses where the cannon shell landed, but it was nowhere near the rum boat's bow. The gunners landed their second shot closer. He saw it splash, but the boat continued to pull ahead.

Suddenly, just as it seemed the rummy would disappear in the failing light of evening, they got a break. The taxi slowed. She had hit something in the water, the skipper speculated, or thrown a prop, or blown a cylinder. Whatever had gone wrong on the heavily laden boat, the subchaser caught up slowly.

"They'll dump the booze and run for it," said the skipper.

Van Dorn adjusted his binoculars. But he saw no frantic figures throwing contraband overboard. The boat just kept running for the night.

"Gunner! Another across his bow."

The Poole gun shook the deck again, and a shell splashed in front of the rumrunner. "They'll pull up now."

The warning shot had no effect and the rumrunner kept going.

Van Dorn made a quick count of the cases

of whisky he saw heaped on deck, estimated the amount she could hold belowdecks, and calculated a minimum cargo of five hundred cases. If the bottles contained the "real Mc-Coy" — authentic Scotch that had not been stretched or doctored with cheap grain alcohol — the boatload was worth thirty thousand dollars. To the crew of a rum boat, who before Prohibition had barely eked out a living catching fish, it was a fortune that might make them more brave than sensible. For thirty thousand dollars, six bootleggers could buy a Cadillac or a Rolls-Royce, a Marmon or a Minerva. For the fishermen's families it meant snug cottages and steady food on the table.

The skipper switched on an electric siren. CG-9 screamed like a banshee. Still, the rum boat ran. "They're crazy. Fire again!" the skipper shouted down to the gun crew. "Get 'em wet!"

The shell hit the water close enough to spray the crew. The rum boat stopped abruptly and turned one hundred eighty degrees to face the subchaser that was bearing down on them in a cloud of blue smoke.

"Stand by, Lewis guns!"

Grinning Coasties hunched over the drum-fed machine guns mounted on pedestals each side of the wheelhouse. Van Dorn reckoned that good sense would prevail at last. The Lewis was a wonderful weapon — fast-firing, rarely jamming, and highly accurate. Rumrunners could be expected to throw their hands in the air before the range got any shorter and let their lawyers spring them. Instead, when the cutter closed to a hundred yards, they started shooting.

Shouts of surprise rang out on the Coast Guard boat.

A rifle slug crackled past the mast, a foot from Van Dorn's head. Another clanged off a ventilator cowling and ricocheted against the cannon on the foredeck, scattering the gun crew, who dived for cover. Van Dorn whipped his Colt .45 automatic from his coat, rammed his shoulder against the mast to counter the cutter's roll, and took careful aim for a very long pistol shot. Just as he found the distant rifleman in his sights, a third rifle slug struck the Coastie manning the starboard Lewis gun and tumbled him off the back of the wing to the main deck.

The big detective climbed down the ladder as fast as he could and squeezed into the wing. He jerked back the machine gun's slide with his left hand and triggered a three-shot burst with his right. Wood flew from the taxi's cabin, inches from the rifleman. Three more and the rifle flew from his hands.

"Another taxi!" came Asa Somers's high-pitched yell from the crow's nest. "Another taxi, astern."

Van Dorn concentrated on clearing the rumrunner's cockpit. He directed a stream of .30-06 slugs that made a believer of the helmsman, who let go the wheel and flung himself flat.

Somers yelled again, "Taxi coming up behind us!"

Fear in the boy's voice made Van Dorn look back.

A long, low black boat was closing fast. Van Dorn had never seen a boat so fast. Forty knots at least. Fifty miles per hour. Thunder chorused from multiple exhaust manifolds. Three dozen straight pipes lanced orange flame into the sky. Triple Liberty motors, massed in a row, each one as powerful as the turbo-supercharged L-12 on Isaac's flying boat, spewed the fiery blast.

The gun crew on the foredeck couldn't see it.

Charging from behind, slicing the seas like a knife, the black boat turned as the subchaser turned, holding the angle that screened it from the cannon. The port machine gunner couldn't see it either, blocked by the wheelhouse. But Joseph Van Dorn could. He pivoted the Lewis gun and opened fire.

The vessel began weaving, jinking sharply left and right, agile as a dragonfly.

A cold smile darkened Van Dorn's face.

"O.K., boys. That's how you want it?" He pointed the Lewis gun straight down the middle of the weaving path and fired in bursts, peppering the black boat with a hundred rounds in ten seconds. Nearly half his shots hit. But to Van Dorn's amazement, they bounced off, and he realized, too late, that she was armored with steel sheathing.

He raked the glass windshield behind which the helmsman crouched. The glass starred but did not shatter. Bulletproof. These boys had come prepared. Then the black boat fired back.

It, too, had a Lewis gun. Hidden below the deck, it pivoted up on a hinged mount, and Van Dorn saw in an instant that the fellow firing it knew his business. Scores of bullets drilled through the subchaser's wooden hull right under where he manned his gun and riddled the chest-high canvas that protected the bridge wing from wind and spray. Van Dorn fired long bursts back. A cool, detached side of his mind marveled that he had not been hit by the withering fire.

Something smacked his chest hard as a thrown cobblestone.

Suddenly, he was falling over the rim of the bridge wing and plummeting toward the deck. The analytical side of his brain noted that the taxi they were chasing was speeding away, covered by machine-gun fire from the black boat, and that, as he fell, the Coast Guard cutter was wheeling to bring the Poole gun to bear. In turning her flank to the seas, she took a wave broadside and heeled steeply to starboard, so that when he finally landed it was not on the narrow deck but on the safety railing that surrounded it. The taut wire cable broke his fall and bounced him overboard into bitter cold water. The last thing he heard was Asa Somers's shrill, *"Mr. Van Dorn!"*

2

"Powwow in the alley. Hancock, you cover."

Isaac Bell appeared to wander casually through the Hotel Gotham's sumptuous lobby. Four well-dressed house detectives drifted quietly after him, a smooth exodus unnoticed by the paying guests. When all four had assembled in the dark and narrow kitchen alley out back, Bell addressed two by name.

"Clayton. Ellis."

Tom Clayton and Ed Ellis were typical Van Dorn Protective Services house dicks — tall, broad-shouldered heavyweights, not as sharp as full-fledged detectives but handsome as the Arrow Collar Man. Tricked out in a decent suit, clean white shirt, polished shoes, and four-in-hand necktie, neither of the former Southern Pacific Railroad detectives appeared out of place in an expensive hotel. But pickpockets, sneak thieves, and confidence men recognized bruisers to steer clear of.

"What's up, Mr. Bell?"

"You're fired."

"What for?" Clayton demanded.

"You sullied the name of the Van Dorn Agency."

" 'Sullied'?" Clayton smirked at his sidekick. " 'Sullied'?"

Ellis said, "I'm with you, pal. 'Sullied'?"

Bell stifled his impulse to floor them both. The others in their squad had resisted taking bribes. For the good of the agency, he seized the opportunity to remind the honest ones what was at stake and to give them courage to resist temptation. So he answered the mocking question, calmly.

"Mr. Van Dorn built a top-notch outfit that spans the continent. We have offices in every city linked by private telegraph and long-distance telephone. We have hundreds of crack detectives — valuable men who know their business — and thousands of Protective Services boys guarding banks and jewelry shops, escorting bullion shipments, and standing watch in the finest hotels. But the outfit isn't worth a plugged nickel if clients can't trust our good name. Van Dorns do not accept graft. You did. You sullied our good name. That is what 'sullied' means, and that is why you are fired."

"Listen here, Mr. Bell, it's human nature to share the wealth. The bootleggers are hauling it in."

Ellis chimed in. "The bellhops get their cut delivering bottles to the guests and it's only fair we get our cut for allowing the booze in the door."

"Not every bellhop."

Clayton and Ellis traded a cagy glance. They knew what had happened.

"The bootlegger you took bribes from tried to throw a boy off the roof last night. That boy's employer, Hotel Gotham, pays us to protect their property, their guests, and their workers. You two let that boy down. Don't let me see you near this hotel ever again."

"Are you threatening us?"

"Spot on, mister. Get lost."

Clayton and Ellis stepped closer, light on their feet for big men. The honest house dicks exchanged looks, wondering if they should come to the chief investigator's defense. Bell stayed them with a quick gesture. A barely perceptible hunch of his shoulder telegraphed a roundhouse right to end the scrap before it started.

Clayton saw it coming. He stepped lithely to his right. The by-the-book evasive move had the unexpected effect of driving his chin straight into Bell's left, which rose from his knee like a wrecking ball and tossed the house dick backwards.

Ellis was already piling on, swinging a quicksilver left too powerful to block. Bell slipped it over his shoulder and returned a right cross to the side of Ellis's head, which slammed him across the alley into Clayton, who was clinging to the wall.

Containing his anger, Isaac Bell said, "If I ever see you on the streets of New York, I'll throw you in the Hudson River."

"Mr. Bell! Mr. Bell!"

A Van Dorn apprentice — a fresh-faced kid of eighteen — burst from the kitchen door. "Mr. Bell. Mr. Van Dorn was shot!"

"What?"

Isaac Bell turned in horror toward the piping voice, so stricken that he failed to register the boy's eyes tracking sudden motion.

Ellis had launched a powerful right hook. Bell succeeded in rolling with part of it, but enough glancing drive landed to knock him off his feet. He sprawled on the greasy concrete. Clayton bounded at him like a placekicker, reared back for maximum power, and launched a boot at his head. Bell tried to block it with his hand, but the boot brushed it aside and came straight at his face. Bell caught Clayton's ankle in his other hand, held tight with all his strength, and surged to his feet in a double explosion of fury and despair.

He hoisted Clayton's leg high above his shoulder, dumped him backwards to the concrete, and whirled to meet Ellis's next punch, a pile-driver left aimed straight at his jaw. Bell ducked under it. Ellis's balled knuckles burned across his scalp. He ducked lower, seized Ellis, and used the heavier man's momentum to drive him at Clayton, who was rising to his feet. The house dicks' faces met nose to nose, mashing cartilage and cracking bone. Bell dropped Ellis in a moaning heap and gripped the apprentice's shoulder with an iron hand.

"Where is he?"

"Bellevue."

Bell took a deep breath and braced himself. "Hospital? Or morgue?"

"Hospital."

"Let's go! The rest of you, back to work. Tell Hancock he's in charge."

The boy had the wit to have a cab waiting.

Bell questioned him closely as it raced across Midtown. But all anyone knew so far was that sometime after Isaac Bell put Joseph Van Dorn aboard the Coast Guard

33

cutter, the Boss had been wounded in a gun battle with rumrunners. Bell thought, fleetingly, that he was probably tying up his Loening at the 31st Street Air Service Terminal when it happened.

"How did they get him ashore so quickly?"

What Joe would call the luck of the Irish had come to his rescue. An alert shore operator had relayed the Coast Guard radio report to the New York Police Department, and the Harbor Squad had dispatched a fast launch, which was already patrolling for rummies off Sandy Hook. It rendezvoused with the much slower cutter and raced Van Dorn up the East River to Bellevue Hospital. Bell would have preferred a hospital with more renowned surgeons than practiced at the overworked, understaffed municipal hospital, but the cops had chosen the one closest to the river.

"Soon as you drop me, take the cab straight back to the office. Tell Detective McKinney that I said that all hands are to hunt the criminals who attacked Mr. Van Dorn." Darren McKinney was a young firecracker Van Dorn had brought up from Washington to run the New York field office.

"Tell him I said to call in markers from every bootlegger in the city; one of them

34

will hear who did it. Tell him to look for a shot-up rum boat. And tell him to look for wounded in the hospitals."

The cab screeched to a stop on smoking tires.

"Off you go! On the jump!"

Bell stormed into the hospital lobby.

At the desk, they told him that Joseph Van Dorn was in the operating room.

"How bad is he?"

"Three of our top surgeons are attending him."

Bell steadied himself on the desk. Three? What grievous wounds would require three?

"Has anyone called his wife?"

"Mrs. Van Dorn is in a waiting room. Would you like to see her?"

"Of course."

A grim-faced receptionist led Bell to a private waiting room.

Dorothy Van Dorn fell into his arms. "Oh, Isaac. It can't be."

She was considerably younger than Joe, a brilliantly educated raven-haired beauty, the daughter of the Washington Navy Yard's legendary dreadnaught gun builder Arthur Langner, the widow of naval architect Farley Kent. Dorothy had been at Smith College with Joe's first wife, who died of pneumonia. Bell had watched with joy when

35

what had seemed a commonsensical cou-
pling of widowed parents with young chil-
dren blossomed into a marriage that
brought unexpected passion to the prim Van
Dorn and a longed-for steadiness to the
tempestuous Dorothy.

"Isaac, what was a man his age doing in a
gunfight?"

There were several answers, none of which
would help. There was no point in assuring
his terrified wife that Joe Van Dorn was the
steadiest of men in a gunfight, ever cool,
alert, and deadly. Nor did Bell see any
purpose in relating that his only fear when
he put him aboard a United States Coast
Guard cutter armed with two machine guns
and a cannon was an accidental dunking.
Now, of course, he wished he had insisted
that Joe take a man with him. There was
plenty of room in the Loening's four-
passenger cabin. He could have assigned a
couple of men to look out for him.

"I don't know yet what happened."

"Who shot him?"

"We're already investigating. I'll know
soon."

He hugged her close, then let go to shake
hands with Joe's oldest friend who had accompanied Dorothy to the hospital. Captain
Dave Novicki, broad and sturdy as a moor-

ing bollard, was a retired ocean mariner. He had taken Joe under his wing years ago when he was a junior officer on the immigrant boat that brought the teenage Van Dorn to America. Bell had met Novicki often at Thanksgiving dinners in the Van Dorns' Murray Hill town house. Joe credited the crusty old sailor's steady influence for much of his success, just as Bell credited Van Dorn's guidance for much of his.

"Thanks for coming," he said to Bell.

Bell motioned Novicki aside to ask in a low voice, "How bad is he?"

"Touch and go. The chief doc promised a progress report in an hour. Two hours ago."

A terrible hour passed. All looked up when a nurse came in. She whispered to Isaac Bell that there was a telephone call for him in the lobby. They handed him a phone at the reception desk. "McKinney?"

"Right here, Mr. Bell."

"What do we have?"

"Ed Tobin found the boat the Coasties were chasing. Half-sunk near the Chelsea Piers. Not the boat that shot him. The taxi they were chasing."

Tobin was a veteran of the New York field office's Gang Squad and a blood relative of Staten Island families of watermen and coal pirates. As such, Ed Tobin knew the harbor better than the Harbor Squad.

"Booze mostly gone. Looks like they off-loaded into smaller boats. Ed says the cops claim they caught one in the East River."

"Anyone show up shot in any hospitals?"

"We're checking every hospital from Bay Shore, Long Island, to Brooklyn, to Staten Island, to Manhattan. Nothing yet."

"No gunshot wounds in any?"

"None that don't have a good story attached."

"Tell me the stories."

"Two guys who plugged each other disputing the right to sell beer to Bensonhurst speakeasies. Guy in a Herald Square hooch hole shot by his girlfriend for two-timing her. Guy in Roosevelt Hospital shot on the El. That's it so far, but the night is young."

"Who shot the guy on the El?"

"Got away. Cops found him alone."

"Which El? Ninth Avenue?"

"Right. Cops took him to the closest hospital."

"Cops? Why not ambulance?"

"He was walking under his own steam. Cops found him stumbling down from the Church stop at Saint Paul's. You know, at 59th?"

"I know where it is."

The Ninth Avenue Elevated Line, which

ran right beside Roosevelt Hospital, started all the way downtown at South Ferry at the edge of the harbor and passed through Chelsea on the way up. A wounded rum-runner could just possibly have come ashore at either of those points and made it to the train.

McKinney said, "I'll send the boys back to Roosevelt."

"No. I'll do it." It was a very slim chance. But it beat hanging around helpless to do anything for Joe Van Dorn.

"How's the Boss?" McKinney asked.

"I don't know yet. They're operating."

"Of all the crazy things . . ."

"What do you mean?"

"That Mr. Van Dorn happened to be there, on that cutter, of all patrols. How many bootleggers go to the trouble of shoot-ing at the Coast Guard? Anyone with half a brain knows it's safer to surrender and let your lawyers bust you loose."

"Good question," said Bell. He hurried back to the waiting room, thinking that Joe had indeed run into an unlikely piece of bad luck. As McKinney said, most rumrun-ners knew it was not worth risking their lives in a shoot-out with the Coast Guard.

Still no word from the surgeons. Bell asked Dorothy, "Are you all right here?

There's something I have to look into." She was deathly pale, and he could see she was nearing the end of her rope.

Captain Novicki flung a brawny arm around her shoulders and boomed, "You get the louses who shot him, Isaac. I'll look after Dorothy and Joe like a mother bear."

Isaac Bell flagged a cab and raced across town through light late-night traffic. It was less than fifteen minutes from Bellevue to Roosevelt Hospital, a giant three-hundred-fifty-bed red brick building. The hospital and the fortresslike Roman Catholic church of St. Paul the Apostle stood between the Irish and Negro slums of Hell's Kitchen to the south and San Juan Hill to the north. "Blind pigs," windowless illegal drinking parlors, darkened the ground floors of tenements. A train rattled overhead as he ran under the El and into the hospital. He gave the front-desk receptionist a look at his gold Van Dorn chief investigator badge, slipped him five dollars, and asked to speak with the patient admitted earlier with a gunshot wound.

"Top floor," the receptionist told him. "Last room at the end of the hall. Private room, with a police guard."

"How badly is he wounded?"

40

"He made it under his own steam."

In the elevator, Bell folded a sawbuck for the cop.

The elevator opened on the soapy odor of a freshly mopped floor. The hall was empty, the tiles glistening.

Bell hurried down the long corridor. The elevator scissored shut behind him.

Ahead, he heard the sharp bang of a small-caliber pistol.

He ran toward the sound, pulling his Browning from his shoulder holster, and rounded the corner. He saw a stairwell door to his left. The door to the room to his right was half open. He heard a loud groan and saw on the floor blue-uniformed trouser legs and scuffed black brogans. Cop shoes. He pushed inside. A New York Police Department officer lay on his back, holding his head, eyes squeezed shut. He groaned again, "It hoits awful."

On the bed, a blond-haired man in hospital garb lay on his side, curled like a fetus, his chin tucked tightly to his chest. The gunshot Bell had heard had been fired point-blank. A tiny red hole half the diameter of a dime pierced the back of his neck, with a ring of blood seared around the rim.

41

3

The window was open.

Bell thrust his head out. The square top of St. Paul's south tower stood at eye level across the street. Beneath the window, the hospital's sheer façade dropped twelve stories to the pavement.

He ran to the stairwell, opened the fire door, and listened for footsteps. Silence. Had the killer stopped some floors down? He couldn't have reached the ground floor yet. Had he bolted out of the stairwell into a lower corridor? Had he climbed the stairs to the roof?

Pistol in hand, Bell raced up the flight, pushed through a door onto the tar-surfaced roof. A smoky sky reflected the dim lights of the neighborhood. Elevator-machine penthouses, stairwell penthouses, and chimneys loomed in the dark. Skylights cast up electric light from the rooms under them. He listened. Far below, another El rattled past. A shadow flickered behind the glow of a skylight, and Bell sprang after it.

He ran in silence, footfalls light on the soft tar, saw the shadow pass another skylight, and put on a burst of speed. He was twenty feet behind when the figure ahead stopped abruptly and whirled around.

Bell dived through the air, tucked his shoulder, clasped his gun to his torso, and rolled as he hit the tar. Two shots cracked in rapid succession, and lead flew through the space he had occupied an instant before.

The killer ducked behind an elevator house.

Bell ran around the other side. He saw a flash of light. A stairwell door opened just wide enough for a man. Bell pegged a shot at the strong, supple, reptilian silhouette, but it slipped away with fluid grace.

He ran to the door, ducked low, and yanked it open. He heard the running man's boots pounding the stairs and plunged after him down two switchback flights. A foot-long brass nozzle flew at his head, swung from a canvas fire hose. Bell ducked under it. It clanged on the steel banister and bounced back at his face. He twisted aside, but in avoiding the heavy nozzle, he lost his footing and fell to one knee. Disoriented for a second, he sensed the man brush him.

Two shots exploded loudly in the confined space, echoed to the roof and down to the cellar. Two slugs buried themselves in plaster beside his head.

Bell jumped to his feet and tore after the killer.

Suddenly, he had a clear shot. For a precious instant he was looking straight down at the crown of the man's flat cap. He aimed his Browning, the modified No. 2 that he had carried for years. At this range he could not miss. He turned smoothly to keep the running killer in his line of sight. Gently, he started to squeeze the trigger. As he did, still moving to line up the shot, something bright as snow intruded on his field of fire.

It was a tall white cap of folded linen, the woman wearing it a nurse in a spotless white dress and pinafore apron. He jerked the gun aside and let go the trigger, a hairsbreath between the life and death of an innocent. Two innocents, he realized as he thundered down the stairs: the nurse, and the doctor who had been embracing her in the privacy of the stairwell and now was shielding her with his body.

"It's not what you think," cried the doctor.

Bell heard glass shatter below and

pounded past them.

Three flights down, the stairs were dark. His boots crunched on broken glass. The killer had smashed the lights. Bell charged down the stairs into the dark. He stumbled, tripped up by a fire hose draped shin-high between the banisters. He snagged a banister with one hand, righted himself, and kept going.

Forced to go slowly in the dark, he heard a door slam. He climbed down two more flights. There was light again, marking where the killer had stopped breaking bulbs and exited the stairwell. He pushed through a door and found himself abruptly outside, bursting into an alley between the hospital and a stable — one of the many on Manhattan Island's West Side that had not yet been converted to an auto garage. There was a tang of manure in the air and a sweet smell of straw.

The alley led to 58th Street, a long block of tenements. The sidewalks were deserted at this hour, the buildings' windows mostly dark. The killer could have run into any of a score of doorways or ducked into a blind pig on Ninth Avenue to the east or Tenth Avenue to the west. The stable door was wide open. He ran inside. A night watchman and a groom were seated on beer kegs, playing checkers on a whisky barrel. The killer would have had to run past them to hide in the stable.

Bell wasted no time in plunking down the folded sawbuck meant for the cop. "You boys see a man with a gun run by?"

"Nope," said the groom.

"Didn't even see a man without a gun," said the watchman. He looked pointedly at Bell's pistol and asked, "Friend of yours?"

"Get out of his way and give a shout if you see him coming."

Over on Ninth Avenue, another El screeched into the Church station. If the killer was already vaulting up the steps to take the train, Bell knew he could never catch up before it left the station. He backed onto the side way, stymied, and looked around. Fifty feet down the block he saw an incongruous sight, a Packard Twin Six town car. The chauffeur was just closing the front hood. He stepped back into the car and started the motor.

Bell holstered his weapon and hurried toward the car, straightening his coat.

As he approached, a side window in the passenger cabin lowered.

Expecting at this hour and in this neighborhood a wealthy old man calling on his mistress or visiting a brothel, Bell was surprised to see a beautiful young woman in a sleeveless sheath dress. She had strings of Baltic amber beads around her neck, a long cigarette holder perched in her fingers, and a cloche hat on her bobbed chestnut hair.

He reached automatically to sweep his hat off his head. He had lost it in the chase.

She had almond eyes, a mischievous smile, and a lovely contralto voice. The gin on her breath was the good stuff, not bathtub. "You look like a gentleman who can't find a taxi."

"Did you see a man run past moments ago?"

"No."

"No one? Either side of the street?"

"Let me ask my driver. He was fiddling with the motor." She swiveled a voice tube to her Cupid's bow lips. "Did you see a man run past moments ago?"

She held the tube to her ear, then she turned back to Bell. "I'm sorry. He didn't either. I wish I could help you. Although . . ." Another smile. "The car's running again. If you truly need a taxi, I can offer you a ride."

Bell looked up and down the street. He hadn't a hope of finding him. His best bet was to go back to the hospital on the chance the cop had caught a close look at who banged him on his head.

"If I see him, should I —"

"Don't go near him."

"I won't," she promised. "I meant, if I should see him, I can report him to you. You should give me your card."

Bell gave her his Van Dorn Detective Agency business card and introduced himself. "Isaac Bell."

"A detective? I suppose that makes him a criminal."

"He just shot a man."

"You don't say!" She fished her own card from a tiny clutch and extended her hand. "Pleased to meet you, Mr. Bell. I'm Fern Hawley."

Bell knew her name from the society columns, and her family's name as well, having attended college in the city of New Haven. She was the sole heir of a Connecticut hardware-and-firearms magnate. And he was familiar with her sort, having been in France in the latter days of the war when independent, adventurous American heiresses indulged by their fathers — or left their own fortunes by their mothers and were therefore under the thumb of no man — flocked to Paris. Many came to do good, nursing the wounded or feeding starving refugees. Many had come to have a good time, run around with European aristocrats, and pay the rent for bohemian painters and writers.

He wondered why she had been on this slum street when her limousine broke down, but the fact was, New York's wealthy young went where they pleased. Possibly headed to West 54th, where Park Avenue society "rubbernecked" at the drunks and brawlers marched through Men's Night Court. Or exiting a side door from a private visit with a hospital patient.

"Are you sure I can't offer you a ride, Mr. Bell?"

"Thank you, Miss Hawley, but not tonight." He glanced up and down the street again. Back to the hospital to interview the cop before his sergeant arrived.

"Good night." Fern Hawley tapped the chauffeur's partition with her cigarette holder. The Packard Twin Six glided from the curb and turned uptown on Tenth Avenue.

Fern Hawley opened the chauffeur's partition and said, "I tried. The man just would not get in the car."

"Have you lost your touch?"

"Don't make me laugh . . . Is Johann all right?"

"Dead."

"*Dead?* How can Johann be dead? He walked into the hospital on his own two legs."

Marat Zolner pulled off his visored chauffeur hat and dropped it beside his pistol. His hair was soaked with perspiration and he was breathing hard from running.

"The detective shot him," he told her.

4

The cop guarding the murdered rumrunner had not seen the man who knocked him for a loop. That was all that Bell could learn from the angry police detectives swarming the hospital. A uniformed officer gave him his hat, which he had found in the stairwell. His derringer was still in it. Bell thanked him with a double sawbuck and raced back to Bellevue Hospital.

Joe Van Dorn was finally out of surgery.

The exhausted surgeons made no promises. "If he makes it through the next hour, he'll have a chance in the hour after that. At least he's strong. I can't recall a man his age so fit."

"Heart like a cathedral bell!" boomed Captain Novicki with a reassuring glance at Dorothy Van Dorn.

Dorothy asked, "How many bullets?"

"Madam," said the surgeon. "This is hardly the time nor place, nor a topic to discuss with a woman."

"My father was a scientist and an engineer. We discussed his work daily. I am asking you how many bullets struck my husband, where the bullets hit, and their effect on his condition."

The chief surgeon looked at Isaac Bell.

Bell said, "Answer her."

"All right. He was struck three times. One creased his skull and almost certainly produced a concussion. Two more passed through him. One pierced his upper arm, fortunately missed the bone, but severed the artery. The other punctured his chest. They were small bore rounds with a hard covering to take the grooves in the rifled barrel, which increased their penetrating power, so neither lodged in his body . . . Shall I go on?"

"How did he survive a severed artery?"

"The petty officer on the Coast Guard cutter arrested the hemorrhage by tourniquet."

"And the bullet through his chest?"

The surgeon shook his head. "We did what we could. To some extent, the bullet pushed blood vessels, tendons, and ligaments aside. Immersion in salt water reduces the probability of septic infection. And the petty officer poured iodine over and around the wounds. We are of the impression that the cold seawater had the effect of slowing his heartbeat and lowering his blood pressure at that critical moment, which might possibly explain the miracle that he is alive."

"Thank you, Doctor. May I see him now?"

"You may sit with him. I doubt he'll speak yet. If he does, don't tax him."

Dorothy went into the room. A disapproving nurse moved from the chair beside the bed to a chair in the corner.

Bell and Novicki waited outside.

"Doctor?" Bell called as the surgeon was leaving. "You mentioned he was in the water. Any idea how he got out?"

"They said a Coast Guardsman dived in after him."

Captain Novicki watched the surgeon shamble away. "There's a man who needs a stiff drink and a good night's sleep. Did you have any luck?"

"Caught up with one of the crew from the rum boat they were chasing. He died."

"Good."

Not at all good, thought Bell. The dead man could shed no light on his gang. He said, "We found the boat shot up. That's about it. I'll try to interview the Coast Guard people in the morning."

"Get some sleep, Isaac. I'll stay here."

"In a while."

"Isaac! He's awake. He's asking for you."

Bell stepped silently into the room. Van Dorn lay flat on his back, his eyes closed, his cheeks oddly slack, and it took Bell a moment to realize they had shaved his beard and whiskers. His head was bandaged from crown to eyebrows. The biceps of his left arm wore another bandage, as did the crook of his right elbow where the tubing for blood transfusions had been inserted into his vein. Just visible below the hospital bed-sheet was the top of an enormous dressing that encircled his chest. His eyes were closed. His lips were moving.

"Put your ear to him," Dorothy whispered. "He's trying to speak to you."

Bell leaned close to do as she asked.

"Isaac."

"I'm here, sir."

"Listen."

"Right here."

"You must . . ."

Bell looked at Dorothy. "We shouldn't tax him. He should rest."

"Listen!" she shot back. "He won't rest until he talks to you."

Isaac Bell spoke in normal tones. "I'm

here, Joe. What do you want me to do?"

"Protect the outfit," Van Dorn whispered.

"Yes, sir."

"It's in worse shape than I am."

"You'll be fine."

"Stop lying. I'm touch and go. So's the outfit . . . I lost Justice."

Bell knew he meant his longtime contract to help the Department of Justice pursue bank robbers, motorcar thieves, and white slavers across state lines. He was not surprised. The Bureau of Investigation had greatly increased its force of special agents during the war and consequently was no longer willing to pay for nationwide investigations by a transcontinental detective agency.

Bell said, "We knew that was coming."

Van Dorn whispered, "Treasury threw me a bone."

He meant, of course, the Coast Guard contract that had gotten him shot. A favor from one of Joe's many Washington friends, it would be canceled tomorrow morning when officials demanded to know why a civilian detective was in a gunfight on a Coast Guard vessel. No matter that investigating who in the Guard took bribes from bootleggers was for the good of the Service, the contract was lost.

But that was the least of the agency's troubles.

Bell leaned closer.

"How'd you make out with Ellis and Clayton?"

"They're leaving town."

"Iceberg," Van Dorn whispered.

The nurse jumped up. "That's enough. He's hallucinating."

"No he's not," said Bell. He nodded sharply at Novicki to get the nurse out of his way. Van Dorn was saying that his life's work was threatened by the corrupting effect of Prohibition. Two house dicks taking bribes were only the tip of the iceberg. The new men replacing detectives lost to the war and the flu pandemic were susceptible to corruption. And when the word about him firing Ellis and Clayton got around, how many Protective Services boys would quit to sign on with less scrupulous agencies with lower standards?

"Isaac."

"Right here."

"I'm counting on you . . . Protect the agency."

"Rest easy," said Bell. But he had his work cut out for him. It was less a matter of protecting the agency than saving it.

5

Haig & Haig Scotch whisky, twenty thousand cases in a freighter from Glasgow, landed in British colonial territory at the Bahaman port of Nassau. Import duty was paid and the whisky was locked in bonded warehouses. Six thousand of the cases were sold to the captain of the Bahamas-registered staysail schooner *Ling Ling*. He paid the export duty and cast off immediately for Long Island's Rum Row.

During the warm and pleasant Gulf Stream sail north, *Ling Ling*'s crew worked on deck. The contents of twelve thousand bottles were stretched — doubled to twenty-four thousand — by mixing the authentic Haig & Haig with grain alcohol and distilled water and adding tea for color. They pasted counterfeit labels that guaranteed the contents on the extra bottles and sealed them with corks boiled in tea to make them look old. Then they repackaged the bottles in ham-shaped burlap bags holding six each, padded with straw, for ease of handling.

Ling Ling arrived off Fire Island on a dark night when the Coast Guard cutter CG-9 was picketing the schooner *Aresthusa,* steaming circles around it to keep taxis from picking up booze. A few miles away, flat-bottom boats slipped alongside *Ling Ling.* They loaded a thousand "hams" and sped to Fire Island, keeping a sharp eye peeled for "Prohibition Navy" patrols and for hijackers. Approaching the beach, they waited for the lights of a foot patrol to pass by. Then they landed in the surf, several miles east of the Blue Point Coast Guard Station.

The hams of Haig & Haig were loaded into carts that men trundled across the narrow island on a boardwalk laid in the soft sand. Fishing boats with oversize engines raced them five miles across Great South Bay and up an unlit channel and into a narrow creek. Cars and trucks were waiting at a dock just beyond the bright lights of a rambling wood-frame hotel. Music and laughter drifted across the marsh from which the creek had been dredged.

The Haig & Haig was quickly moved off the boats into the cars and trucks. The hotel's handyman and dishwasher helped

58

with the loading and were rewarded with a bottle each. Farm trucks, laundry trucks, and milk and grocery vans hurried off in various directions. Some small cars followed, Fords and Chevrolets with hidden compartments for their owners to smuggle a dozen bottles.

Last to leave were the big cars driven by professional bootleggers. Buicks, Packards, and Cadillacs — with seats removed to make more room for the Haig & Haig and with heavy-duty springs added to carry and conceal the extra weight — formed a convoy on the Montauk Highway and headed west toward New York City, seventy miles away.

The two-lane, all-weather road was dark. The towns it passed through were small, consisting of little more than a white church and a shuttered general store or filling station. They drove fast with their lights off, trusting to a starry sky and a sliver-thin moon.

A town constable and two Prohibition officers spotted the convoy and gave chase in a Ford. The bootleggers in the Buick that was protecting the rear of the convoy saw their headlights.

"Cops?"

"Hijackers?"

Either way, they weren't stopping.

The Prohibition officers started shooting their revolvers.

"Hijackers!" shouted the bootleggers.

"Hold on!" The driver stomped hard on the Buick's four-wheel brakes. The car stopped abruptly. The Ford, equipped only with two-wheel brakes, skidded past, the officers shooting. The Buick's occupants, convinced that the cops were hijackers, opened fire with automatic pistols, wounding the constable.

Ahead lay Patchogue, a fair-size town, with a lace mill, streetlamps, and a business district along the highway, which was renamed Main Street as it passed through. The Women's Christian Temperance Union had called an emergency meeting to denounce the Suffolk County sheriff for failing to arrest the bootleggers who were racing across Long Island nightly. The meeting was running late. The guest speaker — a wealthy duck farmer and a leading light in the Ku Klux Klan, which had declared war on rumrunners and bootleggers — was likening the sheriff to "an un-American Bolshevik," when he was interrupted by a telephone report that an auto chase had resulted in the murder of a constable.

"Men!" bellowed the duck farmer. "If the sheriff won't stop 'em, we will!"

He led a citizens' posse into the street to ambush the bootleggers' autos. The volunteer fire department stretched their hook and ladder across the highway.

The bootleggers, fearing more trouble in a larger, better-lit town, and still fifty long miles from the city, pulled their cars to the side of the road and sent a scout ahead. He reported that the fire department had blocked the highway and citizens were arming themselves with squirrel guns. The drivers turned to the boss — a former stickup man from Brooklyn who had put up the cash on behalf of associates there to buy the Haig & Haig from the fishermen — and hoped he had a plan.

His name was Steven Smith. But his men and the New York police called him Professor Smith, because he was always thinking and could usually be counted upon to come up with some way out of a fix like this one.

"Does the town have a church?" the Professor asked.

"A whole bunch," said the scout.

Professor Smith chose one a distance from Main Street and sent two of his cousins to splash gasoline on the front steps and set it afire. Flames leaped to the steeple. When the fire department ran to put it out, and the citizens followed to watch, three Buicks, a Cadillac, and a Packard raced on toward New York with their Haig & Haig.

Hours later, the Brooklyn bootleggers finally felt close enough to New York to sigh in relief. Almost home. Less than a mile to the garage that the Professor had rented under the Fulton Street Elevated.

Marat Zolner had a five-ton Army truck that had been modified with a bigger motor and pneumatic tires. When fully loaded, it still wouldn't top thirty-five miles an hour, but whoever chased it would have to contend with five armed men wearing blue uniforms in the Oldsmobile behind it.

"What's taking them so long?" asked Zolner's driver, a member of a once powerful, now rapidly fading West Side gang called the Gophers. The driver knew the tall, lean Marat Zolner only as Matt, who hired him often for high-paying jobs.

They had parked under the El and had been sitting there for hours. The driver was jumpy. Marat Zolner was patient, an icy presence in the shadows, unmoving, yet taut as a steel spring.

"They might have broken down. They might have run into cops. They might have run into someone who wanted to take it away from them."

"Like us," the driver snickered.

"Here they come."

Five big town cars weighted down with heavy loads were pulling up, drivers blinking headlights for their garage to open its door, unaware that the man inside was tied up with a gag in his mouth. Zolner waved to his men in the Oldsmobile and they piled out with guns drawn.

The driver of the Cadillac stopped short. "This don't look good."

"Relax," said Professor Smith. "It's only cops."

"I thought you paid them off."

Suddenly, Smith didn't like the look of this either. He said, "I did."

"Looks like they want a raise."

"I don't think they're cops," he said too late. The sight of the uniforms had discouraged the bootleggers from pulling their guns. Now guns were pointed in their faces and pressed to their temples. Smith saw no way out. At best, even if they managed to win a gun battle in the street, the noise would attract the real cops. Even though they had already pocketed his payoff money, they would have no choice but to confiscate his Haig & Haig when a shoot-out woke up the neighborhood.

Smith raised his hands, signaling the others to give up. They were ordered out of the cars and frisked. Their guns were taken away. One of the bogus cops pointed at a five-ton truck parked across the street. "Load the truck."

Again, Smith saw no way out of the fix. The booze was lost. But the hothead in the last Buick, the one who had shot at the Long Island constable's Ford, grabbed for the nearest gun. He was a big man, and fast. He clamped a powerful hand around the phony cop's wrist and squeezed so hard that the man cried out and dropped the gun into the Buick driver's other hand. A hijacker stepped behind him, jammed a pistol against his spine, and pulled the trigger. The driver's body muffled the shot, but it was still loud.

"Load the truck!"

Smith's men rushed to obey before anyone else got shot or the cops came. In less than ten minutes all the cars had been emptied and the five-ton truck was rumbling away on groaning springs, trailed by an Oldsmobile full of exultant gunmen.

Marat Zolner and his driver took the truck across the Brooklyn Bridge, ditched three of the least reliable gunmen, and worked their way uptown, stopping twice to sell Haig & Haig to a speakeasy in the old Tenderloin and a chophouse whose owner was desperately trying to lure back the patrons he had lost to joints serving illegal liquor. The majority of Zolner's haul was destined for popular speakeasies on 52nd and 53rd streets whose customers the newspapers had dubbed "the rich and fast."

The sky was getting bright. It was nearly seven in the morning and people on the sidewalks were heading to work. A cop was waiting outside Tony's.

Marat Zolner said, for the benefit of passersby, "Officer, we have a delivery for this establishment. Could you possibly direct traffic around the truck so we don't jam up the street?"

He slipped the cop a fifty-dollar bill and the cop muttered, "Where you guys been? My shift's almost over."

With the cop overseeing the operation, Marat Zolner's men passed ham after ham of Haig & Haig across the sidewalk and down to the speakeasy's cellar entrance. Zolner carried a leather satchel with gold buckles to the heavy front door and knocked. A peephole opened.

"Joe sent me."

The door swung open. "Hey, pal, how's it going?"

"Long night. How about you?" He handed the bouncer ten dollars.

"We had one for the books. Park Avenue dame lost her pearls on the dance floor. Searched napkins, tablecloths, and floor sweepings. No dice." He lowered his voice. "There's a guy with the boss. I'd look out if I was you."

Zolner pulled a bottle of Haig & Haig from his bag to thank the bouncer for the warning. Then he walked through the empty joint where a sleepy waiter was upending chairs onto tables and knocked on the owner's office door. Tony himself opened it. He looked worried. "Come in," he said. "Come in. How'd you make out?"

"Am I interrupting you?"

"No. No. Just talking to a fellow here who wants to meet you."

Zolner said softly so only Tony could hear, "I know it's not your fault."

"Big of you," Tony muttered back.

"Do me a favor. Count what I brought and hold my money out front." He stepped aside to let Tony pass, then entered the office and shut the door. The office was a small, dingy inside room but furnished comfortably, with a carpet and a leather couch in addition to Tony's desk. A heavy-set thug in a good suit rose from the couch. He was wearing his hat.

"How's it going?"

"Long night," said Zolner as he placed the satchel on the desk.

"I'll let you go in a minute."

"How much?" asked Zolner.

"Half."

"Half? That would make you the richest Dry agent in the country."

"I'm not a Prohibition agent. I'm a businessman and you're doing business on my block. It costs half to do business on my block."

"You're not a government agent?" asked Zolner.

"I just told you."

"I had to be sure," said Zolner. "Half, you say?" He dropped one hand into the satchel and the other into his pocket.

"Half — Hey!"

Zolner had crossed the space between them in a single swift step. He smashed the thug's teeth with a blackjack in his right hand and swung a twelve-inch length of lead pipe against his temple. "Businessman?"

The thug swayed, eyes popped wide, feet frozen to the floor, blood pouring from his mouth. Zolner dropped him to the carpet with a second bone-smashing blow of the lead pipe.

At the front door of the speakeasy he counted the money Tony had waiting, piled it into his satchel, and returned fifty dollars.

"What's this for?"

"You need a new carpet."

Before crossing Central Park to Fern's town house, Zolner made one more stop on the Upper West Side to buy a Prohibition agent breakfast at the Bretton Hall Hotel. For five hundred dollars, the federal officer told him about a government raid planned against a leading whisky runner's downtown warehouse.

"Where will they take the booze?"

"Customs. The Appraisers' Stores, down in the Village."

Zolner passed the agent a bottle wrapped in burlap.

"What's this?"

"The real McCoy. Haig & Haig."

6

"Everyone down here is praying for Mr. Van Dorn . . . Well, not everyone, but you know what I mean."

Dr. Shepherd Nuland, the New York County Medical Examiner, indicated a crowd of unclaimed corpses hanging upright in a refrigerated vault and then shook Isaac Bell's hand warmly. It was an elevator ride and a short walk from Joe Van Dorn's hospital room to Bellevue's morgue.

"How's he doing?"

"The docs aren't making any promises," said Bell.

"And how are *you* doing, Isaac?"

"I'll feel better after I've seen the rumrunner who got shot at Roosevelt Hospital."

"Figured you might. I'll do him myself. You take notes."

He gave Bell a white apron and a gauze face mask scented with oil of cloves and led him to a postmortem table where the body of the murdered rumrunner waited under a sheet. A stenographer was standing by. Nuland told him to go to lunch, and tugged off the sheet.

The Medical Examiner's blithe disregard for official procedure was a wrenching reminder of Joe Van Dorn's great gift for friendship. Rich, powerful, and accomplished men across the continent would jump to lend him a hand. Gather debts but never flaunt them, he had taught Bell from the first day of his apprenticeship. Forgive small sins. Offer help. Give favors, they'll be returned.

Isaac Bell opened his notebook to take Nuland's dictation.

"Caucasian male. Twenty-five to thirty years old. Sturdy. Muscular."

Bell saw a large bandage around the man's left thigh that the bedclothes had hidden last night. The Medical Examiner cut it off with scissors and whistled in amazement. "One tough hombre to walk on that."

Two bullets had perforated the flesh. The examiner measured them as an inch and a half apart. He glanced at Bell. "Tight pattern."

"Lewis gun."

Bell wrote rapidly in a clear hand as Nuland went on to describe numerous healed bullet and knife wounds that scarred limbs and trunk, a broken nose, and missing teeth. The examiner noted that some of the scars were quite old, acquired in childhood.

"Your classic street-gang kid . . . All right, let's see what finally caught up with him."

Nuland noted the absence of an exit wound in the throat, mouth, and face, then wrestled the body onto its belly. There were more healed scars on the back of the torso and a single large hole in the posterior thigh where the Lewis gun slugs had exited jointly. Finally, he addressed the tiny, half-a-dime-size wound that Bell had seen just under the hairline in the nape of the neck.

"Point-blank range, small bore . . . Twenty-five caliber, probably . . . Powder tattooing around the flame zone . . . Powder grains embedded in the corneum . . . Powder grains in the mucosum . . ."

He scraped the grains from the skin's outer and inner layers onto glass slides.

"Denser pattern of powder tattooing below the wound . . ." He looked up at Bell. "This Frenchman during the war worked out a system to gauge whether a bullet wound was courtesy of the Germans or self-inflicted . . . The Army wanted proof to prosecute malingerers who tried to get out of the trenches by shooting themselves in

71

the leg. If we can believe Monsieur Chavigny, the heavier concentration under this wound indicates the bullet entered on an upward slant. Hand me that saw — let's go find it . . . How you holding up, Isaac, need a bucket?"

"Getting hungry . . . Shall I run and get us sandwiches?"

"Corned beef . . . But let's find the bullet first."

Bell handed him a hammer and a chisel.

"Thanks . . . Where . . . ? Oh, thanks." He took the forceps from Bell. "Aha! That's why it didn't come out his mouth. It's in his brain! . . . Here we are. A little .25, just like I told you."

Isaac Bell stared at the mangled remains of the man who had either been the thug who machine-gunned Joe Van Dorn or an accomplice.

"Why?" he asked.

"Why what?" said Nuland, holding the slug to the light.

"Why didn't it exit from his mouth?"

"Good question . . . Looks to me like the guy's head was bent forward — sharply — chin to chest." Nuland demonstrated by tucking his own chin to his chest. "Bullet angles into the nape, under or through the occipital bone — through, in this instance

— and *up* into the skull. Easy on the victim. Dead in a flash, no pain."

"Easy on the killer, too," said Isaac Bell.

"How do you mean?"

"No death struggle, no blood."

"Do you have time to see me off, Isaac?" asked Pauline Grandzau.

The doctors allowed no one but Dorothy, Captain Novicki, and Isaac Bell in Joseph Van Dorn's room, which didn't stop detectives from rushing to Bellevue to offer condolences to his wife and wish the Boss well and donate blood in the event of additional operations. The most striking visitor, by far, was Fräulein Privatdetektive Pauline Grandzau, chief of the Berlin field office.

The beautiful young German had won her detective spurs before the war when she was a teenage library student who helped Isaac Bell solve the Thief case.

"Are you going back already?" Bell asked. He was rushing off to the police laboratory, where, he had just learned, they were examining a pistol shell found in the murdered rumrunner's hospital room. "Seems like you just got here."

"I'm afraid so. *Nieuw Amsterdam* sails this afternoon."

He reached automatically for his pocket watch, then shot his cuff instead to check the time. Strapped to his wrist was the perfect substitute for a man who had his hands on the controls of an airplane, racing boat, or motorcar — a Cartier "Tank," which Marion, his wife, had given him for their anniversary.

"I'll do my best to get to the boat," he promised. Pauline, after all, had risked her life to help him behind German lines.

Holland America liners sailed from a Hoboken pier.

Bell made it with only minutes to spare, and when he boarded the Rotterdam-bound *Nieuw Amsterdam,* an aging seventeen-thousand-tonner, he found two Van Dorn detectives already crowded into Pauline's little cabin. Research Department chief Grady Forrer — a scholarly giant of bull-like proportions — and young, pale-skinned, bantamweight James Dashwood — the finest pistol shot in the agency — who had brought her flowers. The giant and the rail-thin youth gripped their bouquets like clubs.

Pauline appeared oblivious to her dazzling effect on either of them.

"Isaac! I'm so glad you could make it." She turned to Dashwood and Forrer. "Boys,

74

thank you so much for coming. And thank you for the beautiful roses, Grady, and the lovely peonies, James. I'll see you when I'm back in the autumn. Good-bye. Thank you. Good-bye."

Grady and Dashwood shuffled out, reluctantly, and Bell had to hide a smile. The skinny little German student with yellow braids, freckles, bright blue eyes, and the moxie of a Berlin street fighter had grown up. A stylish bob replaced her braids. Her enormous eyes were deep as oceans. God alone knew where the freckles had gone. But the moxie was still there, hidden like a sleeve gun, ready when needed.

For a long moment, they stood looking at each other.

Bell broke the silence, speaking German — partly because people were shuffling by in the corridor and partly for old times' sake — the college German she had helped him hone to stay alive.

"I attended the rumrunner's autopsy."

"What did you learn?"

"There was something a little odd about the way the killer shot him. He was shot point-blank. Not between the eyes or in the temple, where you'd expect, but in the back of his neck."

Pauline's eyes settled on him curiously.

"Where in the back of his neck?"

"Just at the hairline."

"The nape?"

"Exactly."

"Next, you will tell me that the bullet did not exit."

"How did you know?"

"It didn't?"

"No. Straight up in his brain."

"Was he American?"

"I assume so. He told the doctors his name was Johnny. Why?"

"Could he have come from abroad?"

"Why do you ask?"

"You just described a *Genickschuss.*"

"*Genickschuss?* What is that? Neck shot?"

"A bullet in the nape of the neck."

"There's a German word for everything," Bell marveled.

"Actually, it's Russian. The word is German, but the Russians coined it for the favored method of execution of the Russian Communist Cheka."

"Soviet secret police?" asked Bell, equal parts intrigued and surprised. Cheka was short for the All-Russian Extraordinary Commission for Combating Counter-Revolution and Sabotage.

"A long and fancy name for the engineers of the Red Terror," said Pauline. "*Genick-*

schuss is how they kill. Quickly, cleanly, efficiently."

"The coroner thought it was efficient," said Bell. "How did a Russian method of killing get a German name?"

Pauline reminded him that millions of Germans lived in Russia before the war. "There was plenty of mixing. And many a German worked for the Russian Revolution. Starting, if you will, with Karl Marx."

"Funny way for a rumrunner to get shot . . . What would the Cheka be doing in New York?"

"Strictly speaking, they would not be Cheka but Comintern, the Russian Communists' foreign attack force. The Comintern would be in New York for the same reason they're in Germany. To lead revolution."

Bell shook his head. "They call it revolution, but what they really want is to replace the old empires the war destroyed with new ones."

"What gun did the killer use?" Pauline asked.

Bell looked at her curiously. "The boys at the police laboratory are pretty sure it was a Mann pocket pistol."

"German. Why do they think it's a Mann?"

"The cops found a shell that had expansion marks from the chamber groove."

"That could only come from the new model. The 1920. Or the '21."

"That's what the cops said. Apparently the 1920 model has a circular groove to permit an ultralight slide. I've not seen one yet."

"You will love it," said Pauline.

She reached under her skirt. Bell caught a flicker of a shapely white thigh encircled by black lace. She pressed a tiny semiautomatic pistol into his hand. It was smaller than a deck of cards, finely machined, and amazingly thin — less than three-quarters of an inch. It was too little for his hand, perfect for hers.

"Five shots," she said. "Isn't it beautiful?"

The aluminum grips were warm from her skin, and Bell wondered, not for the first time, why such a beautiful girl had neither married nor kept a steady boyfriend.

"She is secretly in love with you," Marion had told him.

"She knows my heart is spoken for," had been Bell's reply. He admired Pauline's courage and her razor-sharp mind, and there was no denying she was wonderful to look at. But he, as he told Marion, was already in love.

"Is it accurate?"

"I trust it to twenty feet."

Bell handed it back.

Pauline slipped it in its holster. She looked up with a smile. "Doesn't it seem that our murdered rumrunner has experienced a more complicated death than an ordinary Prohibition gangster?"

"It might," said Bell. "Except Prohibition's get-rich-quick promises tempt all sorts."

The liner's whistle thundered overhead.

Pauline walked him to the gangway, where officers were urging visitors to disembark. "*Auf Wiedersehen,* Isaac. It was lovely to see you. Thanks for coming."

"Glad I did. Your *Genickschuss* was worth the ride to Hoboken. Not to mention meeting your little Mann."

She stood on tiptoe, kissed his cheek, and switched to English. "Please, give my warm regards to your wife."

"I will as soon as I see her. She's making a picture in Los Angeles."

Deep in thought, Bell stood out on deck as the Hoboken Ferry steamed across the Hudson River. He looked back when it landed at 23rd Street. The tugs were turning *Nieuw Amsterdam* into the stream. For an instant, his keen eyes picked out Pauline among the passengers lining the rails, her hair a fleck of shining gold.

If Marion was right, he'd have to find a way to change Pauline's mind.

He hurried into the terminal, searching for a coin telephone.

"Mortuary."

"Dr. Nuland, please . . . Shep, I saw you retrieve powder samples."

"Smokeless powder doesn't leave a lot."

"Enough to ascertain origin?"

"Possibly."

"Would you ask your lab boys to trace where it came from?"

The formulas for smokeless powder were constantly refined. The latest included Ballistite, Cordite, Rifleite, French Poudre. Based on his conversation with Pauline, he wondered would the powder recovered in the postmortem be German military powder or Russian powder.

7

Newtown Storms, senior partner of Storms & Storms, a Wall Street brokerage founded by his great-grandfather to sell stock in the Erie Canal and expanded by succeeding generations to fund railroads and telegraph lines, welcomed Fern Hawley to his office effusively. She was a handful, with a perpetual smirk that implied she was privy to secrets unknown by ordinary mortals. But she was beautiful, she was very rich, and her father had allowed Storms & Storms to manage a full third of the Hawley fortune. With her was a tall, lithe Russian in a fine blue suit, whom Miss Hawley introduced as "My friend Prince André. We met years ago in Paris."

Prince André — "late of Saint Petersburg," as the Russian put it — was carrying an expensive leather satchel with gold buckles. When he put it down to shake hands, Storms saw that his cuff links were set with large diamonds. But he did not let down his guard. He had seen enough Russian refugees sniffing around Wall Street since their revolution to know that despite appearances, they were usually hard up. So, after sufficient small talk to demonstrate to Miss Hawley that he had not forgotten that she was a valued customer, Storms asked, "To what do I owe the pleasure of this visit?"

"Prince André is unable to return to his estates in Russia . . . at this time," said Miss Hawley.

Storms looked sympathetic, while congratulating himself on getting the Russian's number. Dollars to donuts, Miss Hawley had paid for those cuff links. And his suit, too. He made a mental note to have private detectives look, discreetly, into how much the prince was trying to take her for. Why otherwise intelligent, hardworking fathers allowed these foolish women unfettered access to their money was a mystery raised regularly over cocktails at his club.

Storms said, "I understand. If a loan is required, there are people with whom I can arrange introductions."

Prince André turned to Fern Hawley and laid on the Russian accent with a trowel. "Loan? Vat is 'loan'?"

Fern laughed. "Mr. Storms. I'm afraid

82

you're confused. Prince André is looking to invest. Not borrow."

"Invest?" Storms placed both hands on his desk and sat up in his chair.

"Unable to gain access to his estates," said Miss Hawley, "Prince André has been forced to sell other assets. Jewels, mostly, and some French properties. Some of them, at least, in hopes of starting a new life in New York. Show him, André."

Zolner unbuckled the satchel and threw it open.

"Oh?" Storms peered inside at tightly packed banded banknotes. "Oh. How much were you considering?"

"Prince André thought he would open an account with ten thousand dollars to see how you make use of it."

"I think we could handle that very nicely."

Then suddenly Prince André was speaking for himself, his accent all but unnoticeable, and his gaze alert, even challenging. "Miss Hawley thinks buying stocks is a good idea. But do not stock prices continue down?"

"The stock market should turn around any day now," said Miss Hawley.

"But they have been going down for a year and a half," said the Russian. "Since before Christmas in 1919?"

Newtown Storms hastened to take her side of the argument. "Miss Hawley, who has considerable experience in the market, is correct. They must go up."

"Why?"

"Abnormally rapid speculative enhancement of prices for existing stocks caused them to go down. Which, frankly, many experts blame on a reckless class of people new to the discipline of investment. Fortunately, President Harding and Treasury Secretary Mellon are purging the rottenness out of the system by cutting taxes and making the government more efficient."

"Unemployment remains high," said Prince André. "People wander the streets in rags."

"Because the extravagant cost of government saps industry with a withering hand. Don't forget that labor is quiet, and will stay quiet. The steel strike fixed their wagon, as did the sailors' strike in the spring. I can safely predict that wages will stay down where they should and lower the high cost of living. People will work harder and live a more moral life. Enterprising people will pick up the slack from less competent sorts. Uncertainty is bound to end, and business is about to boom. It will roar, Prince André. Now's your chance to get in on the ground floor."

Marat Zolner kept a straight face even though Fern was teasing him with an arched eyebrow. He said to the stockbroker, "You pose a most convincing-sounding argument."

"And keep in mind, Your Highness, once you've opened an account, you can borrow against it in the event you ever need funds."

"Why would I need funds when the market roars?"

Storms greeted such naïveté with a kindly chuckle. "I meant, to borrow against your account to buy more stocks to put into it."

"I am convinced," said Marat Zolner. He cast Fern Hawley a princely smile and shoved the satchel across Storms's desk.

"You can take my word for it," said the broker. "This is the beginning and you're getting in on it. So if you decide to sell any more jewels, you know where to come."

"Let us see, first, how you make out with this."

"Never fear," said Newtown Storms, who fully expected that President Harding and Secretary Mellon would set a great bull market in full swing before most of Wall Street realized it. "You will get rich quickly."

"In that case," said the prince, extending

a surprisingly powerful hand. "We will see you again, quickly."

As Storms rose to usher them out, Fern Hawley said with her knowing smirk, "Next time we stop by your office, you can offer us a drink," and handed him from Marat Zolner's satchel a bottle of Haig & Haig.

Isaac Bell paced the Van Dorn bull pen like a caged lion, flowing across the room in long strides, turning abruptly, flowing smoothly back, wheeling again. His gaze was active, and every detective in the room felt the chief investigator's hard eyes aimed at him.

"It's four days since Mr. Van Dorn was shot. Who did it?"

The squad of picked men Bell had drafted to track down the rumrunners who shot Van Dorn had nicknamed themselves the "Boss Boys." They ran the gamut of Van Dorn operator types from deadly knife fighters who looked like accountants, to cerebral investigators who looked like dock wallopers, to every size and shape in between. Few appeared to have slept recently. There was a collective wince around the room when Isaac Bell repeated, "Four days. This is your city, gents. What is going on?"

The wince dissolved into shamefaced

shrugs and sidelong glances in search of someone with something useful to say. Finally, the bravest of the Boss Boys, grizzled Harry Warren, who had headed the New York Gang Squad since the heyday of the Gophers, ventured into the lion's den.

"Sorry, Isaac. West Side, East Side, Brooklyn, none of the gangs know who these guys are. I spoke with Peg Leg Lonergan and even he doesn't know."

Detectives stared at Harry in amazement and admiration, wondering how he had wangled a conversation with the close-mouthed Lonergan and managed to return from Brooklyn alive.

Harry acknowledged their esteem with a modest nod. "If the leader of the White Hands doesn't know about these guys, none of the Irish know these guys."

"What about the Italians?" asked Bell.

Harry, who had changed his name, was known and respected in Little Italy. "Same thing with the Black Handers. Masseria, Cirillo, Yale, Altieri — none of them know."

"What about Fats Vetere?"

"Him neither."

"What makes you think they're telling you the truth?"

"The bootlegging business is heating up. Gangsters and criminals are pushing out the amateurs. There's so much money to be made. So if the White Hand or the Black Hand knew about these guys, they'd be wanting to get in touch either to buy from them or hijack them. But when I fished, they never fished back. The fact they didn't try to pump me says the guys who shot the Boss are strangers to the gangs."

Bell kept pacing. "What about the bootleggers?"

Several men cleared their throats and answered, briefly, one after another.

"The bootleggers I know don't know, Isaac."

"I went around the warehouses. They swear they don't know."

"Same thing on the piers, Isaac."

"And the speakeasies. They've got no reason to lie to us, Isaac. It's not like we're arresting them."

"It's not like *anyone*'s arresting them."

Bell paced harder, boot heels ringing. "What about the black boat?"

"Yeah, well, the Coasties *say* they saw this black boat. No one else did."

"Except maybe Mr. Van Dorn. Is he talking yet, Isaac?"

"Not as much as the first day," Bell answered, adding, quietly, "In fact, not at all, for the moment." His surgeons feared an infection had settled into his chest. Dorothy was beside herself, and even Captain Novicki was losing faith.

"Watermen," said Bell. He turned to the barrel-chested, broad-bellied Ed Tobin. A brutal beating by the Gopher gang when Tobin was a Van Dorn apprentice had maimed his face with a crushed cheekbone and a drooping eyelid. "Ed, have none of the watermen seen it?"

"None that will talk to me."

"Have you asked Uncle Darbee?" Donald Darbee, Tobin's great-uncle, was a Staten Island coal pirate with sidelines in salvaging cargo that fell off the docks and ferrying fugitives from New York to New Jersey.

"I asked him first off. Uncle Donny's never seen the black boat, never heard of it. Though he did like the idea, and he asked me could I find out whether it's got Liberty motors and, if so, how many, and are they installed in-line or side by side."

Knowing laughter rumbled about the bull pen, and when even Bell cracked a faint smile, Tobin said, "Can I ask you, Mr. Bell, how are you making out with the Coast Guard?"

Bell's smile vanished like a shuttered signal lamp. "I will continue trying to interview the cutter crew." He had had no luck so far. The Coast Guard was keeping CG-9 at sea. When Bell offered to fly out in his plane to interview the crew, his offer was refused.

"McKinney!" Bell turned to the new chief of the New York field office. Darren McKinney was built short, wiry, and supple as chain mail. "You reported that the cops caught a lighter in the East River that had off-loaded the sinking rummy. What sort of booze were they carrying?"

"Dewar's blended Scotch whisky. The real McCoy."

"From *Arethusa*?" *Arethusa* was the famous McCoy's schooner that cruised international waters off the coast of Fire Island.

"McCoy just sailed up a shipload from Nassau. But the guys the cops arrested in the East River swear that they got the stuff from somewhere other than the shot-up rummy — understandable, considering the circumstances."

"Did they or didn't they?" Bell demanded.

"Harbor Squad claims they followed them from the sinking rummy. These guys saying otherwise are understandably reluctant to be linked to a shooting that might have ki—"

A flicker of violence in Isaac Bell's eyes silenced the detective mid-word.

"— That is to say, led to the wounding of

the proprietor of the Van Dorn Detective Agency."

Bell said, "I want that reluctance felt by every bootlegger in this city. Find out if they knew the guys on the shot-up rummy."

"The rummy guys are in jail."

"No they're not," said a gang unit detective hurrying into the bull pen. "Someone bailed 'em out."

"Now's our chance to find out. Run them down."

"Sorry, Isaac, that won't be possible."

"Why not?"

"They just got fished out of the river . . . That's why I'm late."

The Van Dorns met the news of slaughtered witnesses with stunned silence. Criminals fearing the electric chair killed accomplices, not ordinary rumrunners and bootleggers.

Bell turned to Detective Tobin. "Ed, get on a boat. Go out to *Arethusa* and ask McCoy who he sold to that day. If he didn't sell it, he might have some idea who did."

"I'm not so sure he's interested in helping, Mr. Bell."

Bell said, "If he insists on protecting the buyer, tell him we'll buy him a Lewis machine gun — he'll need one for protection, the way things are going. Tell him what

Harry Warren just said, criminals are moving in on bootlegging. If that doesn't change his mind, make it damned clear to him that *I* will make his life on Rum Row immensely unpleasant by persuading the Coast Guard to assign a cutter to circle his schooner day and night for a month."

Tobin started for the door.

"Wait," said Bell. "Take two boys and plenty of firepower. And warn McCoy if he did do business with this roughneck element, he's in danger. Whoever we're looking for has a strong aversion to witnesses."

Tobin turned to Harry Warren. The head of the Gang Squad assigned two of his hardest cases with a brisk nod, and Tobin led them to the weapons vault.

"We'll take a new tack," Bell told the rest. "The rumrunner who got shot at Roosevelt Hospital told the docs that his name was Johnny. Johnny was about twenty-five years old, medium height, strong build, blond hair cut short, bunch of scars. It's possible he's not American. He didn't do much talking at the hospital with a couple of holes in his leg, so no one heard whether he had an accent. Get out there and find his friends."

The detectives trooped out quickly and in seconds Bell was alone, racking his brain for what else he could do. The front-desk man telephoned.

"Lady to see you, Mr. Bell."

"What's her name?"

"Won't say," the desk detective whispered. A steady fellow normally, with a pistol under his coat and a sawed-off shotgun clamped beside his knee, he sounded almost giddy. "She's a knockout."

Bell went to the reception room.

The most beautiful woman he had ever seen was smiling, facing the door, in a tailored traveling suit with an open jacket and a skirt that hung straight to the middle of exquisite calves. She had straw-blond hair, sea-coral-green eyes, and a musical voice.

"I'm no lady. I'm your wife."

"Marion!"

Bell swept her into his arms. "I'm so happy to see you." He held her so close, he could feel her heart racing. "What are you doing here? Of course, you came to see Dorothy. She's at the hospital."

"I'll see Dorothy later. How are *you*?"

"Working an angle on the gang that shot Joe. Hard to tell how he's doing, but he's hanging in there."

"I meant, how are you getting on?"

"Plugging away," he answered quickly, uncharacteristically repeating himself.

"Staying on top of it. The boys are terrific. Everyone's pitching in, working at it overtime."

Marion Morgan Bell had traveled three thousand miles to examine her husband with a clear, cool gaze. She saw a shadow of apprehension in his eyes for the friend who was his mentor. She saw cold resolve to pursue Joe's attackers. And she sensed that the man she loved with all her heart had somehow managed to brace every muscle in his body with hope.

"Good," she said, greatly relieved. "I'll go see Dorothy now."

She held Bell's hand as he walked her downstairs to put her in a taxi.

"I didn't tell you I was coming because I didn't know for sure when I'd arrive and I knew you'd have your hands full."

"How did you get here so fast?"

"I caught a lift to Chicago on Preston and Josephine's special." Preston Whiteway owned a chain of newspapers. His wife, Josephine, was a famous aviatrix. Their private train, absurdly overpowered by a 4-8-2 ALCO locomotive, had set the latest speed record for Los Angeles to Chicago. "I just missed the Twentieth Century Limited, so I got Josephine to sneak me onto her pilot friend's mail plane. The new De Havilland?

94

You would have loved it. We averaged one hundred nine miles an hour."

"I wasn't aware that airmail planes had room for a passenger."

"It was a tight squeeze. I was practically in the pilot's lap, but he was so sweet about it."

"I'll bet."

"We beat the Twentieth Century by four hours!"

"How long can you stay in New York?" Bell asked.

"The Four Marx Brothers asked me to direct a comedy in Fort Lee."

"Aren't they a vaudeville act?"

"They're hoping a two-reeler will get them to Broadway."

The St. Regis doorman hailed a cab. Bell helped Marion into it. He leaned in and kissed her. She whispered, "I booked a suite upstairs," and began to kiss him back.

The cabbie cleared his throat, loudly. "Say, mister, why don't you just ride along with us?"

"Pipe down," said the doorman. "You got something against love?"

Below the ferry terminal at West 23rd Street, Marat Zolner lost sight of the Hudson River behind an unbroken wall of warehouses, bulkhead structures, and dock buildings. On the other side of that wall was a Dutch freighter in from Rotterdam. One of her crew was about to jump ship.

Zolner stopped in one of the cheap lunch-rooms scattered along West Street that catered to seamen. It was across from a door in the wall beside a guard shack. Every seaman who stepped out had to show his papers to prove he had a job on a ship. Zolner ordered a cup of coffee and watched.

Antipov stepped through the door with three others. He was dressed like they were in a tight peacoat and flat cap, but his wire-thin silhouette and steel-frame eyeglasses were unmistakable. They showed their papers and crossed West Street. The three entered a blind pig. Antipov waited outside. He removed his glasses, polished them with a bandanna he pulled from his peacoat, then tied the bandanna around his neck.

Zolner joined him and they walked inland on a side street past unlit garages and shuttered warehouses.

Antipov spoke English with a heavy accent. "Where is Johann?"

"Dead. I'm glad you've come. I counted on him."

"How did he die?"

"He was wounded by the Coast Guard.

Police took him to the hospital. He knew too much."

"Pity," said Antipov.

"Needless to say, Fern believes he was shot by a detective."

"Of course. Who are those men following us?"

At no point had either Russian appeared to look back.

"Neighborhood thugs," answered Zolner. "They rob immigrants who sneak off the ships."

Antipov stopped where the shadows were thickest. "Do you have a cigarette?"

"Of course." Zolner shook a Lucky Strike out of the pack. Antipov struck a match, let the wind blow it out, and struck another and lit the cigarette, shielding the flame this time expertly. The charade gave the thugs time to catch up. Three Irish, Zolner noted, two of them half drunk, but not enough to slow them down. The third floated with a boxer's smooth gait. They attacked without a word.

Zolner retreated to his right, Antipov to his left. To the thugs, they looked like frightened men stumbling into each other, but their paths crossed as smoothly as parts of a machine, and when they finished exchanging places in a dance as precise as it was confusing, the thug charging Zolner was suddenly facing Antipov, and the thug lunging at Antipov was facing Zolner. Zolner dropped his man with a blackjack. Antipov stabbed his with a long, thin dagger.

The boxer scrambled backwards. Zolner and Antipov blocked any hope of running back to West Street or ahead to Tenth Avenue. He opened his hands in the air to show he was not armed.

Antipov spoke as if he were not standing five feet away. "Would it not be ironic to fall at the hands of common criminals?"

"Not likely," said Zolner.

The boxer, seeing that flight was hopeless, closed his big hands into ham-size fists and went up on the balls of his feet.

"He is brave," said Antipov.

"And handles himself well," said Zolner. "What is your name?"

"What's it to you?"

"We are deciding whether to kill you. Or pay you."

"Pay me? Pay me for what?"

"Whatever we require. Tell me where you hang out and I will pay you when there's a job to be done. Easy money."

"Are you nuts?"

"We are bootleggers. We pay easy money for muscle. What is your name?"

"Ricky Newdell."

"What do your pals call you?"

"They call me Hooks. 'Counta my left hook."

Marat Zolner stared at him.

"My best punch," Ricky Newdell explained.

"Where do you hang out?"

"Lunchroom at 18th and Tenth."

"O.K., Hooks. You'll hear from us. I'm Matt. He's Jake. Turn around and walk back to West Street."

"What about these guys?" The man Zolner had blackjacked was out cold. The man Antipov stabbed had not moved since he fell.

Zolner and Antipov wiped the blood off their weapons on the men's coats.

Ricky Newdell said, "These guys are Gophers."

Antipov looked at Zolner. "Goofer?" he asked, pronouncing the gang name as Hooks had. "What is Goofer?"

"Neighborhood gangsters. Used to rule the Hell's Kitchen slum. Leaders dead and in prison."

Antipov shrugged. "What do we care?"

"The Gophers ain't gonna take this lying down," warned Newdell.

"Hooks," said Zolner. "This is your last

99

chance. If you want easy money, turn around and walk away."

Hooks Newdell turned around and walked toward West Street. Behind him he heard laughter, and the knife guy with the thick accent saying, " 'Goofers'? Like 'goofy'?" Hooks did not look back. Something told him with these guys moving into the neighborhood, the Gophers' days were numbered.

8

Marat Zolner steered Yuri Antipov toward Tenth Avenue.

"Where are we going?"

"I have an auto."

Antipov's mouth tightened at the sight of the Packard Twin Six, as Zolner had expected it would. Wait until he saw the place Fern had rented for a hideout.

Zolner drove across the Brooklyn Bridge and east for two hours, over the Brooklyn line into Nassau County, and across Nassau on the Merrick Road to Suffolk and through a dozen villages on the Montauk Highway. The towns were dark, their people sleeping. The farms and forest between the towns were darker, except where roadhouses lit the night, like liners at sea, with colored lights, electric signs, and the headlights of expensive motorcars in parking lots.

Music spilled from the blazing windows.

"A cabaret!" said Antipov, breaking the

silence that lay heavily between them.

"They're called roadhouses in the country, cabarets in the city."

"In the middle of nowhere."

"Their patrons own automobiles."

"And drink alcohol so openly."

"Americans are avid lawbreakers."

Zolner turned off the highway onto a narrow, dark, empty road. He drove for a mile until it ended at a substantial stone building with a tall, wide, iron-studded door in the middle. A warm, wet wind reeked of marsh and salt water. Overhead, through breaks in the trees, stars shone softly in a hazy sky.

"You have a big house," said Antipov.

"This is the gatehouse."

Zolner turned the lights on in the car and blew the horn. They waited.

"Aren't you expected?"

"They have orders to make sure that we are not hijackers or Prohibition officers."

At last, a big man in a leather cap stepped from the shadows with one hand in his pocket. "All clear, boss."

Zolner said, "This is Yuri. He has the run of the property. Yuri, this is Trucks O'Neal. You can count on him."

Trucks O'Neal took a close look and said, "I'll remember you, Yuri."

The iron-studded door swung open, and

Zolner drove the Packard through it.

"Why did you tell him I was 'Yuri' instead of 'Jake'?"

"Trucks is an American Army veteran and war profiteer turned bootlegger. He is loyal."

"How can you be sure? He's not a comrade."

"I saved his skin in Germany, and I am making him wealthy and powerful here. In return, Trucks O'Neal is loyal. Better yet, he's intelligent enough to stay loyal."

He steered onto a curving bluestone driveway. The headlights swept hedgerows and gardens, tennis courts and greenhouses.

"Czar Nicholas would enjoy this," Antipov remarked disapprovingly.

"Czar Nicholas is out of business," Zolner shot back. He turned off the main drive, which went to the estate house whose roof could be seen darkly against the dim stars, and the tires rumbled over railroad tracks. "This is a private siding that connects to the main line to New York."

"Is that a railcar?" The starlight reflected on cut-glass windows.

"A private car."

"Does it belong to Fern?"

"Of course not. We would not risk any connection to Fern. Everything's rented in cash by agents. In case we have to break

103

camp quickly, none of this can be traced to her." He stopped the Packard, climbed out, and stretched the kinks from the long ride. Antipov stood beside him. "What is that?" he asked, pointing at the silhouette of a tall spire.

"The hothouse chimney," said Zolner. "It conceals a radio antenna. The signal guides our boats ashore."

"What is out there? I see no lights."

"Great South Bay. Forty miles long, five miles wide. Across it is Fire Island Inlet, and, through the inlet, the Atlantic Ocean."

"What is around us on the land?"

"Other estates of similar size. All private."

He walked Antipov to a large garage, led him in a side door, and turned on the lights to reveal a canvas-topped stake truck and six Packard and Pierce-Arrow automobiles. "The autos have strengthened suspensions so they don't sag when loaded."

"Why don't you deliver it by rail? From your siding?"

"Have you forgotten trains are trapped on tracks? Rails are easily choked. The Prohibition agents would love nothing more than the opportunity to seize a railcar full of booze. We scatter it on the highways. If they're lucky, they catch one auto in ten."

"But you concentrate it here."

"Many miles from the market in a dark and lonely place."

"How do you get it here?"

"The boats."

He turned out the garage lights and walked a gravel path to another large building on the bank of a still creek. The boathouse had no windows, so only when Zolner opened the door did Antipov see that it was brightly lit inside. Two large boats were tied in separate bulkheaded slips. One was broad beamed, a forty-foot freight boat with two huge motors.

"She carries a thousand cases at twenty-five knots," said Zolner. "The price fluctuates according to demand, but in general her cargo will earn us fifty thousand dollars. A lot of money for a night's work."

"You have made a success of bootlegging."

"The boats are the rum-running side of the business. Distributing and selling it is the actual bootlegging. I've made a success of that, too."

"What is that other boat?" It was much longer than the freight boat and much narrower.

"My pride and joy," said Zolner. "She, too, will carry a thousand cases, but at *fifty* miles an hour. And if anyone gets in her way, look out. She'll gun them down. Her name is *Black Bird*."

"Your pride?"

Zolner ignored the mocking note in Antipov's voice.

"Her sailors are Russian — the best seamen in the world."

"Why have they disassembled her motors?"

The heads were off all three Liberty engines. Carborundum growled against steel, cascading white sparks as a mechanic ground valves.

"The price of speed," shrugged Zolner. "These motors burn up their valves on a regular basis."

"Intake or exhaust?" asked Antipov.

"I forgot, you apprenticed as a mechanic. Exhaust, of course. It's the heat that builds up. No one's come up with a good way to cool them, though not for lack of trying every trick in the book, including hollow valves filled with mercury or sodium. Fortunately, the United States built seventeen thousand Liberty engines, most of which were never used in the war. We buy them for pennies on the dollar."

He gestured at wooden crates stacked against the rear wall. "Believe it or not, it is often more efficient to replace the entire motor than waste time on the valves."

"I would believe almost anything at this point."

Antipov spoke softly, but he was seething with anger.

Now was the time, Zolner decided, to get this out in the open.

"What is it?" he asked. "What is troubling you, Yuri?"

"What of the revolution?"

"What *of* the revolution?"

"You are a Comintern agent, Comrade Zolner. You were sent here to spearhead the Bolshevik takeover of America."

9

"What precisely have you done to spearhead the Bolshevik takeover of America?"

The boathouse mechanic switched off his electric grinder. For a long moment the only sound Marat Zolner heard was the lap of water echoing in the slips.

The Communist International — the "Comintern" — was Soviet Russia's worldwide espionage network. The Russian Communist Party had launched it as its foreign arm when it seized control of the revolution that brought down Czar Nicholas II. The Comintern's mission was to repeat that victory everywhere in the world and overthrow the governments of the international bourgeoisie by all available means — spying, sabotage, and armed force.

Marat Zolner was a battle-hardened soldier of the revolution. During the war he had provoked entire regiments to shoot their officers. He led the Soviet unit that captured the czar's train, fought with the Bolsheviks to subvert the democratic provisional government, and shone in cavalry battles with White Loyalists in the Russian Civil War. Beyond the Russian border, he proved versatile, rallying Berlin street fighters to the barricades. Antipov had fought at his side.

"Go get something to eat!" he called to the valve grinder, a Russian, too. When they were alone, he said to Antipov, "Come here!"

He strode to the wall of spare motors. Sitting on one of the crates was a steel strongbox.

"Open that!"

Antipov flung back the lid. The box was crammed with cash, banded stacks of bills in denominations of one hundred and one thousand dollars.

"Where did you get this?"

"Profits," said Zolner.

"Profits?"

"Money earned smuggling alcohol from Rum Row to Long Island roadhouses and New York speakeasies."

"I ask of the revolution and you answer like a banker. Profits?"

"What I am doing costs money."

"And what precisely are you doing?"

Marat Zolner said, "Masking our Comintern network of assassins and saboteurs as a liquor-bootlegging crime syndicate."

"You wear your mask too well. You boast of pride and joy. You boast of gangsters, smugglers. Bootleggers. Where are the comrades?"

"*Black Bird*'s sailors are comrades — loyal Russian Bolshevik comrades of the Workers' and Peasants' Red Fleet. *Johann* was a comrade. *You* are a comrade."

"And you?"

"My smugglers and gangsters obey me. I am their *bootlegger* boss. They don't know I'm Comintern. They won't know why I expand to Detroit and Miami — nor why our empire spreads to the South, the Midwest, the Pacific Coast."

"Are *you* a comrade?"

"Have you not heard a word I said? Of course *I* am a comrade."

Antipov shook his head.

"What is wrong, Yuri?"

"The Comintern sent you to New York to provoke revolution."

"Precisely what my empire will achieve."

"What part did you take in the strikes of Seattle shipyards? How did you aid the Boston police strike? What was your role in the coalfield strikes? Who did you co-opt in

110

the nationwide steel strike? What of the May first seamens' strike? Are you co-opting the IWW Wobblies? Have you seized control of the American Communist Party?"

Zolner laughed.

"I do not see the joke," Antipov said heavily.

"The Wobblies and the American Communist Party and the labor unions are all in decline. The Congress, the newspapers, and the American Legion sow panic about 'Reds.' But the fact is, as you saw at the roadhouses tonight, Americans of every class are having too much fun defying Prohibition to care about politics, much less class struggle. Gangsters are their heroes. This is why my American Comintern unit fights under the guise of bootlegging."

"Perhaps you will invest your profits on Wall Street," Antipov said sarcastically.

"I already have."

"What?"

"Why shouldn't I build an empire of activities on Wall Street? It will finance operations. Guns aren't cheap. Neither are trucks, cars, boats. Not to mention bribes. Money is influence. Money is access to powerful allies. I have a broker steering excellent investments our way."

"A broker?"

"To buy stocks. To raise money for the scheme."

"Your scheme is tangential and slow."

"I will not be rushed."

"Worse, you veer from the revolution."

Marat Zolner stared down at Antipov. "Listen to me very carefully, Yuri. I am established here. You just arrived. I will explain to you what is going on here. The United States of America emerged from the World War as the new leader of international capitalism, did it not?"

Antipov conceded that the old German and British empires were laid waste by war.

"Toppling capitalism's most powerful industrial empire is too important to rush to defeat."

"You're not toppling capitalism. You're joining it."

"You forget our defeats. We rushed into battle against the international bourgeoisie in Hungary, and lost. We rushed again into the streets of Germany. And lost. Again. Of all the fights I'd fought, I had never seen anything as hopeless as our insurrection in retreat."

"After we win the war, who cares if we lost a battle?"

"We had no fortress to run to, nowhere to rest, no hospital to doctor wounds, no armory to reload our empty guns. I stopped to help a poor girl whose jaw was shot away. Freikorps thugs came along, shooting the wounded. I played dead. She moaned. They heard. They killed her. I cowered under her body to save my own skin, and I swore that I would find a better way to fight the international bourgeoisie."

"Joining them?"

"Beating them at their own game," Zolner retorted.

"You were sent to make war on the state!" Antipov shouted. "Not play games!"

"Prohibition is America's Achilles' heel," Zolner answered quietly and firmly. "Prohibition — this absurd law that people hate — will rot the state and make bootleggers rich."

He smiled down at Antipov, far too confident in his scheme to raise his voice.

"I have learned to fight in wars that I've lost and in wars that I've won. There isn't a bootlegger in America who can stand up to me. I will be the richest. My 'profits' that you disdain will finance the Comintern's attack on the U.S. government. My profits will subvert officials, corrupt police, and destroy the state."

Yuri shifted tactics. His voice grew soft. "Comrade Zolner — Marat — you know why Moscow sent me. Do I have to remind you, my friend, of the Red Terror? Do I have to remind you that the Cheka annihilates counter-revolutionaries?"

"I am not a counter-revolutionary."

"The effect of failure is counter-revolutionary."

"I will not fail."

"Moscow decides what is failure."

"Let Moscow tend to Russia. Let me tend to the United States. I will give America to the Comintern on a silver platter."

"They would be just as happy to have it on base metal."

Staring hard at each other, suddenly both men laughed, acknowledging their surprise that Antipov had made a joke.

"And happy to forgive me, too?" Zolner asked.

They laughed again.

But it was the laughter of deception. Both men knew the truth: The Comintern never forgave freethinking.

Zolner suspected another even grimmer truth: His once bold comrade, his blood brother of the street battles, had grown weary. Yuri Antipov had slipped into the role of functionary, an *apparatchik* obsessed with meaningless details instead of grand schemes. How many like Yuri would seize control of the revolution before they killed the revolution?

"Fern is waiting to see you," he said.

Antipov brightened. "She's here?"

"In the house." He picked up a telephone. "I'll call her. I'll tell her you're here."

The estate house was a limestone mansion built by a railroad magnate thirty years ago in the Gilded Age. Zolner led Antipov through the sculpted entry into a great hall with painted ceilings depicting a history of land transportation that linked Egyptian chariots to crack express trains thundering across the Rocky Mountains. Antipov stared up at the mural. His jaw set like steel.

But when Fern Hawley swept down the vast curving staircase, Antipov melted as he always did in her presence. A big grin lit his stern face, and he extended both hands and shouted, "Midgets!"

Fern took his hands and laughed. "You will never let me forget that, will you?"

"Never."

To greet her with "Midgets!" was to remind her of her conversion on a beautiful summer day in Paris. Victorious Allied regiments were marching down the Champs-Élysées. Bands were playing, crowds cheered, and the sun shone bright. Sud-

115

denly, she had cried out in astonishment, "Midgets!"

"What do you mean?" asked Zolner, who was holding her hand.

An English regiment was marching in strict order — rifles aligned perfectly on their shoulders, uniforms immaculate — but the soldiers were tiny miniature men, not one taller than five feet.

"They're so little," she said. "Little tiny midgets."

"So they are," said Zolner. "Still, they beat the Germans."

But Yuri Antipov gave her a look of withering disdain.

"What is it?" she asked. "What did I say?"

"Don't you know why they are small?"

"No. What do you mean?"

"It's a Lancashire Regiment. From the English coalfields."

"Yuri, what are you talking about?"

"They have mined coal for four generations. They are paid a pittance. Neither they nor their fathers nor their grandfathers nor their great-grandfathers have ever eaten enough food to grow tall."

Even tonight, separated from that moment by three years and three thousand miles, Fern Hawley winced at the memory of such ignorance and such callousness. "They're hungry," she had whispered, and Antipov had reached around Zolner to grip her arm and say, "They will stay hungry until the revolution."

Thanks to Antipov, she believed with all her heart that the international revolution of the proletariat should abolish government. Thanks to Antipov, she passionately supported the Russian proletariat's struggling new state — the Socialist Republic of Workers, Peasants and Soldiers.

"Have you eaten?" she asked.

She pulled a bell cord. A butler appeared.

"What would you like, Yuri? Champagne? A cold bird?"

"Bread and sausage."

Later, upstairs, alone in their palatial bedroom, she asked Zolner, "Why didn't you tell me Yuri was coming?"

Marat Zolner had seen Fern Hawley in action and he admired her bravery and her coolness under fire. She did not panic when police charged with pistols and rubber truncheons. When they bombed the barricades with mine throwers, she could retreat without losing purpose, a rare gift. The revolution needed her sort to fight battles. But she was a naïve romantic. If the Comintern ran to pattern, when the war was finally won brave naïve romantics would be shot in the interest of stability. For romantics would be seen as dangerous as free-thinkers.

Until then, he saw great advantage to teaming up with her.

She already helped him escape execution in Europe, staring down cops as she had the private detective at Roosevelt Hospital. In America she had shown him the ropes and provided extraordinary cover. Together, they had worked up disguises that allowed him to move freely. He had learned to ape the pretensions of the elegant White Russian émigrés fleeing to New York, San Francisco, and Los Angeles. Or, wearing laborer's duds, he could pass as just another of the faceless foreigners who toiled in the docks, mines, and mills. And to mingle with their bosses, he had only to stroll into the opera or a high-class speakeasy with Fern Hawley on his arm.

"I didn't tell you that Yuri was coming because information that you do not need to know endangers both you and our mission. What if you were forced to reveal what you knew?"

"What are you talking about? This isn't Russia or Germany. We're in the United States."

"You think there is no torture in the United States?"

Fern Hawley laughed. "They'd know what torture was when my lawyers got through with them."

Marat Zolner said, "I'm sorry. Old habits die hard."

"I am only asking you to trust me. You should have told me. Yuri is my friend."

"Yuri Antipov is no one's friend."

"He's *your* friend."

"We fought together. We are brothers in blood. But he is not my friend. He is Comintern from the soles of his feet to the hair on his skull."

"I know that. That's why he likes me. He knows that I'm as devoted as he is to the proletariat."

"He is Comintern," Zolner repeated. "If Moscow ordered him to throw you in a fire, he would without a second thought."

"So are you Comintern."

"I use my brain to think. They hate thinking that they can't control."

"Would Yuri throw you in that fire?"

Zolner gave her a thin smile and turned out the light. "Only if they told him to."

"Marat," she whispered in the dark. "I am grateful to Yuri Antipov and I admire Yuri Antipov. But I could never love him the way

I love you."

"Why are you grateful to him?"

She sat up in the canopied bed and hugged her arms around her knees. The sky had cleared, and through the French windows she saw a sliver of moon hanging over the bay. "Yuri helps me understand a world I never knew until I met you two. He's like a wise uncle. But you are my muse. Yuri was my guide. But you are my comrade-in-arms."

"Wait until they force you to choose," Zolner said bleakly.

"I will fight at your side."

10

The first mail delivery of the morning brought a letter from the Chief Medical Examiner's Office to the Van Dorn field office.

Dear Isaac,
The powder on Johnny's bullet wound was manufactured by the Aetna Explosives Company of Mt. Union, Pennsylvania. Hope it helps.

Sincerely,
(Signed) Shep

Bell was familiar with the powder plant, a sprawling factory he had often seen from the Broadway Limited on the Pennsylvania Railroad's main line between Altoona and Harrisburg.

"Dear Shep," he wrote back,

So much for hunches. That Russian neck

121

shot gave me a feeling the powder was from Germany or Russia. Next time you're on Fifth Avenue, let me buy you a drink of strong tea.

Warm regards,
(Signed) Isaac

Isaac Bell hurried from the Sayville train station to a one-story white clapboard building that had Ionic columns supporting a wide triangular pediment in the Greek Revival style. Lettering carved in relief and painted black read:

THE SUFFOLK COUNTY NEWS

Under his arm were several recent editions of the Long Island weekly he had ordered up from Van Dorn Research. He went inside and spotted his quarry, a retired private detective named Scudder Smith. Smith was wearing shirtsleeves, banded at the elbow, and a red bow tie. He was behind his desk, reading a long yellow galley that reeked of wet ink.

Bell said, "The Research boys found me your stories about rumrunners. Spellbinding."

Smith looked up, dropped the galley, and jumped to his feet. "Isaac! How in the heck are you?"

"Scudder." Bell shook his hand. "It's been too long."

The two men cast keen eyes on each others' faces.

Bell, Smith thought, looked as youthful and robust as ever despite the years and the war that had marked so many. Smith, Bell thought, looked like he hadn't had a drink in years and consequently was much less gnarly than when last he had seen him.

"What are you doing out here?" Scudder asked. "On a job? . . . Wait a second. How did you know I was here? Newsies don't hawk the *Suffolk County News* on the sidewalks of New York."

"Mr. Van Dorn's wife showed me the note you sent to the hospital."

"How is he doing?"

"He's hanging on. Left me in charge, and I've got my hands full trying to keep the agency afloat. But I do know that he hopes there are no hard feelings."

"Hell no. Getting fired for over-imbibing was the best thing that ever happened to me. Sobered up. Married the girl of my dreams. Helen promptly inherited the paper. So I'm back in my original business, writing news. Beats mixing it up with thugs half my age. And I don't have to hang out, drinking burnt coffee, in the criminal court pressroom. I walk home for lunch with my beautiful wife, write what I please. I'm even a pillar of the community. You'll love this, Isaac. They made me an Odd Fellow, a Moose, and a Mason, and the fellows starting a Lions Club asked me to join them, too."

"Doesn't it get a little quiet?" Bell asked. As a reporter turned detective, Scudder Smith had been famous at the Van Dorn Agency for knowing every street in the city, every saloon, and every brothel. And there was no better guide to a Chinatown opium den.

Scudder said, "Quiet? Not since Prohibition."

Bell nodded. "I got the impression sniffing the air it's been greeted with open arms. I smelled more booze on the sea breeze than salt."

"Half the town has fired-up home stills. The only ones who don't smell booze cooking are the cops." He picked up the galley. "This is my editorial about cops seen treating chorus girls to supper in expensive roadhouses. I don't know who'll read it. The entire South Shore is having a ball."

"Does your wife work on the paper?"

124

"She can. Practically ran it for her dad for years."

"So I heard."

"You heard? What do you mean?"

"Could she take over for a while?"

"Why?"

"So you could come back to New York and lend a hand 'til I get things straightened out."

"Isaac, old son," drawled Texas Walt Hatfield. "Shore Ah'd love to help you out, but Hollywood's got me tangled tighter than a roped calf."

Texas Walt Hatfield, another former Van Dorn detective, had become a matinee idol who starred in scores of western movies. His drawl had grown thicker and his choice of words more cowboy-ish, but he was still as lean and lethal-looking as a Comanche scalping knife. Bell had run him down in the Plaza Hotel's Palm Court. Patrons at other tables were gaping, and several people had stopped by to ask for Walt's autograph, which he supplied with a powerful handshake for the men and an I'll-meet-you-later smile for the ladies.

"Ah mean, if Ah could get out of my contract, Ah'd be with you lickety-split."

"Are you sure about that?" asked Bell.

"Heck yes. Ah hanker to get in a gunfight with real bullets."

Bell nodded discreetly to the maître d' who was awaiting his signal.

Walt changed the subject. "Ah'm mighty relieved the Boss is hanging on. How you doing running down the varmints who shot him?"

"The Coast Guard's stonewalling, won't let me near the crew, so I haven't had a word from the witnesses, and the cops are stonewalling, being embarrassed they let a killer in the hospital room with a witness they were guarding. But the fellow's post-mortem examination was interesting . . ." He filled Walt in on the *Genickschuss.*

"You wouldn't want to try that with a .45," drawled Hatfield. "You'd have to rustle up the swampers to mop the walls . . . And how's the fair Marion? Forgive my not asking sooner."

"She's shooting a comedy over in Fort Lee."

"So you got your gal with you! That's plumb perfect."

The maître d' reappeared leading a waiter, who was carrying a stick phone with an immensely long cord.

"Excuse me, gentlemen. There is a long-distance telephone call from Los Angeles,

California, for Mr. Texas Walt Hatfield."

"Excuse me a sec, Isaac. Like Ah say, they're jest all over me like paint."

He took the phone, held it to his mouth and ear. "Yup. This is Texas Walt. Who's there?"

He sat up straight, covered the mouthpiece, and muttered to Bell, "It's Mr. Andrew Rubenoff. He owns the moving picture studio — Yes, suh, Mr. Rubenoff. Yes, suh. Yes, suh . . . You don't say . . . Ah see. O.K. Thank you . . . What's that? Hang on, he's right here."

Texas Walt passed the telephone to Isaac Bell. "Damnedest thing. Just let me out of my contract temporarily. Now he wants to talk to you. His name's Rubenoff. Andrew Rubenoff."

Bell took the telephone, said, "Thank you, Uncle Andy," and hung up.

Texas Walt stared. A slow grin creased his craggy face. "Isaac. You son of a gun."

"I thought you were itching to get in a real gunfight."

"Is he really your uncle?"

"I just call him that to razz him. He's an old banking friend of my father's."

"Well, you got me. What are you going to do with me?"

"Put you to work."

127

They were interrupted again, by ladies wanting Walt's autograph. He signed their books and dazzled them with a smile. When they had gone, he said to Bell, "Ah hope you aren't fixing to have me do any masquerading. This old face has gotten too famous to operate incognito."

"I'm going to hide you in plain sight."

"How?"

"Ever been to Detroit?"

"Detroit? What the deuce is in Detroit, except a bunch of automobiles?"

"Bootleggers," said Bell. "The place is crawling with them."

"Shore. Because it's one mile from Canada. What's that got to do with me?"

Bell looked Hatfield in the eye and said, "Walt, I just got word they've corrupted our Detroit field office from top to bottom. Our boys are taking payoffs to ride shotgun on liquor runs and shaking down the bellhops."

"*Our* boys?" the Texan asked with a wintery scowl. "Are you sure, Isaac?"

"I don't know who's still on the square. I want you to pay them a visit."

Walt strode directly to the hatcheck, threw down a quarter, and clapped his J. B. Stetson on his head. Bell intercepted him at the front door.

"Here's your train ticket. I booked a

stateroom on the Detroiter."

"Ah can afford my own stateroom ticket."

"Not on a detective's salary, you can't. Wire me tomorrow."

A cable was waiting for Isaac Bell in the New York field office, which was three blocks down Fifth Avenue from the Plaza, on the second floor of the St. Regis Hotel.

PARIS CHIEF WOUNDED.

PRIVATE MATTER.

WIFE NO THIS.

COVERING.

ARCHIE

Bell crumpled it in his fist. He had been counting on his best friend, Archibald Angell Abbott IV, to come back from Europe, where Van Dorn had sent him to reinvigorate the Paris, Rome, and London offices. This meant he had to find another right-hand man to help him straighten out the agency. McKinney was busy ramrodding the New York office. Harry Warren was busy with the Gang Squad, and, even if he weren't, a detective who knew every gangster in New York hadn't the national knowledge Bell needed. Nor did Scudder Smith. Tim Holian, out in Los Angeles, and Horace Bronson, back from Paris to his old post in San Francisco, were needed there to hold down the western states.

"Where's Dashwood?"

"He's at the rifle range, Mr. Bell."

Bell walked quickly up Park Avenue to the Seventh Regiment Armory and down into the basement. The sharpshooters and marksmen of the regiment's crack shooting team were practicing for a match in the double-decked rifle range. He waited behind the firing line, breathing in the lively scent of smokeless powder, until the clatter of .22s ceased. Targets were snaked in. The riflemen inspected them, then passed them to the range captain.

The range captain compared them for the tightest patterns around the bull's-eyes and held up the winner's target. In the center of the black eye was a hole so clean it might have been cut by folding the paper in two and cutting a tiny half-moon with scissors. "Number 14? Number 14? Where are you, sir?"

Detective James Dashwood descended from the upper deck. He looked paler than

130

ever, Bell thought. His skin was dead white, and he was thin to the point of gaunt. His suit hung loosely on his frame.

"Of course," said the range captain. "I should have guessed. Gentlemen, meet former lieutenant James Dashwood."

The name drew respectful murmurs from the marksmen and sharpshooters. His service as an American Expeditionary Forces sniper in the trenches was legend.

"James," the captain asked with a knowing smile. "Would you please show them your 'rifle.' "

Dashwood gave a diffident shrug. He had a boyish voice. "That's O.K., Captain."

"Please, James. Your 'rifle.' "

Dashwood looked around, clearly unhappy to be the center of attention. He saw Bell watching from the back. A pleased grin lit his face. Bell gave his former apprentice a proud thumbs-up.

Dashwood drew a pistol from his coat, held it up for all to see, and ducked his head shyly at the cheers.

When they were alone, walking down Park Avenue, Bell asked, "How are you feeling?"

"I'm O.K."

"I asked for a reason," said Bell. "How is your health?" Dashwood had been caught in a German gas attack and the chlorine had played havoc with his lungs.

"I have good days and bad. At the moment I'm doing O.K."

"When's the last time the coughing laid you low?"

"Last month. I got over it. What's up, Mr. Bell?"

"I think you should start calling me Isaac."

"O.K., Isaac," Dashwood answered slowly, working his way around the unaccustomed way of conversing with the boss who had been his teacher, sage, and adviser all in one. "Why do you ask about my condition?"

"I promised Mr. Van Dorn to look after the agency until he recovers. I need a right hand. And a troubleshooter I can send around the continent."

"Why not Archie Abbott?"

"Archie's stuck in France."

"Isn't there anyone else?"

"None I'd prefer." Bell stopped walking, looked Dashwood in the eye, and thrust out his hand. "Can we shake on it?"

"Telephone, Mr. Bell. Dr. Nuland at the morgue."

"Hello, Shep. Thanks again for reporting on that powder."

"Would you happen to be looking for a Russian?"

Bell felt a surge of excitement. "It's likely that neck shot was by a Russian. Why?"

"I looked a little deeper when I got your note. About your hunch? Turns out in 1914, 1915, and 1916 the Aetna Explosives Company filled huge contracts to supply the Russian government with smokeless powder."

After Bell put down the phone, he called someone he knew in the New York Police Department laboratory. He was a bullet expert who was paid well and regularly to do private work for the Van Dorn Detective Agency. "I'm calling about that shell casing they found at Roosevelt where a shooting victim was murdered. The one with the expansion ring from a Mann pistol. Any idea where it was manufactured? . . . What's that?"

It sounded to Bell as if the expert was whispering into a mouthpiece muffled by his hand.

"Like I already told you, Mr. Bell, they got egg on their face, and it'll cost me my job to speak a word. I'm really sorry, Mr. Bell. But they'll sack me if I get caught."

"No hard feelings," said Bell and hung up. He was not surprised, but it had been worth a try. He had run into similar resistance with the Coast Guard. Every time he tried to interview the crew of CG-9, he was told she was out of reach, far at sea, or her radio was broken. The truth was, the Coast Guard brass were just as embarrassed about Van Dorn's shooting as the cop brass were about the bungled police protection at the hospital.

He *had* managed to wrangle a glimpse of the report on the slug that Shepherd Nuland fished out of Johnny's skull. But it had offered no clue to its source of manufacture. Which made the possible Russian source of the smokeless powder the only information as close to a fact that he could get his hands on.

He composed a Marconigram in Van Dorn cipher. The Radio Corporation of America would transmit it from the former Marconi Wireless Station in New Jersey to the liner *Nieuw Amsterdam:*

NECK SHOT POWDER POSSIBLY RUSSIAN.

It wasn't much to go on. But it would give Pauline Grandzau something to think about on the boat. And when Pauline put her mind to something, something interesting often came of it.

11

Hooks Newdell's new bosses, Matt and Jake, thought big, bigger than anyone Hooks had ever met up with — bigger than the Gophers, bigger than the White Hand Gang, even bigger than the Italians who were taking over the docks. Just looking at the huge government building they were going to break into made him nervous.

Matt and Jake were in the backseat of a Marmon parked on Greenwich Street under the Ninth Avenue El in Greenwich Village two blocks from the piers. Hooks was in front at the wheel. High above the El loomed the government building, a stone-and-brick monster rising ten stories in the night and filling the entire block bordered by Christopher, Greenwich, Barrow, and Washington streets. Hooks had always called it the Customs Building, but it was also known as the Appraisers' Stores and the Samples Office, a huge storehouse where

U.S. Customs took samples of imported goods to appraise how much they could tax the foreign shipments. Built like a fortress, it was also where the government stashed confiscated liquor and smuggled jewels and antiques and anything else valuable they got their paws on, like last week when customs agents intercepted a bunch of submachine guns being shipped to Ireland for the Sinn Féin. It was the kind of place that guys dreamed about busting into.

Matt and Jake were actually going to do it. A liquor deal to end all liquor deals.

Matt had bribed a Prohibition agent. The agent had told him when a big booze raid was planned and where the goods that the Dry agents seized would be stored — ground floor, right inside the Christopher Street entrance. This made things easy, Matt had explained. The building had acres of storerooms. There were ten elevators and three miles of hallways. Seven hundred clerks worked in it during the day. Near the front door made it easy, quick and easy in and out. Late at night even better. So Matt said.

But it made Hooks nervous and he couldn't stop talking. As they waited for the signal from Matt's man inside, he tried again to break the silence that they wrapped around themselves like armor.

"The guys in the car were saying that you mighta shot a detective, Matt."

Matt did not answer.

"Did ya?"

Marat Zolner was assessing whether Hooks Newdell had potential. He needed an American to represent him when he didn't want his face or accent noticed. But he was beginning to doubt that Hooks was the man. "Did ya what?"

"What the guys say. That you shot a private dick."

"Hooks, did it ever occur to you that whoever said that stands a good chance of getting shot himself?"

Hooks Newdell backpedaled madly. "They didn't mean nothin'. They was just guessing. It's just that we — *they* — were wondering, are you the guys who shot Joseph Van Dorn?"

Zolner remained silent, and the nervous Hooks sealed his doom. The fool simply did not know when to shut his mouth.

"Did you guys go bonkers?" he blurted. "You shot Joe Van Dorn? Do you know who that is?"

"Only a detective."

"It's bad enough shooting any Van Dorn.

Even a house dick. But you guys shot their boss."

"It's not like a cop."

"The Van Dorns got a saying: 'We never give up! Never!' "

"Words."

"Except you never hear word of 'em giving up . . . So you did shoot him?"

Yuri moved like lightning, and the tip of his dagger was suddenly pressing up against the soft flesh under Ricky Newdell's chin. "Stop talking!"

"O.K.! O.K.!"

"Shut! Up!"

Hooks Newdell pressed his lips together and sat motionless.

Antipov glanced at Zolner. Zolner shook his head. Hooks would be useful alive for a couple of more hours. Antipov sheathed his dagger.

Zolner tugged a Waltham railroad watch from his pocket and angled it to the light of a streetlamp. "Start the motor."

A minute later, a man dressed like a clerk, in a suit, necktie, and a bowler hat, walked up Greenwich Street from the direction of Barrow. He shot an anxious glance at the Marmon, ducked his head, and hurried on.

"Slowly," said Marat Zolner. "Keep him in sight."

The man turned left on Christopher.

"Pull over. Come with us."

Yuri was out of the car before it stopped rolling. Zolner was right behind him, signaling for Hooks to stick close. They rounded the corner. The clerk was knocking at the front door, head down, afraid to look in their direction. Light spilled onto the sidewalk as the door was unlocked and swung inward. The clerk said, "Thank you. I'm working late tonight in the Verifier's office."

The guard he spoke to answered, "Yes, sir, Mr. Knowles — Hey!"

Antipov shoved Knowles into the guard. Marat Zolner struck Knowles to the floor, clearing the way for Hooks Newdell to punch the guard to his knees before he could draw his revolver and knock him unconscious with a fist to his jaw.

Zolner closed the door, leaving it open a crack. His five-ton truck careened around the corner of Washington Street, screeched to a stop, and roared backwards across the sidewalk and up to the front door. Dock wallopers leaped out from under the tarpaulin that covered the cargo bed and made a beeline for the room where the confiscated booze was stored. Within sixty seconds they were lugging cases of Canadian rye into the truck.

"Hooks! Come with me and Jake."

Zolner headed for the central elevator bank at a dead run. All but one of the cars were dark at this late hour, and the operator slouched in it was yawning. It took the man a moment to realize something was wrong. It was too late. At Zolner's signal, Hooks blackjacked him. They piled in, and Zolner ran the car down a level to the subbasement, where Knowles had reported the telephone switchboard was located. Hooks pummeled the night operator unconscious. Zolner and Antipov switched off the trunk lines. Then they ran back to the elevator. Zolner leaned hard on the control wheel and the car shot up.

"Hey, where you going?" asked Hooks when they passed the first floor.

"Shut up," said Yuri.

Zolner ran the elevator to the tenth floor, the top. He and Yuri stepped out, guns drawn. Hooks followed with his bloody blackjack. The hall, empty and unguarded, was lined with blank steel doors. Zolner counted four from the elevator bank.

"Hope you have a key," said Hooks, lumbering close behind.

Antipov shoved him aside and pulled from his pocket a quarter stick of dynamite. He secured it to the doorknob with electrician's insulating tape and lit a short fuse with a match. Hooks ran down the hall. Antipov and Zolner hurried after him. The charge exploded with the sharp report of a very large firecracker and blew the door into a vault room that was heaped with four-foot-long canvas bags.

Antipov slashed one open with his dagger. He pulled out a weapon that looked like a short rifle or shotgun with two handgrips and a stick magazine, pointing straight down, and no butt stock.

"What's that?" asked Hooks Newdell.

"An Annihilator," said Zolner, tucking it tightly against his hip and pointing it straight ahead. He quickly gathered bags of the weapons and bags of extra magazines.

"What's an Annihilator?"

"A submachine gun."

"A machine gun you can carry around?" Hooks was amazed. Guys back from the war talked about Lewis machine guns. But Lewis guns were heavy — thirty pounds — and four or five feet long, and you had to mount them on something solid. This thing you could tuck under your coat.

"Fires .45 pistol ammunition. Twenty shots in a stick, reloads in a second."

"I never seen one before."

"Neither has anyone else in New York.

Pick that up and let's go."

"Say, wait a minute. These are the Thompson guns the customs agents found on the ship. These are Sinn Féin's guns."

"No," said Yuri Antipov. "They are ours."

"Yeah, but —"

"Hooks, what is that you dropped?"

Hooks bent his head and looked down at his feet. "What?"

Yuri Antipov pressed his revolver to the nape of the boxer's neck and pulled the trigger. Hooks collapsed in a heap.

Zolner asked, "What did you do that for?"

"You were going to kill him, were you not?"

"You should have waited. He could have helped us carry the guns."

12

"I blame the Irish."

"For which, the guns or the booze?"

"Both. The booze was a Sinn Féin smoke screen to get their submachine guns back."

"Some smoke screen. Seventy-five thousand bucks of twenty-year-old Canadian Club. Sinn Féin oughta stop the civil war and open a speakeasy."

So went the conversation among detectives hurrying in and out of the Van Dorn bull pen while Isaac Bell, who had set up a desk prominently in the middle of the room to keep everyone on his toes, combed through empty report after empty report on the Van Dorn shooting.

It was the morning after a daring and brilliantly executed late-night raid on the Appraisers' Stores. The newspapers, which had printed less than half the story the private detectives had pieced together, were having a ball castigating Prohibition, Prohibition officials, Dry agents, U.S. Customs, the Treasury Department, and the New York City police.

"Just wait," said Darren McKinney, "until they find out about the submachine guns. Heads will roll." The New York cops and U.S. Customs had kept the gun theft out of the papers, but the story had to come out eventually.

Harry Warren burst in at a dead run. "Isaac! Wait 'til you hear the latest. I was just talking to a customs agent, and he —"

"If it doesn't have to do with Joe Van Dorn, I don't want to hear it —" But even as he spoke, Bell thought better of it and changed his mind. Any clues to the raid that were snagged in the Van Dorn net could stand them in good stead with the federal government. "Hold on, I take that back. What's up?"

Harry leaned in close and spoke in a low voice. "Something's fishy. They found a dead guy in the machine-gun room. A kid named Newdell. Ricky 'Hooks' Newdell. Small-potatoes thug dreaming of prize-fights."

"What's fishy?"

"He hung out in a lunchroom on 18th. Customs guy didn't know it, but that's a Gopher joint. Hooks was a Gopher."

"You're kidding. What was a Gopher doing in that operation?"

"My question, too. The Gophers have been washed-up since before the war. The bunch that moved to Chelsea couldn't pour water out of a hat with directions stamped on the crown."

"Could they have been hired by Sinn Féin?" Bell asked dubiously.

"Sinn Féin aren't stupid, and they've got plenty of gunmen without tapping Gophers."

"How did he die?"

"Shot."

"First I've heard there was gunplay."

"No, no, no, not by customs agents. No, it sounds like one of his pals nailed him."

Isaac Bell said, "That makes no sense. By all accounts we've heard, it was a smooth operation. Guys on that smooth an operation don't usually kill each other on the job."

"I agree, but a Gopher where a Gopher shouldn't be is dead. Something's up."

Bell and Harry Warren were interrupted by Ed Tobin. The head of the Boss Boys squad looked like he'd slept under a pier. His suit was rumpled, his hat battered, his complexion sallow. But his eyes glowed with triumph.

"Found a friend of your Johnny," he said.

145

"I'm pretty sure."

Isaac Bell surged to his feet. "Where?"

"Oysterman I was buying drinks for — Staten Island fellow named Tom Kemp — said a bootlegger he knew disappeared just when he was hoping the guy was going to hire his boat to taxi booze. The bootlegger looked like your description of Johnny, and he had a German accent."

"Was his name Johnny?"

"We didn't get that far. Kemp's pal came into the blind pig and recognized my mug. Soon as he spilled I was a detective, Kemp clammed up."

"I'll get it out of him," said Bell.

"He won't talk to a detective. He thinks we're the same as cops. Can't blame him, if he's hoping to make a living running booze — Hey, where're you going, Isaac?"

"Tell the garage to send over a Stutz Bearcat."

The tall detective strode to the costume room, stripped off his clothes, and put on a one-hundred-thirty-dollar pin-striped navy suit that he had waiting in a closet. Its coat had a pinched waist and was cut to accentuate his broad shoulders. He knotted a silk necktie, folded a matching handkerchief and inserted it in the breast pocket, and transferred the contents of his pockets. From a rack of hats, he chose one carefully, a dark Borsalino, then studied his reflection in a full-length mirror. He laced spats over his boots and looked again.

Something else was missing.

He unbuttoned his coat and rearranged his belongings. He closed it, pulled the Borsalino low over his eyes, and returned to the bull pen. "Let's go."

Tobin said, "That's why you want a Stutz. It'll make you look like a high-class bootlegger."

"That, and the fact that it has a three-hundred-sixty-cubic-inch engine that puts out eighty horsepower," said Bell. "The image ought to convince your man I intend to hire his boat."

"I like the gun bulge."

"Don't tell my tailor."

Bell opened his coat to show Tobin the notebook he had shoved behind his shoulder holster, deliberately puckering the cloth that his tailor had so skillfully crafted to conceal the Browning.

They drove the Stutz to the Battery and took it across to Staten Island on the ferry. From the St. George landing, they drove past the mansions and resort hotels of Richmond Terrace and along the Kill Van

Kull, a narrow, winding strait of water that separated Staten Island from New Jersey and led to New York Harbor in either direction. Tobin got out of the car at Bridge Creek and pointed Bell in the direction of Tom Kemp's oyster boat.

Bell drove within sight of the boat and parked the car on the side of the road where Kemp would see it when he looked up from the motor he was working on. Then he swaggered down the gangway onto a rickety floating dock. Kemp's vessel was typical of the workboats that New York oystermen had been converting from sail to motor power since long before the war. It was broad and flat and thirty feet long. The motor sat in a hole in the deck, and Bell saw immediately that it was anything but typical. He recognized an eight-hundred-twenty-five-cubic-inch, six-cylinder Pierce-Arrow that Tom must have pulled out of a wrecked touring car. A maze of tubing indicated that he had added on an oversize oil pump to keep it lubricated when the boat angled its bow up at speed.

"How fast does this thing go?" he asked the figure crouched over it with tools scattered beside him.

"Who wants to know?" Kemp said without bothering to look up.

Bell stepped onto the boat without being invited — a sin, Ed Tobin had told him, that a waterman would equate with burning an American flag or insulting his mother. Kemp jumped to his feet. He was a big man with arms and shoulders that bulged from lifting oyster tongs since boyhood. Bell moved closer, two feet from the man, close enough for him to smell his cologne and have to crane his neck to meet his cold gaze.

"*I* want to know. How fast does your boat go?"

Tom Kemp took note of Bell's expression. His eyes fixed on the bulge under his coat. "Thirty knots."

"What's that in miles per hour?"

"Jeez, mister, I don't know. Thirty-five?"

"How fast when it's loaded?"

"Depends with what."

"Booze."

"Mister, booze is —"

"Profitable," said Bell, and before Tom could say anything else, "I hear two different stories about you, Mr. Kemp. One says you're available to run rum. The other says you've already been hired. Which is it? Are you available or not?"

"I'm available."

"You're sure?"

"Yeah . . . You don't believe me?"

"What happened to the German guy?" Bell shot back. Now he had to wait. Would Kemp answer, What German guy? Would he say, The German guy disappeared?

"How do you know about the German?" Kemp demanded.

Bell repeated, coldly, "What happened to the German guy?"

"I don't know. He was hanging out, looking for a boat. I thought we had a deal. But he never showed."

"When was this?"

"What do you care?"

Bell said, "When I learn a lot about a fellow who I'm going to trust with ten thousand bucks of my booze, I also learn what questions to ask to see if he lies to me. When did the German say he would show?"

"Sunday."

Bell nodded. Johnny had died Saturday. He could have been intending to make another run Sunday.

"When did he tell you Sunday?"

"Last week."

"O.K. You're doing pretty good so far. Next question: What's his name?"

"He called himself Johnny."

"I know he called himself Johnny. What's his real name?"

"What do you mean? It's Johnny."

150

"Germans don't call themselves Johnny."

"Oh yeah. Well, Johann. Something like that. Johann."

"You're doing O.K., Tom. Tell me his last name and we're in business."

Tom Kemp wet his lips. Bell suspected that the oysterman knew Johann's last name but didn't want to tell. He wondered why it mattered to him.

"Tom, I thought we're on the square."

"Kozlov. Johann Kozlov."

"Good," said Bell. "Very good." Finally, a breakthrough, but he still wondered why Tom hesitated to reveal Kozlov's name. He pulled a large roll of bills from his pocket and peeled off a hundred-dollar bill.

"Down payment," he said. As Tom Kemp reached eagerly for the money, Bell asked, "Did you know him long?"

"Nope."

"Then how'd you meet him?"

Tom wet his lips again.

Bell held tightly to the bill. "How did Johann know where to find you?"

"I don't know. He just found me."

"Why would he trust you?"

"I got an uncle works on the ships. Stoker. He hooked up with Johann Kozlov when the Wobblies were trying to put some backbone in the seamen's union."

"Johann Kozlov was a Wobbly?" Bell could not conceal his surprise. The Wobblies, the Industrial Workers of the World, were passionately dedicated to the dream of labor taking control of production. They strived to make the established conservative craft unions demand more and fight harder, usually without success.

"The strike in the spring?" asked Bell. The International Seamen's Union had struck every port in the nation on May 1 and lost so badly they had to accept a quarter cut in pay.

"The union kept the Wobblies out, and with no Wobblies to give 'em guts, the owners broke the strike."

Broken so badly, Bell wondered, that a dedicated labor organizer threw up his hands and became a rumrunner? The Wobblies had been accused of many failings, but never greed.

"Where is your uncle?"

"Bound for Singapore, last I heard."

"What line?"

Kemp got truculent again. "What the hell does a bootlegger care what line my uncle's stoking for?"

The tall detective shifted smoothly back to his bootlegger act. "I don't pay a man until I know whose side he's on," he said coldly, and started to stuff his roll back into his pocket. "What line owns the ship your uncle is working on?"

"No line will hire him since the strike. He shipped out on a tramp."

"Johann Kozlov's name," said Grady Forrer, chief of Van Dorn Research, reporting next morning to Isaac Bell, "suggests both German and Russian heritage. He was, in fact, a German-born alien radical."

"Was he a Wobbly?"

"We've found no evidence of an IWW connection yet. But he did join the Communist Party, which had some Wobblies in it. In fact, Kozlov joined both wings of it simultaneously, which is odd because the Communist Labor Party and the Communist Party of America couldn't stand each other. Moscow ordered them to merge, but even that didn't take until this spring when they finally formed the so-called United Communist Party. You can imagine the shoutfests at their meetings."

"Could Moscow have sent Kozlov to America to deliver the order from Moscow to merge?"

"Interesting thought," Grady mused, "if not likely." He made a note. "I'll look into it."

"But you found no evidence of a direct link to the IWW? Remember, I was told he was organizing for the Wobblies in the sailors' strike."

Grady shrugged. "We found no evidence of involvement in the sailors' strike. And no *record* of his joining the IWW. Which is not surprising, considering that he was deported."

"Deported? When?"

"Kozlov was arrested in the Red Scare roundups — the Palmer Raids — in the first wave, at the end of 1919. The Justice Department deported him back to his native Germany."

The government raids on alien radicals' homes, schools, and businesses had been launched in late 1919 by Attorney General Mitchell Palmer after an Italian anarchist bombed Palmer's Washington home. Bell said, "I'm not sure what to make of that. It's a heck of a background for a rumrunner."

Bell pondered the curiosity. How big a leap was it from radical to criminal? He had encountered labor radicals and he thought it a big leap indeed for those dedicated to a cause. On the other hand, how many in the bootlegging line even considered themselves criminals? They told themselves they were providing a service. Or, as Scudder Smith had put it, "having fun." At least until the real criminals started beating them up to steal the profits.

"How many were arrested in the Palmer Raids?"

"At least ten thousand," Grady answered.

"How many were deported?"

"Eight hundred."

"One in twelve? That puts Herr Kozlov in select company."

"Or just unlucky."

"How so?"

"He got deported early, before Palmer's fellow cabinet members accused the attorney general of seeing a Red behind every bush. Palmer was scheming to deport tens of thousands. But pretty soon the Red Scare was leaking steam."

Bell shook his head in puzzlement. How did any of this get him closer to the rum gang that shot Joe Van Dorn?

Grady gathered his notes. "How's the Boss doing?"

Bell brightened. "Better. Much better. The infection did not take hold. Dorothy just telephoned that he wants to see me. The docs said they'll let me in tomorrow if he keeps improving."

"Thank God. Give him my best. By the

way, Isaac, this *Genickschuss* neck shot you told me about? We looked into it. Pauline was right. The Cheka perfected the technique."

"I haven't seen her wrong yet," said Bell, and, with that in mind, sent another Marconigram to the *Nieuw Amsterdam.*

JOHNNY IS JOHANN KOZLOV.

RED SCARE DEPORTED TO GERMANY.

KOZLOV ASSOCIATES?

HOW DID KOZLOV RETURN TO THE UNITED STATES?

In the event she had landed already, he sent copies of it by transatlantic cable care of the Holland America Line to their Rotterdam pier and to the Van Dorn field office in Berlin.

"I've discovered one man who actually knew Johann Kozlov," Isaac Bell told Marion over a midnight supper of Welsh rarebit and a bottle of Mumm champagne from the cellar Archie Abbott had installed in his East Side town house when the Volstead Act was passed. They were in their suite at the St.

Regis, Bell sprawled in a comfortable armchair, Marion lounging on the couch. Happily home from a long day of chasing vaudevillians around Fort Lee, she had dressed for supper in a green silk peignoir that matched her eyes.

"Unfortunately, he's somewhere in the middle of the Pacific Ocean on a tramp steamer that doesn't have a radio."

Bell often talked over his cases with his wife, whose judgment he respected mightily. Marion had a law degree from Stanford University, a razor-sharp mind, and a knack for approaching clues from an unexpected angle. She was unusually observant. She was also an optimist.

"At least you have a name. And Grady's Research boys say Kozlov joined the Communist Party. And you're pretty sure he was a Wobbly."

"But I can't reckon how an anti-capitalist who wants to abolish the wage system becomes a rumrunner."

"Maybe he was not that dedicated an anti-capitalist."

"Dedicated enough to get deported," said Bell.

"The Palmer Raids were an abomination," said Marion, who had many foreign-born friends in the moving picture business.

Bell said, "The vast majority were turned loose."

"I had one friend, a French actor, who was released within a week. Another, a brilliant Russian camera operator, spent three months in a filthy jail."

"At least Mr. Palmer got his comeuppance when his party decided he was not their ideal candidate for president."

"Funny, isn't it?"

"What's funny?"

"Your Herr Kozlov had the last laugh when he made his way back to New York to radicalize the sailors' union."

"Until he became a rumrunner."

"Which," said Marion, "you still find to be an unusual change of career."

She paused for his answer, but he did not speak.

Bell was finding it increasingly difficult to concentrate on the case. Marion's peignoir clung intriguingly, and she had loosened her hair, which she usually wore up to keep it out of the camera eyepiece. It framed her beautiful face like gold leaf.

"Don't you?"

"What?"

"Don't you find it an unusual change of career?"

"Why don't we sleep on it?" he asked.

She eyed him over the rim of her champagne flute. "Yes. We both have busy mornings."

"Then we would be doubly wise," said Isaac Bell, "to go to bed."

"Wise," Marion agreed. She put down her glass and headed into the bedroom.

Bell followed close behind.

"But!" said Marion, her eyes suddenly flashing.

"But what?"

"Johann Kozlov risked arrest, imprisonment, even his life, sneaking back into the country. Then he risked exposure by organizing the sailors' strike. Labor organizers are arrested routinely. He was willing to risk getting caught. Wouldn't you call that dedicated?"

Bell said, "But that does not change the fact that less than two months later, Johann Kozlov was wounded running rum."

"But does that mean that he changed his career?"

"That," said Bell, "is a very interesting question. You're asking, was he running rum for some other reason than getting rich quick?"

Marion climbed under the sheets. "Are you *ever* coming to bed?"

13

Pauline Grandzau trotted briskly down the *Nieuw Amsterdam*'s gangway, carrying her bag in one hand and Isaac's Marconigram in the other. She deciphered the Van Dorn code in her head.

Isaac's last query was the easiest.

**HOW DID KOZLOV RETURN TO
THE UNITED STATES?**

Steamer ticket and false passport, if he had the means. Or try to snag a berth as a sailor and desert when the ship landed, which was difficult with tens of thousands of merchant seamen on the beach waiting for shipping to recover from the end of the war. Or, if Herr Kozlov was especially valuable to the Communist Party, then passage would be arranged by the Comintern Maritime Section, which not only organized seamen's mutinies but used their network to move Communist agents around the world disguised as ships' officers and seamen. Kozlov's execution by *Genickschuss* suggested that he could have been that valuable, an operative who knew too much to be allowed to talk.

"Red Scare deported to Germany" and "Kozlov associates?" were matters that she had to address, gingerly and face-to-face, with her contacts in the police and the Foreign Service. A copy of the Marconigram was waiting with her steamer trunk, courtesy of the Holland America Line's chief purser, which showed her exactly how important Isaac thought this Kozlov was. She would find a third copy at the office.

She took the train to Amsterdam, and on to Berlin, and arrived in Germany's capital as night fell. Outside the railroad station, she found the streets of the government districts in Tiergarten and Mitte blocked by thousands of boys singing the "Internationale" and chanting, "Up and do battle! Up and do battle!"

Tense security police were guarding banks, newspaper offices, and public buildings.

Searchlights played across the façades. Armed bicyclists patrolled the streets in the uniform of the anti-Communist Freikorps. Headlines on news kiosks shrilled the battle

cries, and fears, of the political factions vy-
ing for power in post-war Germany:

COMMUNISTS TO DYNAMITE MONUMENTS

ULTRA-REACTIONARY ARMY OFFICERS
TO LAUNCH COUP

BOLSHEVIKS BURN BOURGEOISIE
NEWSPAPERS

FREIKORPS COMMANDEER POLICE

REDS HIDE RIFLES IN MINE SHAFTS

Provocateurs abounded. There was unrest
in Saxony, open rebellion in the city of
Halle, and in Hamburg, Germany's second-
largest city, rumor that the Communists
would hoist the red flag over the shipyards.

Pauline gave up trying to get to her office
and retreated to the train station to telephone central police headquarters. All lines
were busy. Back outside, the streetcars and
trams had stopped running. She refused to
be stymied. Berlin was her city, and she was
proud to know every neighborhood and
nearly every street. She had had the briefest
apprenticeship of any Van Dorn field chief,
but she had observed her mentor, Art Cur-

tis, in action and had learned by his example to cultivate friends in places both high and low.

She waded through the crowds, racking her brain for whom among her network of friends and informants in government, business, the military, police, and criminals could help her find at least the beginning of Kozlov's trail.

She cut down to the Unter den Linden and walked a mile on the boulevard through thickening crowds. The police headquarters at Alexanderplatz was surrounded by poor and chaotic neighborhoods fought over by Reds and anti-Communists. The building looked under siege behind a wall of Freikorps trucks and police armored cars parked around it end to end.

She hurried back to the train station to send telegrams to her police contacts. Thankfully, the telegraph was working. But only one friend wired back.

PRATER.

She walked as fast as she could to the Prater Garten, a beer garden set under chestnut trees in Prenzlauer Berg. It was just far enough beyond Mitte to offer sanctuary from the tumult shaking the

163

center of the city. Klaxons could be heard faintly, accompanied by a rumble of armored car engines, but at least the demonstrations and fights were too far off to be seen.

She spied a cadaverous man at a table under the trees and took a chair across from him. He had been the powerful Kommandeur of Berlin's center Polizeigruppen until he resisted Freikorps demands. Desperate to regain his power, he was hungry for information. *Give,* Isaac Bell had taught her, *and you shall receive.*

"Thank you for coming," she said.

He eyed her bleakly and puffed smoke from a cigarette in the corner of his mouth. Finally, he muttered, "The worst part of being demoted into semi-retirement is that beautiful private detectives no longer call on me for favors."

"This must come as a great relief to your wife."

Fritz Richter laughed out loud. "Pauline, Pauline, you always did brighten the day."

Pauline answered him formally. "You will please remember, Herr Polizeikommandeur, that I asked for information — not favors — and I always give you information back."

"It's been too long a time, Fräulein Privatdetektive."

"I'm home from the United States only this evening. You are the first old acquaintance I have called on."

"Go back, is my advice. Make a new life in a new country. Our Germany is exploding again."

"I don't want a new country."

"There's a new one coming whether you want it or not. Our warring Nationalists and Communists and Social Democrats and National Socialists and Freikorps and Red Hundreds — a plague on all their houses — are not fighting for their supposed ideals. They are fighting for the spoils of the World War."

"Our chief investigator told me that not ten days ago in New York."

"How unusual. I don't think of Americans as taking the long view. Did he tell you, too, that the winner — the best organized and most ruthless — will dictate the future of ordinary people who are trying to avoid the fight?"

"Semi-retirement has brought out the gloomy philosopher in you."

"There will be no gracious winners, no knights in shining armor." He signaled the waiter. "May I buy you beer, young lady?"

"No. Let Van Dorn pay." She ordered beer and, suddenly realizing she was starving: "I haven't eaten all day. Will you join me?"

Richter nodded and lit a new cigarette from the ember of the old. He wouldn't eat but she ordered anyway. *"Weisswurst."*

Richter raised his glass. *"Prost!"*

"Cheers! I'm tracking a man named Johann Kozlov who was deported last year by the Americans. He made his way back to America, where he was shot in the Cheka way."

"Comintern. Yes?"

"I would say, yes. Who can I talk to?"

He eyed her appraisingly. "What is it worth to you?"

She returned a look that put Fritz Richter in mind of an alpine blizzard. "If I would not sleep with an important police commander for information, why would I sleep with a demoted, semi-retired old lecher?"

Before he could think of an answer, she broke into a smile that left him no choice but to smile back, duck his head, and murmur, "You can't blame an old lecher for trying."

Which led to an introduction to someone she did not know at the Foreign Office.

At Bellevue Hospital, Isaac Bell found Joseph Van Dorn propped up on pillows and gazing expectantly at the door. He had a week's growth of new beard on his cheeks, which made him look a little healthier. His eyes were clearer but hardly piercing, and Bell had to work hard to put a smile on his face. The founder of the Van Dorn Detective Agency looked old and very, very tired.

"There you are," Van Dorn whispered.

"Came as soon as they let me. How are you?"

Dorothy Van Dorn and David Novicki were hovering. Novicki said, "I was just entertaining our pal here with tales of my retirement, wasn't I, Joe? 'Barnacle Bill' is home from the sea. Joe won't believe that I was driving a trolley on Long Island."

Van Dorn whispered, "Passengers have no idea what a hand they have at the helm."

"Trolley went bust," says Novicki. "I'm going to drive a taxi."

"Dorothy," Van Dorn whispered. "Why don't you and Dave grab yourself some lunch. I need to talk with Isaac."

"Not too much," she said.

"We'll behave ourselves. Don't you worry."

Dorothy kissed him on the forehead and leveled her silvery gray eyes on Bell. "Go easy. He's not out of the woods yet. But he's been clamoring to see you."

"Don't worry. I won't tire him."

Van Dorn waited until his wife and friend

were out the door. Then he asked Bell in a hoarse whisper, "How's it going in Detroit?"

"Worse than we thought."

Bell explained that the entire field office was being undermined by corruption, including the supposedly loyal detective Van Dorn had put in charge.

"We have to clear 'em out and rebuild from scratch."

"Send Kansas City Eddie Edwards," Van Dorn replied in a voice so low Bell could barely hear. "He'll straighten them out."

"Eddie's not getting any younger," said Bell. "And Detroit's getting tougher. I sent Texas Walt."

"Hatfield? Isn't he out west, making moving pictures?"

"Walt's taking time off."

"I hope he hasn't gone soft. All that Hollywood high living."

"If Walt's gone soft, it doesn't show."

Van Dorn closed his eyes. He lay silent, his chest barely moving with his breath. When he finally opened his eyes again, Bell said, "I do have better news about Protective Services."

"What's that?"

"Darnedest thing, but when the word got out that Clayton and Ellis were let go, our hotel dicks took notice all around the country."

"How do you know?"

"I sent agents disguised as bootleggers to offer bribes."

"Good for you!"

"The boys told them to get lost. Several were so emphatic, they threw punches."

"That is a great relief. How are we doing with the Coast Guard?"

"I'm sorry, Joe. They canceled the contract."

"Damnation!" Van Dorn erupted, which set him to coughing. Bell held a handkerchief for him and then gave him water. Van Dorn caught his breath. "I was really hoping we could parley new government work out of that. I got shot *and* lost the client. No justice in the world."

Bell was relieved to see a wry smile on Van Dorn's bristly cheeks. He said, "I'll try and learn what our chances are when I finally get through to the Coast Guard chief of staff."

"O.K. . . . . How are we doing with the gang who shot up the cutter?"

"One of them showed up at Roosevelt Hospital, wounded. Before I could interview him, someone killed him."

Van Dorn whispered, "What for?"

"I don't know. Maybe they thought you were dead and they'd be facing murder charges if they didn't kill the witness. At any rate, I almost caught the guy who shot him, but I lost him. I doubt I'd recognize him if he walked in the door. But we got the dead man's name. Alien radical, deported to Germany, sneaked back in. I have Pauline working on who his friends were over there."

"That's a good start."

"I am hoping you can help me, hoping you might remember a little more."

"Shoot," Van Dorn said weakly.

"The Coast Guard still won't talk to me. So all I know about what happened out there is secondhand from the harbor cops. And the harbor's boiling with rumors. What do you remember about a black boat?"

"It was going like a bat out of hell. Fastest boat I ever saw, Isaac. Had to be doing fifty miles an hour. It had a Lewis gun and a fellow who knew how to use it. And it was armored."

"An armored speedboat?"

"Bulletproof glass in the windshield, too. I thought for sure I'd nailed him. Bullets bounced off it like rain. The only men I hit were on the other boat. The taxi."

"Was the black boat guarding the taxi?"

"That was certainly the effect. Here's the thing, Isaac." Van Dorn sat up taller, his eyes glowing.

"Take it easy. Talk slowly. Don't push yourself. O.K.?"

"O.K.," Van Dorn whispered. "Here's the situation. My head's clearing, and I'm remembering that was one heck of a gun battle."

"Machine guns and armor . . . I should say so."

Van Dorn waved for silence. "I've been in plenty scraps, but not like that one. I thought I was back in Panama. Do you know what I mean?"

Bell nodded. Decades ago, as a young U.S. Marine, Joe Van Dorn had landed on the Isthmus in the middle of a revolution.

"Those boys on the black boat knew their business. They used their speed to hold an angle of engagement the Coasties couldn't cover with their cannon. They'd been to war before."

14

As Newtown Storms had predicted to Marat Zolner, the stock market began to move up.

"I can't promise every week will be as exciting as this one, Prince André," Storms told him on the telephone. "We were especially fortunate with a New York Central offering. The firm had an inside track, shall we say. Your ten thousand dollars is now worth twenty."

"I need ten thousand of it immediately," said Zolner.

"May I strongly counsel, Your Highness, that you plow this windfall back into your account? I see new opportunities every day."

"I see one, too," said Zolner. "Fern will pick up the money this afternoon."

That evening, Marat Zolner took the ten thousand to the Bronx and paid the owner of Morrison Motor Express for a controlling interest in a fleet of seven-and-a-half-ton Mack AC "Bulldog" trucks. He dispatched four of the sturdy, slope-nosed, long-haul vehicles three hundred fifty miles to Champlain, New York, on the Canadian border.

Zolner gave command of the convoy to the powerfully built and aptly nicknamed Trucks O'Neal. Next to each driver rode a guard armed with cash for the booze, the names of the customs agents to pay off, and a Thompson submachine gun to either defend the convoy or, if they ran into a New York–bound shipment, cut short the two-day trip to Canada and hijack it.

Despite, or because of, an introduction by retired police commander Richter, the Foreign Service secretary did not invite Pauline Grandzau to his office. Pauline suggested they meet at the Kronprinzenpalais, where the National Gallery had created a wonderful new museum for modern art.

"That would be splendid," he said, his genuine enthusiasm reminding her that for anyone who loved painting and sculpture and film, it was a magnificent time to be alive in Germany. For artists, the past was over and the future gleamed.

They made eye contact in the bustling front hall — he as handsome as Richter had promised her, she as striking as Richter had promised him — and he followed Pauline upstairs to the top floor, which housed a temporary collection. They wandered separately until, as if by chance, both were standing in front of an exciting Hannah Höch collage, a photo montage, with a title that made it hard to dismiss the violence in the streets.

Pauline read the title aloud, couching it as a question: " 'Cut with the Dada Kitchen Knife Through the Last Weimar Beer-Belly Cultural Epoch in Germany'?"

"Tongue in cheek?" the Foreign Service man asked.

"Let us hope."

Side by side, they continued in low tones.

"We had Kozlov watched from the moment we stamped his passport."

"Is he Comintern?"

The secretary answered that nothing in the Foreign Service files had indicated whether Kozlov served the Russian Comintern. But all in his department agreed that the newly returned emigrant would be a fount of up-to-date information about radicals in the United States and therefore a potential agent to be smuggled back in.

"We asked who would approach him, this revolutionary who knew America. It did not take long. They met at the zoo. The agent's name was Valtin."

"Is Valtin Comintern?"

"Of course."

"Where did they go? What did they do?"

The reply was neutral, his voice and expression bland. "The security police made a fateful decision to watch but not intervene. They were hoping, I suppose, to arrest not just two men but an entire network. Thus when they lost track of Kozlov, they lost Valtin, too."

The sweepers were out in force, cleaning the streets of every sign of the demonstrations and marches around Alexanderplatz, when Pauline called on an old friend in the security police. They went out for coffee and pastry.

"You know I can't talk about this."

"Of course you can't," she said. "But, I must ask you" — the clatter of china and silver in the busy confectionary ensured that even the couple holding hands at the next table could not hear them, but she lowered her voice anyway for dramatic effect — "is it true that Valtin and Kozlov escaped surveillance and disappeared?"

"Disappeared?" He sat up straight as a sword. "Is that what the Foreign Office told you? Pauline, how could you believe that for even a moment?"

"I did not think it likely. I imagined you let that story out to get them off your back."

"You imagined correctly. We followed Kozlov's and Valtin's every move. We watched like hawks. We were keen-eyed and we were silent. They never saw us."

"Did Valtin put Kozlov on a boat to America?"

He hesitated. "I am not privy to that detail."

That sounded to Pauline as if the Foreign Office secretary had it right. The security police had indeed lost sight of Kozlov and his Comintern contact. "Where is Valtin now?"

"We are currently tracking him through a young woman who is either a Comintern courier or his lover, or both. We're holding back to see with whom else she makes contact."

It was more likely, she thought, they hoped the girl would lead them back to the agent they had lost. "What is her name?"

"Her name is Anny."

"Anny?" Pauline took a dainty bite of her *Mohnkuchen.* Her tongue crept across her lips to lick a poppy seed. She touched her mouth with her napkin and eyed him over the linen as if it were a veil.

The Polizeioberstleutnant steadied his breathing.

"What is Anny's last name?" she asked.

"You are a devil in devil's clothing, Fräulein Privatdetektive Grandzau. I've spoken too freely already. You know I cannot tell you her last name."

"You can't blame a devil for trying . . . If you can't tell me her last name, you can surely tell me what is the color of her hair and eyes . . . or perhaps where she stays or works . . ."

When Marat Zolner returned to Manhattan from the Bronx, he found that Yuri Antipov had left an urgent message with Fern Hawley.

"He wants you to meet him downtown. He said you'll know where."

Zolner went to a blind pig on Vesey around the corner from the Washington Market. Antipov was taking a small sip of what passed for gin in the place.

"How is your empire?" he asked.

Zolner said, "You know, bootlegging wasn't my idea originally. I got it in Finland. Do you recall the Comintern scheme to raise money for weapons by smuggling liquor past Finnish Customs? It was very

177

innovative until the Comintern's entire Finnish Section passed out drunk on the contraband."

Antipov did not laugh.

"What do you want from me?" Zolner asked.

"I want you to rent a stable in Lower Manhattan."

"What for?"

"Come." Antipov led him around the corner to Barclay Street, where he had parked an old-fashioned coal wagon identical to the thousands that cluttered the narrow streets of Lower Manhattan and drove the truck drivers crazy. A strong horse stood in the traces, nosing an empty feed bag.

"Where did you get this?"

"I brought it over from New Jersey on the ferry. It is high time to do the job we were sent to do."

"What's in the wagon?"

"Dynamite."

Zolner stared at him while he thought how to deal with what was clearly an ultimatum. Antipov gazed back calmly, a man whose mind was made up, determined, utterly sure, and implacable.

"Where did you get dynamite?"

"I memorized Moscow's list of quarries where comrades work," Antipov answered.

"If you will not help me, I'll do it myself."

"I will help you, of course. There is no reason why we can't build and attack at the same time."

"I need a safe stable for the wagon."

"You'll be inside it in one hour."

Antipov looked at him curiously. "You surprise me, Marat. I would have thought you would tell me to go to hell."

"We are Comintern, Yuri. Our goal is the same. Overthrow the international bourgeoisie by every means. Come. Let's walk the horse while we talk."

"Where?"

"I have a stable. Ten short blocks."

"It must be a safe place to prepare the attack."

"Trucks O'Neal will keep it safe."

"Excellent." Antipov had come to see the value of the American, a hard-boiled, clear-headed gangster who could recruit similarly trustworthy men when they were needed.

Zolner took the bridle and coaxed the animal to turn the wagon up Washington Street. "What is our target?"

"Wall Street."

BOOK TWO:
HIJACK

The Comintern Delivers

COAL

15

A patched sail of faded canvas looked common, thought Captain Novicki. Even innocent. And if you hoisted your sail on a slow-moving, old-fashioned, cat-rigged workboat and sat a white-whiskered Barnacle Bill smoking his pipe at the tiller, you'd be damned-near invisible. At least to anyone searching for the get-rich-quick boys.

Or so Novicki hoped as he steered his catboat across Great South Bay. A stiff wind raised a fierce chop studded with whitecaps. The old mariner sailed blithely through it, out the narrow Fire Island Inlet and into the Atlantic Ocean.

Eight miles out in international waters he found a row of wooden schooners and rusty tramp freighters anchored to the shallow bottom and pitching on the swells. Their hulls and rigging were hung with billboards advertising authentic Scotch whisky, English

gin, and French champagne. Captain Novicki tied up at the schooner he had con-
tracted to deliver for and handed over mail
and gifts of fresh fruit and vegetables to the
captain and his family and soda pop for the
kids. The oldest child climbed the mast with
binoculars to watch for the Coast Guard
while the family helped load as many cases
as Novicki's boat would hold.

He was not the only upright citizen taxi-
ing booze to shore. It was evident from the
private yachts and motorboats sailing up
and down Rum Row, bargaining with the
ships selling liquor. But neither they nor
any rum-running taxi that night had a more
valuable cargo — the finest single-malt
Scotch whisky of such a dark color and
pungent smoky aroma that it could be
stretched five-to-one with grain alcohol and
still sold as the real McCoy.

The schooner captain and his wife appeared anxious. Novicki asked what was
bothering them.

"There was another hijacking last night.
At least we think there was. The boat never
came back, and he was in fine shape when
he headed in. I'd keep a weather eye, if I
were you."

"Nobody'll bother a little old catboat."

"She ain't that little, and she's beamy as a

barge," said the schooner captain. "Any gangster who knows his business will see you squeezed in a hundred cases."

Novicki had timed it so he could run for the coast after dark. Eight miles off and ten miles upwind of Fire Island Inlet, he had an easy sail on following seas. He covered two miles in thirty minutes, ears cocked for the sound of engines. A couple of taxis roared past at five times his speed.

Suddenly, he heard the distinctive rumble of tripled-up gasoline motors. He hurried to the mast and dropped the sail and got the canvas on deck seconds before a Coast Guard cutter swept the water with its searchlight. It moved on eventually. He raised his sail and kept listening.

He was almost back to the inlet when he sensed as much as heard distant thunder.

He gauged his position to be too far off to hear the surf on the beach. Nor was it a storm. The sky was clearing and stars were already burning through the haze. He reached over the side and dipped his pipe into the water, dousing the red glow.

The thunder moved closer.

Fire raced over the waves, a bank of dense flame that unveiled in its down glow the profile of a long black boat.

Novicki tied his tiller and hurried forward to drop the sail again. But this time he was too late. The black boat had a searchlight that was bigger than the Coast Guard's. The white-hot beam swept the sea, skipping from wave top to wave top, and suddenly blazed on the sail like a hundred suns. Blinded and confused, the old man stumbled to his tiller as if he could somehow steer his way out of this mess.

A machine gun roared. The barrel spit fire almost as bright as the black boat's exhaust, and almost as loud. Bullets pierced Novicki's decks and sent splinters into his face. The storm of lead blasting the wood, shredding the sail, and screaming past his ears was paralyzing. His hand locked on the tiller. The thundering engines quieted, throttled down, as the boat drew near. But the gun kept firing staccato bursts and the bullets kept flying. In between the bursts he heard men yelling. In all the noise and confusion it took him a moment to realize they weren't Americans. They were speaking a foreign language. He couldn't hear much over the gun, but it might be Russian, a language he had encountered occasionally at sea.

The oddity had the wholly unexpected effect of clearing his head. He couldn't understand their meaning, but whatever language they were shouting, it sure wouldn't translate as "Cease fire!" Confident that the sea held no worse dangers, the old mariner filled his lungs and rolled over the side and into the water.

It was startling cold, cold enough to almost stop the heart. He was dragged under by the weight of his coat, which he had buttoned against the chilly night air. He did not fight it but let it take him deep, away from the riot overhead. The water muffled the thunder of the black boat's engines and the roar of the machine gun. But he heard the purposeful thrashing of many propellers.

He was running out of air. He ripped at the buttons and got out of his coat and swam at an angle to the surface, trying to move as far as he could from the boats. He broke surface at last, gulped air, and looked around. The hijackers were thirty feet away, swarming over his boat, busy loading his booze into theirs. They had switched off the searchlight and were working by flashlight. He swam farther away so they wouldn't see him and dog-paddled, teeth chattering, to stay afloat. As soon as they finished, they attacked the catboat's bilges with axes, chopping holes in the bottom. She started to settle, pulled under by the weight of her centerboard.

The black boat engaged its engines and thundered into the night.

An armored car painted with skulls and crossbones led a gang of anti-Communists into a Berlin alley. They were police-trained and armed with pistols and rubber truncheons. The men trapped inside the Communist bomb factory panicked. The Reds had one gun among them, a rusted revolver. The consignment of brand-new Ortgies 7.65 pistols that the Central Committee had promised had not materialized. Anny, the girl who cooked for them, turned in terror to Pauline Grandzau.

Pauline took her hand.

The bomb factory was hidden in a ground-floor tenement flat in the Wedding working-class district of narrow streets and crooked alleys. If anyone could help her find the truth about Johann Kozlov, it was this girl Pauline had followed here. Anny was a passionate believer in the workers' cause and a reluctant convert to violent revolution, which she called a historic necessity.

Though highly intelligent, she seemed utterly unaware that the security police had been watching her. She would be locked in a cell if they hadn't hoped she would lead them to the Comintern agent, Valtin, who had approached Johann Kozlov. At this crucial moment, Pauline surmised, they had lost track of her and had no idea that their unwitting Judas goat was moments from being badly injured or killed.

The door shook as the anti-Communists hammered on it with truncheons and gun butts. The bombmakers threw their shoulders against the door to hold it shut.

"Help me pull up the rug," Pauline told Anny.

The bombmakers had apparently grown up in neighborhoods less poor than this one and none of them even suspected there was a trapdoor under the filthy carpet. It opened over a wet earthen cellar. The cellar had been dug decades ago by country peasants when they moved to the city in the forlorn hope of storing vegetables grown in tenement shadows.

"How did you know?" Anny whispered.

"When I was a girl, I lived in Wedding with my mother."

If the root cellar was like others Pauline had seen, it would have another door that opened outside into what she hoped would be an interior yard with a fence they could squeeze through and run. It did. Holding Anny's hand tightly, she emerged under a sliver of gray sky spitting rain.

Buildings walled them in on all four sides. Only one had a door.

"What of the others?" asked Anny.

"They'll follow, if they have any sense,"

But before the bomb builders could escape through the cellar, an explosion shook the ground. A cloud of dust burst from the cellar door. Pauline felt the earth tremble under her feet as the entire front of the crumbling tenement collapsed. Brick and timber buried the anti-Communists and their armored car in the alley and the bomb-makers in their flat.

Isaac Bell asked Captain Novicki, "What happened to your face, Dave?"

"Just some splinters."

"Looks like a treeful."

"Listen, Isaac. I have a confession to make."

"What did you do?"

"I got caught running rum."

Bell gave him a brisk once-over. His cheeks above his beard and his forehead were speckled with cuts, and he had one of those new Band-Aids stuck on his ear. He was lucky he hadn't lost an eye. Otherwise, he looked his usual rugged self, a feisty old man who did not think he was old. "Caught running rum? Or *hijacked*?"

"Hijacked."

"Where'd it happen?"

"They were waiting a half mile off Fire Island Inlet. Shot up my boat and stole the . . . cargo. Then chopped holes in the bottom to sink her."

"Sounds like you're lucky you're alive."

"Darned lucky. Thankfully, I don't have to tell Joe right away. Bad enough admitting to you that I broke the law."

"I'm not a cop," said Bell. "And I'm not a priest."

"You're a Van Dorn, that's worse. Joe sets high standards. It would be easier telling a cop or a priest. This is just embarrassing as hell. But I'm telling you for a reason."

"What else happened?"

"I saw the black boat everyone's talking about."

Bell's eyes lit up. "Describe it!"

The old sea captain, not surprisingly, was an excellent witness. He had observed closely and recalled details. He estimated that the boat was sixty or seventy feet long. "Narrow beam. She rides very low in the

191

water, but she'll be seakindly with that flared bow. Three Libertys in the motor box. And there was room in the box for an extra standing by in case one stopped running. Forward cockpit, room for four or five men. She looks small because she's built so fine, but she is one big boat. I'll bet she'll carry a thousand cases."

"Guns?"

"Oh yes. Sounded like the Lewis the Navy had on the subchasers. And a mammoth searchlight. Big as a destroyer's."

"Armor?"

Novicki shrugged his brawny shoulders. "I don't know, I wasn't shooting back."

"How fast is she? Joe thought she turned fifty knots."

"Those Libertys roared like she could."

"It sounds very much like what Joe described. How'd you happen to survive?"

"Took my chances in the drink."

"You swam ashore?" Bell asked, astonished. The seawater was cold and rough and Novicki had to be pushing seventy.

"No. I clambered aboard my boat, stuffed canvas in the holes they chopped, and bailed like mad until we drifted onto the beach. The Inlet Coast Guard Station lent a hand. Lucky the thieves took every last bag of booze, so I wasn't breaking any laws."

"Close call all around," said Bell.

The old man hung his head. "I feel like a damned fool. I was out of a job. Broke. Fellow offered me money to make the taxi run. Sounded like easy money."

"How many runs did you do?"

"It was my first."

"Want some advice?"

"Yeah, I know. Don't do it again."

"Running rum will get you killed. The smuggling business is changing, fast — gangsters are taking over."

"Based on last night," Novicki said wryly, "I can't argue with that."

Bell said, "Maybe Barnacle Bill should go back to sea."

"Isaac, I'd love to. Damned few windjammers left since the war sunk so many. No one's going to put a man my age in charge of a steamer."

"I'll bet I can put you on a windjammer," said Bell. "I talked to fellows in the Bahamas liquor business — I'm working every angle in this case — and they operate on the 'lawful' side, shipping Scotch and gin from Britain and rum from Hispaniola to Nassau. It's a legal, aboveboard enterprise — at least until the rumrunners take it from Nassau. How would you feel if I could wrangle you a job sailing a rum schooner from the

Caribbean up to The Bahamas?"

"If they'd hire an old man."

"They'll hire any qualified master who's still breathing. Few young captains can be trusted with a sailing ship. And seafaring geezers are in short supply, what with so many captains taking up the booze business. What do you say?"

"I'd be mighty grateful."

Isaac Bell thrust out his hand. "Put her there. We'll shake on it. And don't worry, Joe won't hear about this from me."

"I'll tell him myself as soon as he's up to hearing it. I won't lie to a friend. But, Isaac, there's one more thing I should tell you."

Bell smiled. "I hope you haven't rifled the poor box."

"Didn't burn down any churches either," Novicki smiled back. "I don't know what it means. I thought I heard the hijackers shouting in Russian."

"*Russian?* Are you sure?"

"The Lewis gun was going to beat the band, but I've sailed with Russians — right good seamen when sober — and I swear they could have been yelling Russian. Sure as heck weren't English."

Isaac Bell dampened his excitement at this news. He did not want to encourage Novicki to embellish beyond what he believed.

"There are many foreign sailors on Rum Row. Could they have been sailors up from the Caribbean?"

"No, I'd recognize the Caribbean dialect."

"There's a slew of Italian gangsters in the booze line. Maybe it was a ship from Italy?"

"No, they weren't Eye-talian. Coulda been German, but the more I think on it, I heard Russian. Or Polish, I suppose. Except Russian doesn't make sense. I mean, I could imagine Russians anchoring on Rum Row to sell the stuff, I suppose, but not running it to the beach. That's for local fellows who know the water."

"I'm glad you came to me, Dave."

"Might this help you nail the thugs who shot Joe?"

"It could," said Bell. Considering, he thought to himself, that a German-Russian rumrunner had been shot, in the grisly Cheka way, with a bullet that could have been propelled by Russian smokeless powder. "Go say good-bye to Joe and Dorothy and pack your sea chest."

"I hate leaving them."

"They'll get by. I'm here, Dorothy's strong, and, with any luck, Joe will continue improving."

"If he doesn't get another infection."

"You being here can't stop an infection,"

195

Bell said firmly. He reached for his wallet. "Buy a train ticket to Miami. I'll have a wire about the ship waiting for you at the station. Depending on where the ship is, you'll have to take a steamer either to Nassau or down to Jamaica or Hispaniola."

"I can't take your money."

Bell was not surprised by Novicki's reluctance and had prepared for it. He extended a thick wad of bills. "It's not my money, it's Van Dorn money. And I'm hiring you to send me a report on the Nassau-to-Miami rum-running before you ship out for the Caribbean."

Novicki set a stubborn jaw.

"It's not charity," Bell insisted firmly. "I'm convinced that the illegal booze business is about to become a national criminal enterprise. If I'm right, then the smuggling and bootlegging at entry points like Detroit and Florida are going to attract the same criminals who are getting rich in New York. I've already put a top man in Detroit. The fact that you are going to Miami means that you can help me out down there."

"I'll get myself down there on my own."

Bell grabbed his hand and pressed the money into it. "I need you there right away. You're alert and observant, Dave. I need all the help you can give me."

He walked Captain Novicki out the door and hurried back to the bull pen, where he leveled an imperious finger at three bespectacled detectives. Dressed in vests, bow ties, and banded shirtsleeves, they looked less like private investigators than hard-eyed, humorless bookkeepers.

Adler, Kliegman, and Marcum gathered around his desk.

"The high-powered armored rum boat that machine-gunned the Boss is prowling the coast again," Bell said. "Grady Forrer will pinpoint the location of boatyards in Long Island, New York, and New Jersey that are capable of building such a vessel. You gents will canvas them to find out which one launched her. Pretend that your bootlegger boss is offering top dollar to buy one like it — only faster. Telephone me the instant you find one and I'll be there with the money."

Something else that the cool-headed old geezer told him about the black boat had lodged in the back of Bell's mind. Despite ducking bullets and swimming for his life, Dave Novicki had recalled in fine detail a long rank of three engines spitting fire from a motor box near the stern. He had speculated that the box had room for a fourth engine. That the fourth was not spitting fire indicated either that it had broken down or, as likely, was a replacement standing by in case one of the three regulars stopped running.

No one knew better than an airplane pilot that Libertys broke down often. A big selling point when he bought his Loening Air Yacht had been the design that perched the motor high atop the wing, which provided for quick removal and replacement of the entire unit. He had not signed on the dotted line until Loening Aeronautical threw in a spare motor and a crate of valves.

"McKinney!"

"Right here, Mr. Bell."

"Do any of your Washington friends work for the War Department's director of sales?"

"They'll know someone who does."

"Find a War Department man who can tell us who buys war surplus Liberty motors and spare parts."

"I don't mean to outguess you, Mr. Bell, but at last count the government had *thirteen thousand* Liberty motors on hand."

"That's why bootleggers buy them. They're fast, cheap, and plentiful. Tell your man to concentrate on motor and spare parts purchases within a hundred miles of New York."

The detectives scattered.

Bell sent a transatlantic cable to Pauline Grandzau.

MORE RUSSIANS.

WHAT OF KOZLOV?

Pauline Grandzau shook the Communist girl Anny awake when the Hamburg train slowed to stop at a small-town station ten miles before the northern port city. They got off the train and walked from the town into the forest where Anny's friend, Valtin, was leading a *Hundertschaften* company of a hundred Communist fighters in maneuvers in preparation to lead an uprising in Hamburg.

"Is Valtin your friend or boyfriend?" Pauline asked.

"We don't do it that way. If a girl likes a boy, she says, 'Come with me.' And if he wants to, he comes. But that doesn't mean you have to be with him every day."

"What if you do want to be with him every day?"

"You can. But if another girl says, 'Come with me,' you would be wrong to try to stop him. The revolution has no room for jealousy."

Pauline Grandzau found that utopian

fantasy even harder to believe when Anny pointed out the tall, handsome, dark-haired Valtin. Even seen at a distance through the trees, he looked like a man who could provoke an array of jealousies with a smile.

At the moment, he was concentrating mightily on drilling a hundred tough-looking merchant seamen armed with ancient czarist army rifles, a variety of pistols, including a handful of new Ortgies, some powerful World War stick grenades, and numerous old-fashioned Kugel grenades. Of the hundred, she noticed on closer inspection, at least twenty were younger men, carrying knives and clubs.

They were rehearsing signals for assault and retreat as they advanced and fell back along forest paths that represented city streets and gathered around trees that stood for tenement buildings and factories. A huge heap of fallen trees and limbs became a street barricade.

Valtin ordered a break. The men sprawled on the forest floor and shared cigarettes. Valtin sauntered over and kissed Anny on the mouth without taking his eyes off Pauline. "Who are you?"

"This is Pauline," said Anny. "She saved me from the Bürgerwehr."

"How?"

Anny explained how she'd been trapped in the bomb factory. Pauline said, "All I did was find a way out."

"Why were you there?"

"She is looking for someone named Kozlov."

"Johann Kozlov," said Pauline. "I had hoped one of the bomb builders knew him, but the Bürgerwehr attacked before I could ask."

"Why do you ask about Kozlov?"

Pauline had rehearsed her answer. "My brother is in prison in America. Kozlov tried to get out of being deported by testifying against Fritz. I want Kozlov to retract his false statements."

"Why would he?"

"To free a wrongly accused honest man."

"Are you out of your mind? Kozlov is a revolutionary. He can't operate by 'honest man' morals."

Valtin was not aware that Johann Kozlov had been killed in America. Pauline thought that odd if Kozlov had been his recruit. Of course, Valtin had been hiding and preparing for the assault on Hamburg and cut off from regular intelligence. But it struck her that Valtin hadn't necessarily recruited Kozlov to the Comintern. What if Kozlov was already a Comintern agent and Valtin had been sent either to test his loyalty since his arrest in America or to give him instructions from Moscow?

Valtin was eyeing her suspiciously. "Who are you? What do you do? How do you make your living?"

"I am a librarian."

"Where?"

"Berlin." She gave him a card.

"Prussian State Library," he read aloud. "You have degrees. You are a specialist. Where did you grow up?"

She told him her mother's last address in Wedding. He raised his eyebrows. "You've come a long way."

"Education elevates."

"You do not speak with the accent of a Berlin street urchin."

Pauline said, "I was ambitious to leave all that behind."

"Not very far behind in a Wedding bomb factory. And now you're standing in a Red encampment."

"I go where I must to help my brother. I ask you again, where should I look for Kozlov?"

"Berlin. He was a street fighter in the uprising."

"Who were his comrades?"

"He fought beside Zolner," Valtin answered offhandedly as if Zolner was a name she should know. A hero and a famous leader. Excommander Richter would know the name. From Hamburg she could telephone Richter and ask what the police knew about Zolner.

"Do you know where Zolner is now?"

"I am hoping the Central Committee will dispatch Zolner to lead the fight in Hamburg. Why don't you come with us?" He spoke offhandedly again, but it was clearly a challenge. Or a test.

"What is Zolner's first name?"

"Why don't you ask him in Hamburg?"

It was dark when the *Hundertschaften* began marching along a railroad track toward Hamburg and she was alone with Anny. The women's job was to carry first-aid kits at the back of the line.

"What is Zolner's first name?"

"I don't know," Anny whispered back. "They say he once danced in the ballet."

16

"Oh, I'm so sorry, Mr. Bell. It looks like CG-9 got new orders. They never came off patrol."

The Coast Guard lieutenant assigned to oversee Isaac Bell's interview of the captain of cutter CG-9 did not look one bit sorry that the Staten Island slip where Bell had been told the cutter was docked was empty. "Too bad you had to come all the way out here."

"Don't worry," said Bell. "I have a friend in Staten Island. It's a nice day. We'll go for a boat ride."

Bell drove to the docks at Richmond Terrace and for two hundred dollars chartered a boat skippered by Detective Ed Tobin's great-uncle Donald Darbee. It was a broad, low, flat-bottomed oyster scow, but unlike a vessel actually used to tong oysters, it had a gigantic four-barrel Peerless V-8 motor for outrunning the Harbor Squad. Since passage of the Volstead Act, the long-haired, grizzled Darbee had installed a modern radiotelegraph to keep track of the Prohibition patrols. The radio was operated by his pretty teenage granddaughter, Robin. Robin was cool as a cucumber and knew Morse code.

Bell told the old man his plan and, together, they removed everything from the boat that could be construed as illegal, leaving on Darbee's Kill Van Kull dock the leftovers of booze, opium, and ammunition that had fallen under the bilgeboards. "With no contraband on board," Bell explained, "when the Coast Guard catches us, they can't arrest us."

"Don't like the idea of getting caught," Darbee grumbled.

"Grandpa," said Robin, rolling her eyes. "Mr. Bell just told you why."

"I know why. I'm old, not stupid. He wants to get on that cutter. But I don't like getting caught. It goes against my nature."

Bell piloted the oyster boat across the busy harbor, through the Narrows between Staten Island and Brooklyn, and out the Lower Bay, past the Ambrose Lightship, and into the ocean. Darbee and little Robin crouched under the forward cubby, exchanging radio transmissions with Staten

Island watermen who were already at sea, heading for Rum Row. Cousins and cronies helped Darbee pinpoint cutter CG-9's position within a few miles.

Bell opened up the throttle and steered east-northeast. An hour later, ten miles off Long Beach, he spotted the distinctive high-bow, swept-stern profile of the former submarine chaser. The Coast Guard vessel stayed to its course, its lookouts failing to spot the low gray oyster boat.

"O.K., Mr. Darbee. Show 'em we're here."

Darbee poured motor oil through a specially constructed funnel. The oil dripped into the hot exhaust manifold. His boat trailed a huge cloud of smoke.

"First time I ever used my smoke screen for bait."

The cutter wheeled about and headed toward them, carving a bright bow wave. Bell throttled back until he had just enough way to keep the boat headed into the seas. The cutter drew near. Seen from the low oyster boat, it looked enormous, its deck gun formidable, its twin Lewis guns lethal.

Isaac Bell and Uncle Donny and young Robin raised their hands in the air. The cutter swung alongside, banged hard against their hull, and sailors jumped aboard with drawn guns. They made lines fast and began searching the boat.

Bell saw the cutter's white-haired petty officer staring down at him. In a moment he would recognize him as the pilot who had delivered Joseph Van Dorn in a Flying Yacht. He had to get aboard the cutter before he did or the game would be up.

"Uncle Donny," he muttered. "Could you manage to do something to annoy them?"

Donald Darbee, who despised authority in general and rated the Coast Guard even lower than the New York Police Department Harbor Squad, curled his lips to show yellow teeth in a mocking smile.

The sailor guarding them shouted, "What are you grinning at?"

"I haven't had this much fun since a foggy night I 'helped' a police boat run into the Statue of Liberty."

"Shut up, old man. Watch your mouth."

Now Bell raised his voice in righteous indignation. "Watch *your* mouth, sailor! That's no way to talk to a gentleman four times your age."

"Shut up or you're under arrest."

Bell shouted, louder, "You can't arrest me!"

"Oh yeah? You're under arrest. March!"

Bell let sailors pull him up onto the cutter's stern deck. The petty officer hurried down to confront him, stopped cold, and said, "I know you from somewhere."

Bell looked him in the eye. "I believe you're the man who saved Joseph Van Dorn's life with a tourniquet. If you are, I'm in your debt."

"That's who you are."

"I wonder if you would do me another favor and tell your skipper I have to talk to him." Just then the boarding party called out that there was no booze on the oyster boat.

The weary-looking skipper, who had been observing from the flying bridge, came down to the stern deck. "What's the big idea with the smoke screen? There's no liquor on your boat."

"We knew you lamebrains would never find us if we didn't help!" Darbee yelled.

The captain ignored him, saying to Bell, "You lured me off station to help your pals' taxis get by. It's a crime to impede a patrol."

Isaac Bell extended his hand. "Captain, I am Van Dorn Chief Investigator Isaac Bell. I'm sure you don't begrudge me investigating who shot my boss while he was on your ship. Do you?"

"Of course not. But —"

"You can get back to your patrol as soon as you tell me exactly what happened when

Mr. Van Dorn was shot on your ship."

"Why the charade?" The captain jerked a thumb at Darbee and his boat.

"The Coast Guard is dodging me. Your superiors won't let me interview you or your crew."

"I wondered about that," the captain nodded. "That's why they've kept us out here. Cook's down to baked beans and water, and we're running low on fuel."

"As soon as you answer my questions," said Bell, "I'll stop bothering them and they'll let you return to harbor."

"I have nothing to hide."

"What struck you most about the black boat?"

"Speed. I've never seen such a fast boat."

Exactly what Joseph Van Dorn had told him. "What next?"

"Tactics," said the captain. "They used their speed to great effect. They took advantage of my vessel's shortcomings, maneuvering behind us so we couldn't bring the Poole gun to bear."

Bell said, "Mr. Van Dorn told me he thought he was back in Panama with the Marines."

"*I* thought I was back in the war," said the captain.

"Lead flying will do it," said the petty officer.

"That, too, but what I'm saying is they conducted their attack like a naval engagement. Isn't that so, Chief?"

"Aye, sir. The rumrunners handled themselves like vets."

"They weren't common criminals."

Again, thought Bell, precisely what Van Dorn had said.

At that moment, with the cutter's deck rolling under his feet, Isaac Bell voiced in his mind what he had been mulling ever since he chased the killer who murdered Johann Kozlov: If they weren't common criminals, if they weren't run-of-the-mill whisky haulers, what were they doing bootlegging?

"That's all I know," said the captain. "Chief, put him back on his boat."

"One more thing," said Bell. "Who pulled Mr. Van Dorn out of the water?"

The captain and the petty officer exchanged uncomfortable glances.

The captain spoke. "Seaman Third Class Asa Somers."

"I'd like to shake his hand."

The chief looked out at the water. The captain said, "Somers was discharged."

"What for? He's a hero."

"His discharge order came straight from headquarters. Someone complained about the wild-goose chases we got sent on — said someone was tipping them off. The brass decided the complainer, or the tipster, was Somers. He was the last to join the ship. They took him off on a launch."

"Was he the complainer?"

"I don't know, but he's a decent kid."

"Smart as a whip," said the chief.

"Where can I find him?"

"Long live Soviet Germany!"

The Communist battle cry was uttered in hoarse whispers by the *Hundertschaften* company as they sneaked into Hamburg in the dead of night. Valtin ordered his men to break into shops to steal jars of kerosene. The Central Committee had promised stick grenades. Until they arrived, the Red shock troops would set fires with lamp oil. Which left Pauline with little hope that the Central Committee would dispatch Zolner as promised. But she was in the thick of it now, an unwilling participant in what was beginning to look to her like a doomed attack by a thousand men against a city of a million.

But as they advanced deeper into the city, they were joined by other *Hundertschaften* companies and ordinary citizens streaming down from the tenements. Their numbers began to swell. The first police station they attacked fell quickly. They marched bewildered policemen out in their own handcuffs — hostages, if needed — and looted the station house arsenals of rifles and pistols, ammunition, and a water-cooled MG 08/15 *Maschinengewehr* mounted on a tripod. Valtin assigned four war veterans to lug the machine gun to a tenement roof that commanded the street.

They continued toward the shipyards, the night dark, the streets deserted. Surprise seemed total. There was no sign of riot brigades, no mobs of Bürgerwehr auxiliaries, no columns of Freikorps. They were advancing stealthily on another police station when its lights went out.

"Attack!" Valtin bellowed, and they charged the building.

The cops opened fire with rifles and pistols. Flashes of red and yellow pierced the dark. Men fell in the street.

Valtin hurled a stick grenade. It smashed the glass of a small window and lodged against wire mesh. But the grenade was a dud and did not explode. The *Hundertschaften* resumed firing their pistols. The police answered with a machine gun. The roar was deafening, the muzzle flashes blinding. Anny pinwheeled into Pauline. Pauline tried to keep her from falling. She caught her in her arms. The girl was deadweight.

Pauline forced herself to look at her face. To her horror, she saw a dark hole between her eyes. Anny had been killed instantly. We were inches apart, Pauline thought, still holding her.

Three teenage boys, brave beyond reasoning, ran at the building, throwing jars of kerosene. Braver than they would be, Pauline thought, if they had been standing with Anny. Bullets cut them down. Glass shattered, kerosene splashed. A fourth boy ran to it with a burning rag. A bullet hurled him back and he fell on the burning rag. An old man who had joined them moments before the attack stepped forward. Bullets stormed past him. Pauline waited for him to die. He flicked a cigarette. It sailed through the dark like a shooting star. The front of the police station caught fire, and flames tumbled in the windows.

The door opened and policemen ran out, beating at their burning tunics with bare hands and rolling on the cobblestones to put out the flames. Pauline thought in the confusion that the Reds were helping the police put out the flames. But her eyes told the terrible truth. They were leaping over the bodies of the fallen boys to knock down the cops and kick them to death.

Pauline knew in that moment that her hopes for Germany had been hijacked exactly as ex-Kommandeur Fritz Richter had predicted they would be: no gracious winners, no shining knights.

She eased Anny's body to the cobblestones with an awful feeling that the worst would thrive and the dreamers would die. Valtin's Red Hundreds left the burning police station and raced toward the shipyard. Afraid to be left behind, Pauline ran after them.

Government posters at street corners proclaimed the death penalty for possessing weapons. The fighters tore them down. They crossed a broad thoroughfare, which Pauline recognized as one that led to the central railroad station where she could telephone long-distance to Richter in Berlin. She had seen no sign of the mysterious Zolner, and, in all the fighting, he might well be dead. She slowed and let the stragglers overtake her. As she began to turn away, she handed her first-aid rucksack to the last man in line.

He stared over her shoulder, his eyes suddenly widening with terror.

A column of squat gray armored cars was roaring up the thoroughfare.

"Run!"

The survivors of the Red Hundreds sprinted for the neighborhood of narrow, winding streets that housed the shipyard workers. The workers, who had been striking for days, had blocked the streets with massive, well-constructed barricades of overturned wagons, trucks, and furniture. They were reinforced with cobblestones and protected from above by snipers on the roofs.

The armored cars attacked, spitting machine-gun fire from narrow slits in their steel fronts. As Pauline had seen in Berlin, they were painted with skulls and cross-bones. Stick grenades plummeted down from the rooftops. The powerful explosives blasted sheet armor loose from the attacking cars, exposing their drivers and machine gunners to rifle fire from above. Several cars stopped, immobilized. One caught fire. Another exploded. And the rest retreated.

Workers and Red Hundreds cheered and embraced.

Moments later, there was a huge explosion in the middle of the main barricade, tearing it apart and hurtling men and debris in the air.

"Minenwerfer!" Bomb throwers.

Another ten-pound mortar shell screamed

down from the sky. And another.

"To the shipyard!"

Fleeing the ruined barricade, the survivors stampeded toward the shipyard.

The strikers opened the gates to let them in. Pauline emerged from the narrow streets, her ears ringing from the mortar explosions. She saw the ribs of a steamer under construction reaching for the open sky. A searchlight leaped along sheds and tall gantries and swept across the frame of the half-built ship and locked suddenly, brilliantly, on a huge red flag billowing in the wind.

The workers' cheers were drowned out by gunfire from the river.

Hamburg police in armed motorboats raced toward the builders' ways, firing rifles and mounted machine guns. Strikers and *Hundertschaften* dived for cover. The cops stormed ashore. Pauline saw the red flag illuminated by the searchlight descend swiftly down the mast and out of sight. Moments later, the police ran it up again, soaked in gasoline and burning fiercely.

17

The retreat was chaos, every man for himself. The Reds threw away incriminating weapons and ran for the oldest slums of crooked alleys where they might hide, protected by the criminals who lived there. Pauline walked in the shadows of the buildings, head down, empty hands visible, eyes alert, watching for the police. A man still holding a gun raced by. In the wake of the insurrection the cops had retaken the rooftops, and a sniper cut him down.

She saw Valtin in a doorway. He had been shot. His peacoat was soaked with blood. It took him a confused moment to recognize her.

"Where is Anny?" he asked.

"Anny is dead. Put your arm over my shoulder. I'll help you to a hospital."

"Are you crazy? Wounds will tell them who we are."

"Where is Zolner?"

Valtin was struggling to breathe. "If the Central Committee sent him, I didn't see him."

"What's his first name?"

"Why do you keep . . . Oh yes, your poor betrayed brother."

"What's his first name?"

"Marat. Marat Zolner."

"Marat Zolner."

"It's only his *nom de guerre.*"

"What's his real name?"

Valtin closed his eyes. "Sometimes he is Dima Smirnov, spelled with a *v.* Sometimes Dmitri Smirnoff spelled with *f*s. Sometimes . . . Who knows? Who cares?" He sagged against the door. His chin slumped to his chest. His feet skidded out from under him. Pauline knelt beside him. When he opened his eyes, what she saw there told her that nothing would save him. He whispered something she couldn't hear. A bubble of blood swelled on his lips. She leaned closer.

"What?"

The bubble made a wet *Pop!* against her ear. "Run!"

His hat had fallen beside him. Pauline laid it over his face and hurried away.

Looters were battering open shops and running from them with bread and milk and beer and coats and hats. Now it was the police who were erecting barricades, stringing barbed wire across the larger streets. She pressed into a doorway to wait for an armored car to creep past on an intersecting street. The men inside flung open their hatches and stood in the open, no longer afraid. It passed from her view.

An empty bottle smashed at her feet. Two looters lurched toward her. Before she could move, they had cornered her in the doorway. They were drunk, reeking of schnapps.

One grabbed her from behind, the other reached for her legs. She kicked out, knowing her only chance was to get to her gun before they found it. He caught her ankles. The man behind squeezed tighter. She went limp.

"Right," he laughed. "Might as well enjoy it."

He let go of her arms to turn her toward him and as he bent and pressed his reeking mouth to hers, she reached under her skirt with both hands, pulled her Mann, and cocked the slide. She shot the one who was holding her ankles first. He fell backwards with an expression of surprise. The other, oblivious because of gunfire ringing in the streets, kept trying to kiss her. She twisted the gun between them and pulled the trigger and he dropped to the cobbles, wounded, though not mortally, by the small-caliber gun.

Before Pauline could move ten feet, steel-helmeted cops stopped her and saw the gun she was trying to hide in her skirt. They shouted that she was under arrest.

"They tried to rape me," she protested. "I had to protect myself."

"Death is the penalty for weapons."

"I have a license." She showed them her genuine *Ausweiskarte* and a Van Dorn business card. She took the time they read her papers to calm herself.

"What in the name of God are you doing in Hamburg in the middle of a riot, Fräulein Privatdetektive?"

Pauline affected the confident manner of a Prussian aristocrat. "The Van Dorn Detective Agency intends to establish a field office in Germany's second-largest city."

"Take my advice. Wait until we've exterminated the rabble."

She aimed a curt nod in the direction of the looters she had shot. "I would appreciate it if you accept these two as my contribution to the effort and escort me to Central Station."

Startled by her audacity, the police officer looked down at the woman. She was small and slight and uncommonly pretty. But she had a field marshal's icy eyes. He returned her pistol, offered his arm, and walked her to the station.

The telephones were working. She reached Richter by long distance. Germany had the most highly developed telephone system in Europe and the connection was so clear he could have been across the table in the Prater Garten.

"Hamburg? Are you all right? We have reports of heavy fighting."

"It's over," she said.

"How bad was it?"

"Worse than even you could imagine. How is it in Berlin?"

"Quiet as a tomb. The Comintern got their signals crossed. They called off the Berlin and Bremen attacks. The fools in Hamburg were left in the lurch."

"Who is Marat Zolner?"

She listened to the lines. They made the faintest hissing sound of falling water. Finally, Richter asked, "How did you find out about Zolner?"

"Johann Kozlov was his right-hand man."

"I did not know that."

"Didn't I tell you I would bring you information?"

"Very good information," Richter admitted.

"Now it's your turn. Where is Marat Zolner?"

"Fellow here to see you, Mr. Van Dorn," said Isaac Bell.

Van Dorn's haggard face lit with a weak smile. The boy was standing in the doorway in civilian clothes, fidgeting with his hat. "Seaman Somers! Come on in, son. Don't let that nurse dragon scare you. Come by the bed where I can see you. Dorothy! This boy saved my life."

"Are you getting better, sir?"

"Tip-top," Van Dorn lied. "Have they made you captain yet?"

Somers hung his head. "They discharged me."

What?" The outraged eruption set him coughing, and the rib-racking cough turned him pale with pain. When he finally caught his breath, he waved the nurse aside and demanded of Bell, "Isaac? What's going on?"

Bell explained how Somers had run afoul of the Coast Guard brass.

"That's outrageous. They should have struck a medal . . . So you need a job?"

"Yes, sir, I do. But who would hire me being discharged?"

"Who will hire you? *I'll* hire you. Starting here and now you're a Van Dorn Apprentice Detective. Isaac, make it so!"

"Yes, sir, Mr. Van Dorn," said Bell, not at all surprised by the turn of events, having engineered it. He didn't doubt that young Somers had the requisite courage, daring, and enterprise to become a Van Dorn.

As for the Boss, he suddenly sounded invigorated.

"Welcome aboard, Somers. Of course we'll have to clear it with your parents."

"I'm an orphan, sir. I never knew my father. My mother died of tubercular trouble, working in the mill."

"Kiss of death?" asked Van Dorn.

"Yes, sir." To save money, mill owners held on to the old shuttles that required threading the eye with a suction of breath.

"Who will you start him under, Isaac?"

"Grady Forrer."

"Research?"

"It's clear talking to him that Asa's read every magazine printed. He'll get a good start with Grady, and we'll move him around from there."

Bell turned to a noise at the door. A Van Dorn messenger was knocking softly. "Mr. Bell? Cable from Germany."

KOZLOV COMMUNIST FIGHTER BERLIN
UPRISING.
RIGHT HAND TO COMINTERN AGENT MARAT
ZOLNER,
ALIAS DMITRI SMIRNOFF,
ALIAS DIMA SMIRNOV.
ZOLNER ESCAPED GOVERNMENT DEATH
SENTENCE.
SINCE KOZLOV IS DEAD I AM TRACING
MARAT ZOLNER.

A name at last.

Isaac Bell raced back to the St. Regis and burst into the Van Dorn offices, calling out for Grady Forrer. The Research man lumbered up to Bell's desk in the middle of the bull pen. Under one massive arm was a cardboard file folder, bulging to capacity.

"Russia again," said Bell. "Pauline found another Bolshevik connection. Find out everything you can about a Comintern agent named Marat Zolner. And I want a full report on the Comintern."

"The Comintern is the foreign espionage arm of the Russian Revolution," said Grady Forrer. He heaved the file folder onto Bell's desk, where it landed like a blacksmith's anvil.

"What's this?"

"Your report on the Comintern."

"What?"

"I suspected you would want it after your interest in Cheka *Genickschuss* — neck shots."

A pleased smile warmed Isaac Bell's face. It was right and fit that the crime-fighting operation Joseph Van Dorn had taken such pains to build had shifted smoothly into top gear to bring his attackers to justice.

Grady patted the folder lovingly. "The gist is, the Comintern exports the Communist revolution around the world to, quote, 'overthrow the governments of the international bourgeoisie by all available means — spying, sabotage, and armed force.' "

"How are they doing?"

"They fell on their face in Hungary and, so far at least, they're falling on their face in Germany. I predict they will fare better in India and much, much better in China."

"What about here? How are they making out in America?"

Grady adjusted his wire-rimmed glasses. Bell was familiar with his deliberate expression. He had seen it often. Grady's central belief — a tenet he drilled into his apprentices — was that generalizations murdered facts.

"Interesting question, Isaac. And difficult

225

to answer. America is different. We were not destroyed by the World War. Despite the current business recession, we are not starving. And I see no evidence that the Comintern has united the warring American Communist factions in any manner that made them stronger."

"What about the anarchists?"

Grady Forrer shook his head. "The Bureau of Investigation would have us believe the Bolsheviks have teamed up with radicals and anarchists. That is simply not true."

"Why not?"

"The Comintern are cold, ruthless, and eminently practical. They despise anarchists as hopelessly impractical."

"Do you have any evidence the Comintern conspires with the IWW?"

Again Grady shook his head. "The Wobblies may be radicals, but they are essentially romantics. The Comintern has even less time for romantics than anarchists. Don't forget, they invented *Genickschuss* to execute impractical radicals and romantics."

Bell said, "You are telling me that the Comintern will attack America on its own — independent of our homegrown conspirators."

"The cold, ruthless, practical ones might," Grady amended cautiously.

"Aren't they already attacking?"

Grady smiled. "Isaac, I am paid to keep heads level in the Research Department. Somehow, you have maneuvered me into speculating that the coldly efficient bootleggers who shot up a Coast Guard cutter, nearly killed Mr. Van Dorn, executed their wounded, and are currently wreaking havoc on street gangs and hijacking rumrunners and whisky haulers are actually attacking the United States of America."

"I couldn't have put it better myself."

"But bootlegging profits," Grady Forrer cautioned, "are incalculably immense. Getting rich quick is as powerful a motivator as ideology."

Chief Investigator Isaac Bell had heard enough.

He raised his voice so every detective in the bull pen could hear.

"Pauline Grandzau linked the bootleggers who shot Mr. Van Dorn to the Russian Bolshevik Comintern. As of this minute, the Van Dorn Agency will presume that these particular bootleggers — led by one Marat Zolner, alias Dmitri Smirnoff, alias Dima Smirnov — have more on their minds than getting rich quick."

18

Bill Lynch, a portly young boatbuilder already famous for the fastest speedboats on Great South Bay, and Harold Harding, his grizzled, cigar-chomping partner, watched with interest as a midnight blue eighty-horsepower Stutz Bearcat careened into Lynch & Harding Marine's oyster-shell driveway.

A fair-haired man in a pinch-waist pin-striped suit jumped out of the roadster. He drew his Borsalino fedora low over his eyes and looked around with a no-nonsense expression at the orderly sprawl of docks and sheds that lined a bulkheaded Long Island creek.

Lynch sized him up through thick spectacles. Well over six feet tall and lean as cable, he had golden hair and a thick mustache that were barbered to a fare-thee-well. There was a bulge under his coat where either a fat wallet or a shoulder holster resided.

Lynch bet Harding a quarter that the bulge was artillery.

"No bet," growled Harold. "But I'll bet *you* that bookkeeper nosing around here yesterday works for him."

"No bet. Looking for something, mister?"

"I'm looking for a boat."

Bill Lynch said, "Something tells me you want a speedy one."

"Let's see what you've got."

In the shed, mechanics were wrestling a heavy chain hoist to lower an eight-cylinder, liquid-cooled Curtiss OX-5 into a fishing boat hull that already contained two of them. The driver of the Stutz did not ask why a fisherman needed three aircraft motors. But he did ask how fast the Curtisses would make the boat.

Lynch, happily convinced that their visitor was a bootlegger, speculated within the realm of the believable that she would hit forty knots.

"Ever built a seventy-footer with three Libertys?"

Lynch and Harding exchanged a look.

"Yup."

"Where is she?"

"Put her on a railcar."

"Railcar?" The bootlegger glanced at the

weed-choked siding that curved into the yard and connected to the Long Island Railroad tracks half a mile inland. "I'd have thought your customers sail them away."

"Usually."

"Where'd she go?"

"Haven't seen her since."

The bootlegger asked, "Could you build a faster one?"

Lynch said, "I drew up plans for a seventy-foot express cruiser with four Libertys turning quadruple screws. She's waiting for a customer."

"Could I have her in a month?"

"I don't see why not."

Harding bit clean through his stogie. "We can't do it that fast."

"Yes we can," said Lynch. "I'll have her in the water in thirty days."

The tall customer with a gun in his coat asked, "Would you have any objection to me paying cash?"

"None I can think of," said Lynch, and Harding lit a fresh cigar.

Lynch unrolled his plans. The customer pored over them knowledgeably. He ordered additional hatches fore and aft— Lewis gun emplacements, Lynch assumed, since he wanted reinforced scantlings under them — and electric mountings for Sperry high-intensity searchlights.

"And double the armor in the bow."

"Planning on ramming the opposition?"

"I'd like to know I can."

They settled on a price and a schedule of payouts keyed to hull completion, motor installation, and sea trials.

The customer started counting a down payment, stacking crisp hundred-dollar bills on a workbench. Midway, he paused. "The seventy-footer you built? The one with three motors. Was it for a regular customer?"

"Nope."

"Someone you knew?"

"Nope."

"What was his name?"

"Funny thing you should ask. He paid cash like you. Hundred-dollar bills. After he brought the third payment, I said to Harold here, 'You know, Harold, we don't know that fellow's name.' And Harold said, 'His name is Franklin. Ben Franklin.' Harold meant because his face is on the hundred-dollar bill."

Harold said, "You want to hear something really funny: The man with no name named the boat. He called it *Black Bird.*"

"Black Bird?"

" 'Counta the boat was black. I asked him should we paint *Black Bird* on the transom.

He said no, he'd remember it."

"What will you name yours?" asked Lynch.

"Marion."

"Should we paint *Marion* on the transom?"

"In gold."

He still hadn't resumed counting money. "What did the fellow look like?"

"Tall man, even thinner than you. Light on his feet, like he seemed to float. Dark hair. Dark eyes. Cheekbones like chisels."

"Did he speak with a foreign accent?"

"A bit," said Lynch.

"City fellow," said Harding. "They all got funny accents."

"Russian, by any chance?"

"They all sound the same," said Harding.

Lynch said, "We hear Swedes around here, and Dutchmen. Real ones from Holland. I doubt I ever heard a Russian."

"We got less Russians than Chinamen," said Harding.

"So for all you know," said the bootlegger, "he could have been French?"

"No," said Lynch, "I met plenty of Frenchies in the war."

"And French ladies," Harold leered. "You know, Billy won a medal."

"By the way," said Lynch, gazing intently at the half-counted stack of money, "we include compass and charts free of charge."

"And fire extinguishers," said Harding.

"What color do you want your boat?" asked Lynch.

The tall bootlegger pointed down the creek where it opened into the bay. The sky was overcast and it was impossible to distinguish where gray water ended and leaden cloud began. "That color."

Isaac Bell found a new cable from Pauline when he got back from the boatyard. She had sent it from the North Sea German port of Bremerhaven.

POLICE LOST MARAT ZOLNER
BREMERHAVEN.
ALIAS SMIRNOFF SAILED NEW YORK,
NORTH GERMAN LLOYD RHEIN,
RENAMED SUSQUEHANNA.

Bell checked "Incoming Steamships" in the *Times*'s "Shipping & Mails" pages. He found no listing for the *Susquehanna*. But under "Outgoing Steamships Carrying Mail" she was listed as sailing the next day to Bremerhaven with mail for Germany and Denmark. Which meant she was at her pier now.

Regardless of who owned them, North

233

German Lloyd ships sailed from Hoboken as they did before the war. Bell hurried there on the ferry, went aboard and straight to the chief purser's office.

The purser was American, a disgruntled employee of the U.S. Mail Shipping Company that had leased a fleet of North German Lloyd liners seized in the war. Bell listened sympathetically to an earful of complaints about the new "fly-by-night" owners who hadn't paid the Shipping Board "a dime of rent they owe — not to mention my back salary."

"Yes," said Bell. "I've followed the story in the newspaper. Your company claims there's a plot by foreign lines to sabotage American shipping?"

"Wrapping themselves in the flag won't pay bills. The company is nothing but paper. Mark my word, the Shipping Board will foreclose on the boat, and where will I be?"

Isaac Bell took out his wallet and laid a hundred-dollar bill on the purser's desk. "Maybe this could tide you over. There's something I have to know."

"What?" asked the purser, eyeing hopefully the better part of two weeks' salary.

"Early last spring in Bremerhaven, a Russian named Dmitri Smirnoff booked passage to New York on your ship. What do you

234

recall of him?"

"Nothing."

"Nothing?" Bell's hand strayed over the bill, covering it. "He might have called himself Dima Smirnov, spelled with a *v.*"

"Smirnoff never came on board. He switched places last minute with another passenger."

"Is that allowed?"

"It's allowed if the chief purser says it's allowed. The new passenger made it worth my while. It didn't matter. Nobody got cheated. The company got their money. I just changed the manifest."

"Who was the new passenger?"

"A New York hard case. Charlie O'Neal."

"What do you mean by a 'hard case'? A gangster?"

"Something like that. He had a nickname. He called himself Trucks. Gangsters tend to do that, don't they? Trucks O'Neal. Sounds like a gangster."

"Could you describe Trucks?"

"Beefy bruiser, like the moniker implies. Quick-moving. Black hair, high widow's peak. His nose had been mashed a couple of times."

"How tall?"

"Six foot."

"Eyes?"

"Tiny little eyes. Like a pig."

"What color?"

"Pig color."

"Pigs have pink eyes," said Bell.

"No, I meant kind of brown, like the rest of the pig." The purser ruminated a moment and added, "By the way, I don't mean to speak against him. Trucks didn't cause any trouble or anything. He just wanted to get home."

Bell removed his hand from the hundred and took another from his wallet. "Do you recall where 'home' was?"

"I think I have it somewhere in my files." He opened a drawer and thumbed over folders. "Reason I remember is there was some problem with customs. By the time they worked it out, O'Neal had gone on ahead. So we delivered his trunk. Here! Four-sixteen West 20th Street, across the river in New York."

"Chelsea," said Bell, rising quickly. "Good luck with the Shipping Board."

"I'll need it," said the purser. But by then the tall detective was striding as fast as his legs would thrust him across the embarkation lobby and down the gangplank.

West 20th street was a once elegant block of town houses that overlooked the gardens of an Episcopal seminary. Many of the homes had been subdivided into rooming houses for the longshoremen who worked on the Chelsea piers. Number 416 was one of these, a slapped-together warren of sagging stairs and tiny rooms that smelled of tobacco and sweat. Bell found the elfin, white-haired superintendent drinking bathtub gin in a back apartment carved out of the original house's kitchen. A cat had passed out on his lap.

"Trucks?" the super echoed.

"Charlie 'Trucks' O'Neal. What floor does he live on?"

"He left in May."

"Did he leave a forwarding address?"

The super took a long slug from his jelly jar of cloudy gin and looked up quizzically. "I wouldn't know how Park Avenue swells do it, mister, but down here on the docks men who adopt nicknames like Trucks do not leave forwarding addresses."

"Trucks O'Neal," said Harry Warren of the Gang Squad and proceeded to demonstrate why the Van Dorn Research boys swore, enviously, that surgeons had exchanged Harry's brain for a Dewey decimal system gangster catalogue.

"Heavyweight, six-two, busted nose, black

hair. Enlisted in '17, one step ahead of the cops. Army kicked him out with a dishonorable discharge after the war for some sort of profiteering shenanigans. Came home and took up with his old crowd."

Isaac Bell asked, "Is he a Gopher?"

"No," said Harry. "He hates the Gophers and they hate him. That's how he got his nose broken. You know, I haven't heard much of him lately. Any of you guys?"

One of Harry's younger men said, "I saw him on Broadway couple of months ago. Chorus girl on his arm, looking prosperous. I figured he was bootlegging."

Another Gang Squad man said, "I don't know how prosperous. I'm pretty sure I saw him driving a truck down on Warren Street. Scooted into a stable before I could get a good look."

"A truck full of hooch," said Harry Warren, "would make him prosperous."

"Find him," said Bell. "Pull out all stops."

"This is a wonderful business," said Marat Zolner. He strutted restlessly about his improvised bottling plant on Lower Manhattan's Murray Street. Trucks O'Neal was snoring softly on a cot in the back. A covered alley connected the former warehouse to the stable that Zolner had rented on Warren Street for Antipov's horse and wagon.

"Smell!" He thrust an open bottle of single-malt whisky under Yuri's nose.

Antipov recoiled. "It stinks like a peasant hut in winter."

"That's peat smoke, craved by connoisseurs. Smell this." He extended a bottle of clear fluid.

"I smell nothing."

"Two-hundred-proof industrial grain alcohol from a government-licensed distillery in Pennsylvania. So pure, it's flammable as gasoline." He splashed it on the concrete floor, flicked Antipov's cigarette from his lips, and tossed it. Blue flame jumped waist-high.

"And this."

He held another bottle over the flame. Antipov stepped back.

Zolner poured its contents on the fire, dousing it. "Water."

"Listen to me, Marat. I am through waiting."

But Zolner's exuberance was not to be derailed.

"So! One part malt whisky, which cost us nothing but *Black Bird*'s gasoline. Ten parts pure two-hundred-proof grain alcohol, which cost bribes of fifty pennies per bottle, plus ten pennies per bottle for Trucks O'Neal's payments to thugs to guard the shipment from the distillery. Ten parts water, free from the tap."

He held up a bottle with a yellow label. " 'Glen Urquhart Genuine Single Malt Whisky' counterfeit labels, indistinguishable from the original, a penny apiece. Empty bottle and cork, two pennies. Tea for color.

"Voila! One hundred hijacked cases become two thousand cases. Gangsters who have no idea they work for us peddle it to speakeasies and roadhouses for a small cut of seventy-five dollars a case. Rendering pure profit of one hundred twenty thousand dollars for the exclusive use of the Comintern."

"It is time to take direct action against the capitalists," said Antipov. "Are you with me or against me?"

"With you, of course."

He signaled silence with a finger to his lips and led Antipov quietly past the sleeping O'Neal and through the covered alley that connected the back of the bottling plant to the back of the stable.

The strong horse that had pulled Yuri Antipov's wagonload of dynamite from New Jersey had grown restless cooped up in the stall. It snorted eagerly as Zolner and Antipov heaped hundreds of three-inch cast-iron window sash slugs around the explosives and concealed them under shovelfuls of coal. But it grew impatient when Zolner crawled under the wagon to connect the detonator to a battery-powered flashlight and a Waterbury alarm clock — leaving one wire loose, which he would connect only after the wagon stopped lurching and banging on the cobblestones.

The horse began kicking its stall.

"Easy," Zolner called soothingly. "We're almost ready."

The animal calmed down immediately.

"How do you do that?" marveled Antipov, who had never fought on horseback.

"He knows I like him," said Zolner. "He would never believe what we have planned for him. Would you?" he asked, approaching the animal with an apple.

Yuri, the least sentimental of men, asked, "Couldn't we unhitch him?"

"The Financial District is crawling with police. The streets and sidewalks are jam-packed at lunch hour. We'll be lucky to get away on foot, much less leading a horse. All right, are you ready?"

"I've been ready for days!"

"I am talking to the horse."

Zolner opened the stall, said, "Come along," and hitched the animal to the wagon.

They dressed in workmen's shirts, trousers, boots, and flat caps, all smudged with coal dust, and rubbed dust on their hands and faces. Zolner climbed up on the driver's bench and took the reins. Antipov slid open the stable door.

A man who looked like a plainclothes police officer stepped in from the sidewalk. He looked around with quick, hard eyes, took in the horse, Zolner seated in the wagon, and Yuri Antipov frozen with surprise. He opened his coat, revealing a gleaming badge pinned inside the lapel, and a fleeting glimpse of a heavy automatic pistol.

"Have either of you gents seen Charlie 'Trucks' O'Neal?"

Zolner spoke first in Russian, saying to Yuri, "I will distract him for you," and in heavily accented English, "Ve not know such person."

"Big guy, six-two, broken nose, black hair."

"Ve not know such person."

"That's funny. 'Cause I hear he rents this stable. And here are you guys with a horse and a wagon, which are staples of the stable business, if you know what I mean."

"Are you policeman?"

The man stared a moment, appeared to make up his mind, and suddenly sounded more friendly. "Don't worry, gents, I'm not a cop. Van Dorn private detective. Harry Warren's my name. I don't mean to keep you guys from going about your business. Though I'm not sure who's going to buy your coal in the middle of the summer."

He opened his coat again, took out a wallet, and flashed a ten-dollar bill. "Are you sure you haven't seen him?"

Marat Zolner reached for the money and stuffed it in his pocket. "Man who rent stable . . . desk there." He pointed at the office door.

"Thanks. You gents go on. I'll wait for him in there."

Harry Warren was halfway to the office door when Antipov started after him, dagger drawn.

"Was that Russian you were speaking?" asked the detective, turning suddenly and drawing his pistol with blinding speed. He fired once, into the stable floor, an inch from Antipov's shoe. The Comintern officer skidded to a stop.

Harry Warren glanced at the distant door

to the street. No one had been passing by, no one was peering in for the source of the gunshot, which was good. He needed time with these two without the cops.

He said to Zolner, "Translate to your pal to drop his knife before I shoot him. And you keep your hands where I can see them."

Zolner spoke. Antipov let the dagger fall from his hand.

Warren did not know what he had stumbled into while looking for Trucks O'Neal, but it looked promising. Particularly with the Russian connections Isaac Bell kept turning up. He addressed Zolner in a deliberately conversational tone while watching closely for the man's reaction. "The reason I ask about Russian is we keep running into a Russian connection to this case we're trying to solve about who tried to kill our boss. Could be coincidence, though, if it is, your pal's attempt to stick a knife in my back will require some explaining."

Marat Zolner and Yuri Antipov stood still as bronze statues. Not even their eyes moved, not even to track the sudden motion of Trucks O'Neal entering silently from the covered alley and clutching a full bottle of counterfeit Glen Urquhart Genuine by the neck.

Harry Warren sensed the rush and whirled. The bottle aimed at the back of his head smashed against his temple, fracturing the thin bone and rupturing the artery under it.

Marat Zolner shut the stable door. Antipov and Trucks O'Neal slung the detective's body into the wagon beside the dynamite and covered it with more coal.

"Why," Zolner asked, "are the Van Dorns looking for you?"

"Me?"

"He asked if we had seen you. Why?"

"Say, wait a minute. I didn't do nothin' to bring 'em after me."

"Don't come back here. We're done with the stable. We're done bottling."

"But there's eighty thousand bucks of Scotch next door."

"It's more like one hundred fifty thousand," Zolner said quietly.

"Are you blaming me?"

"I'm sending you to Detroit before they catch up with you."

"I'm not starting over in Detroit."

Zolner stepped very close and stared down into Trucks's eyes. "Trucks, I've never questioned your loyalty. Remove anything of yours that is incriminating. I'll have people meet your train. Go! Now!"

O'Neal backed away, spun on his heel, and hurried through the covered alley.

"Kill him," said Antipov.

"Capitalists first. Open the door."

Antipov opened the door again.

They sat side by side on the driver's bench. The horse plodded slowly through the clogged streets of Lower Manhattan, down Broadway to Trinity Church, and turned onto Wall Street. Zolner reined in and set the brake outside No. 23 Wall on the corner of Broad. Left to his own devices, he would have parked the dynamite around the corner at the New York Stock Exchange, the nucleus of the Financial District. But Yuri had chosen the marble headquarters of J. P. Morgan.

He climbed down and adjusted the horse's feed bag, then knelt by the wagon, pretending to adjust the swingletree while he connected the final detonation wire.

"Cops!"

Yuri Antipov had spotted a policeman coming their way. Marat Zolner climbed back up, sat beside him, and took the reins. The cop pushed closer through the crowd.

Antipov fingered the dagger under his shirt.

"That won't help this time," said Zolner.

"Wait on the wagon until I've dealt with him. I'll be right back." He jumped down again.

Yuri Antipov watched Marat Zolner intercept the cop. Would he bribe him? Or blackjack him? Not in front of all these people who thronged the busy intersection. Suddenly, both the cop and Zolner hurried away and melted into the crowd. What had Marat said to him? Antipov was trying to figure out what was going on and what he should do when he heard an alarm clock ring.

19

Isaac Bell heard the explosion four miles away in the Van Dorns' St. Regis office. Wildly divergent reports flooded in on the wires and telephones, blaming a dynamite accident on a Jersey City dock, a Lower Manhattan gas main, a subterranean New York Steam Company pipe, then a powder mishap at one of the many Financial District construction sites.

Bell received an urgent call from police headquarters.

"Inspector Condon would appreciate if you'd come down to No. 23 Wall Street."

The fastest way downtown was on the subway. Bell got as close as he could and ran the rest of the distance from City Hall Station, where they had stopped the trains. He was blocks from Wall Street when he saw windows blown out of buildings. Nearer the explosion, the carnage was horrific. He estimated scores had been killed and hundreds injured. Trucks and taxis were turned upside down, scattered like toys. The dead were huddled on the sidewalk under coats. The street was deep in broken glass. From it, Bell gingerly extracted a cucumber-shaped piece of cast iron with a hole through its length.

He spotted Inspector Condon directing an army of plainclothes and uniforms from the front steps of the Morgan Building. Its windows were smashed from basement to attic, its marble walls pocked with shrapnel and blackened by coal dust. The mutilated carcass of a dray horse lay on the curb. Only the animal's head was intact, blinders covering its eyes.

"Thanks for coming, Isaac," Condon said gravely. He was a youthful-looking, fresh-faced son and grandson of cops and universally believed to be the department's fastest-rising star. "I'm awful sorry, but I have to show you something."

He handed Bell a battered piece of gold.

"Van Dorn shield."

"I'm afraid so, my friend."

Senior men carried gold. Bell held it to the light. He could just make out the engraved No. 17 and it shook him to the core.

"Harry Warren."

"Oh, for God's sake!" Condon inhaled sharply, blinked, and looked away. "Always the wrong man . . . Any idea what Harry was doing down here?"

"Last he told me, he was nosing around Warren Street."

"Of all the ways to go," said the cop. "Harry busted into more gang dens than you and I could shake a stick at and here he ends up an innocent bystander."

"Where's his body?"

"I don't know that we'll ever find it. He must have been right next to the damned thing. His badge landed in the Morgan lobby."

Bell put it in his pocket. "Does the Bomb Squad have any idea what caused it?"

"Not yet. They found a wagon shaft and this horse with its guts blown out. Could have been some damned fool transporting powder. Some people saw a wagon right there where you see all the burn marks. And there are three or four foundation excavations nearby where the contractors would store dynamite. Fire department has the Bureau of Combustibles checking permits. But considering J. P. Morgan was every Bolshevik's Bogey Man, I will not be surprised to learn it was a bomb."

"It *was* a bomb," said Bell. "It wasn't an

accident."

He handed Condon the chunk of iron he had picked up.

"Recognize this?"

"Sash cord slug," said the inspector, naming the counterweight used to open windows. "Could have blown out of one of these buildings."

"You don't find sash slugs in modern skyscrapers. Besides, see how it's burnt? It could have been in the explosion."

Condon grew red in the face. "If that's so, then some cold-blooded radical was deliberately trying to kill or maim as many people as possible."

"If it was," Bell spoke with cold fury, "then the Red Scare boys deported the wrong radicals."

Tragically, the foreigners like Johann Kozlov — not to mention Marion's movie-folk friends — rounded up and deported in the Red Scare were immensely less dangerous than whoever detonated the bomb.

"Innocents," he told Inspector Condon, "paid the price."

His angry gaze fixed on the dead horse.

"Dick? Do you mind if I take a shoe?"

Isaac Bell brought Harry Warren's badge back to the office and dictated a directive:

"The Van Dorn Agency will establish its own Bomb Investigations Department and contract to provide better information to the government than the Justice Department is getting from its Bureau of Investigation."

He put Grady Forrer in charge of hiring the best specialists, made a note to ask Joe Van Dorn who his best contact was at Justice, and instructed Darren McKinney to find the sharpest Washington lobbyist that money could buy.

Next, he assembled the Gang Squad. Grieving detectives circled his desk.

"Does anyone know what Harry was doing on Wall Street?"

"He said he was going to Warren Street, Mr. Bell."

"That's what he told me."

"How did he get down to Wall Street?"

They looked at Ed Tobin who had apprenticed under Harry. Ed said, "He could have spotted Trucks O'Neal on Warren Street and followed him down to Wall Street."

"And then," Bell asked, "he had the worst luck in the world walking past that wagon just when it went off?"

"Maybe."

"I don't like coincidences," said Bell.

"And I don't believe there's a detective in this room who likes them either."

"No argument there, Mr. Bell."

Bell said, "Here's how we find whether Harry Warren followed Trucks O'Neal to Wall Street. Keep searching for Trucks O'Neal. Check morgues and hospitals. If O'Neal's among the victims, that'll settle it. But if we find him alive and unhurt, we'll have proof Harry wasn't near Trucks when the dynamite went off. *Find Trucks O'Neal!* Start on Warren Street. Find that stable Harry was looking for. There can't be that many still in business down there."

A detective said, "I just got back from there, Mr. Bell. The only stable I found was locked up."

"Go back. Watch the place. Meanwhile, look at this."

Bell laid the battered scrap of gold on his deck. "Harry's badge. Number 17. Cops found it blown through the front door of the Morgan Building."

Around it he placed a horseshoe with a jagged nail and a patch of rubber stuck to it.

"From the horse that pulled the wagon that blew up . . . Find the farrier who shoed the horse that pulled the wagon that transported the dynamite that killed Harry

Warren. The farrier will tell us who owned the wagon."

"Yuri died a hero of the revolution," Marat Zolner told Fern Hawley.

She was red-eyed and crying inconsolably. "Don't pretend that you're not glad that you lost your overseer."

"Only until Moscow sends the next."

"They'll never find another like him."

That, thought Zolner, is certainly my hope.

And not an empty hope. Ironically, Yuri's Wall Street bombing would buy him time. With nearly forty dead, four hundred wounded, and photographs of the wreckage in every newspaper in the world, the Comintern had plenty to celebrate. So he was a hero, too, and it would be a while before the *apparatchiks* got brave enough to challenge him again.

Trucks O'Neal posed an immediate threat. When the Van Dorns caught up with him, the gangster knew too much. There was no doubt they would. Trucks had refused to hide in Detroit, so the only question was how soon. Worse, by now Trucks had had time to realize that he was a threat, which meant he would not let Zolner near enough to kill him. But Trucks was greedy. And greedy men were predictable.

Grady Forrer pulled a recent issue of *International Horseshoers' Monthly Magazine* from the Van Dorn Research Department's library stacks and opened it on a desk in front of Apprentice Somers. Next to it he placed the horseshoe that Isaac Bell had brought back from the Wall Street bombing.

"What we have for our search for a particular farrier is a horseshoe and a nail and a scrap of rubber from what was likely a horseshoe pad. Now, this monthly is chockful of interesting articles about the goings-on in the International Union of Journeymen Horseshoers of the U.S. and Canada. But what we are interested in are these advertisements for horseshoes, horse nails, and horseshoe pads. Are you with me so far?"

"Yes, sir, Mr. Forrer."

"Why don't we start with the horseshoe itself. Describe it to me."

"It's worn thin."

"Do you see the manufacturer's name or trademark stamped on it?"

Somers turned it over in his hands. "No, sir. No name. No stamp."

"So how are we going to compare it to these ads? You think on that. I'll be back."

When Forrer returned, Somers pointed excitedly at the advertisement for Red Tip horseshoes made by the Neverslip Manufacturing Company of New Brunswick, New Jersey. "Look at this ad, Mr. Forrer. It tells you all about how to make a horseshoe. You could make one yourself after you read this ad."

"Yes," said Grady. "But when researching for information about something specific like where was this horseshoe made, you've got to be careful not to get sidetracked. You and I *could* read every word in every ad in the magazine. But should we? Because while we're learning to make horseshoes, the criminals who shot Mr. Van Dorn are at target practice, improving their aim to shoot the next detective. Unless we stop them first. Now, why don't you tackle this nail. I'll be back."

When Grady Forrer returned, young Somers had disappeared. An hour passed and he burst excitedly into the newspaper library where Forrer was assembling a report on Detroit's gang wars.

"Apprentices go to lunch when they're told to, Master Somers."

"I didn't go to lunch. The nail is worn down like the shoe, so there's no special marks on it. But I noticed something on the shoe so I ran over to Third Avenue and showed it to a carter. See this little wedge? The carter told me the farrier brazes it onto the shoe to lift the back of the hoof if the horse is standing wrong on it."

Grady turned the shoe over in his huge fingers. "Horse podiatry?"

"Now look at this mark." Somers peeled the rubber off the wedge and touched a fingernail to a faint mark pressed into the metal.

Forrer snatched up a magnifying glass. "What is this? . . . 'RDNJ'?"

"*NJ* could mean New Jersey. So *RD* might be the farrier's initials."

"Sounds like you ought to get over to New Jersey and find RD."

"How?"

"Remember those advertisements in *Horseshoers'* for shoes and nails and pads. Where did they tell the farrier to buy their products?"

"The jobber?"

"Work up a list of New Jersey jobbers for blacksmith supplies."

The bleary-eyed Gang Squad detective, who hadn't slept in the twenty-four hours after the bombing, made a believable-looking derelict as he pretended to snooze in a doorway across Warren Street from the stable he was watching.

"It took us a while to catch on," he told Isaac Bell, who hadn't slept either, when Bell crouched beside him, pretending to give him a cigarette. It was late at night and the streets were empty.

"This guy who looks exactly like Trucks — Ed Tobin swears it's him — goes in the stable in this side, then he drives out on Murray Street. The backs of the buildings butt together in the middle of the block. He just went in again. Ed's watching on Murray."

"Stay here," said Bell. "Nail him if he comes out. I'll cover the other side."

He ran full speed to the corner, down Greenwich, and turned onto Murray.

Ed Tobin was waiting inside a butcher's van, eye to a peephole. Tired as he was, he flashed Bell a predatory grin. "I snuck close. He's got one truck left. Loading booze now."

"How many helpers?"

"None. He's clearing the place out all alone."

Bell said, "Looks like he knew Harry was close."

"If Harry was getting close, what was he doing on Wall Street?"

"Maybe Harry got too close," said Bell.

"And Trucks killed him? And put him in the wagon?"

"That's a stable on Warren Street. Where would you put a wagon while you collected dynamite?"

"The same guys."

The chief investigator and the Gang Squad chief's onetime apprentice exchanged a grim look.

"I've been asking myself something similar," said Tobin. "Harry shadowed suspects close as glue. Trucks doesn't have a mark on him. So Harry couldn't have been following close when he got blown up. But Harry had no reason to be in front of the Morgan Building. He was supposed to be eleven blocks uptown, here at the stable."

"What you are speculating," Bell said, "is that Harry was in the wagon."

"I didn't want to say it. It sounds too crazy."

"It's not crazy," said Bell. "It *is* speculative. And it would be purely wild speculation if we were not tracking possible Comintern agents hell-bent on sowing terror."

"So what if Harry, looking for Trucks, got the drop on them in the stable? What if they turned the tables and killed him?"

Isaac Bell nodded. "That could be why

Trucks is running for it, if he knew that Harry was a Van Dorn. Van Dorns don't come alone. He's grabbing what he can of the booze before we catch up with him."

"You want to bust in the door?"

"Very much so," said Bell. "But I'd rather see where he goes. If anyone knows who Marat Zolner is, it's the gangster who came back home on Zolner's steamer ticket."

"Door's opening!"

"Can you trust this thing to keep up?"

"It's running O.K."

A heavyset man pulled the doors inward. The streetlight fell on his face. His skin gleamed with perspiration. He had removed his hat, revealing a distinct widow's peak.

"That's Trucks," said Tobin. "No question. See what I said? Not a mark on him."

Trucks O'Neal stepped back into the warehouse and a moment later drove out in a Dodge delivery van, riding low under the weight of a heavy load.

Bell said, "He didn't close the door this time. He's finished. He's not coming back."

Tobin jumped behind the steering wheel and stepped on the electric starter.

"Stick close," said Bell. "I'd rather he spots us than we lose him."

They followed the Dodge downtown for eight blocks, into the Syrian quarter, and across Rector Street to West Street and down a block. Trucks O'Neal rounded the corner, half a block ahead of Isaac Bell and Ed Tobin. They followed, turning into a dark street that was suddenly ablaze with muzzle flashes.

A staccato roar echoed off the buildings like a thunderstorm of chain lightning. A line of bullets stitched holes in a row of parked cars. Tobin slammed on the brakes.

Isaac Bell threw open the passenger door, collared Tobin with his free hand, and dragged him out with him. As they rolled across the cobbles the butcher van resonated like a tin drum, its sides and windshield punctured repeatedly.

"Thompson .45 submachine gun." Bell rolled to a crouched position behind a bullet-riddled Model T and whipped his Browning from his coat.

"What are they shooting at us for?" Tobin shouted over the roar, which continued at the same deadly pitch.

"They're not."

"Could have fooled me."

"They're shooting at the guys shooting back."

A scattering of pistol fire confirmed that the Van Dorns had driven into the middle of someone else's gunfight. Tobin drew a short-barreled belly gun, which would be of even less use against the Thompson than Bell's automatic.

Another storm of bullets raked the street. This time no one shot back. When it stopped, Bell raised his head to look for O'Neal. He saw the Dodge with its tires flattened and its driver's door open, but no sign of the gangster. A Locomobile burst from a warehouse, careened past the Dodge, and raced around the corner on squealing tires.

And suddenly it was quiet.

Bell knew he had the briefest of moments to find whether Trucks O'Neal had survived before the cops came and took charge. Trailed closely by Tobin, who watched their backs, the tall detective approached the Dodge. It had been riddled, like the Van Dorn van and most of the vehicles in sight. It reeked of spilled alcohol from hundreds of broken bottles. There was no one inside.

Bell heard a groan. They followed the sound into the warehouse from where the automobile had just raced. Cases of whisky were stacked around the walls.

"Glen Urquhart Genuine," said Tobin. "Same stuff Trucks had at Murray Street. Looks like he got hijacked."

"But where is Trucks?"

Deeper into the warehouse they found a flashy-looking man in a gaudy suit who had been creased in the shoulder by a bullet. He was struggling to sit up and reach for a pistol that had fallen beside him.

Bell kicked the gun away and knelt by him. "Who shot you?"

"Who shot me? What are you, a cop?"

"Van Dorn."

"Same thing."

"Who shot you?" Isaac Bell repeated coldly.

"No one."

"What happened here?"

"Beats me."

"Where's Trucks O'Neal?"

The gangster surprised Bell. He laughed. "Trucks? Trucks went for a ride."

"Where?"

"I don't talk to cops."

"You'll wish we were cops," Tobin growled over Bell's shoulder. To Bell he said, "This guy I recognize is Johnny Quinn, who sells hooch for Lonergan. Isn't that right, Johnny?"

Quinn nodded. "I need a doctor."

"You'll need an undertaker if you don't give us O'Neal," said Tobin, and then he spoke to Bell as if the gangster was not sprawled on concrete between them. "The way I read it, Trucks is selling the stuff to this guy. Hijacker with the Thompson tries to take the stuff. Mr. Quinn and his friends hold them off. Quinn's shot, friends run for it. Hijackers get some but not all of O'Neal's product."

"No," said Bell. "I see no truck to take it in. And they shot up the Dodge. They didn't hijack the booze. If they hijacked anything, they hijacked O'Neal."

Bell turned his attention back to the gangster. "Where did they take him?"

"Nowhere."

An electric police siren howled nearby. Bell's hand flickered toward his boot. He held his throwing knife in front of the gangster's face, then threw a headlock around his neck and slipped the knifepoint inside his ear. "I asked, where did they take him?"

"You're not a cop?"

"We already established that. Which way?"

The gangster wet his lips. "Listen, this is between Trucks and them."

"You know who grabbed him, don't you?"

"Yeah, and I ain't telling you because whatever you do to me they'll do worse."

"You want to bet?" asked Bell.

The gangster twisted his head to look imploringly at Ed Tobin. "Listen, buddy.

You know who I'm talking about? The guys taking over the docks. Pushing out Lonergan and the rest."

"Black Hand," said Tobin.

"The Black Hand set Trucks up. They was waiting for him."

Isaac Bell and Ed Tobin exchanged a glance. That the Italians, who were shoving the Irish out of the lucrative control of longshore labor, were gunning for Trucks O'Neal was a wrinkle unconnected to the Comintern and Marat Zolner.

Or was it unconnected? Bell wondered. What if Zolner was teaming up with partners? What if he had teamed up New York's new top dogs? If he had formed a working alliance, then it was very possible that those new partners were doing Zolner a service eliminating a witness who knew enough to threaten their joint schemes.

"Where did the Black Hand take Trucks?" Bell asked.

Tobin leaned closer to whisper. "You better tell us. I have no control over what this guy does to you."

Bell emphasized Tobin's warning by sliding his blade deeper into the gangster's ear. The point grazed his eardrum. Quinn went limp. Bell said, "You already told us they took Trucks for a 'ride.' *Where?*"

"I don't know for sure. They usually take guys to Brooklyn."

"Brooklyn's a big place."

"Fulton Street."

"Fulton Street's a big street."

"Come on, mister, you're going to get me in all kinds of trouble."

"You're in all kinds of trouble."

Ed Tobin interceded again, in a manner now less kindly than fatalistic. "Think of this guy as your priest. God's the only one he'll tell your confession to and God probably doesn't care. Where on Fulton?"

"Down by the ferry. Under the bridge."

It was less than a mile across Lower Manhattan to the Brooklyn Bridge, even skirting the barricades in the Wall Street area where the police were still investigating the explosion. On the bridge, with the sky turning pink and the wind whistling through the bullet holes in the butcher van's windshield, Ed Tobin asked, "Comintern and Black Hand? Funny combination."

"Five'll get you ten the Black Hand doesn't know that Zolner is Comintern. Just a top-notch bootlegger smart enough to make friends. We can ask Trucks, but you have to step on the gas before they kill him. Go! On the jump!"

They careened through the snakes' nest of exit ramps on squealing tires and down, down, down to the derelict ferry-landing neighborhood where Fulton Street petered out under the bridge in a slum of flophouses, blind pigs, and greasy spoons. Vagrants slept in doorways. Bell saw no cops anywhere.

The sun had yet to light the Gothic towers of the bridge, but it was reddening the top girders of the skyscrapers under construction across the river on Wall Street. The ferry to Manhattan, which few rode since the bridge had effectively put it out of business long ago, no longer ran at night. Along the waterfront, the shacks and docks and piers appeared abandoned, with peeling paint and splintery decks.

"There's their Locomobile."

They pulled up behind the auto they had seen race from the warehouse on Murray Street. It was parked beside a truck in the shadows at the foot of a pier under a broken streetlamp.

"Out on the pier," said Bell, breaking into a run.

Far away, at the end of the long wooden structure that thrust into the river, a gang of six or seven surrounded a man they were half carrying, half dragging toward the water. Bell pulled his gun, stopped running, and took aim. Careful not to hit Trucks, he fired twice, close, over their heads. A hat flew. A gangster ducked and threw himself flat. The rest held tight, reached the end, and threw Trucks O'Neal into the river.

Isaac Bell ran full tilt. The gangsters peeled away and scattered, running back toward their auto, watching Bell carefully and making room for him to run past them. The river was at slack tide, the serene surface disturbed by a single round dimple. Trucks had plunged into the water like an anvil and sank straight to the bottom.

Bell tore off his coat, kicked out of his boots, and dived after him.

Piercing the center of the dimple that marked O'Neal's entry, he drove straight down, stroking and kicking and reaching into the dark. Descending fifteen or twenty feet, he hit bottom, felt mud, banged into something hard — the foot of a piling. He felt around frantically and something soft closed around his outstretched hand and held on tight.

Bell could hardly believe it. It was a near miracle. But in diving straight down, he landed on the bottom next to O'Neal, who was clinging to his hand with all his might.

Bell planted his feet in the mud and kicked off to pull him to the surface.

Bell could not lift him.

He tugged harder on the man's hand as if to shout *Push off! Help me lift you!* Where was his natural buoyancy? Even a man who couldn't swim would float partway to the surface, but Bell could not budge him from the mud.

He was running out of air.

He pulled himself down by the gangster's hand, braced again in the soft mud, and tried to push off. But again he could not lift the man. Now he was out of air. He could hear his heart pounding. There was a roaring in his head. He had no choice but to swim to the surface, fill his lungs, and dive down to help him again. O'Neal's hand tightened around his with the superhuman strength of desperation.

Isaac Bell pried his fingers loose, one by one.

He heard a sudden hollow rush. Bubbles of air rubbed past his face. O'Neal was drowning. His grip slackened. Bell yanked free and kicked with his last strength toward the light overhead. He held his breath until he could wait no longer and when he opened his mouth and inhaled, he was amazed to discover he had made it to the air.

"Get a rope!" he yelled. "Ed get a rope!"

The resourceful Tobin was already sprinting back from the ferry landing. He threw a long rope. Bell filled his lungs and dragged it under. Unhindered by the slack water, he dived directly to the drowning gangster, looped the rope under his arms and tied it around his chest and shot to the surface.

"Pull!"

Twelve feet above him on the pier, Tobin had been joined by a couple of vagrants, who shouted for others to help, and they heaved on the rope like men who worked on boats and slowly lifted Trucks O'Neal out of the water. His head broke surface. He was, Bell feared, dead, but he shouted for them to hoist him up to the pier. They did, then dropped the rope for Bell. He climbed out and discovered that the gangsters who had thrown Trucks in the river had tied concrete cinder blocks to his ankles.

Ed was laboring over Trucks's prone body, pressing on his back and raising his arms, attempting artificial respiration, expelling water and making his lungs draw fresh air. But it was hopeless. O'Neal was dead.

Cops arrived.

"Well, that's a new one. Cement over-shoes."

"Who was he?"

"He was," said Isaac Bell, "the Van Dorn Detective Agency's best lead."

"Can I get a gun from the weapons' vault, Mr. Forrer?"

"Apprentice Van Dorns don't carry guns."

"I learned how to shoot in the Coast Guard."

"Nix. I am sending you to Newark to interview a jobber of farrier supplies. It is highly unlikely that a man who makes his living selling horse nails and anvils will engage you in a shoot-out."

Somers looked so disappointed that Forrer elaborated.

"Mr. Van Dorn believes that a young man with a gun is less observant than he should be, imagining that he can shoot his way out of difficulty. But a young man dependent upon his wits to survive learns to be more observant . . . A necessary detective skill, wouldn't you agree, young man?"

Somers took the train to Newark.

In the Ironbound District, near the freight station, he found the warehouse that belonged to the New Jersey horseshoe jobber that he and Mr. Forrer had settled on as the likely purveyor of the horseshoe Mr. Bell had retrieved on Wall Street.

The jobber told him that the rubber scrap stuck to the horseshoe could have been either a Revere Rubber Company Air Cushion Pad or a Dryden Hoof Pad.

"How about Neverslip Manufacturing from New Brunswick?" asked Somers.

"Coulda been."

"Do you have any idea which farrier might have bought it from you?"

"No. It could have been anyone."

"What if that same farrier also bought this Neverslip shoe?"

The jobber turned the worn shoe over in his hands. "Coulda."

Somers showed him the mark stamped in the wedge. "How would this get marked like this?"

"The farrier has his initials on a punch. Smacks it with a hammer to make his mark. He signs it. Like a trademark."

"Do you recognize the initials *RD*?"

"Sonny, why are you asking all these questions?"

Asa Somers straightened his skinny shoulders and stood tall. "I am an apprentice Van Dorn private detective. We are investigating the bombing on Wall Street."

"I thought the government does that. And

the cops."

"Could he be one of your customers?"

"Could be."

"Do you remember the farrier's name?"

The jobber shrugged, as if deciding that Somers was an earnest lad who posed no threat to his customer. "His name is Ross. Ross Danis."

"Where can I find him?"

"I don't know where he sleeps these days. He used to be farrier and blacksmith on Mrs. Dodge's estate 'til they let him go."

"For what?" asked Somers, whose own firing by the Coast Guard still stung despite his wonderful new job with the Van Dorns.

"They say *Mr.* Dodge," snickered the jobber, "was getting green-eyed, if you're old enough to know what I mean."

"Do you mean that Mr. Dodge was jealous of Mr. Danis's attentions to Mrs. Dodge?"

"The lady was smiling like she hadn't in years."

"Where would I find Mr. Danis when he's working?"

"Seeing as he just bought himself a spanking new Boss leather apron and a fresh set of Disston rasps, he's probably shoeing horses at the Monmouth County Fair — unless Mr. Dodge is in attendance."

■ ■ ■ ■

"But what of the revolution?" asked Fern Hawley.

She was staring sullenly at an untouched glass of genuine champagne that had been poured for her by former heavyweight champion Jack Johnson, the owner of Harlem's Club Deluxe.

Marat Zolner had hoped a late-night outing would take her mind off Yuri.

"Bootlegging," he reminded her again, "is our path to revolution."

"Yuri didn't think so."

The famous black prizefighter's Lenox Avenue speakeasy was Fern's favorite cabaret. A hot jazz band drew the cream of the Park Avenue crowd. They came uptown in limousines and taxis, dressed to the nines, after private dinner parties, theater, and the opera. Zolner enjoyed it, too, especially while playing the part of an aristocratic Russian émigré out on the town with his American benefactress. It was great fun to be rich, fun to slum with movie stars and gangsters and young flappers in short hair and shorter skirts.

"Yuri did not understand," he said gently. "But he was coming around to seeing

America the way it is going."

"But where are *we* going?" asked Fern. She had been impatient for results before Yuri was killed. Now she was obsessed.

"We are going to a city where a narrow river, which a speedboat can cross in minutes, is all that separates a legally wet nation from a legally dry nation."

"Detroit," said Fern, who had kept up to date on every aspect of Prohibition since Zolner first hatched his scheme.

"Detroit. Three of every four drinks poured in the United States come from Detroit. Detroit sells to Saint Louis, New Orleans, Kansas City, and Denver, the West, Midwest, and South."

"But the Purple Gang and the River Gang are fighting to control it. They own the police. They own the politicians."

Marat Zolner reached under the table and took her knee in a firm grip. "That is why we are going to Detroit."

"But what of the revolution?" Fern repeated defiantly. She looked away, refusing to meet Zolner's eye. Her own eyes fell on the smiling Jack Johnson, who was greeting a striking couple at the door.

"Look! There's Isaac Bell."

20

"Welcome back, Isaac. And Mrs. Bell, what a pleasure to see you again."

Former heavyweight champion Jack Johnson — a remarkably fit-looking forty-three-year-old black man — cut a splendid figure in a dark suit with chalk-white stripes. He bowed low over Marion's hand.

"Would it be too much to hope that you are making a new picture in New York?"

"From now on, I'm shooting all my movies in New York. Nothing in Hollywood can hold a candle to Club Deluxe."

Johnson accepted the compliment with a hearty laugh.

"By the way, Isaac, thank you for the cigars."

"You thanked me already, Jack. They were the least I could do."

Johnson had served a stretch at Leavenworth — railroaded into the penitentiary on a false Mann Act charge — and Isaac Bell, like many of the great prizefighter's admirers, had sent boxes of the finest La Aroma de Cubas to help him through the year. "I see you're looking to fight Dempsey. Or is that just newspaper talk?"

"What do you think?"

"I think you're a mighty fit forty-three and Jack Dempsey's twenty-six."

"I believe I could lick him. I'm feeling tiptop, in better condition than ever."

"You look it," said Bell.

"I don't want to fight any second-raters and neither does Dempsey. It'll be a heck of a battle. I'll tell you this, though." Jack Johnson lowered his voice. "I better win. The hoodlums are moving in on me here. I won't own this joint much longer."

"Who?" asked Bell.

"Some bootlegger gangster they're about to set loose from Sing Sing. I'm told he's planning to buy me out cheap and redecorate with 'jungle' stuff, palm trees and all that. I won't have much say in it unless I want to go to war with guns and knives, and *that* I am too old for."

"Which gangster?"

Jack Johnson looked out at his busy cabaret. He smiled at the sight of the packed tables, rushing waiters, and crowded dance floor. "Don't know yet, though I wouldn't be surprised if he's got some scouts in here watching me right now. Like I say, it's time for me to go back in the ring."

Marat Zolner recognized the man talking to Jack Johnson as the Van Dorn detective who pursued him the night he executed Johann Kozlov.

"Are you sure he never saw your face?" Fern asked.

"Absolutely."

"But you were close enough to see him shoot Johann."

"I said I *heard* the shot. I didn't see it."

"So it could have been someone else who killed Johann?"

"I saw no one but Bell." And then, to steer Fern off the subject of the shooting, he asked, "Who's the gorgeous creature on his arm?"

"His wife. Marion Morgan Bell. The movie director."

"Director? Such a beauty should be the star."

"Would you like me to ask Mr. Bell to introduce her to you?" Fern asked icily.

"I meant nothing to get sore about, only that at a distance, at least, she appears to be extraordinarily beautiful."

"Such a handsome man," Fern shot back,

"deserves at least one beauty."

She watched Isaac Bell rake the speakeasy with a probing gaze that missed nothing. His violet blue eyes settled on her and darkened in recognition even as he smiled hello.

Fern waved.

"What are you doing?" asked Zolner.

"Here's your chance for a close-up."

Bell and Marion made their way slowly across the crowded speakeasy, stopped repeatedly by fans jumping up to tell Marion how much they liked her moving pictures. Few directors would ever be recognized by the general public, but when Marion appeared in a movie magazine, her face was remembered.

"I'd like to stop at Fern Hawley's table," Bell told her.

"Who's the man with her?"

"Let's find out."

The society woman's companion rose politely when they stopped at the table. He stood with poise and grace, a trim and elegant man as tall as Bell and slightly thinner. He had an easy manner but a sharp gaze. Fern introduced him. "My old friend Prince André, late of Saint Petersburg."

Bell and Prince André shook hands firmly.

Bell introduced Marion. Pleasantries were exchanged. They agreed to sit for a moment.

Prince André engaged Marion in a technical conversation about film, drawing on the Russian model. Marion told him that she was shooting a comedy about a Russian ballet company stranded in New York.

"What will you title it?"

"Jump to New York."

"What could be better? We should all 'jump to New York,' should we not, my dear?"

Fern Hawley said to Bell, "My friend is laying on the charm for your wife."

"I'm used to it," said Bell.

"How often does it end in fisticuffs?"

"No more than half the time."

Fern's grin made her eyes even more opaque. She pursed her Cupid's bow lips to ask, "And the outcome when it does?"

"They don't do it again. Is Prince André a recent arrival?"

"I knew him in Paris."

"Was he a refugee then?"

"Far from it. His family had estates in France."

"And also in America?"

"None I know of," Fern said. "May I ask you a question?"

"Of course," said Bell with a glance at Prince André and a private smile for Marion.

"A blunt question," Fern said.

"Blunt away," said Bell. "What's on your mind?"

"When we met the first time, when you were chasing . . . whoever you were chasing?"

"Yes?"

"I had the impression that you could, under the right circumstances, like me very much."

"I've always liked characters," said Bell.

"Good characters or bad characters?"

"I mean, different types — nonconformists, bohemians."

"I'm not sure I've been complimented."

Bell grinned. "You're positive you're complimented. You love standing out."

"So you could like me?" Fern smiled. Her almond eyes slid toward Marion. "Under the right circumstances."

"They don't exist," said Bell. He turned to Prince André. "We've entertained you far too long, sir. Forgive the interruption."

Marion slipped her hand into his arm and they continued across the speakeasy. "I've yet to meet a Russian refugee who wasn't a prince or at least a count."

"He's a tough-looking prince," said Bell.

"I thought so, too. Did you see his hands?"

"Powerful. His shake felt more American than European."

"He told me he fought in the cavalry."

"I hope Miss Hawley knows what she's doing."

Marion said, "Miss Hawley strikes me as a woman who has known what she was doing since the day she broke every heart in kindergarten. Do you find her attractive?"

"I certainly would," said Bell, "if I weren't with the loveliest woman in the world."

"How would you feel if I bobbed my hair like hers?"

"I like your hair the way it is. But I'd take you bald, if it made you happy. Where do you suppose Fern Hawley found Prince André?"

"If broke aristocrats find rich American heiresses in New York the way they do in Hollywood, he would have wrangled introductions so he could show up in some place she was comfortable — a country club or an expensive restaurant."

"She told me they met in Paris."

"I'm sure Miss Hawley was comfortable in Paris."

"May I have this fox-trot?"

They danced to a jazzed-up "Melancholy

Baby," Bell sweeping Marion around other couples in order to pass repeatedly close to Fern and Prince André's table. The heiress and the Russian refugee were deep in conversation.

When Bell and Marion returned to their table, Marion said, "Despite her stick-it-in-your-eye smirk, Miss Hawley is not happy."

"Why?"

"I think she's disappointed."

"Could the bloom be off the rose?"

"No, that rose is still blooming. It's something else."

Bell noticed a broad-shouldered man in evening clothes watching Fern's table from the bar, his highball glass untouched. When Prince André looked toward him, he straightened up slightly, as an employee might, confirming Bell's strong impression he was a bodyguard. The Russian's active gaze wheeled his way. Before he could see Bell watching, Bell turned to Marion.

"Speaking of blooming roses, I forgot to tell you Pauline sends her warm regards."

Across the room, Prince André rose to his feet and extended his hand to Fern Hawley. He guided her onto the dance floor and took her in his arms.

Marion said, "You see what I mean about the rose? These two enjoy each other. Isn't he a wonderful dancer?"

Bell agreed. "He looks like he trained in the ballet."

"He's tall, for the ballet."

"Maybe he was a short boy. At any rate, I'm shopping around for the right fellow for Pauline."

"Who?"

"Dashwood is nuts for her."

Marion looked skeptical. "I've always thought that Dashwood is uncommonly close to his mother."

"She starred in Buffalo Bill's Wild West Show and taught Dashwood how to shoot."

"Mr. Freud would have a ball with that one. On the other hand, if anyone could wean Dashwood, it would be Fräulein Grandzau."

Bell glanced through the crowds again. "Do you suppose you could get Fern Hawley to open up to you?"

"I'll try. How can we get the prince out of the way?"

"I'll ask the waiter to tell him he's wanted on the telephone."

"What do you want to know?"

"I want to know how Miss Hawley happened to be sitting in her limousine on a slum street outside the back door of Roosevelt Hospital the night the killer who shot

Johann Kozlov got away from me. I wondered then, and I wonder more now. It had to be a coincidence. But . . ."

"But you hate coincidences. I'll try and work my way around to it . . . Too late, there they go!"

Bell watched closely as Fern and Prince André left straight from the dance floor. A waiter ran after them with the feathered boa she had left on her chair.

"You're right," said Bell. "She is disappointed in him. There's something in the angle she holds her head."

"You should be a detective . . . Where are you going?"

Bell's reply was a terse, "Don't follow me."

The man he had observed at the bar moved quickly to escort Fern and Prince André out of the speakeasy. Bell followed. A thug in a topcoat, who Bell had noticed lounging under the electric canopy earlier, blocked a newspaper photographer trying to snap a picture of Fern and the prince. Moving to stop Bell, he put a hand on his arm.

"Save yourself trouble, mister. Go back inside while you have teeth."

The tall detective knocked him to the pavement.

But by then the bodyguard — Bell had no

doubt anymore he was that — had shut Fern and the prince's car door. The chauffeur stepped on the gas and sped into busy Lenox Avenue. The bodyguard faced Bell, took in his partner on the sidewalk with a swift glance, and opened his coat to show his pistol. "Want something, mister?"

Bell opened his own coat, closed a big hand around his Browning, and started toward him. But late-night revelers were swarming the sidewalk, and loaded taxis were hauling up to the curb.

The Packard carrying Fern Hawley and Prince André cut in front of a trolley and disappeared. The bodyguard helped his partner stand and they left in a taxi, leaving Isaac Bell to wonder whether they were guarding the wealthy young woman or her pampered gigolo who looked thoroughly capable of guarding himself.

In the limousine, Marat put his arm around Fern.

She turned her face away. "The bank's closed."

"Bank? What bank?"

"It's an expression. It's the way a girl says she's not in the mood."

"Since when?"

"Since . . . I have the heebie-jeebies about Yuri."

"The bank did not appear to be closed to Isaac Bell."

"Oh, for God's sake, Marat. He's a detective. That's all we need."

"You were falling all over him."

"He's married."

"Do you ask me to believe that would stop you?"

"It would stop him — don't you know *anything*?"

They rode in silence until the car stopped in front of her town house. The driver jumped out. Marat Zolner signaled through the glass not to open the door.

"Now what?" said Fern.

"How long will this bank be closed?" he asked.

"Not forever. I just need a little time." She patted his hand. "Don't worry, it'll be O.K."

"We have much to do. You keep asking about the revolution. The revolution requires intense focus. Nothing should distract from it. Therefore, we will do the following: You will stay here while I'm away. Use the time to think. I'll send for you once I'm established. If you want to come, you'll come."

"Where are you going?"

"I told you. I am expanding our operation. I am ready to take Detroit."

"Who is 'I'? Who do you mean? I the bootlegger? I the Comintern officer?"

"We are one," said Marat Zolner. "I. The bootlegger. And the Comintern. This is the plan. This has always been the plan."

"What of the revolution?"

"We *are* the revolution."

"Yuri was the revolution. Johann was the revolution. Look what happened to them."

"Yuri lost his way. He lost his focus. Dynamite does not forgive mistakes. Johann had the bad luck to run into the wrong detective."

"You won't escape the Van Dorns in Detroit."

"What makes you think that?"

"They have field offices everywhere, including Detroit."

Zolner reached out and squeezed her leg hard.

"Stop!"

Zolner squeezed harder and said, "The Van Dorn Detroit field office is going out of business."

21

Thirty miles to the east, that same night, Uncle Donny Darbee was running an oyster boat full of Scotch from Rum Row toward Far Rockaway Inlet. Progress, he was thinking, was a wonderful thing. The modern world worked better than the one he had been born in. Fog lay thick on the water, but a radio signal kept him on course like magic. The big Peerless V-8 his nephews had lifted out of someone's new automobile made his boat faster than an old-fashioned twenty-horsepower Ford and beat the pants off sails and steam engines. And Prohibition, God bless the politicians who passed it, made running rum far more bankable than pirating coal and easier on an old man's back.

It looked like the fog had scared off the marine police and the Coast Guard.

Guided by the crash of breakers, he slipped in near silence through the stone breakwaters of the inlet. He continued with his heavily muffled engine throttled way back into Reynolds Channel, a sheltered strait that paralleled the ocean between Long Beach Island and Long Island. Listening for other boats, so as not to collide in the dark, and paying close attention to the changing currents, which indicated his position in the narrow channel, he headed on the course indicated by Robin's radio. They had two more miles of waters he knew well to a boathouse owned by a Long Beach hotel that would buy his booze.

"Grandpa!"

"What?"

"The radio's going haywire."

The next moment, Darbee heard the thunder of ganged Libertys. He looked over his shoulder and saw the blood-red glare of their fiery exhaust. Too late, he realized, the radio signal was a trap and the black boat everyone was talking about was trying to hijack him. A big searchlight burned through the fog, passed over his low gray hull, and swooped back like a hungry sea hawk.

"Hunker down by the engine before they start shooting."

Robin obeyed instantly. "What are you going to do, Grandpa?"

"I'm going to hope to heck he don't spot us."

He eased his throttle forward and picked up speed, reasoning that they wouldn't hear him over the roar of their own engines. But suddenly their engines grew quiet. They had either slowed down to listen or shifted their engine exhausts through heavy mufflers, as he had shifted his when he entered the inlet.

The searchlight blazed back toward him. They were not making a secret of their presence, and Darbee suspected it wasn't the fog that cleared out the cops but payoffs. Which meant he and the little girl were entirely on their own. He poured on as much speed as the Peerless would give while muffled. The searchlight swung close. He saw the glow touch Robin's face. She looked frightened, but she was cool — one of the reasons he took her along on these jaunts.

Now they saw him.

He opened his cutouts for more speed. The Peerless roared.

Behind them the Libertys got very loud, and the big boat sprinted after him.

Robin asked again, "What are we going to do, Grandpa?"

"We're going to run him onto Hog Island."

"What's Hog Island?"

"Summer resort. Dancing pavilion, restaurants, bathhouses, carnival on the boardwalk."

She looked ahead into the empty dark, looked back at the Cyclops eye of the searchlight catching up, and looked worriedly at her grandfather. His long hair was streaming in the wind. He had one gnarly hand draped casually on the tiller. The expression on his face was weirdly serene, considering they were being chased by something scarier than cops, and she wondered, with a stab of heartbreak, *Had the black boat frightened the old man out of his wits?*

"I don't see any island, Grandpa."

"Neither does he."

"But where is it?"

"Hurricane washed it away."

"What hurricane, Grandpa?"

"I don't remember — back thirty, forty years ago. Before your mother was born, if I recall."

"Where is Hog Island now?"

"About three feet under us."

"Oh!" she burst out in relief. He was O.K. "A sandbar! But, Grandpa, we draw almost three feet."

"He draws *five.*"

At that moment, behind them, they heard

the big engines stop.

"They found it!" said Darbee. He slowed down and engaged his mufflers. In the near silence, they listened to men shouting in fear and anger.

"What language is that, Grandpa?"

"Hell knows, but I can tell you what they're yelling: We're hard aground on a sandbar, the tide is going out, and if we don't get off it right now we'll be sitting ducks when the sun comes up."

Darbee leaned on his tiller. They doubled back and listened from a distance. The black boat's engines thundered and died, thundered and died, as they repeatedly risked their propellers trying to back her off. An engine suddenly revved so fast, it screamed.

"Busted a prop," Darbee said cheerfully. "Or a shaft. Oops, there goes another one. He's got one to go. Let's hope he don't bust that one, too."

"Why? Let him bust all three and we'll get out of here."

A single engine churned cautiously, revved a little, and slowed.

"Hear that?" Darbee exulted. "He got off. Good."

"Why good, Grandpa?"

"You just watch."

■ ■ ■ ■

The black boat limped east at ten knots.

Darbee followed. They passed Jones Inlet, but stayed in the inner passage, as he suspected they would. They did not dare go back out into the ocean with only one propeller, a propeller thumping from a bent shaft.

"Grandpa, what are we doing?"

"Gonna find out where he lives."

"Why?"

"Why? What do you mean why? I want that boat."

"How are we going to steal a boat from all those gangsters?"

"Haven't figured that out yet."

They followed for hours as it picked its way carefully through the twisty channel and finally out into South Oyster Bay and across it to Great South Bay. A dim gray dawn began to lighten the east. Soon the old man and his granddaughter could see the faintest hint of the black boat silhouetted against it.

"Where are we, Grandpa?" Robin whispered.

"Off Great River, I believe."

"Have you figured out how we're going to

steal it?"

"Not yet."

"Maybe Mr. Bell could help us."

"That goody two-shoes don't steal boats."

"But if we did him a favor . . ."

Out of the mouths of babes, old Darbee thought. What a smart little girl she was. A chip off the old block.

". . . maybe Mr. Bell would do one back."

"The metal is flying," bellowed Ross Danis.

The big farrier had a handsome head of hair, an amiable grin, and bright eyes. Sweat glistened on his broad chest and streamed from his massive arms. Asa Somers found it hard to believe that a man could have so many muscles. He bulged like the Jack Dempsey advertisements for Nuxated Iron.

It was Babies Day at the Monmouth County Fair.

Following the baby show would be a horse show and then horse racing, which meant Danis was busy at his portable forge. Asa Somers offered to crank his bellows to keep his fire white-hot. This kept both hands free to go at it, in the farrier's own words, "hammer and tongs," fitting shoes, driving and clinching nails into hoofs, finishing with his rasp. It had the side advantage of keeping him talkative.

When Danis finally stopped for a swig of water, and a furtive slug from a flask, Somers showed him the worn Neverslip shoe. "Could you have put this shoe on a horse?"

"Hope not. Looks like the animal threw it, which would make me look bad."

"He didn't throw it."

"Where'd you get it?"

"Wall Street."

"Never worked on Wall Street."

"I didn't mean you did it on Wall Street."

"Not only did I never work on Wall Street, I find it hard to imagine a horse I shoed ever being on Wall Street. That's across the river in New York City. Is it a swell's carriage horse?"

"Is this your mark on this wedge?"

Danis leaned over it to look, dripping sweat on Somers's arm. "I'll be darned. Where'd you find this?"

"The horse was pulling a coal wagon."

"Coal wagon? I don't understand. No teamster's going to drive his coal wagon all the way to New Jersey to shoe his horse."

"What if the horse was sold to a New York coal wagon teamster after you shoed him?"

"Well, I'll be," said Danis, his red face lighting in recognition.

"What do you mean?"

"His name was Redman."

"Who?"

"Big, strong quarry horse. Seventeen hands. Strong as a mule. Good-natured, too. Just the sweetest temper."

"Who owns him?"

"Fellow came in all in a rush. He had just bought him, didn't realize he had a loose shoe. Didn't know a thing about horses. I wondered how he'd ever hitch up the wagon. I figured I'd lend a hand, but Redman was such a sweet-natured animal they worked it out."

"Did you get his name?"

"Redman."

"The man."

"No. He was a foreigner. Had a real thick accent, and he was in a heck of a rush. Gave me two bucks and ran off."

"Was that here?"

"No, no, no. Not at the fair. Up in Jersey City . . . Wall Street? Yeah, that makes sense."

"What do you mean?"

"Last I saw, they were heading toward the ferry."

Asa Somers reported to Grady Forrer and, a while later, he overheard Mr. Bell on the telephone. "We traced the horseshoe to a New Jersey farrier. I'm sorry, Dick, but it looks like a dead end."

Isaac Bell said good-bye to Inspector Condon and hung up the telephone, wondering what next. He was painfully aware that he needed a lucky break or two. But, so far, they weren't flocking his way.

He noticed Somers skulking about. "Why the long face, Asa?"

"The horseshoe didn't help?"

"What? No, don't worry about it. We have to try everything to find what works."

"I wish mine had."

"I could say the same about Trucks O'Neal and the *Black Bird* motors. It's the nature of the game. You just keep plugging away."

"Can I have a gun?"

"Not yet."

"I heard a rumor from some of the boys that when you were an apprentice you bought your own derringer."

"Like most rumors, that's not entirely true."

Somers looked at Bell inquiringly.

"Go on, son. If you're going to be a detective, you have to ask questions. *Ask.*"

"What wasn't true?"

"I didn't buy my derringer. I took a derringer away from somebody. And kept it."

Darren McKinney ran into the bull pen. "Mr. Bell!"

"McKinney."

"My Washington fellow came through."

Shipments to the New York region from the War Department director of sales included a dozen surplus Liberty engines, and crates of spare parts, to the Long Island Railroad freight depot in Bay Shore, sixty miles from the city. Isaac Bell drew a circle on the map, representing the likely distance a truck would drive from a railroad depot, and dispatched detectives to all the South Shore towns within it.

"Blue Point, Sayville, Patchogue, Great River, Bay Shore, Islip, West Islip."

"Needle in a haystack," said McKinney.

But Isaac Bell was optimistic. "We were looking in a hundred-mile haystack. Now we're down to ten."

The Van Dorn operator rang. "Long-distance telephone from Texas Walt Hatfield."

"Detroit?"

"Yes, but not on the private line."

It was a fairly decent connection. Bell could hear hints of Walt's drawl. "Ah busted some heads, cleaning up the office. We're down to two good men."

"Are you sure about them?"

"Plumb sure. Exceptin' we had a mite of trouble. They're both in the hospital, owing to a bushwhacker lobbing a hand grenade into the premises."

Bell asked how badly they were hurt.

"They'll recover, but they're not tip-top at the moment."

"Who threw the grenade?"

"I'd say the Purple Gang."

"The Purple Gang are street kids."

"The little tykes are growing by leaps and bounds. Partly on account of their vicious habits. Partly due to the Eye-talians killing each other off leaving the Purples to play the big time. Most of the Detroit big boys are sleeping in the river. There's been a complete change of gang bosses."

"Close the office."

"The hand grenade sort of did that already. I've got a real estate fellow looking for a new space."

"Close it. Permanently."

"Now, hold on, Isaac," Texas Walt drawled. "These hydrophobic skunks will get the wrong idea if we slink out of town with our tails between our legs."

"We'll come back — undercover."

"I already told you it won't do having folks stopping me for my autograph while I'm masquerading as a criminal."

Isaac Bell said, "And I told you I'm going to hide you in plain sight —"

Bell looked up at a sudden commotion. Ed Tobin burst into the office, grinning like a bulldog that had sunk its teeth into a steak.

"— Hold the wire, Walt." Bell put down the phone. "What?"

"Uncle Donny found the black boat."

"Where?"

"Great River."

Bell stood up. "Great River?"

"It's way out on Long Island."

"I *know* where it is," said Bell. "Eight miles from the Bay Shore freight house, where the War Department shipped a dozen surplus Libertys. Where are they keeping it?"

"Stashed it in a boathouse on a private estate."

Bell grabbed the phone. "Walt, I'll call you back when I can. Meantime, tell your real estate agent to rent a big place out of town for a roadhouse."

"Roadhouse?"

"You heard me. Rent a roadhouse!"

Bell banged down the phone.

"How did he find it?"

"It tried to hijack him. Uncle Donny followed it, hoping to steal it."

"What changed his mind?"

"Too many of them. And he had little Robin with him. So now he's hoping when we catch it, we'll give it to him."

"Fair enough. But that's a lot of boat for one old man. Aren't his nephews in the jail-house?"

"Jimmy and Marvyn got set loose for good behavior — actually, a paperwork error in their favor. Wes, and Charlie, and Dave and Eddie, and Blaze are up for parole, eventually."

"Wait a minute. How did that oyster scow manage to keep up with a fifty-knot express cruiser?"

"She ran aground. Busted props and driveshafts."

Isaac Bell headed for the door. "We'll get there before they fix her. Where's Dashwood? James, round up the boys! And get ahold of some Prohibition agents you can trust."

"Trust? How much?"

"More than the rest. But don't tell them where we're going."

Outside the St. Regis Hotel, grim-visaged detectives piled clanking golf bags from the Van Dorn weapons vault into town cars. The lead motor was an elegant Pierce-

Arrow packed with folding ladders and grappling hooks to scale walls and axes and sledgehammers to breach them.

Bell gave the order to move out. Then he took Ed Tobin, Uncle Donny, and two detectives who were strong swimmers to the 31st Street Air Service Terminal. The mechanics at the Loening factory next door had his flying boat warmed up and ready to take off. Coiled in the passenger cabin were several hundred yards of light manila line and wire rope.

22

Great River opened into the bay between a golf course under construction on one side and marshland on the other. The channel moved inland on a northerly route through flat shores that were speckled intermittently by the lights of mansions. A mile or so in, the river narrowed to a width of five hundred feet. Tall trees grew close to the shore. A small tributary entered from the west. Its dredged channel led from the main river to an enormous boathouse that showed no lights when night fell.

Isaac Bell had seen this water route from the air in the last of the daylight. After Uncle Donny pinpointed the boathouse, he got a good look at a huge mansion behind it, the road in, which was blocked by a substantial gatehouse, and a spur that connected a mile inland to the Long Island Railroad.

As soon as it was dark, he set detectives to

work in strict silence. The swimmers crossed the tributary with a manila rope. Climbing out on the other side, they used it as a messenger line to pull the heavier wire rope after them and clamped the wire around thick trees. In the event the black boat had been repaired already and tried to make a run for it, the channel was blocked.

Bell ordered a pair of the heaviest town cars to be parked nose to nose across the road a short distance from the gatehouse. He had invited Prohibition officers on the raid — partly to process arrests, mostly to stay on friendly terms with government agencies that might contract with Van Dorn. They stayed in the blockade cars under James Dashwood's watchful eye. The Dry agents were impatient, fiddling with their guns and whispering bad jokes. Bell had not told them yet who they were raiding, nor would he until he had every bootlegger on the property in handcuffs.

"Ready when you are, Mr. Bell," said Ed Tobin.

"Now," said Bell. Before a night owl neighbor telephoned the police about the roadblock.

The stone gatehouse was dark, with no sign of sentries. But nothing short of dynamite would budge its massive iron-studded door, so they left the battering ram in the Pierce-Arrow and scaled the walls with knotted line and grappling hooks. The first men up — Bell in the lead, followed by Tobin — carried folds of heavy canvas slung over their shoulders. The wall was topped with strands of barbed wire, reminding veterans of the trenches, minus artillery and machine guns. The masonry under the wire was impregnated with broken glass. They clipped the wire, covered the glass with the canvas, and left the ropes and canvas in place for the next men.

Eight detectives cleared the wall. Bell sent two to open the gatehouse door from inside for Dashwood and the Dry agents. The rest followed him to the boathouse on a route he had sketched from the air. They skirted the tennis courts and removed a stone pillar from under a birdbath in the formal gardens. Stumbling in the dark on the railroad siding, they followed the rails to the boathouse.

Bell signaled with whispers and shoulder taps to hold up at the door, which he could see dimly by the thin light of the stars. There were a few lit windows in the mansion, which loomed in the distance, but no lights shone in the boathouse. It seemed a miracle, but, so far, no one had heard them.

That was about to change.

"Break it down."

The birdbath pillar made an excellent battering ram, and the door flew inward with the third thunderous blow. They spilled through, Bell in the lead. It was darker inside than out and eerily quiet, but for the lapping of water.

"Where is everybody?"

"Find the lights."

Flashlight beams poked the dark until they found a big electrical box. They threw its knife switches and lights shone down from the rafters on two slips. One held a fair-size booze taxi with twin engines. The other was empty.

The black boat had vanished.

"Go get Uncle Donny."

The detectives whom Bell had sent to the gatehouse had opened it, and the town cars streamed through and up the driveway, playing headlights on the mansion and the empty railroad siding. The Prohibition agents swaggered into the boathouse and looked around, big-eyed.

"Some operation."

"Look at all that giggle water."

"One hundred percent."

Barrels of two-hundred-proof pure grain alcohol were stacked against the inland wall, sharing the space with some crated Liberty airplane motors and a strongbox with its lid propped open.

"Mr. Bell," a detective called. "There's no one in the house."

"Gatehouse is empty," said another.

"There you are, Uncle Donny." Bell took him aside. "No black boat."

"Damn."

"Are you sure you saw him come in here?"

"Sure as I know my name."

"In this boathouse?"

"I saw him from a distance. So did little Robin. You don't believe me, ask her."

"I believe you, sir."

"Don't start calling me sir."

"Could this have been the boat you saw come after you?"

The old man gestured disdainfully. "There's only two motors on that boat. And it ain't black. The boat that chased me was black, longer, and had three motors."

"You heard all three?"

"Heard 'em bust two props. Followed them home on their third."

"But it's not here. Where did it go?"

"Didn't get past that wire."

Bell asked whether the black boat might have sunk in the channel before it reached the boathouse.

308

Darbee shook his shaggy head. "First of all, the channel ain't deep. If he sunk, we'd see him sticking up. Second, I saw him go in here. And I saw them close that door."

Bell beckoned Ed Tobin. "Bring your light." Tobin and Darbee followed him outside. "Point it at the tracks."

Ed shone his light on the rail. They knelt down and inspected it closely. "Son of a gun," said Tobin. "Almost no rust on top."

Bell ran his fingers along the side of the rail. The base and the web were heavily encrusted with iron oxide, but the running surface atop the head was almost smooth, the rust ground away recently by the wheels of a train.

"The builders told me," said Bell, "that whoever bought the boat took it away on a railcar. Looks like they did it again."

"Where?"

"They've had the better part of a day to take it anywhere. There's a telephone inside. Call the railroad and get started tracking a flatcar. Where's Dashwood?"

"Right here, Isaac. I was just checking the mansion."

"Let's see what they left behind."

They stepped back into the lit boathouse.

Bell saw the blood rush from Dashwood's face. His skin went dead white, and he seemed to be holding his breath. "Are you all right, James?"

Dashwood narrowed his eyes and appeared to be looking everywhere at once.

"James."

"Sorry, Isaac." His color returned as quickly as it had faded. But he still looked tense. "Threw me, for a second, back to the war. When we broke out of the trench and took a village, I'd climb the church belfry or the town hall cupola for a shooting position. When the Germans retreated, they'd booby-trap the place. My spotter stepped on the stairs and it blew him to kingdom come."

"What did you see here?" Bell asked sharply. "What set you off?"

"It was the emptiness, I think. Deserted. Like we found in France."

Bell saw the Prohibition agents clustered around the open strongbox. "What have you got there, gents?"

"That's O.K., Mr. Bell. We'll be confiscating this. It's government property now."

"Is there something in that strongbox?"

The agents moved closer, shielding it with their bodies.

"What is in there?" demanded Bell.

"Just a couple bucks. Looks like they took

the money and ran and forgot a couple of bucks."

"Don't touch that money."

"Don't worry, we'll count it up and take proper care of it. You go about your business."

"Don't touch it!" Bell roared. "It's a booby trap."

The Dry agents ignored him and grabbed the cash.

Isaac Bell caught one glimpse of what looked like thousands of dollars, not "a couple of bucks," as he yanked Dashwood and Ed Tobin backwards through the door. With a flash of light and hollow *Boom!* an explosion erupted under the barrels of grain alcohol. Flaming liquid leaped to the rafters, and the whole place was afire in seconds.

■ ■ ■ ■

Book Three: Gangland

■ ■ ■ ■

The Black Boat Attacks

23

Marat Zolner drove *Black Bird* the length of Lake Erie in a single dark night.

With new propellers and driveshafts, and her Libertys freshly tuned, she cruised the two-hundred-forty-mile voyage from Buffalo Main Light to the mouth of the Detroit River at an easy-on-the-valves, fuel-stretching thirty miles an hour. Zolner kept her so far offshore, straddling the invisible border between Canada and America, that all he could see of the lights of Erie and Cleveland were low halos to the south. She slowed only twice: for heavy seas, when a squall lashed the western flats with wind and rain; and, earlier, to sink with her Lewis gun a wooden customs boat, which could never catch her but had a radio to report her presence.

Nearing the Detroit River, Zolner stopped off the Pelee Passage Light and flashed an Aldis signal lamp. A motorboat sped out from Point Pelee, driven by a Comintern Maritime Section agent with a smuggler's knowledge of the long, narrow strait's labyrinth of coves, islands, and inlets. He led the black boat up the Pelee Passage, past the Bar Point Shoal Lighthouse and into the Amherstburg Channel. Reserved for inbound shipping, the channel ran north between Bois Blanc Island and the Canadian mainland. They overtook monster shadows in the dark, six-hundred-foot iron ore carriers, riding high in ballast.

"What a wonderful place," said Marat Zolner.

City lights and chimneys belching fire marked the office buildings, automobile plants, and foundries of Detroit on the American side of the river. On the Canadian side — ninety seconds at *Black Bird*'s top speed — were the "border cities" of Windsor, Riverside, Ford City, Walkerville, Sandwich, Ojibway, and La Salle. Their population was a mere tenth of Detroit's, but they were as brightly lit, their waterfronts crammed with distilleries, breweries, and the government export docks where customs cleared alcohol for export. The cleared booze was absolutely legal until it crossed the international border in the middle of the river.

The boat leading them veered toward Windsor and pointed the way to a hidden inlet that led to a brick boathouse that had been built before the war for an industrialist's yacht.

Black Bird rumbled into it. Men lowered the door, and she was safe.

Isaac Bell ordered a dozen Van Dorn detectives to track the flatcar that had taken *Black Bird* from Marat Zolner's Great River estate. He had no proof that Zolner had rented the estate; whoever had had paid cash through brokers who had disappeared. Vanished, too, were the agents who had arranged for the railroad to move the car. But if not Zolner, who else? Besides, Zolner or not, the black boat served the Comintern.

The Van Dorns started at Zolner's siding, the remnants of a passenger spur that had served the exclusive South Side Sportsmen's Club. The spur connected to the Montauk Branch of the Long Island Railroad. Detectives went west toward New York City and east toward Montauk Point. In both directions were many towns with freight sidings near creeks, inlets, and harbors.

Bell himself headed three station stops to the west to the railroad's district freight yard at Babylon. On the chief dispatcher's blackboard was a record of a "special," an extra, unscheduled train, consisting of a locomotive, tender, caboose, and a flatcar, serial number 55461.

He asked to speak with the engineer, but the man was out on another train. The locomotive's fireman was "around somewhere," but neither in the freight house, where large items were stored, nor in the express house, which handled packages. "Try the engine house." Skirting piles of sand and gravel and a clamshell bucket loading hopper cars, Bell found the fireman oiling a 4-6-0 and asked if he had a look at the boat.

"What boat?"

"On the flatcar."

"Is that what it was? It was wrapped under canvas. Sure, could have been a boat, I suppose."

"Didn't you wonder?"

"Weren't about to ask. They were a tough bunch."

"How many men?"

"Six or seven, I believe. They holed up in the caboose, made the brakeman ride up in the cab with me and the engineer."

"Where'd you take it?"

"I rode as far as Jamaica."

From the Long Island Railroad's central

freight junction at Jamaica, in the New York City borough of Queens, car number 55461 had been sent to the East New York freight yard. From East New York, it was shunted to the waterfront Bay Ridge Terminal and rolled onto a car float. A Pennsylvania Railroad tugboat shepherded the car float across the Upper Bay to Jersey City's Greenville Terminal, where 55461 disappeared.

Bell made a contribution to the railroad police "benevolent fund" and blanketed the yard with his own detectives to search for it. But it was nowhere on the property. Nor did the Pennsylvania Railroad have any record of the flatcar heading south or west on "Pennsy" track.

An angry Isaac Bell stormed that a flatcar carrying a seventy-foot speedboat, covered in canvas or not, could not simply vanish. A frightened dispatcher finally admitted that shortly after the car had arrived at Greenville, someone had lifted some papers from the chief dispatcher's files. Bell recalled from Grady Forrer's report that, when penetrating a foreign nation, the Comintern routinely infiltrated railroads and dockyards with low-level agents.

"What would happen," he asked the Greenville dispatcher, "if flatcar 55461 had continued down the line with no record of its existence?"

"That would have caused great confusion and immediate consternation."

Bell sent his men on a search for what competing railroad line the flatcar might have been transferred to. They picked up the trail nearby in Jersey City at the Weehawken junction. Number 55461 had been coupled to a New York Central freight train. The New York Central freight had headed north on the Central's West Shore Division, which meandered four hundred twenty-five miles from Weehawken, New Jersey, to Buffalo, New York.

Isaac Bell sent detectives after the freight. But with a fair idea of *Black Bird*'s ultimate destination forming in his mind, Bell himself raced to the Delaware, Lackawanna and Western's Hoboken Terminal. The Phoebe Snow, a high-speed passenger limited, whisked him straight to Buffalo.

The Buffalo Yardmaster at the New York Central West Shore Division Terminal told Bell the freight train had already been broken up. Some of the cars had unloaded in Buffalo and some were dispersed to other railroads. "A boat, you say?"

"Under canvas."

"Well, if it was a boat, go talk to the Buffalo Creek Railroad. They switch cars to the waterfront."

Bell hitched a ride on a Buffalo Creek switching engine, a little 0-6-0, that pushed a string of empty hopper cars back to the waterfront, where giant bulk carriers from the Midwest were moored to grain elevator docks. The engineer dropped the last empty, and the little engine huffed a few hundred yards to the end of the line. The rails stopped beside a crane on the edge of Lake Erie.

"Dropped him right here."

The engineer lit a cigarette. Bell climbed down beside the murky water and stared west.

"A boat," said the engineer, "can go anywhere from here."

"Detroit."

"Anywhere. The Great Lakes are all connected. It could be Detroit. Could be Chicago, Milwaukee, even Duluth — though I don't know who'd want to go to Duluth — Cleveland, Toledo, or even up Lake Ontario to Toronto."

"Detroit," said Bell.

The ingredients for three of every four drinks consumed in America were smuggled across the Detroit River. Where else could

Marat Zolner and his *Black Bird* be but Detroit? Bell was sure it was Detroit. But he was less sure why.

The Van Dorn Detective Agency had bloodied his nose in New York, taking his Long Island estate and his bottling plant in Lower Manhattan. Had Zolner fled to Detroit? Or did he already have New York in the bag, despite a bloody nose, and had gone to Detroit to expand his empire?

"Good luck," a Canadian stevedore at the liquor export dock muttered as the long black whisky hauler rumbled into the dark. "You'll need it when the Purple Gang hears you coming a mile away."

He and his mates were placing bets. The new boat, which had taken on a full thousand cases of Canadian Club, made a hell of a racket. Who would catch it first? Customs picketboats? Or the hijackers? The hijackers were the favorites. Side bets were placed on the notoriously vicious River Gang. The smart money inclined toward the rival Purple Gang, dubbed "monstrous" by a newspaperman whose head was found soon after floating in Lake Erie.

Any whisky hauler with any brains at all used mufflers. And if the black boat's noise didn't cut its odds to near zero, it was nowhere as fast as it looked. The newcomers had overloaded it. Crossing a stretch of river where a whisky hauler's only friends were speed and stealth, it rode low in the water, its engines laboring, at the pace of a steamer on a Sunday school outing.

The River Gang boss, "St. Louis Pete" Berelli, son of Sicilian immigrants, had grown up in a Jewish slum. Initiated as a boy into the neighborhood's exceptionally violent street gang, Berelli had nothing against the Jews. Until he hauled whisky in Detroit and ran up against the Purple Gang. Their so-called Jewish Navy whisky hijackers made the gangsters back in St. Louis look like choirboys. There was absolutely no reason to club every man on his boat and throw their bodies into the river. And even less reason to tow him behind the boat by a rope tied around his ankles to drown him slowly.

He was half dead when the rope slackened. The boat had stopped. Frantically flapping his arms to hold his head above water, he heard a loud motorboat passing in the dark. His blood ran colder than the water. A veteran of whisky crossings — and a savage hijacker himself — St. Louis Pete knew what the Purples would do next. In about two seconds, he would be drowning again, but not so slowly.

In the cockpit of the Purple Gang's speed-
boat, the Jewish Navy's "Admiral Abe"
Weintraub had lost interest in St. Louis Pete
Berelli.

"Shut up . . . Listen!"

Weintraub thought he heard what sounded
like a very big boat on a night run to
Detroit. There it roared again, motors
straining to move a heavy load.

"Get him!" he shouted at his driver, and
they tore after it.

His boat was a powerful Gar Wood with
monster Allison supercharged motors and a
semi-displacement hull. Towing the River
Gang boat they had just hijacked, and the
Sicilian behind it, diminished its speed by
very little. But, oddly, while they caught up
close enough to see the red glare of the
nightrunner's exhaust pipes, they couldn't
quite overtake it.

"Faster!" Admiral Abe yelled.

The driver, a loan shark enforcer by day,
feared Admiral Abe as every sensible gangster did. He coaxed every bit he could out
of his engines.

Suddenly, the red glare they were following disappeared. The Gar Wood was enveloped in a dark cloud of thick, choking

smoke. They were coughing on the smoke when the boat they were chasing fell silent.

"Where'd he go?"

"Stop!"

The driver jerked back his throttles. The bow dropped into the water, and the Gar Wood slowed so quickly that the boat they were towing crashed into their stern with an impact that splintered mahogany and knocked all but Admiral Abe off their feet.

"Kill 'em!" he yelled, pulling a heavy Colt Navy automatic and shooting into the dark where he sensed a long black hull sliding alongside. A searchlight blazed, and in the half second before it blinded him, he saw a Lewis machine gun on a sturdy mount. It spat fire in short bursts that cut his men down even as they pulled pistols. The noise was deafening and then over.

The black boat slammed alongside. Fighting men swarmed aboard, scooped the fallen gangsters off the decks, and threw them in the river. A rifle barrel knocked Weintraub's gun out of his hand. Men grabbed him. He fought. They beat him to the deck and hog-tied him, with his wrists behind his back and tight to his ankles.

"Who are you bastards?"

A tall, lean figure with his face masked

smashed a blackjack against Weintraub's mouth.

The searchlight went out.

Abe Weintraub spat blood and teeth. "I said, who are you bastards?"

"New partners."

Weintraub spat another tooth. "I don't need a partner."

"Not *your* partner," came the scornful reply, "your boss's partner. Who is he?"

"We're the Purple Gang," Weintraub shot back. "Leave the booze and run while you can."

They looped a line to the rope that tied his wrists to his ankles and threw him in the water. Weintraub held his breath, waiting for them to pull him out, waiting for the rope to jerk his wrists and drag him toward air. He waited until he could wait no more and had to breathe. He gulped for air but inhaled water.

They jerked his head out of the water. He gasped, coughed, gagged, and threw up. They dropped him back in the water. The second time they pulled his head back to air, the guy who had knocked his teeth out leaned over the side of the boat and addressed him conversationally. "There's a drowned guy hanging off the boat you were towing. Any idea who he was?"

Weintraub answered — the wop didn't matter, and it would buy time before they dunked him again. "St. Louis Pete."

"With what gang was Mr. Pete affiliated?"

"What?"

"Who'd he hang with?"

"River Gang."

"Poor Mr. Pete. Horrible way to die. Put him back under!"

They brought him up sooner than before, but he was gagging out of control. It seemed to take forever to get actual air in his lungs. When he could speak, Abe Weintraub said, "We're the Purple Gang. We own the river. We own the city. What do you think you're doing?"

"Doing? I am terrorizing you. What do you think I'm doing?"

"Why?"

"To beat you into submission. Do you want to die slowly? Or would you prefer to be beaten into submission?"

"No one beats Abe Weintraub."

"There's a first time for everything, Mr. Weintraub. You're looking at yours. You will turn on the phonograph and tell me who's your boss."

"What's the difference? You'll kill me either way."

"There is a third way. Work for me. Trespasses are forgiven if you're my man. Would you like that?"

"Go to hell."

"Put him back under."

24

An electric sign of multicolored bulbs as dazzling as any in Asbury Park glared atop a fresh-painted, veranda-draped hotel on an all-weather highway ten miles outside Detroit:

TEXAS WALT'S HIGH SOCIETY ROADHOUSE

The parking lot was full of Pierce-Arrows, Packards, Cadillacs, Rolls-Royces, Marmons, and Minervas, and it looked like a safe bet there were movie stars inside. If they were, then a new kind of lighted sign imported from Paris — neon gas set aglow inside clear tubes shaped like a martini glass — left no doubt they were drinking cocktails. Music gushed from the open windows, a sweet tune from a Broadway hit. It was played by Detroit's favorite twelve-piece society band, Leroy Smith's, and the cream of the Motor City's fast and rich spilled onto the verandas, dancing and singing along with "Kansas Nightingale" Amber Edwards:

"Till it wilted she wore it,
she'll always adore it
Her sweet little Alice blue gown."

A lime green V-8 Cadillac Sport Phaeton pulled up under the porte cochere.

Texas Walt Hatfield himself strode down the front steps to greet it. The tall western star was wearing his signature J. B. Stetson hat, a turquoise silk shirt, string tie, brocade vest, and ostrich-skin boots. Twin Colts were holstered low on his hips. Strapping doormen flanked him.

"Good job, Walt," said Isaac Bell, stepping down from the Phaeton in his bootlegger outfit. "The joint is jumpin'."

"Just like you ordered. Music, gambling, pretty gals, and the best booze south of Canada. Now, will you tell me *why* I'm operating an illegal alcohol establishment?"

"What do you mean illegal? The cops are directing traffic."

"And the town council's in the bar, toasting the mayor. Dammit to hell, Isaac, why is the Van Dorn Detective Agency running a roadhouse?"

"Information," said Bell. "Moneymaking roadhouses attract gangsters offering 'protection' for a cut of the profits. We'll put the question to every shakedown thug who tries to horn in on us."

"What question?"

"The same question Marat Zolner is asking: Who is Detroit's top dog? He's looking for a bootleg partner, like the Black Hand in New York."

"Detroit's different. Top dogs get shot, dynamited, and throat-slit on a regular basis. Every time the cops reckon who's running things, the sidewinder gets ambushed. It's bootleg war."

"I'm betting the Comintern has the muscle and the money to swing the war their way. The boss who Zolner backs will win the war. When we learn who Zolner chooses, *we* will do the ambushing."

"Looking forward to that," said Texas Walt. "Meantime, we're making money hand over fist. More than enough to cover the bribes — Good evening, Mr. Mayor. Good evening, Judge," he greeted two plump men in new suits. "Your fair ladies asked me to tell you they're getting a head start in the bar."

"Wouldn't it be funny," said Bell, "if the

Comintern were up to the same scheme we were?"

"Ah'd put nothing past Bolsheviks," said Walt. "But how do you mean?"

"Bootlegging to pay for the revolution."

Walt Hatfield laughed. "Personally, Ah'd say the heck with the revolution, Ah'm getting rich off Prohibition."

"Of course, you're not a Bolshevik."

"Not when last Ah looked. Hold on! There's trouble. Be right back, Isaac, gotta bust a head."

"Need help?"

"There's only three of them."

The tall Texan bounded up the steps and inside where a bootlegger in a flash suit was pummeling a waiter held by a pair of husky bodyguards. Walt's anvil fists flew. Within moments Walt Hatfield was walking the bootlegger, who now had a bloody nose, and a limping bodyguard to the parking lot. Ed Tobin, dressed as a floor manager in a tuxedo, followed him with an unconscious thug over his shoulder.

Bell headed inside, asking himself how odd was the idea of bootlegging whisky to fund the revolution. Invading armies fed off the land, foraging as they marched. Grady Forrer had chronicled Communist holdup gangs robbing czarist banks: "Stick 'em up in the name of the revolution!" Sinn Féin had paid to smuggle Thompson .45 submachine guns by robbing banks. Bell's own father, a Union intelligence officer in the Civil War, had hunted down Confederate raiders robbing express cars. Why wouldn't a Russian Comintern espionage agent plotting to overthrow the United States mask his Bolshevik assassins and saboteurs as a bootlegging crime syndicate?

The bar was seventy feet long and lined three deep.

Bell ordered a napkin and a glass of ice.

Scudder Smith sidled up with a *Brooklyn Eagle* press card in his hatband and dark tea in a highball glass. Most in the bar were too drunk to notice they knew each other, but, just in case, it paid to keep things private and appear to have just met.

"Brooklyn Eagle?" asked Bell. "You're out of your territory."

"The paper sent me to write a feature story on Prohibition in Detroit."

"Have you found any?"

"I haven't seen evidence of Prohibition, but I've heard rumors about a hooch tunnel under the river. Have you heard about the tunnel?"

"This is the first I've heard."

"Sounds loony, except they all say the Polish gang dug it, which makes sense. The Poles emigrated from Silesia, where they mine coal. So they're good at digging."

Bell lowered his voice. "Scudder, find me that black boat. Pretend you're writing about speedboats. Detroit's famous for hydroplanes. There's a guy named Gar Wood who builds the fastest."

Walt joined them. "Ain't had so much fun since Ah rode with Pancho Villa. That's the fourth ruckus tonight and it ain't hardly dark. Same thing last night."

The bartender passed him a dampened handkerchief to wipe the blood from his knuckles.

Scudder asked, "Since when did you ride with Pancho Villa?"

"Back when Isaac was in short pants at Yale. Where you going, Isaac?"

"Have a chat with your sparring partners."

He found the three in the parking lot, slumped against a Marmon, under the watchful eye of a Van Dorn. The unconscious bodyguard was still out cold. Bell hauled the bootlegger to his feet, walked him out of earshot, and handed him the glass of ice and the napkin. The bootlegger wiped the blood off his face and pressed ice to his nose.

"Thanks, buddy."

"Would you answer some questions for me?"

"Are you a cop?"

The TEXAS WALT's sign lit the parking lot bright as day. Isaac Bell gestured at his expensive suit, his handmade boots, and his rabbit-felt Borsalino. Then he shot a cuff, revealing diamond links and his gold Tank watch.

"Do I look like a cop?"

"You buddies with that damned cowboy who punched my nose?"

"I just got into town. Trying to get the lay of the land. But I'm hearing strange rumors."

"Like what?"

"Rumor has it," said Isaac Bell, "there's a casino out in the middle of Lake Erie on a big ship."

"Oh yeah?"

"Ever hear that?"

The bootlegger shrugged. "I heard they got a speakeasy in a dirigible."

"Like the Germans bombed London with?" asked Bell. He had heard it, too. It was one of the crazier Prohibition tales floating around the Motor City. No one was clear how the giant airship remained invisible in daylight or how the customers got from the ground to the hovering casino.

"How do they get up to it?"

"They must have figured out how to land an airplane on it."

Bell said, "I think I'll stick to roadhouses. What's your name, by the way? I'm Joe."

The bootlegger gave him a long look and decided to play it safe. "I'm Joe, too. Pleased to meet you, Joe."

They shook hands. Bell said, "I also heard about hijackers with a black boat."

"There's a lot of black boats on the river."

"This one's got a Lewis gun."

Joe nodded sagely. "You can't go wrong with Lewis guns."

"Ever hear about a tunnel under the river?"

"Sure. They got a train tunnel."

"For hauling whisky?"

"Yeah, you grease a brakeman and slip some on a freight car."

"But you never heard about a tunnel just for booze?"

Joe looked Isaac Bell in the eye. "A tunnel would be a surefire way to haul hooch. If I had heard it, it would be my tunnel and I sure as hell wouldn't tell anybody about it."

Isaac Bell went back to the bar. Another fight broke out. It looked to Bell to be a staged battle intended to intimidate the paying customers and impress upon the owners the wisdom of paying for protection.

"Tarnation!" said Texas Walt. "Here we go again."

Hatfield waded in. Ed Tobin joined him, trading his silver cocktail tray for a blackjack, and laid two men on the floor. The thug directing the theatrics pulled a gun.

Bell and Scudder moved swiftly to help. They needn't have bothered. Light glinted on Hatfield's scalping knife, and the gun fell from a hand flayed to the bone. Van Dorn waiters wrapped it in napkins and marched the gunman through the kitchen door. A woman stepped up for Walt's autograph and the movie star obliged.

"Pay dirt!" he grinned when he got back to the bar. "We have finally attracted a higher grade of extortionist. He threatened to sell me protection 'insurance.' A step up from plain old 'protection.' "

Bell said, "I'll see if you put him in a talking mood."

He found the gunman propped up on a keg outside the kitchen door, clutching his hand and guarded by an enormous Protective Services man. The napkins reeked of whisky that the Van Dorns had doused it with to prevent infection. He was white-faced with shock. But he retained the in-charge demeanor of a racket boss used to running the show.

Bell drew up another keg. "Hurt much?"

"What do you think?"

"I think you pulled a gun on the wrong guy."

"No kidding. Where'd a movie star learn to use a knife like that? I thought they was all mamma's boys. I never seen it coming."

"In Hollywood," Bell said, maintaining a serious expression, "they teach the actors the fighting that goes with the kind of movies they're in."

He passed his flask. The gunman pulled hard on it.

"Who are you working for?"

"You a cop?"

Isaac Bell took back his flask. "Do I look like a cop?"

"Then who are you?"

"I'm Gus," said Bell, using the other standard name for the speak-easy doorman. "What should I call you?"

"I'm Gus, too," said the gangster. "But it happens to be my real name. Who are you really?"

"I'm a guy who won't pay for a shakedown but will pay for information."

"Where'd you come from?"

"Chicago," said Bell, a city he knew

intimately, having apprenticed there under Joseph Van Dorn.

"Where in Chicago?"

"Grew up on the West Side."

"You know the Spillane brothers?"

"I put them out of business."

This was true, although sending them to Joliet Penitentiary was not the way Gus interpreted it, judging by a look of respect and a knowing assessment of Bell's high-priced duds.

"What are you doing in Detroit?"

Bell skipped his black boat rumors gambit and went straight to the heart of his scheme. "I'm looking for introductions."

"To who?"

"Potential partners."

The gangster perked up. "I thought Texas Walt owned the joint."

"I have an interest in it. We're looking for guys who know their business. So far, you are not a shining example of knowing your business, but maybe you're just having a slow night."

"Partners? That's what I offered that son-of-a-bitch movie star."

"You offered him protection insurance."

"Any fool knows that means partners. You can't run a business in Detroit without pro-tection."

"He doesn't seem to need protection."

"What kind of partners?"

"Supply partners. Partners we can count on for steady liquor. Do your bosses happen to be in the hauling business?"

"What makes you think I have a boss?"

"Bosses don't barge into a joint waving a gun."

"They do in Detroit."

Bell regarded him thoughtfully. "Is that a fact?"

The gunman stood up. "Here's another fact: You can go to hell."

Isaac Bell drew his Browning and aimed it at the gangster's as yet unwounded hand. "You want another crippled paw? Sit down!"

Flummoxed, the gangster gripped the blood-soaked napkins, sat back down on the keg, and cradled his hand in his lap. "What is going on?" he protested. "Where are all you guys coming from?"

"What do you mean, what's going on? What guys?"

"Always in Detroit we fight each other. Now we got outsiders, torpedoes shoving into our operations. Hijackers."

"What hijackers? Boats on the river?"

"You take your life in your hands on the river."

"Have you run into a big black boat?

Machine gun? Armor plate?"

"No."

"Have you ever run up against the Jewish Navy?"

"Once."

"What happened?"

"Nothing I'd want to happen again."

Bell said, "It sounds like they put you out of business."

"I'm waiting for winter. Drive across the ice."

"It's summer. How are you making a living in the meantime?"

"Snatch racket."

"Who are you kidnapping?"

"Guys that can't go to the cops."

Isaac Bell indicated familiarity with the kidnapping business by raising a pertinent objection. "Guys who can't go to the cops can be a handful."

"Sure can. You gotta be careful who you snatch. You wouldn't want to kidnap a Jewish Navy guy. You want guys with dough from bookmaking, whisky hauling, and girls; you want payroll bandits, loan sharks, auto thieves — except if they're Purples. Purples would chase you all the way to Mexico."

If Marat Zolner intended to make a criminal alliance in Detroit, as he had with the

Black Hand in New York, the leader of the rising Purple Gang would be high on his list. The difficulty would be identifying him. As Walt had noted, Detroit bosses were killed right and left by the warring gangs, and even the cops were never sure who was on top.

"Who's the Purple's boss?"

"You have a lot of questions, mister."

"I have a lot of curiosity," said Bell. "What's his name?"

"Forget it."

"Would you like to go for a ride?"

"Where?"

Gus followed Bell's gaze, past the kitchen and across the lot to a black Stutz sedan parked in the shadows, and his meaning sunk in. Leaning against it were Harry Warren's toughest Gang Squad detectives. Grieving for the murdered Harry, they had no difficulty looking like gangsters who would kill without hesitation and enjoy it. Gus shook his head. "Look, mister . . ."

"What's his name?"

"Saying it could get me killed."

"Not saying it *will* get you killed. What's his name?"

Gus looked around, ducked his head like a turtle, and whispered, "Stern."

"First name?"

"Max."

"Where do I find Max Stern?"

"I ain't that high up, mister. You gotta believe me."

"Where do you guess he hangs out?"

"The big guys don't hang out. Too dangerous."

Bell believed him. At least he had a name of the boss Zolner might go to. He switched tactics. "I keep hearing stories about that black boat."

"Boats are old hat."

"What do you mean?"

"Driving whisky sixes across the ice will be old hat, too."

Bell said, "What are you talking about?"

"When they get the tunnel."

"What tunnel?"

The gangster backpedaled. He was either reconsidering the truth of the rumor or the wisdom of talking about it. He said, "If you ask me, it's talk. Like the dirigible. Like the floating casino."

"What's the talk?"

"They're almost done digging it. Just talk."

"Where?"

Gus repeated almost word for word what "Joe" had told Bell in the parking lot. "If I knew where, I'd own it, which I don't. If I did, I wouldn't need the money for shaking down your roadhouse. Or if I knew and I didn't own it, I'd be dead."

"Why dead?"

"You can't move a tunnel. Only two ways to hide it: pay off or kill off everybody who knows about it."

Bell said, "If that were true, wouldn't you hear about workmen — masons, bricklayers, maybe even sandhogs — floating facedown in the river?"

"The river's full of bodies. Everyone thinks they're hijacked whisky haulers. Could be some other reason. Could be guys digging tunnels." The gangster hunched over his wounded hand and fell silent.

Convinced that he had gotten as much as he could out of Gus, Bell walked up the paved path that led to the front of the roadhouse. He was feeling discouraged. This tunnel talk was interesting, but he did not feel one foot closer to Marat Zolner and the Comintern.

It was getting late. Cars were pulling away, and he saw a line of red taillights, driving home to Detroit. The cops directing traffic had called it a night. As he approached the front steps, he exchanged nods with Dashwood, who was keeping an eye on things from the far side of the veranda. Stragglers lingered, swells and flappers prolonging good-byes with hip flasks.

Suddenly, Bell saw headlights blazing up the road, racing against the Detroit-bound traffic. The auto, a seven-passenger Packard, passed the parking lot. But instead of turning under the porte cochere, it stopped out front on the road. A man leaped out, gripping a stick grenade by its long handle. He jerked the detonating cord and wound up like a fastball pitcher aiming to burn one over the inside corner.

Isaac Bell sprang into motion, running as fast as he could.

The grenade flew on a flat trajectory, under the high roof of the porte cochere, straight at the veranda where men and women were shaking hands and hugging good night. A tipsy flapper stumbled on the steps. James Dashwood glided to her rescue and she fell into his arms instead of down the stairs.

25

The girl laughed, her face bright in the glare of the TEXAS WALT'S sign. The shadow of the grenade swooped across it like a bat. Dashwood turned toward it, too late. Isaac Bell was drawing near, sprinting among the revelers, long arm reaching, hand outstretched. He was so close that he recognized the grenade as the German Army *Stielhandgranate.* If it was a newer Model 24, it was loaded with almost two pounds of TNT, enough high explosive to kill everyone within fifteen feet.

It smacked into his hand like a line drive.

The 24s had a five-second delay. Bell had two seconds left to throw it as far as he could. His finger caught in the carrying hook. He grabbed the wooden handle with his other hand, wrenched it off his finger, and hurled it with all his might.

The Packard raced away. The thug who had thrown the grenade gaped, mesmerized, as it sped back to him like a boomerang.

Bell and Dashwood opened their arms wide and dragged as many people as they could down on the steps and floor of the veranda. The grenade detonated. A flash of light threw shadows on the front wall. A shock wave slammed Bell and Dashwood into the people. The explosion was deafening and blew out the front windows and half the lightbulbs in the TEXAS WALT'S sign.

In the light that remained, a cloud of dust hung heavily on the road. There was nothing to be seen of the gangster who had thrown the stick grenade. Through the ringing in his ears, Isaac Bell heard screams of fear. The roar of a powerful motor cut through the screams.

The Packard had turned around. It was racing back, windows bristling with rifles and pistols. Dashwood and Bell stumbled to their feet and staggered to the road.

The driver of the Packard saw two men emerge from the dust cloud the grenade had kicked up. He floored his accelerator. Tony, the boss beside him in the front seat, and the boys in the back started shooting, jerking their triggers as fast as they could.

The two men stepped into the middle of the road, turned sideways, raised pistols, and started firing back. A bullet shattered the windshield and knocked the driver's hat sideways. Another broke a headlight.

"Get the big one!" shouted Tony. They shifted fire, and a lucky shot from the swaying auto knocked the bigger man off the road. The smaller, a skinny scarecrow, stepped into the lights, gun raised like a target shooter.

"Run him down!"

Flame lanced from his pistol. A left front tire blew, and the wheel jerked in the driver's hands. The scarecrow fired again. The right front tire blew, and the heavy auto skidded and screeched on smoking rims straight at him.

James Dashwood drifted aside like a matador. The Packard slid past. He fired a shot into each rear tire, and the car swerved into a tree with a loud bang. Three men were thrown to the pavement. The driver was impaled on the steering column. Van Dorns swarmed from the roadhouse and surrounded them. Dashwood ran to where Isaac Bell had fallen.

"Isaac!"

"I'm O.K."

Dashwood mopped Bell's brow with a handkerchief. "You don't look O.K. You're covered in blood."

"Scalp, I think."

"He's fine," said Walt Hatfield, who hurried up with a shotgun. "Just leaking a little."

Hatfield handed Bell a bandanna. "You're O.K., old son, aren't you?"

The Texan's anxious expression scared Dashwood more than the blood.

"Where are they?" asked Bell. His ears were ringing, his head spinning. He saw the wrecked Packard wrapped half around a tree. Bloodied gunmen sprawled beside it. "Anyone else hurt?"

"Folks on the porch are mostly shook-up."

A siren howled in the distance.

Bell surged to his feet and stood, swaying. He gripped Dashwood's skinny arm and pointed at the gunmen. "Give the cops all those louses except the boss. Bring him to the cellar. On the jump! They'll be here any second."

"Attempted murder," said Isaac Bell. "Even in Detroit they'll lock you up."

"Not for long," said the gangster manacled to a cellar post. He had a gash on his head that had splattered his clothes as bloodily as Bell's. Bell hoped that the man had a headache worse than the one that was jackhammering his own skull. He had left the doctor Texas Walt called to stitch his scalp cooling his heels upstairs until he had wrung everything he could out of the gangster. The whisky he poured on it to stop the bleeding had hurt worse than the bullet that parted his hair, and he could not quite see straight. It took no acting talent to sound vengeful.

"Long," he said. "Very long. I'll hand you to the U.S. Marshal. He'll get you on a federal offense."

"This ain't federal."

"Ever heard of the Espionage Act? The Congress wrote it with your name on it. Radicals throw bombs. Aliens throw bombs. Communists. Bolsheviks. The United States Attorney will put you in the big house for life."

"They can't pin that on me."

"Thirty witnesses saw your gang throw a grenade. Thirty witnesses saw you rake a crowd of people with rifle fire."

"They don't have the guts to testify. I'll be out in a day."

"I've got the guts to testify," said Texas Walt.

"So do I," said Ed Tobin.

"Me, too," said Dashwood.

"Even I will muster the courage," said

Isaac Bell. "That's four of us."

"Mister," said Texas Walt, leaning in to put his hawk face an inch from the gangster's. "You've got one greasy foot in the federal penitentiary and another on thin ice. It is high time you start talking."

The gangster pressed his free hand to his bloody head. "What do you want to know?"

Bell studied their prisoner carefully. The thug would expect Bell to ask who had ordered him to bomb the roadhouse. Fear and criminal pride would make him resist turning in someone he knew.

"Your name."

"Tony."

"Tony what?"

"Big Tony Sana."

"Who gave you the grenade, Tony?"

"War surplus. They're all over the place."

"It was a *German* stick grenade. How did you happen to get your paws on a grenade from the Kaiser's army?"

Bell reckoned that the Comintern was the likeliest source. Such a powerful grenade would also explain the phenomenal damage Bell had seen at the former Van Dorn offices. The Detroit mobs hadn't yet figured that the Texas Walt roadhouse was a Van Dorn masquerade. But the Comintern might well have.

The gangster shrugged. "I don't know. One of the guys got a box of 'em somewhere."

Bell thought that Tony Sana looked genuinely puzzled that of all the questions the roadhouse torpedoes could ask, who cared where a hand grenade came from? Had Marat Zolner paid Tony's gang to attack Texas Walt's? Had he allied with them as he had with the Black Hand in New York? No. Tony was small-time. If anything, Zolner was playing Tony's boys for suckers, as he had the Gophers.

"I want to know who gave you the grenade."

"Maybe some doughboy brought souvenirs home from the war."

"Which one of your guys did he give it to?"

"I think it was Little Angelo."

"We'll deal with Angelo later. Now, what's this I heard about a hooch tunnel under the river?"

"I didn't hear nothing about no tunnel."

Bell said, "People tell me boats are old hat. And come winter, driving whisky sixes across the ice will be old hat, too."

"Yeah, well, there oughta be plenty of business for everyone."

"Who's your boss?"

"I'm my boss."

"What about the cable sub?"

Tony looked glad to discuss a topic outside his own business. "These dumb Polacks, they got a long rope and a crank. They sink the booze in the river in steel kegs. The rope drags it across the bottom."

"From where?"

"Some island."

"Where does it go?"

"Poletown."

"Who runs it?"

"I told ya, Polacks from Poletown."

"Poles from Poletown?"

"Yeah, except the Jaworski gang says it ain't them. Lying bastards. They was speaking Polack."

"Polish? Who was speaking Polish. The cable sub?"

"That's what I heard."

"Speaking Polish? Or Russian?"

"Same thing, ain't it?"

Bell exchanged glances with Dashwood and Tobin. Suddenly, there were two Dashwoods and two Tobins. It took a moment to realize that the shot that had creased his skull was giving him double vision. He blinked. There were still two of each detective. He turned to two Tonys.

"Tony, you say you don't have a boss. If

you did have a boss, who would he be?"

Big Tony Sana looked intrigued by the thought. He said, "Bosses come and go."

"Let's say one came."

"Could be a bunch of guys."

"Max Stern?"

Tony looked surprised. "Where'd you hear that?"

"Around. Could it be Max Stern?"

"Could be."

"Where do I find him?"

"Who knows? I'm telling you, Max Stern ain't my boss."

"Admiral Abe," said Marat Zolner. "Aren't you glad you saw reason?"

They were dining on sweetbreads, the most expensive item on the menu at Detroit's classy new Hotel Wolverine and one that Weintraub could chew without many teeth.

Abe Weintraub shot a murderous glare across the table. He had a moon-shaped face with a small nose, ears, and mouth. He looked, Zolner thought, innocuous, even gentle, except for his dark dead eyes.

"Don't get the wrong idea. I ain't no pushover."

"You made that clear," said Zolner, who had seen enough Cheka torture chambers to admire a thug as determined as Abe Weintraub not to be broken. His conversion had taken so long that it was a miracle they hadn't accidentally drowned him. But Weintraub had been worth the trouble. He commanded the Purple Gang's Jewish Navy by dint of brains, unmatched brutality, and ruthless determination. He knew every Detroit criminal worth knowing, saw them with a clear eye, and knew their weaknesses and their strengths. He would make an aggressive captain of foot soldiers in any revolution.

"Now what?" asked Weintraub, mopping his plate clean with a slice of bread.

"Now you will tell me who to kill."

"What are you talking about?"

"Tell me which gangsters to get out of our way. Starting at the top."

"*Tell* you? Or kill 'em for you?"

It was like discussing terms with a wolf or a shark. Or the hotel's namesake wolverine. Weintraub understood destruction and only destruction, but he understood it very well. Zolner had set up a number of gangsters like him in New York — to control supply and demand — but none so ferocious.

He said, "You will help me locate them. We will ferret out the chinks in their armor. Then we will kill them."

"Why would I do that?"

"Because I will allow you to pick up the pieces."

Weintraub stared in disbelief. "I thought I heard it all. This takes the cake."

"I am offering you the city of Detroit," Marat Zolner said.

"When I'm done, it will be my city. I don't need you."

"Would you prefer to wait five years in hopes your enemies all kill each other off? Keeping in mind that the one who survives will emerge strong. Or do you want to get to it right now?"

"Now."

"Starting at the top, Abe, who do we kill first?"

"Max Stern."

"Is that a fact?" the Bolshevik asked coldly.

"Max Stern," Weintraub repeated.

The agents whom Zolner had sent ahead to scout Detroit and Windsor had predicted that the top boss would be a Jew. The Italian gangs had decimated themselves in the murderous Giannola–Vitale mafia wars. A Purple Gang killer named Max Stern had been rated most likely to emerge top dog.

"I've heard that, too," said Zolner. "Now you hear it from me."

"Except that I also hear that Stern has

disappeared." The gangster had vanished the very night *Black Bird* rumbled into her Windsor boathouse.

"Yeah, well, these boss guys lay low. For their health."

Marat Zolner's features hardened. "Max Stern was incinerated in a brewery furnace over in Windsor."

"Oh yeah?"

"You have one more chance, you lying son of a bitch."

Abe Weintraub did not protest the insult. "O.K. Just testing who you are. I don't know how you know this stuff, but you're the real thing."

"Last chance, Abe: *Who do we kill first?*"

"Sam Rosenthal."

Zolner settled back in his chair. At last. "I wondered if it was him."

"Wonder 'til you're blue in the face," said Weintraub. "Rosenthal is bulletproof."

"Isn't Sam Rosenthal digging a tunnel under the river?"

Abe Weintraub ignored the question — a clue, Zolner knew by now, that the tight-lipped gangster knew the answer — and said, "Nobody gets close enough to shoot him. Nobody's seen him outside in a year."

Zolner had been hearing that more Canadian booze traveled *under* the river than on it. Some was smuggled in railroad freight cars. A Polish gang was said to pull submerged containers on the bottom of the river by a windlass cable, which sounded slow and cumbersome. But another story held great promise, a smuggling tunnel that would make the Comintern's fortune. The tunnel would lock up Detroit and add the biggest transit point to the operations he set up in New York.

"Is Sam Rosenthal digging a tunnel under the river?"

"When'd you hear that?"

Zolner laid both big hands on the tablecloth and leaned forward. "Abe, it's too late to turn off the phonograph."

"Go to hell."

"Do you really want to go back in the water?"

Weintraub half rose from the table.

"Abe, look around the lobby."

Weintraub glared. "I've got torpedoes, too."

"Look again, Abe. See the salesman with the big sample case? See the long-haired violin player? . . . Mine are tougher and smarter, and they've got your boys covered with Thompson .45s . . . Besides, do you really want a shoot-out? Or would you rather accept my offer of Detroit? Do you know where Rosenthal is digging?"

"No."

"I hear he's digging from one of the Canadian islands," said Zolner. "That would make sense, tunnel only half a mile instead of a full mile all the way across, and start in friendlier territory."

"Oh yeah?"

"Find out which."

"Tell you this. When it's dug, it will put your black boat out of business."

Black Bird would soon "fly south for the winter" on a railcar to Miami, a fact that Zolner kept to himself. He said, "Rosenthal's tunnel will put your entire Jewish Navy out of business."

Weintraub fell silent.

He knows about the tunnel, thought Zolner. His agents were spot-on about the rumors. The tunnel was almost finished. But it was maddening that no one knew where it was.

"Surely you understand that the future of hauling Canadian booze is moving huge volumes of it through Rosenthal's tunnel, not lugging it on boats and trucks on ice."

"So the tunnel is why you want to kill Rosenthal?"

"And why I want to give you Detroit — so you can help me hold on to the tunnel."

"But Rosenthal could be good for business if he stops the wars. Divvy up territories. Lay down some rules."

Marat Zolner asked, "Do you really believe that Rosenthal can stop the wars without sinking your Jewish Navy? Better *we* lay down the rules."

For the first time since Marat Zolner hijacked Abe Weintraub's boat, he saw the Jewish gangster smile.

26

"Why's a Jew getting buried by the Catholics?" Scudder Smith asked the Detroit police captain whose blue-coated squads were struggling to keep ten thousand spectators on the sidewalks.

The Van Dorn detective had notebook and pencil in hand and his *Brooklyn Eagle* press card in his hat. It was a hot, sunny morning on Detroit's west side. Across Dexter Avenue stood St. Gregory the Great, a sturdy red brick church with a limestone façade. The doors were open, and pallbearers were staggering down the front steps under the weight of a fifteen-thousand-dollar silver coffin.

"His mother was from Ireland," said the cop. "She made him go to Saint Gregory's school straight through fourth grade."

Scores of polished autos were lined up to follow the hearse and flower cars to the cemetery. Bronze stars attached to bumpers identified autos that belonged to city department functionaries, and Scudder Smith said from the side of his mouth as Isaac Bell passed by, "Gives the official touch to the ceremonial procession. Look at all those five-thousand-dollar motors. You'd think they were burying the king of England."

Bell moved restlessly among the crowd, disguised as a workman in plumber's overalls and a flat cap that covered the bandage on his throbbing head. Fitful bouts of double vision flipped the sidewalk into a funhouse ride.

Tobin was here, too, as was Dashwood, trying to identify the hoodlums and beer runners and whisky haulers attending the lavish funeral. The newspapers were calling it the Purple Gang's biggest-ever "send-off."

The flower cars behind the hearse carried wreathes with the dead man's name in gold letters.

OUR PAL MAX

OUR BROTHER MAX

LOVE TO MAXIE FROM
UNCLE HANK AND AUNT HELENE

Bell was deeply disappointed and thoroughly disgusted by this latest setback. Inside the coffin was a heap of bone and ash discovered by Windsor brewery workers while cleaning a firebox. The bones had been identified by their owner's prized blackjack. The nickel-stainless grip engraved with his initials *MS* had survived the flames.

With the gangster Bell had hoped would lead him to Zolner now dead, Bell could do little but draw on his photographic memory to compare wanted posters and police mug shots to Max Stern's gangster friends and family lining up their luxurious automobiles. In one of those splendid autos could be the new boss of Detroit's Purple Gang — the gangster with whom Marat Zolner would join forces.

Cops on motorcycles and horseback cleared a lane in the middle of Dexter Avenue, and the biggest wreath by far came up the avenue towed on a trailer hung with black crepe. Thousands of red roses depicted a full-size replica of a Rolls-Royce Silver Ghost. A golden banner ran its length.

FROM SAM

"What's the word on Sam?" Bell asked Scudder, who had been buying liquor lunches, dinners, and breakfasts for Detroit's newspapermen to get the latest on the gangs.

"The boys in the pressroom were taking bets whether Sam Rosenthal would show his face, figuring he's safe with Max dead."

"The new boss?"

"They say he's smarter than Einstein. And the other contender hasn't been heard from lately."

"Admiral Abe?"

"Abe Weintraub. With Abe out of the picture, Sam could be Marat's new pal."

Bell focused on a real Rolls-Royce behind the trailer, a slab-sided sky blue Silver Ghost town car agleam with glass and nickel. A window rolled down, and he saw a sun-starved, hatchet-faced figure observing the crowds with a cold smile. Rosenthal looked young, strong, and triumphant.

"Judging by Mr. Rosenthal's floral contribution," said Bell, "you might be right. You and Ed and Dash stay here. I'll follow that Rolls."

The funeral cortege began pulling slowly from the church. Bell followed on the sidewalk, battling through the crowd to pace Sam Rosenthal's Rolls-Royce. Suddenly, his senses jumped to even higher alert.

A Pierce-Arrow Limousine Landau slipped out of a side street, and the police blocked the cars behind it so it could join the file three cars ahead of Rosenthal's. What had drawn Bell's eye was a glimpse of the passenger, a mourning woman in a black cloche hat with a veil. Max's wife? No, a wife would not be alone in the car but surrounded by family. His mistress, was more likely. He could not quite see her face behind the veil, but something about the cock of her head was familiar.

Fern Hawley? But how could a rich society girl be riding in a gangster parade? Yet, he could swear it was her. He had observed the heiress closely when he and Marion had bumped into her and Prince André at Club Deluxe. If it was Fern, he saw no sign of Prince André. Unless he was driving. Not likely. Bell tried to see the driver behind the front window, but reflections in the glass revealed only the silhouette of a chauffeur's cap.

He was struck by an even more peculiar thought. Prince André, as he remembered

Fern's friend, looked similar to speedboat builder Bill Lynch's description of the man who bought *Black Bird*. As with most big ideas, as soon as it coursed through his mind he wondered why it hadn't occurred to him earlier. The answer was context. It was probably nothing, but there was a simple way to find out. Bell made a mental note to have Research show Lynch a photograph of Prince André from the society pages. He returned his attention to pushing through the spectators packing the sidewalks to keep up with the Rolls-Royce.

He heard music — strings — piercing the blare of motorcycle and auto engines, and loud voices ohhhing and ahhhing over the limousines and flowers. On a street corner far ahead, he saw a band of violinists in black coats and slouch hats. They were serenading the cortege with a slow and halting arrangement of "O Sole Mio."

A Neapolitan love song seemed an odd choice of music to bury an American gangster of Jewish and Irish heritage. Maybe, thought Bell, it was the only tune they knew. They sounded painfully shrill, even at a distance. Maybe it was his headache, but in fact two were wielding their bows like carpenter saws and had their eyes fixed desperately as drowning men on the tall, wraith-thin violinist in the middle, who seemed to be carrying the lead.

Bell felt his every sense drawn to him. The musician's face was shrouded by the broad, low-swept brim of his hat, his instrument, and his bowing arm. But Bell had seen his silhouette before, the same supple reptilian grace he had seen on Roosevelt Hospital's roof, and again — it hit him with electric force — on the dance floor of Club Deluxe.

The Pierce-Arrow wheeled out of the cortege as suddenly as it had slipped in and disappeared around the corner where the band was playing. No chance for another look at whether it was Fern Hawley in back. But at this moment, what Bell wanted much more was an up close look at the tall violinist.

He peered over a rippling sea of ladies' cloches and men's cloth caps and fedoras. There were hundreds of people between them. The crowd jammed the sidewalk, from the buildings to the police line at the curb, weirdly multiplied by a spasm of double vision. He squinted his eyes to clear the carnival.

The hearse and the limousines gathered speed.

Sam Rosenthal's Silver Ghost passed Bell. It was almost a full block ahead when it reached the musicians. Rosenthal extended his pale white hand to toss them a tip. Gold coins flew through the air, glittering in the sun. The people murmured, acknowledging his gesture: The new king was generous. The music stopped abruptly.

Isaac Bell saw the musicians duck to the sidewalk to pick up the coins. They popped up in unison. All five were cradling Thompson .45 submachine guns, bracing them against their ribs by their double handgrips.

The tall, thin violinist triggered his first.

His henchmen followed his lead with an earsplitting roar.

Shards of glass flew as hundreds of slugs riddled Sam Rosenthal's Rolls-Royce. The sight of flame-spitting guns stampeded the people nearest to the car. They turned and ran, the bigger trampling the smaller. Those farther off who heard the shattering blast of gunfire threw themselves to the sidewalk.

Isaac Bell leaped over prone forms and shoved past people too stunned to duck. He ran toward the gunmen, who continued to rake the Rolls-Royce even after the lifeless bodies of Sam Rosenthal and his bodyguards and driver had spilled onto the avenue. Before he could get halfway there, the car caught fire. The shooting stopped. The gunmen stuffed their Thompsons into instrument cases and ran down the side street.

Bell reached the pile of violins and violas in time to see the Pierce-Arrow limousine that he thought was Fern Hawley's speed away from the carnage. A cop ran after it, waving his pistol. A burst of .45 slugs cut him down.

27

Cold-eyed men who traveled light arrived from Cleveland, Toledo, Chicago, Milwaukee, Minneapolis, and Pittsburgh, and jumped to the Michigan Central platforms before their trains stopped rolling. They hurried on their way, across town to a former Wells Fargo Express office that Isaac Bell had rented on Woodbridge Street.

The building was in the freight district between the Michigan Central and New York Central depots, a block from the Detroit River. Thick walls, small windows, and steel doors made for a fortified headquarters. The out-of-town detectives — valuable men who knew their business whom Bell had summoned from the Midwest field offices — were greeted by the sobering sight of workmen wiring mesh over the barred glass to keep out hand grenades. What even the sharpest-eyed did not see were the snipers James Dashwood had installed atop a water tower that overlooked the approaches.

Having housed an express company, the new Detroit headquarters, which the detectives nicknamed Fort Van Dorn, was wired for a variety of telephone and telegraph lines. Within hours of taking possession, Bell had local and long-distance telephone connections, private telephone and telegraph lines to the rest of the field offices, a Morkrum telegraph printer, and an overseas cable link.

"I underestimated Marat Zolner," he reported to Joseph Van Dorn at Bellevue Hospital by long distance. "And I overestimated the effect of what I thought was a body blow we gave them in New York. The Comintern did not *flee* from New York. Zolner *expanded* to Detroit."

"Interesting hunch," said Van Dorn.

"It's more than a hunch."

"But you could just as easily conclude that Zolner machine-gunned the boss of the Purple Gang out of desperation." Van Dorn's voice was stronger, and Dorothy told Bell when she answered the telephone that he was sitting up in a chair. "You drove him from New York and he's desperate to start over in Detroit."

"No," said Bell. "Zolner is fighting from strength, not weakness. We bloodied his nose in New York, but we did not break up his alliances. The profits from his New York bootlegger partners are funding the expansion."

"If bootlegging made him that rich, why didn't he buy his way into Detroit? Why'd he pounce with all four feet?"

"No one can buy Detroit. It's too volatile. He has to beat the gangs to control the bootlegging."

"That has a greater ring of fact than your expanding from New York theory for which you have no evidence."

Yes, thought Bell. The Boss is sounding a little more like himself. He was marshaling his arguments when the Morkrum printer clattered. James Dashwood ripped a message off the paper roll and handed him the curly sheet.

"Hold the wire, Joe."

The New York office had forwarded a long overseas cable from Germany. Bell decoded the familiar Van Dorn cipher in his head.

Pauline Grandzau had discovered that Comintern agents had chartered the twelve-thousand-ton tanker *Sandra T. Congdon* and loaded it with two-hundred-proof pure grain alcohol. The tanker had sailed from

Bremerhaven bound for Nassau, The Bahamas.

Bell whistled in amazement.

"What?" Van Dorn growled into his phone.

"Proof," said Bell. "A shipload of *two hundred* proof."

"What are you talking about?"

"Proof that Marat Zolner is not only still operating in New York but expanding. The Comintern is gearing up to supply Rum Row on a whole new scale."

He read Pauline's cable aloud to Van Dorn.

They discussed its ramifications. Possession of grain alcohol was a not to be missed opportunity to dilute genuine liquor. Such a big ship could carry well over a hundred thousand barrels — five hundred railroad tank cars — easily stretched to fifty million bottles.

"Enough liquor," said Van Dorn, "to plaster the adult population of the East Coast through the Christmas and New Year's holidays."

"And pour a hundred million dollars into the Comintern's treasury."

"That is fifty times the federal budget for enforcement of Prohibition," said Van Dorn. "Good for Pauline. Will you send her to

Nassau as she asked?"

"Absolutely."

"Even long-distance, I can hear a gleam in your eye, Isaac. Just don't forget that Zolner has proved himself a mastermind. And he's got the entire Comintern on his side."

"I'm not sure about that," said Bell. "I have a hunch he's a one-man show."

"They're making a great success of getting away with every crime in the book," Van Dorn countered drily.

"But nothing that he's built so far can last without him. When we stop Zolner, we stop the Comintern."

"Nothing's stopped him yet."

"The way to stop him is to use against him the one thing I admire about him," said Bell.

"Admire?" Van Dorn's explosion of indignation spiraled into a coughing fit.

Bell listened to the wracking cough, praying for it to ease, but it knocked Joe breathless. Bell waited, gripping the phone. The doctors had warned there'd be setbacks, and he'd just set one off.

A woman spoke into the phone. "Mr. Van Dorn will telephone you back when he is able."

"Marion?"

"Isaac!"

"Is he O.K.?"

"I don't know. I just walked in. Here's a nurse . . . And a doctor . . . They've got him . . ." She lowered her voice. "Oh, the poor man. It breaks your heart. He's better one moment, then falls back. They've got him now, Isaac. Don't worry. How are you?"

"Tip-top," Bell lied, gingerly rubbing his itching stitches. He pictured her lighting up Joe's room in a smart suit and hat. "And how are you?"

"They gave me another movie. I'm having fun filming all day and missing you at dinner."

"How about after dinner?"

"Worse. The New York papers said there was a shooting in Detroit."

"It's the national pastime out here. Bigger than baseball."

"This one sounded like a war."

"I will tell you all about it when I see you."

"Can't wait. Here's Joe . . . He claims he's 'tip-top.' Where do you suppose he learned that expression? Good-bye, darling. So lovely to hear your voice."

Van Dorn did not sound much recovered. He took a few shallow breaths and wheezed, "How could you possibly admire a murdering, thieving, treacherous, bomb-throwing,

godless Bolshevik who slaughters innocents?"

"He leads from the front. In the thick of
the fight. He is no coward."

"Neither is Satan."

"It's his Achilles' heel. I'll find him where
the lead is flying. And that's where I'll finish him."

Van Dorn fell silent.

Had the long-distance connection broken?
Or something worse? "Are you O.K., Joe?"

"I was just wondering if a villain weren't a
villain, would he be a hero's best friend?"

Isaac Bell was in no mood for philosophy.
"I would not be one bit surprised that Marat Zolner manned the Lewis gun that shot
you. And I have absolutely no doubt he was
there when Harry Warren was killed and
personally loaded his body — dead or dying
— into that wagon."

"All right," Van Dorn whispered. "I know
what you're saying. What's your next move?"

"Drive Zolner out of Detroit."

"How?"

"Find out who Zolner installed in place of
Rosenthal. Question his girlfriend, Fern
Hawley. Send Pauline to Nassau to throw a
monkey wrench in whatever he's up to with
that tanker. And find that whisky tunnel,
because if the Comintern doesn't own it

already, it will soon. When they do, they will be so rich it could be impossible to stop them."

Pauline's cable had ended:

REQUEST ASSIGNMENT NASSAU.

LIQUOR IMPORT-EXPORT GUISE,
WHISKY AGENT FOR GLASGOW DISTILLERY.

EAR TO GROUND.

During the war, Bell recalled, she had smuggled a downed Scottish flier out of Germany. The pilot's grandfather had founded a distillery. Bell cabled back.

GO NASSAU SOONEST.

The reply he received was not from Germany but from France, where Archie Abbott remained in temporary command of the Van Dorn field office.

YOUR CABLE FORWARDED PARIS.

I'M COVERING FOR BERLIN.

PAULINE SAILED YESTERDAY,
SS AQUITANIA,
CONNECTING NASSAU.

Isaac Bell laughed. So much for "request." "Fräulein Moxie" was off to the races — Cunard express liner *Aquitania* from Le Havre to New York; Havana Special, overnight train to Miami, Florida; and the new flying-boat service to Nassau. Pauline would be across the Atlantic and in The Bahamas in seven or eight days. While a war-weary, ten-knot tanker was still on the high seas, she would have time before it landed to establish a business front in Nassau with a Market Street import-export office under a shingle that read:

PAULINE GRANDZAU

LICENSED TO SELL

WHOLESALE SPIRITS & LIQUORS

The Wolverine, the express train that connected with the 20th Century in Buffalo, brought photographs of Fern Hawley that Van Dorn Research had clipped from the New York society pages. That the one shot of the heiress gallivanting included Prince

André doubled Bell's suspicion that the Russian and Marat Zolner were the same man. His picture was out of focus, blurred by motion. It looked to Bell as if, caught by surprise climbing out of a limousine, he was trying to turn his face from the camera.

Bell wired Grady Forrer.

PRINCE ANDRE CAMERA SHY.

SHOW PICTURE TO
LYNCH & HARDING MARINE.

Bell armed his detectives with Fern's photographs and sent them to query desk clerks and managers at Detroit's top hotels. In none of the fancier places where he would expect her to stay was the Connecticut heiress recognized. Nor was Prince André. They polled second-rate hotels, and garages that rented limousines, with no results.

The society reporters wrote, repeatedly, that she had served as a volunteer war nurse in France. Bell cabled Archie Abbott to inquire about her and Prince André.

At Michigan Central Station, Bell's detectives found no evidence of her arriving recently on any of the extra-fare limited trains like The Detroiter or The Wolverine that a wealthy woman would ride. On the other hand, thought Bell, she was uncommonly wealthy. He went personally to the private sidings. New York Central Railroad detectives, always eager to help a Van Dorn executive in hopes of future employment, had no memory of Fern Hawley arriving by private car from New York.

"What about New Haven?"

A rail dick recalled that a car from Connecticut had parked for several days on a private siding. "Left yesterday at noon."

Only hours after the machine-gun attack on Rosenthal.

"Where did it go?"

They questioned dispatchers. The private car had been coupled to a New York Central passenger train bound for Cincinnati that connected with the Southern Railway's "Royal Palm" to Jacksonville, Florida.

With an idea forming of where she was headed, Bell asked, "What line does the Southern connect to in Jacksonville?"

"Florida East Coast Railway."

Isaac Bell slipped him a double sawbuck and his card. "If you need something from the Van Dorns, drop me a line."

The tall detective returned to the main passenger terminal and found a coin telephone to call James Dashwood at Fort Van Dorn.

"She's gone to Miami! I'm booking you a through ticket on the Royal Palm. Get down to Florida and find out what she's up to."

"Is Zolner with her?"

"He can't leave Detroit until he's installed his replacement for Rosenthal and they finish that tunnel."

"Do you think Zolner sent her away to keep her out of danger?"

"Possibly. Or she could be fed up with him and gone south early for the winter. Except I've got a very strong feeling that Fern Hawley's gone on ahead to lay the groundwork for his next move."

Dashwood played the devil's advocate as Bell had taught him to. "Based on what?"

"Based on Pauline's report that the Comintern sent a shipload of grain alcohol to The Bahamas. Nassau is only a hundred eighty miles from Miami, Bimini's even closer, and Florida is a booze funnel into the entire South. He'll have New York in the East, Detroit in the Midwest, and Florida in the South.

"At that point, he can paste a new label on millions of bottles — 'Genuine Old Cominterm, America's Favorite.' "

■ ■ ■ ■

Isaac Bell paced impatiently.

"Whisky haulers have heard about a booze tunnel under the Detroit River. Strong-arm men have heard about this tunnel. The cops have heard about this tunnel. Crooks have heard about this tunnel. Gangsters have heard about this tunnel. Wouldn't you think that Detroit newspapermen have not only heard about this tunnel but would also have some inkling of where it is?"

"It's a big story," Scudder Smith agreed. He was toying with his hat and looked like a man who was reconsidering not drinking.

"You're picking up bar tabs for every reporter in town," Bell reminded him. "One of them must be writing the big story."

"No editor would run it. It would get the reporter shot — which wouldn't trouble most editors excessively — but it could get the editor himself shot, too, and that possibility *would* trouble him."

Isaac Bell did not smile.

"Funny enough," said Scudder. "You know who's really looking for the tunnel?"

"Volstead officers," said Bell. "The payoffs would make them rich men."

"Or dead."

Bell said, "Go back to the pressrooms, go back to the blind pigs where newspapermen hang out. There must be some cub reporter out there scrambling for a scoop that would make his name."

Scudder Smith came back much sooner than Bell had expected.

"Now what?"

Scudder grinned ear to ear. "I have redeemed myself."

"Did you find a reporter who found the tunnel?"

"No. But I found several reporters who know who might have shot Sam Rosenthal."

"*Might* have?"

"I don't know who actually pulled the trigger, but I definitely know who replaced him. Abe Weintraub, like we guessed. Admiral Abe."

"I thought he disappeared. I thought he was dead."

"So did I. So did they. But then I caught a rumor that the admiral was seen gumming his supper at the Hotel Wolverine."

" 'Gumming'?"

"Apparently someone — an amazingly formidable someone — knocked Abe's teeth out. I checked. I found a Wolverine waiter who said he ate sweetbreads. Sweetbreads and champagne. Sweetbreads are expensive. A meal you eat when you're celebrating. As if you became the new Purples' boss."

"And easy to chew," said Bell. "Any idea who knocked his teeth out?"

"Everyone agrees that whoever did it must be dead by now."

"Was he dining alone?"

"That's the best part. I showed the waiter Prince André's photograph. He thought Prince André might be the guy Abe was eating sweetbreads with."

Bell thought that this was too much to hope for. The most that Bill Lynch and Harold Harding had conceded, when shown the out-of-focus photograph, was a dubious "maybe" that it was the bootlegger who had commissioned *Black Bird.*

He asked, "Why was the waiter so talkative?"

"He needed money to leave Detroit."

"Why?"

"I persuaded him, after I suggested that Abe might be the new boss of the Purples, that any association with Admiral Abe could be dangerous for his health. Including — or especially — witnessing who he eats sweetbreads with. Rightly or wrongly, the waiter decided to start over a thousand miles away. I — or, strictly speaking, Mr. Van Dorn —

provided the means."

"But it's not impossible that the waiter told you what he thought you wanted to hear," said Bell.

"May I suggest," said Scudder, "that we have a field office full of valuable men to follow up on this?"

James Dashwood telegraphed on the private wire that he had traced Fern Hawley's railcar to a Palm Beach, Florida, siding that served an oceanfront estate seventy miles north of Miami. Neither the car nor the estate was owned by her.

PALACE CAR RENTED.

ESTATE RENTED.

FERN FLOWN.

There was nothing innately suspicious about renting cars and estates. She could, indeed, be setting up early for the winter in Florida, where more and more of the rich headed when the weather got cold. Typically, though, society people of Fern's means were building elaborate homes in Palm Beach and Miami. She could be testing the waters. But for what? Winter holidays

385

or Marat Zolner's empire?

The answer came in a contrite wire from Dashwood.

MISSED BLACKBIRD FLATCAR
YESTERDAY MIAMI.

"Couple of Prohibition dicks asking to see you, Isaac," said Texas Walt.

Bell looked up from the sandwiches he was sharing at the kitchen chopping block with Leon Randolph, the Texas Walt's Roadhouse cook whom he knew from the days Leon had cooked on the Atchison, Topeka and Santa Fe's Overland Limited.

"How did they know to find me here?"

"I wondered, too. I persuaded them to leave their artillery with the hatcheck."

The bar was empty at this hour but for a bartender who was polishing a sawed-off shotgun.

Bell's stern features darkened with such anger when he recognized the Volstead agents that Texas Walt's hands would have strayed toward his Colts if the bartender didn't already have them covered.

"We got to talk, Mr. Bell."

Tom Clayton and Ed Ellis, the former Protective Services house detectives Bell had fired from the Hotel Gotham, looked

386

prosperous. Their cheeks were pink from the barbershop, their hair slick. They wore signet rings on their fingers and remained somewhat handsome, despite imperfectly healed broken noses.

"We've already bribed your superiors," Bell answered coldly.

"We know," Ed Ellis said. "Bureau chief told us Texas Walt's is hands-off."

"It should be for what it cost us. Did you inform your chief that we're Van Dorns?"

"No!" cried Clayton.

"We wouldn't squeal on you!" said Ellis.

"Why not?"

"We don't want to gum up your case."

"Mighty big of you," Bell said, more than a little puzzled.

"Can we talk in private?" asked Clayton.

"How'd you happen to land in Detroit?"

Clayton ducked his head.

Ellis rubbed his nose. "We knew we weren't welcome in New York anymore."

Clayton immediately said, "Hey, no hard feelings, Mr. Bell. We got what we deserved."

"We just thank God they didn't kill that little kid."

"Detroit," said Bell. "I asked how did you two end up in Detroit?"

"We figured the Detroit Prohibition Bureau had to be a gold mine, with all the booze coming from Canada."

"Came out to wangle jobs," said Clayton, and Ellis explained matter-of-factly, "Government doesn't pay much, but the salary's only a start, if you know what we mean."

"You mean graft," said Bell. "Hush money, payoffs, protection."

"We ain't lying to you."

But their story didn't add up. Congress had organized the Prohibition Bureau to be exempt from Civil Service regulations. As a result, its system of hiring agents was completely corrupt, and the bureau was hobbled by cronyism, nepotism, and patronage.

"How did you manage Volstead jobs? Nobody gets in the bureau without some bigwig pulling wires."

"We know a bigwig," said Ellis.

Clayton explained. "A Michigan politician staying at the Gotham was getting in a jam with his missus over a manicure girl."

"We fixed it for him — arranged for a onetime gift — and he was mighty grateful. 'If you boys ever need anything in Detroit, look me up.' "

"We looked him up."

"Presto!" said Ellis and patted his badge.

Isaac Bell turned to Walt Hatfield. "I can handle them."

The bartender put away his shotgun.

Bell took Clayton and Ellis to the cellar where he had interrogated Tony. "It better be good, boys. I'm in no mood to play." Which was putting it mildly. Harry Warren was dead, and Marat Zolner was getting stronger every day.

Clayton and Ellis exchanged significant looks. They nudged each other. Then they chorused, "We heard you're looking for a tunnel."

28

"We can help you."

"Where did you hear we're looking for it?" asked Bell.

"Everybody knows the Van Dorns have a new office down by the tracks," said Clayton.

"Hoods and cops wonder what you're up to," said Ellis.

"They heard you're asking about the tunnel."

"It sort of happens," said Ellis. "Word gets around."

"Questions raise questions," Bell snapped. *"Go on!"*

"Our bosses at the bureau caught wind of the tunnel, too. They're hunting night and day. They reckon it'll be worth a fortune in protection."

"And they're worried you'll get there first," said Ellis.

Clayton said, "Me and Ed knew they

wouldn't share it with us — they hog the big payoffs — so me and him did a little snooping on our own. Thinking maybe we'd get there first. We heard the tunnel guys drowned a bunch of Eye-talians working on it. They weren't hoods, just some bricklayers and stonemasons."

"Murdered 'em because they knew where it was," said Ellis.

"It didn't seem right."

"Making us think that maybe getting rich off Prohibition isn't completely right either," said Ellis.

Bell stared hard at them, wanting to believe that they had stumbled onto valuable information but not clear about their motives. They gazed back, wide-eyed and guileless, and Bell recalled, with growing excitement, that a prison chaplain once told him that he was often surprised by the particular event that shunted a sinner to a righteous path.

"Do you know where the tunnel is?" he asked.

"Pretty fair idea," said Clayton.

"Downriver," said Ellis. "It starts on Fighting Island."

"Comes up under a boathouse in Ecorse."

This sounded pretty good, thought Bell. Fighting Island was logical — a large, empty mid-river island on the Canada side of the international boundary. Ecorse on the United States side was a lawless, wide-open town next door to Detroit with elected officials and cops in the bootleggers' pockets.

"Do you know where the boathouse is?"

"Got some good hunches," said Ellis.

Bell said, "There are two hundred boathouses on the Ecorse waterfront and dozens of slips."

"Gotta be near the creek," said Clayton, narrowing the location considerably.

"Where'd your hunches come from?"

"Heard our boss talking."

"Any theories who dug it?"

"The boss thought Polacks started digging it. Polacks from Poletown. Started in Ecorse. Then Eye-talians pushed 'em out. Then there was talk of Russians."

"Russians?" asked Bell, keeping his own information to himself. "Where did Russians come from?"

"Could be talk, but there's thousands of foreigners in Detroit."

"Where does your boss stand on this?"

Clayton's answer suggested a second motive for their conversion: a healthy desire to seek shelter in Fort Van Dorn. "He died yesterday, killed crossing Michigan Avenue."

"Hit-and-run. Could have been a Ford.

Could have been a Dodge."

Isaac Bell extended his hand. "Welcome back, boys. You're reinstated. On probation, providing you keep your noses clean."

"Oh, we will, Mr. Bell."

"Thanks, Mr. Bell."

"Should we quit our government jobs?"

"Stay at them. I'd like nothing better than a couple of good men inside the Prohibition Bureau."

Neither Abe Weintraub, who was only five and a half feet tall, nor Marat Zolner could stand erect in the Ecorse end of the Comintern's tunnel under the Detroit River. The short, newly dug connecting section was wet, dimly lit, and had a very low ceiling. Water seeped through cracks in the bricks and sandbags and accumulated in a trench between the rails on which rolled eight-foot flatcars stacked with whisky cases.

Pumps on Fighting Island, two thousand feet away, emptied the trench when it filled. The pumps, a dynamo for the lights, and the flatcars were housed in a ferry terminal under construction on the island. There was no ferry, no plans for one, but there were various city of La Salle building permits for the terminal, and the fiction provided a ruse for the machinery.

The main tunnel, discovered by Polish gangsters who then dug the Ecorse connector, was a partially built railroad bore. It was much bigger, better lit, and comparatively dry, a high-crowned cast-iron tube that had been sealed shut and abandoned decades ago when Ecorse was a tiny village and Fighting Island, then as now, consisted of fifteen hundred acres of deserted swampy lowland. The curving ceiling was so high that it felt more like a room than a passage.

Zolner had feared, at first, that the low, cramped, hundred-foot connector between the abandoned tunnel and the Ecorse boathouse shaft would be a choke point. But then he had seen an unusual opportunity offered by the big railroad section — a secret, secure underriver warehouse where he could stash cases by the carload. It already contained a huge stockpile of liquor worth millions, and they were packing in more every day. The amount that he chose to funnel through the choke point would control the American liquor market, raising and lowering the price by adjusting supply.

Only yesterday, when he caught wind that the River Gang had successfully landed ten thousand cases of a whisky labeled "Canadian Club" in Detroit, Zolner had immediately released ten thousand cases from the tunnel. Before the River Gang could sell theirs, Abe Weintraub's distributors hit the streets with the same whisky at half the price. Bankruptcy would loom over a legitimate business. In the hooch trade it meant gunplay. The Purples won the shoot-outs with a Thomas .45 loaned by the Comintern.

Next week, carefully planned hijackings — scheduled to coincide with Volstead raids conducted by bribed agents — would squeeze supply. Zolner would sell more whisky from the tunnel at double the price. Pure capitalism, he joked to Weintraub. Worse than Karl Marx had ever dreamed.

He allowed no one but his own trusted agents near the Detroit side of the tunnel now that it was finished and the last workers executed. The sole exception to the ban was Admiral Abe. Not even Weintraub's bodyguards were allowed near. By now, of course, Weintraub trusted him, even loved him, for the belief had sunk into his savage, one-track brain that Marat Zolner was not only making him rich and powerful but needed him to fend off the other gangs and protect the tunnel.

"Excellent town to hide a hooch tunnel."

Ecorse also looked to Isaac Bell like a fine

place to lam it from the cops.

He was piloting his long green Phaeton through the clogged streets of the cabaret section known as the Half Mile of Hell. No one would notice strangers and newcomers, not with thousands flooding in nightly to drink and career about. Thousands from Detroit and the suburbs got drunk in the ramshackle cabarets, played roulette, blackjack, and craps in gambling parlors, and celebrated in the dance halls and brothels that had sprung to life with Prohibition.

Booze was plentiful and cheap. Steel mills and chemical plants had grown to supply the booming motor factories, and the customers had money to burn. Those who arrived sober quickly remedied their condition and thronged the streets all night. It was a good town to be a gangster and not a bad town for private detectives searching for a tunnel.

If the fancy Cadillac, the pistol bulge in his suit coat, and the Borsalino dragged over his eyes left any doubt Isaac Bell was a bootlegger, the sight of his bodyguards erased it. Scar-faced Ed Tobin rode shotgun, broken-nosed Clayton and Ellis glowered in the backseat. In the unlikely event they were recognized as Prohibition agents, they would not be the first bureau officials to accept freelance employment from a bootlegger who needed protection while prospecting for new opportunities or stalking rivals.

Bell turned onto a street that paralleled the river. The air reeked of mud, beer, and whisky. To his right, every building had a bar on the ground floor. The bars to his left occupied the backs of boathouses that extended from the Ecorse riverbank out over deep water. The tall detective and his men stalked into several. Each had a bar selling every known brand of whisky and gin, each had a free lunch like the old pre-Prohibition saloons, and each had plenty of scantily dressed women livening the atmosphere.

Bell spotted a bar on the waterside that was a bit darker than the others. Drawing closer, he noticed that the people lurching about the sidewalk were giving it a wide berth to avoid the broad-shouldered doormen who were blocking the entrance.

Bell said, "Let's see what makes them unfriendly," and led the way.

The doormen appraised the four men coming at them and reached inside their coats. Bell and Tobin seized their arms before they could pull guns and passed them back to Clayton and Ellis, who sub-

_ed them quickly. Bell pushed through the doors.

It was quiet inside, the bar empty. The bartender reached under it, then raised his hands over his head and gaped down the barrel of the Browning that materialized in Bell's hand. The man looked both frightened and resigned, as if he expected something like this would be happening soon.

"What do you want?"

"Show us your cellar," said Bell.

"Cellar? What cellar? It's a boathouse."

"We'd like to see it anyway."

"Buddy, I'm telling you the truth."

"I want to see why this is the only bar on the street that has no customers. Open that trapdoor."

The bartender pulled open the trapdoor. There was no cellar, only a short ladder that descended to the mud, and no shaft to a tunnel.

They walked through the barroom toward the river and stepped out on a landing. Hidden in the shadows, Bell saw similar landings to the left and right. Suddenly, a man stepped to the end of the dock next door and swung a lantern like a brakeman signaling a locomotive engineer. Then a lightbulb flashed on and off in the second-floor windows. They were signaling the coast was clear of cops and Prohibition officers, Bell realized, as a motorboat towed a barge in from the dark river and tied up at the dock. Two boatmen unloaded quickly. Two came out from their boathouse and ran the cases inside, and the boat towed the empty barge away. A bigger operation commenced on the other side, where a door opened in a boathouse, a deep-laden speedboat slipped in, and the door shut.

Tobin muttered to Bell, "Legitimate whisky haulers, no tunnel."

Bell went in and took the bartender aside. "Take it easy. We have no more business here."

"Glad to hear it."

Bell reached into his pocket and pulled out a fat roll of hundred-dollar bills. "But I have a question. I'm curious about something. If you could help me out, I would greatly appreciate it."

"Maybe I can help," the bartender said cautiously. "Depends. What do you want to know?"

"Business is booming up and down the street. Why does this one joint have those hard-boiled boys keeping out the customers?"

"The boss got shot. We don't know what's going on."

Shot over what?"

"Purple Gang cut the price of Canadian Club in half. Knocked my boss right out of the market. He and his boys caught up with them on Michigan Grand. Before you know it, there's gunplay. You ever hear of a sub-machine gun?"

"It rings a bell."

"The Purples had one."

29

The Van Dorns piled back in the Phaeton and kept hunting. They burst into two more unusually quiet bars. One was deserted. The other had a woman waiting anxiously for a husband who had yet to return from a whisky run. In neither did they find a shaft to a tunnel.

The first red streaks of dawn gleamed across the river. Bell called it a night.

"Beginning to think it isn't here," said Tobin.

Clayton and Ellis looked crestfallen. "Hope we didn't give you a bum steer, Mr. Bell."

"Grab some sleep, boys. We'll try again tomorrow night."

Clayton and Ellis went back to their hotel.

Bell and Tobin returned to Fort Van Dorn. Tobin climbed the stairs to the dormitory where Bell had ordered his detectives to sleep so he didn't have to worry about them being ambushed in hotels. Bell checked the teleprinter. He found a wire from Grady Forrer.

POKING AROUND.

TELEPHONE SOONEST.

Bell boiled water and ground coffee beans while the operators put through the long-distance line. Submachine guns most likely meant Comintern. But why would the Comintern cut the price of booze?

The operator called back. "Ringing, sir."

Grady answered with a wide-awake, "Isaac, you will love this."

"What's up?"

"But first, some background to put it in perspective. Before I walk you through ancient railroad history."

Isaac Bell stifled a yawn and a groan. The night owl Grady was in one of his talkative moods. But the Van Dorn Research Department was arguably the detective agency's greatest asset.

"Go right ahead. Take your time."

"Thirty years ago, American railroads had pretty much overcome the insurmountable engineering challenges that used to impede construction. Advances in grading, bridge

402

building, tunneling, and locomotive design meant they could build almost anywhere they pleased. The main obstacle to building new railroads was other railroads competing for the same markets. Do you understand?"

"No crystal was ever clearer, Grady."

"You remember your old friend Osgood Hennessy?"

"Railroad tycoon," said Bell, "who happens to be our mutual friend Archie Abbott's father-in-law. Go on, please."

"Thirty years ago, way back in 1891, Osgood Hennessy tried to organize another transcontinental railroad by connecting lines he owned east of Chicago to his Great Northern Railway west of Minneapolis. But rival railroads, which had corrupted even more Illinois, Wisconsin, and Minnesota legislators, governors, and judges than Hennessy had, blocked him. He could neither lay new track between Chicago and Minneapolis nor gain a controlling interest of an existing line. But Old Man Hennessy, you may recall, was unstoppable."

"Like a combination Brahma bull and Consolidated locomotive."

"So Hennessy devised a scheme to connect Chicago to Minneapolis by a new route via Detroit."

"Last time I looked at a map," said Bell,

"Detroit was *east* of Chicago."

"Bear with me, Isaac. Stranger railroads were built in the '90s; all sorts of monkey tricks to sell stock. But this was a real one, if roundabout. Hennessy surveyed a line from Minneapolis to Duluth, then up the shore of Lake Superior to Port Arthur and onto the Canadian Pacific Railroad at Port Arthur and around the top of Superior and Lake Huron and down through Ontario to Windsor, where it would connect with the New York Central."

"What would the New York Central get out of that arrangement? The Vanderbilts hated Hennessy."

"They would get access to the tunnel to Detroit."

"What tunnel?"

"The tunnel Hennessy was excavating under the Detroit River."

"There's only one rail tunnel under the Detroit River and it wasn't built until 1910."

"Hennessy started his twenty years earlier."

"He did?"

"He laid a two-thousand-foot cast-iron tube, using the same Beach shield compressed-air method as they did for the Saint Clair Tunnel."

"First? Ahead of the rest of the line?"

"First off, he commissioned a geological survey for the tunnel. Then he went straight to work on it. Probably wanted to be sure that he could build the hardest part of the line before he committed to the rest."

Bell said, "I remember when he built the Cascades Cutoff. He bridged Cascade Canyon first, way ahead of the line. 'Speed,' he used to say. 'It's all about speed.' Why doesn't anybody know about this tunnel?"

"Hennessy had to keep it secret from his enemies or they'd have blocked him in the Michigan State House. He tunneled clandestinely — under the table, so to speak. Which was why he dug from the Canadian side . . . on Fighting Island."

"Fighting Island?" Bell put down his coffee.

"The Canadians were glad to keep mum. The scheme would boost their railroads. Plus Hennessy bought the shield and all of his machinery and cast iron from the same Canadian factories that supplied the Saint Clair job."

"Fighting Island to where?"

"Ecorse."

"Grady, are you sure?"

"All the main lines pass close to Ecorse. Ecorse was the ideal place to connect."

"So where is it?"

405

"Abandoned. The scheme collapsed and Hennessy cut his losses — stopped work just short of Ecorse."

"Is it still there?"

"It must be. He'd have sealed it up, having paid for it, hoping to finish it sometime in the future. But it strikes me that if some smart bootlegger found out, he might have finished the last hundred feet or so and had himself a hooch tunnel from Fighting Island to Detroit."

"So this would be a much bigger tunnel than something hacked out with shovel and pick."

"Bigger? I'll say. Hennessy's section has room for a locomotive, tender, caboose, and twenty-five railcars."

"Grady, you are a genius."

Bell heard a sharp clang on the telephone line. Grady said, "I am raising a glass to that thought. Hope it helps."

"Wait! Find me a map. Somewhere must be engineers' plans and surveys."

"Oh, didn't I tell you? I put it on the night train. You'll have it this morning."

Bell hired a surveyor. The surveyor confirmed with his transit what already looked likely to the naked eye. The jumping-off point indicated on Osgood Hennessy's original tunnel drawings was beneath a large wooden building under construction on Fighting Island directly across from Ecorse. Inquiries in Canada revealed it was to be a ferry terminal, which seemed odd for an island peopled by a handful of recluses. The mystery was cleared up when the Van Dorns discovered that the company building the terminal had also applied for building permits to erect a Ferris wheel and dance pavilion for a mid-river summer resort.

"Maybe," said Bell.

Plotting where the tunnel would emerge in Ecorse would have been a simple matter of perching the surveyor on the half-built terminal and pointing his transit across the water at the compass angle projected on Hennessy's map. But binoculars showed the building site was fenced off. Riflemen were guarding the high wooden wall, confirmation that the tunnel started under the terminal.

Bell presented his New York Yacht Club credentials to gain admission to the Detroit Yacht Club. He bought a river chart and rented two Gar Wood speedboats. He made one a guard boat, manned by Tobin, Clayton, and Ellis, heavily armed, and took the surveyor with him downstream in the other.

"You'll have to be quick," he told the surveyor. "We don't want to be noticed by customs or hijackers."

Nearing Ecorse, Bell throttled back and disengaged the propellers to let the boat drift on the current while the surveyor sighted the terminal. He was quick.

"X marks the spot, Mr. Bell. The original tunnel is directly under us now."

Bell engaged the engines in reverse to hold the boat against the current. The surveyor whipped his transit one hundred eighty degrees to pinpoint where on the Ecorse waterfront the tunnel would emerge, provided the last section continued in a straight line.

"That red boathouse, Mr. Bell, if the extension is in-line with the original."

Bell noted that the chart showed a water depth of thirty feet. He wondered how deeply the crown of the tunnel was buried under the river bottom. A way to attack Marat Zolner was taking shape in his mind. It was instigated by the bartender's tale of his boss getting shot. Submachine guns almost certainly indicated the Comintern had a hand in it. And if they did, he was beginning to realize why they would cut the price of booze in half.

Bell headed downriver, waited for dusk, and went back to the spot between the ferry terminal and the red boathouse. Idling the engines to keep the boat in place, he checked their position relative to the two structures. Then he took compass bearings on a light atop the red boathouse and bearings on prominent lights up and down the river. Returning to this precise spot tomorrow night would be a simple matter of lining up the lights.

30

James Dashwood returned to Detroit with more bad news. He had come within sixty seconds of catching up with Fern Hawley — one minute too late to stop her chartered flying boat from taking off from Miami.

"Florida is a good place to hide if you're as rich as she is. She could be in Palm Beach or the Florida Keys, or Havana, Cuba, or Bimini or Nassau or any other islands of The Bahamas. Or she could have rendezvoused with a yacht at sea. I put the word out to our various people and decided I'd be more useful back in Detroit."

Bell said, "Maybe Nassau — where the booze tanker is headed. In which case, Pauline will deal with her."

"Maybe I should go down and look out for Pauline?"

"Pauline looks out for herself. Do you remember the spy who was sabotaging the Navy's battleships?"

Dashwood grinned. "I remember trying to convince his enormous bodyguard that I was an itinerant temperance orator, not a detective."

Bell said, "Admiral Falconer showed me experiments in a test caisson where armor experts simulated torpedo attacks to measure the impact of explosions underwater. Torpedoes were coming into their own just as the science boys began to understand what made them so deadly."

Blast energy from mines and torpedoes was terrifically amplified and concentrated underwater. By the middle of the war, depth charges were sinking submarines, which gave Bell an idea how to deal with the tunnel and everything in it.

"Round up four cases of dynamite."

Bell wired Grady Forrer for more information from the geological survey that Osgood Hennessy had commissioned for his tunnel.

HOW DEEP TUNNEL?

WHAT IS BOTTOM MATERIAL?

Bell had decreed that gangland Detroit was too dangerous for even a fortified Van Dorn field office to employ apprentices, so he was forced to press tough Protective

411

Services operatives into apprentice tasks. "Run to the library. Look in the 1891 issues of *Harper's Weekly* for an article about the Saint Clair River Tunnel."

"Library?"

"You can count on *Harper's* for a rundown on the big engineering feats. 1891. The librarian will help you find it."

"When?"

"Now! On the jump!"

The broad-shouldered house dick lumbered off, scratching his head.

Grady wired back:

BOTTOM CONSISTS OF SAND, CLAY,
BOULDERS, AND ROCK.

TUNNEL CROWN THREE FEET
UNDER BOTTOM.

"Good!"

But when the Protective Services op returned with the *Harper's* article about the St. Clair Tunnel, Bell ran into a snag he hadn't considered. The cast-iron walls of the St. Clair Tunnel were two inches thick, which would make it immensely strong. Hennessy's abandoned tunnel had been built of similar cast-iron segments.

Stymied, and hoping to see the problem

from another, more productive angle, Bell put it to Dashwood in the starkest terms. "We can't count on explosives breaching the main tunnel. They will easily destroy the connector. But if the connector collapses too far from the main tunnel, the debris will seal it before the water reaches the main tunnel. To guarantee breaching the main tunnel and destroying the Comintern's stockpile, we have to explode the dynamite very near the joint where the tunnels connect."

Dashwood asked, "Why don't we just raid the tunnel? That will shut it."

"It won't stay shut long," said Bell. "The cops and courts are for sale on both sides of the river. They'll put pictures in the papers of a prosecutor swinging an ax at a case of whisky. But hush money will keep that booze safe where it is. Zolner and his partners will lay low 'til the politicians are done demanding another 'drive' against liquor, then back to business — unless we flood the tunnel and destroy the Comintern's stockpile. I told Mr. Van Dorn, and I'll tell you: I will not settle for bloodying his nose this time. I'm going to drive Marat Zolner out of Detroit."

"Where do you think he'll go?"

Bell answered, "Where do I think? Listen."

413

He sat at the private-wire Morse key and tapped out a message to New York.

FORWARD FINAL PAYMENT LYNCH & HARDING MARINE.
DELIVER MARION EXPRESS CRUISER MIAMI.

"We have to stop him from setting up business the way he's doing here in Detroit and back in New York."

"What if he goes to The Bahamas?" Dashwood asked.

"He won't. He has no reason to go to Nassau. Nassau is like Canada, a relatively safe base for legal liquor. Florida is lawless, an import-and-distribution center like Detroit and New York where he can fight to expand and take over."

Bell gave Dashwood a cold smile and added, "If for some reason he does go to Nassau, Nassau is three hours from Miami by fast boat. And *Marion* is going to be one fast boat."

He wired Grady again.

HOW FAR FROM SHORE DID HENNESSY TUNNEL STOP?

Grady telephoned long-distance.

414

"Too complicated for the wire. I found handwritten engineers' notes on the survey that suggest they stopped excavating just where the bank began to slope upward."

Bell spread open his Detroit River chart. "There's a deep channel down the middle, nearer to Fighting Island, and then a narrower one, the Wyandotte Channel, that hugs the Ecorse shore."

"They must have dredged it deeper since the survey. There's no channel mentioned."

"It hugs the shore," said Bell. "The dredge would have struck the crown of the tunnel probably, so just beyond the current Wyandotte Channel is where they must have stopped."

He improvised calipers with two fingers and compared the distance to the chart's scale.

Grady said, "The other reason I telephoned . . ."

"What?" Bell was distracted. It wasn't so much the headache — they were tapering off, and the plague of double vision had pretty much ended. He was puzzling some way to drop his improvised depth charge exactly one hundred feet offshore. "What did you say, Grady?"

"The Research Department is assembling a complete Prohibition file — an up-to-date encyclopedia of bootleggers, gangsters, rum-runners, et cetera, with *curriculum vitae,* photographs, fingerprints."

"Good job. That'll show the Justice Department what we can do."

"I thought I'd pop down to The Bahamas. Get the latest on the Nassau import-export racket. What do you think?"

"I think you'd get in Pauline's way."

"Oh, that's right, she's down there," Grady said innocently. "Is she all right on her own?"

"Pauline is quite all right on her own . . . Actually, you raise a good point. She could use a trustworthy runner. Tell you what, send young Somers to Nassau. I'll cable Pauline."

APPRENTICE ASA SOMERS COMING
YOUR WAY.
GO-GETTER SAVED JVD BACON.

Then Bell called for the Protective Services op, whom he had sent earlier to the library.

"Go buy a rope."

"How long?"

"One hundred four feet."

"One hundred *four?*"

"The four's for a loop. Watch carefully

how they measure."

Jack Payne, a Van Dorn detective on loan from the Cleveland field office, had been a combat engineer in the trenches during the war. Working in an empty backwater slip Bell located near the Detroit Yacht Club, Payne rigged the dynamite with waterproof fuses and detonators and screwed twenty pounds of old horseshoes to each of the forty-pound cases so they would sink fast.

After dark, they tied the cases into one heavy packet perched on the stern of one of the Gar Wood speedboats.

"Just to review your scheme, Mr. Bell," said Detective Payne, "keep in mind that that shock wave will go *up* as well as down. The moment you drop these crates, jam your throttles and get away from there as fast as you can."

"The Bureau chief found the tunnel," reported Ellis and Clayton, arriving winded at Fort Van Dorn.

"Sorry, Mr. Bell. They're dickering the cost of protection right now."

Isaac Bell's response was a fathomless smile.

"Tell me all about it."

"They somehow connected with the

mayor of the city of La Salle and —"

Bell cut him off. "I don't care how. What can you tell me about the tunnel that you didn't know before?"

"It's got more booze in it than we thought. A lot more."

"Guards?"

"Armies. Tons of them at the ferry terminal, tons in Ecorse. Every building around that boathouse is theirs. Including the second one we raided."

"How many guards are in the tunnel?"

"They don't let anyone in the tunnel."

Isaac Bell said, "Good. I was a little concerned about not-so-innocent innocent bystanders." He raised his voice so the others could hear. "O.K., gents, we're doing it now."

Isaac Bell let Ed Tobin drive the dynamite boat. In the dark, a son of Staten Island coal pirates would make a shrewder helmsman than a scion of Boston bankers. The black water seemed to swallow distance. Channel lights, shore lights, and boat lights could be confusing. And gauging position required a smuggler's eye. Bell stood by their improvised depth charge with the hundred-four-foot rope coiled in his hands.

Shadowed by the guard boat, they raced

down the Detroit River. As Ecorse came into view, Tobin lined up the boathouse, shore, and ferry terminal lights. He cut his throttles abruptly and swerved toward the row of boathouses that thrust out from the bank. Guards heard them coming and hurried out on their docks.

Twenty feet from the red boathouse dock, Tobin engaged his propellers in reverse, spun his helm, and raced his engines. The Gar Wood stopped abruptly, pivoted ninety degrees, and thundered backwards toward the dock pilings.

Isaac Bell jumped up on the stern and braced a boot on the dynamite. Ed switched his propellers forward again and rammed his throttles. The boat stopped six inches from a piling. Bell looped the rope around it and knotted the fastest bowline he had ever tied.

"Go!"

Ed Tobin eased forward, slowly paying out the rope. Bell let it slide loosely through his hands and watched for the bitter end. He heard men on the docks shouting for lights.

"Stop!" he called to Tobin.

They were precisely one hundred feet from the dock, over the joint between the two tunnels. Suddenly, searchlights glared down from boathouse roofs. Isaac Bell cut the ropes holding the dynamite. They started shooting.

Bell flicked a flame from an Austrian cigarette lighter made of a rifle cartridge that Pauline Grandzau had given him. Thompson submachine guns sprayed their once seen, never forgotten red flashes. Bullets whipped past, fanning his face and splintering the wooden crates. A bullet blew out the flame.

Bell heard the guard boat's engines and the measured crack of a rifle as Dashwood coolly returned the submachine-gun fire. Bell flicked the lighter again and again, got it going, and touched the blue apex of the flame to the waterproof fuse. The fuse caught with a dazzling burst of sparks. He planted both feet and heaved his shoulder against the crates.

One hundred sixty pounds of dynamite slid off the back of the boat and sank like a stone.

"Go!" he shouted to Ed Tobin.

Ed Tobin rammed his throttles full ahead. The Gar Wood leaped forward. It had traveled barely fifty feet when the dynamite exploded with a muffled, violent thud. A geyser of water shot in the air beside the boat. A shock wave blasted after it, a tremendous eruption that splintered the hull and hurled the Van Dorn detectives into the river.

Inside the tunnel, a half-mile rail line had been converted to an immensely long warehouse. Two endless rows of twelve-bottle crates of whisky were stacked from the rails to the curving crown of the tunnel's ceiling. Between the stacks, which stretched from Fighting Island almost to Ecorse, was a narrow corridor. It was twenty feet high but only three feet wide, barely wide enough for one man at time.

River water rammed into this corridor like a rectangular piston. The water filled the space between the crates on either side, the ceiling above, and the wooden railroad ties below. Marat Zolner and Abe Weintraub ran for their lives.

Weintraub was in the lead.

Zolner was catching up fast, his long legs propelling him twice the length of the shorter man's steps. The lights — bare bulbs hanging overhead and powered by the dynamo on Fighting Island — flickered, and the animal fear that made him flee exploded into human terror. As horrific as the fate thundering after him was, it would be a million times worse in the dark.

A noise louder than the water chased

them, the high-pitched clangor of breaking glass. The river was splintering crates and smashing bottles by the tens of thousands. The water stank of whisky.

Ahead, high in the flickering lights, Zolner saw the walls of crates begin to move. The river had overtaken and flanked them. Squeezed between the tunnel walls and the stacks, the water toppled the highest crates. They fell from both sides into the narrow corridor, strewn like boulders by a mountain landslide, and blocked the corridor. Weintraub scampered up the shifting pile of wood and glass like an ape, racing desperately for the top of the heap, where a sliver of light shone in the last three-foot-wide, two-foot-high opening.

Zolner scrambled after him. The river caught up. Water slammed into his back and hurled him toward the ceiling. Weintraub reached the opening and started to squirm through. Zolner was suddenly in water up to his neck. Weintraub's thick torso was blocking the space. Zolner grabbed his foot. He braced his own feet on the tumbled stack, pulled with all his might, yanked the gangster out of the opening, and dived through it himself.

Weintraub tried to follow. He got stuck and let out a terrified roar: "Help me!"

He was stopping the water like a cork in a bottle, and if Zolner managed to pull him out, they would both drown. He ran to the shaft ladder, which was fixed to the cast-iron wall at the end of the tunnel. Mounting the iron rungs, he looked back.

The river smashed through the barrier. Abe Weintraub flew to the end of the tunnel, hurled on a crest of water and broken crates that dashed him against the cast-iron wall. The water rose to Zolner's chest. He kicked loose from it and climbed up the shaft into the night. Across the river, he saw a motorboat's searchlight probing the dark like a desperate finger.

"Isaac!"

"Mr. Bell!"

"Ed! Ed Tobin. Where are you?"

In the searchlight glare, the Van Dorns on the guard boat saw the shattered speedboat half sunk on its side. It was turning, slowly spinning, picking up speed, spinning faster and faster, as it was sucked into a huge whirlpool. A crater was spinning in the river, a gigantic hole left by a million tons of water plunging into the tunnel.

"Isaac!"

"Here!" Bell shouted. "Behind you!" The river current had helped him and Tobin swim away from the wreckage. Now the vortex was drawing them back.

The guard boat roared alongside them. Strong arms hauled them out of the water, drenched but unhurt, just as the last of the speedboat was sucked under.

Isaac Bell was grinning ear to ear.

"They'll never invite me back to that yacht club."

■ ■ ■ ■

BOOK FOUR:
HURRICANE

■ ■ ■ ■

A Hard Landing

31

Palm trees rustled, the sea was green, and the sky a fine blue. Iced daiquiris frosted their glasses, the finishing touch, like painter's varnish, on a portrait of a dreamy afternoon in tropical Nassau.

Out of nowhere, the dream melted into a detective's nightmare.

Pauline Grandzau had seen to every detail to disguise herself as a plucky businesswoman subtly battling the "no skirts" prejudice of the men in the liquor trade: She was awaiting a consignment of rye from the Glasgow company she represented; the market for Scotch was glutted, and Americans loved their rye; she had to make a deal with a buyer.

"Meantime, I'm talking up a storm to convince the buyers it's coming soon and it will be the real McCoy, so they'll bid up the price."

"Are the buyers the rumrunners?"

"Exactly! They sail it up to the Row."

Fern Hawley, seated across their little round cocktail table, seemed to swallow her story hook, line, and sinker. The Van Dorn detective, who was pretending to be a liquor agent, and Marat Zolner's girlfriend, who was pretending to be a carefree American tourist, were going to be, in Fern's own words, "great pals."

They had climbed the lookout tower on the hotel's roof, where liquor agents were watching the deep-blue sea for their ships, and admired Fern's steam yacht, the biggest anchored in the turquoise harbor. Now on the patio under the royal palms, sharpers and hucksters, bankers and gangsters were bustling about overtime, and the daiquiris were flowing.

But, all of a sudden, just as Pauline eased Fern into a discussion of the liquor traffic — legal in the British colony, legal on the high seas, legal on Rum Row, *illegal* on the wrong side of the U.S. border — who should wander into the all-day, all-night party that Prohibition had made of the Lucerne Hotel than the only human being in all the British Bahamas who knew that she was a Van Dorn detective.

Joseph Van Dorn's oldest friend, whom Isaac Bell had introduced her to at Bellevue

Hospital, spotted her instantly and waved.

"Captain Novicki," she blurted, jumping to her feet and trying to send signals with her eyes.

Dave Novicki churned toward their table, robust as a barrel of beer and guileless as a manatee.

She greeted him in a rush of words, hoping to contain him. "I'm so surprised to see you here, I thought you set sail already, may I introduce my new friend, Miss Fern Hawley of New York? She just landed in her yacht, you must have seen it in the harbor from your ship." She took a breath and turned to Fern. "Captain Novicki commands a schooner that brings my *import-export firm's* rum from, uhhm, Hispaniola, is it, Captain? Or will it be Jamaica next shipment?"

Novicki looked puzzled and about to speak, which could not possibly help.

Pauline stuck out her hand. Novicki took it, and she squeezed his horny paw as hard as she could, saying with a laugh she could only hope did not sound hysterical, "Or will you sail all the way to England to bring me some gin?"

Novicki looked down at her hand. Then he looked into her eyes.

Sea captains must be alert, she thought.

And unusually observant. Surely —

He spoke at last.

"I'm not certain the old girl could sail as far as England, but I would risk it for you, my dear, if you're hard-up for gin. In fact," he added, warming to the fiction, "I would gladly sail her around the Horn to fetch you the wines of Chile or cross the Pacific for Japanese sake."

With that, Novicki gave her hand a little squeeze, let go of it, and seized Fern's. His sharp eyes roamed her beautiful face appreciatively, and when a surprised intake of breath from her revealed that he had her attention, he said, "Pleased to make your acquaintance, Miss Hawley. What yacht did you arrive in?"

"Maya."

"Yes, I saw her come in. Handsome steamer. Beats the newfangled diesels hands down. But may I caution you, if you're discussing business deals with this young lady" — he clapped Pauline on the back — *"hold tight to your fillings and count the spoons!"*

"We're only drinking daiquiris," said Pauline. "This isn't business. We just ran into each other down at the harbor."

"I'm only a tourist," said Fern. "Would you join us?"

Novicki looked like a man who very much wanted to while away the afternoon drinking daiquiris with two beautiful woman. Pauline shot him an eyeful of *No, no, absolutely not!*

"Thank you, Miss Hawley . . . Pauline. Nothing would delight me more. But I don't like the look of that sky. I want deep water under my bottom, the sooner the better."

He made his good-byes, choosing an instant when Fern turned to signal the waiter for refills to give Pauline a solemn grin.

Fern watched him churn away. "Did you notice what was going on with him?"

"What do you mean?"

"He was *flirting* with me."

"Do you want me to call him back?"

Fern burst out laughing. "No! He's way too old."

"Are you sure?"

"O.K., I wouldn't kick him out of bed. But, no, too late. He's gone to his ship."

Pauline shrugged. "All I know is, he's the nicest rumrunner I've ever met. Most of them are pretty rough." She took a sip from her glass.

Fern looked up through the palm fronds.

431

"I don't see what's wrong with the sky, do you?"

"It looks wonderful," said Pauline, "though it could be the daiquiris. Oh, mine's getting empty again."

"I already called the waiter. Here they come . . . What shall we drink to? New friends? I can't believe how we just bumped into each other and, all of a sudden, we're telling each other things like we've been friends forever."

"To new friends and old friends," said Pauline, clinking her glass against Fern's. "And nice rumrunners."

"I'll leave the rumrunners to you. Bootleggers are more my style."

"They're rough, too, aren't they?"

"Sometimes . . . Sometimes they're real louses. Sometimes they're the cat's whiskers."

"How do you tell them apart?"

Fern put down her drink and looked up at the sky. "You don't. Until it's too late."

32

Isaac Bell inhaled the intoxicating mix of fresh paint, clean oil, and gasoline of a just launched, brand-new express cruiser. New she was, and beautiful, a sleek, ghostly gray that seemed to hover more than float on Biscayne Bay. He nudged her throttles and she got lively. He engaged the mufflers and she was suddenly silent.

A fast Prohibition Bureau boat pulled alongside and signaled him to stop. Bell waved good-bye. He cut out the mufflers and hit the throttles and left the revenuers bouncing on his thunderous wake.

He tore around Biscayne Bay, twirling her spoked wheel to cut figure eights past the hydroplane landings, the towering McAllister Hotel, draped in striped awnings, the Boat Club, and the Biscayne Boulevard finger piers, where the fleets of lumber schooners that supplied the building boom were unloading cypress and yellow pine. In the middle of the bay, off the Miami River, floated the pylons that marked the Motor Boat Race Course. Isaac Bell set an unofficial record around the three-mile circuit at sixty miles an hour.

Lynch & Harding had done themselves proud. She handled like a dream.

He circled a long passenger freighter from Baltimore that was transferring people to a harbor launch. A flying boat approached from the east. Bell raced alongside it as it landed. Then he opened her up and headed for the ocean, tearing under the causeway that linked downtown Miami to Miami Beach and pointing her razor-sharp bow at Government Cut at the south end of the bay. He blasted through the shipping channel at top speed and roared down the Atlantic Coast.

In the ocean swells, she felt big and fast and sturdy. Beyond the settlements, along shores thick with jungle broken repeatedly by the raw scars of clearance and construction, a dark boat shot from a mangrove swamp and chased after him. Bell slowed down and let the boat pull alongside. Three men wearing revolvers on their hips looked him over. Any doubts they were hijackers vanished when they reached for their weapons.

Bell tugged a lever conveniently located in the cockpit. A hatch popped open on the foredeck, and a Lewis gun swiveled up within easy reach. The hijackers raced back to their swamp.

Bell turned around and sped back past Government Cut and along the white sand of Miami Beach. He cut figure eights for the swimmers. Then he thundered back into Biscayne Bay and, having drawn the attention of half of Florida to *Marion,* he raced back to the dock.

A crowd of boatmen, tourists, and hotel guests had gathered. Bell landed in an explosive flurry of reversed engines, propeller wash, and flaming straight pipes.

"Wonder what you all are going to use that boat for?" drawled an onlooker with a snicker that everyone knew meant rum.

Isaac Bell said, "I'm going to get rich winning boat races."

"That's a good story for the Dries."

"Want to bet? I'm calling out candidates."

"Heck, who'd race you? That's more airplane than boat."

Bell said, "I heard about a big black boat whose owner thinks he's hotter than jazz. We'll see if he's got the nerve to put his money where his mouth is."

"Where is he?"

"Lying low," Bell grinned, "since he heard I'm here. Fact is, I'll pay a thousand dollars to anybody who tells me where to find him."

"A *thousand* dollars?"

"Call it a finder's fee. Call it a reward. I intend to call him out."

"Show us the money."

Isaac Bell pulled a roll from the pocket of his white duck trousers and flashed a thousand-dollar bill, common currency among top-notch Florida bootleggers. "Tell your friends," he said. "Share the wealth."

He tipped his visored skipper's cap to the ladies and sauntered up the boardwalk to make a public show of lunch on the veranda while the word got around about the thousand. Before he got ten feet, he was waylaid by a beautiful blonde who was wearing a big hat and dark glasses and a white linen sheath dress that the sea breeze shaped to her trim figure.

Marat Zolner focused binoculars on the McAllister Hotel quay.

A long gray rum boat was tied alongside, sleek and muscular as a captured shark. Ten stories above Biscayne Bay, in a top-floor suite, he had watched her slice through Government Cut at sixty miles per hour, streak across the bay, and land just below.

436

He had not been surprised to see Van Dorn Chief Investigator Isaac Bell vault out of her cockpit.

From razor bow to sturdy transom, the gray boat's powerful lines were first cousin to *Black Bird*'s, realized by the same Lynch & Harding who had built his boat. And by now he knew that Isaac Bell was relentless.

The Comintern agent had no time for regrets. But for a moment he indulged in speculating what would have happened if he hadn't shot Joseph Van Dorn. If not for that chance event — a twist of fate that the machine gunner he had shot on the Coast Guard cutter had not been an ordinary sailor — no one could have discovered his Comintern scheme until it was too late to stop him. Thanks to that twist of fate, Isaac Bell had thrown hurdles in his path, repeatedly, and showed no signs of going away.

The tall detective tipped the boat boys who tied his lines — lavishly, Zolner guessed by their bows and scrapes — then engaged the people hanging around the dock in banter. Suddenly, a girl took his arm. She was slim and blond but not his wife.

Zolner recalled that Marion Morgan Bell was taller. This girl was petite. He could not see much of her face under her hat and behind sunglasses, but she carried herself like a woman accustomed to being admired.

"What has caught your attention?" asked the woman who had summoned Zolner to the suite.

She was a Comintern courier, a forthright Italian Bolshevik who was sleeping with a man in Lenin's inner circle and so trusted by Moscow that she could indulge in expensive hotels and speak her mind freely.

"Only a pretty girl."

"I doubt that," said the courier. "There is fury in your face. You look angry enough to kill."

It seemed to Zolner that Bell and the girl were acquainted. Colleagues, he guessed by the familiar manner in which they faced each other. Maybe lovers, although he thought not. She was a colleague. Another Van Dorn detective.

"You misread my expression," he told the courier. "I am *happy* enough to kill."

"First things first, comrade. Your report."

Couriers did not *demand* reports. Moscow had moved more quickly to replace Yuri Antipov than Zolner had predicted. The Italian woman with long black maiden's hair and executioner's eyes was his new overseer.

"One moment," he said, snatching up her telephone without her permission. He gave the hotel operator the number of a speak-

438

easy in a hotel on East Flagler and issued cryptic orders to the gangster who answered. Then he put down the telephone and asked Moscow's woman, "Are you ready for my report?"

Isaac Bell was very surprised to see Pauline in Miami. She must have landed in the flying boat he had run beside.

"You made quite a spectacle of yourself," she greeted him.

He said, "I don't expect Marat Zolner to accept a challenge to race *Black Bird.* But a thousand-dollar finder's fee ought to turn up someone who's seen where he keeps her."

"I hope you'll take me for a ride."

"We should not be seen together, Pauline. Zolner's comrades could be watching."

"I'm sorry. I should have cabled my report. It was foolish of me . . ." Her almost negligible German accent was suddenly evident. "But I just vanted to come. Last minute. An impulse . . ."

Bell had never seen her flustered before, even as a young girl. Nor had he ever seen her so beautiful. He realized, belatedly, that she had dressed with unusual care, even for her, applying lipstick with an artist's hand. And she had changed her hair from the boyish bob he'd seen in New York to stylish marcel waves.

"How'd you make out with Fern?"

"Fern Hawley is deeply unhappy," said Pauline. "It seems that Zolner has somehow disappointed her."

"That's what Marion said. A man had disappointed her."

"Well, good for Marion."

"Any clue as to how?"

"No. Whenever I approach that question, she closes the iron door."

"What are our chances of turning her against him?"

"Mine are nil. *You* would have a better chance."

"How do you reckon that?"

"She likes men. She likes good-looking men. And she likes men who stand out from the crowd. In fact, she thinks such men are her due."

"I gather you don't like her."

Pauline recovered her smooth demeanor. "I didn't say that. And I don't mean to give that impression. She is a woman who has never had to do anything in her life. If circumstances ever forced her to, she might shine. She certainly wants to."

"Go back to Nassau," said Bell. "I'll get out there as soon as I can."

"She's on her yacht. She could leave any minute."

"I'll be there as soon as I can."

Having wrecked, or at least slowed, Zolner's Detroit operation, Isaac Bell knew that the clock was running. It was vital not to give the Comintern agent time to set up in Florida as he had in New York.

"All right," Pauline said, briskly. "I'm off."

"How are things working out with young Somers?"

"He's a bright boy. I was comfortable leaving him in charge of the office."

"Glad to hear it," said Bell. "I thought you'd like him."

Marat Zolner knew that Moscow would never accept the death of their new overseer so soon after Yuri's. He could not kill her yet. He had no choice but to pretend to accept her authority. He said, "I can report that things are going swimmingly. Matters are in hand."

"It does not look that way, to my eye. Nor to Moscow's."

"I will tell you what I told Yuri Antipov before he died. My scheme is the best strategy — the only strategy — to infiltrate the United States and subvert the government."

"Moscow has come to understand that. Moscow agrees that America is a unique situation that requires a unique strategy."

"Do they?" Zolner was amazed. "It sounds to me that certain comrades have been replaced."

"That is not important. What is important is your failure to execute your strategy in Detroit."

"A minor setback."

"Minor? The loss of a liquor stockpile worth millions of dollars?"

His Canadian comrades had betrayed him.

"A regrettable loss," Zolner admitted, "but replaceable."

"And the drowning of your staunchest ally?"

There were no secrets.

He said, "There are plenty more where Weintraub came from. Detroit has no shortage of ambitious gangsters. He, too, is replaceable."

Her next question came like a silken thrust of Yuri's dagger. "And will you replace your stockbroker in New York?"

Zolner concealed his shock. He had underestimated the Comintern's reach. It appeared that while he and Yuri had bombed Wall Street, some obscure branch of the Comintern had managed to infiltrate the stock exchange. Through an underpaid, envious clerk, was his first thought. But it could be higher up, inside a bank or brokerage house, through some privileged romantic "serving the cause" like Fern Hawley. Not Newtown Storms; there was not a romantic bone in the broker's body. But someone with access to inside knowledge, in the finest Wall Street tradition.

He pretended he was bewildered.

"What are you talking about?"

"You have incurred enormous losses in the American stock market."

"I salute you, comrade. I have no idea how you discovered it but your information is golden, if not a little out-of-date. The situation is temporary. Gains follow losses in the market. It is the nature of capitalism to —"

She cut him off.

"The loss of millions in liquor. The death of your staunchest ally in Detroit. Your stock market holdings all but wiped out. Please, comrade. Do you take us for fools? Nothing you've attempted has worked. How long before you're beating on our door, begging for funding?"

Now it was relief, deep relief, that Zolner concealed. They did not know the truth behind the stock market losses. He said, "I don't need a kopeck. I won't ask for a kopeck."

"I find that hard to believe. How will you save this situation?"

"Clear the decks and start over."

" 'Decks'? What are these 'decks'?"

"It's an expression, comrade. It means that I will continue building our network as soon as I have cleared an obstacle out of my way."

"Euphemisms are wasted on me, comrade. Who are you going to kill?"

"The one man making the obstacles."

"Isaac Bell?"

Zolner laid on fulsome praise. "Your intelligence is golden, comrade."

She was an idiot. Who else but Isaac Bell?

She said, "You have twenty-four hours."

Zolner shook his head. "Absolutely not. I will not risk our mission by accepting an artificial deadline."

"It's not your deadline, comrade. It is the deadline Moscow has imposed on me."

"For what?"

"To escort you home."

"Home?"

"You've been recalled."

33

When Marat Zolner drew himself up to his full height, the Italian courier thought to herself that the rumors about the ballet must be true. It was evident in the elegance of his stature that when he was a child somewhere in some benighted province of czarist Russia, Marat Zolner had indeed trained to be a dancer. Haughty as the aristocrats they both disdained and despised, he looked down his handsome nose at her and said, "Comrade, I know that the Comintern demands obedience."

"It is well you remember."

"Absolute and instant obedience makes us strong. Whether we obey out of faith in the revolution or out of loyalty to Russia — knowing that when we carry the fight abroad we keep the international bourgeoisie from invading while the Soviet is still recovering from the civil war — or out of fear."

She said, "You may keep your motives to

yourself."

His shoulders sagged very slightly, and she fancied that she saw the spirit drain out of him. He turned to the window and stared out at the bay and the blue ocean beyond. He opened the window, lifting the sash with the grace that ornamented his every move, and she had the strangest feeling that he would rather step into the sky and fall ten stories to the beach than return to Moscow.

She said, "Surely you are not considering suicide."

Marat Zolner turned back to her, thinking, *Suicide? Why would I commit suicide? I have wealth, I have power, and I have enormous plans. These setbacks are temporary. The future is mine.*

He said, "I am not coming with you."

She raised her voice: "Gregor!"

A heavyset Russian almost as tall as Zolner pushed through the door from the adjoining suite. He held a Nagant revolver as if he knew how to use it. He pointed at Zolner's shoulder and said in Russian, "Put your gun on the table, comrade."

Zolner slowly opened his coat, pulled his automatic out of its holster by the butt, and laid it on the table. He feigned dismay, but surrendering the gun did not trouble him.

He carried it mostly for show, preferring to fight in close.

The courier said, "He carries his blackjack in his left-hand hip pocket."

"Put it on the table."

He had no choice but to produce his blackjack and lay it beside the gun.

"Come closer," said Gregor.

Marat Zolner knew the drill. He had cowed many a prisoner. Gregor would grab his arm in a powerful grip and smash his nose with the Nagant's barrel. He stepped slowly closer, staring at the pistol as if mesmerized, right foot forward, left foot forward. Gregor drew the Nagant back slightly, winding up to strike. Right foot forward, left foot *kicking* toward the ceiling — a symphony of weight, momentum, balance — kicking higher, smashing Gregor's jaw.

He caught the gun as it dropped, pressed it to the staggered man's chest, and jerked the stiff trigger. The Nagant's sealed cylinder made it much quieter than an ordinary revolver, and Gregor's bulk further muffled the report.

The courier was as fearless as he. "Now what are you going to do?" she asked contemptuously.

"If I return home," he answered, "I will

return a hero."

"Hero? You'll spend the rest of your short life running from us *and* the American police."

"They will blame his murder on you."

"Who will believe that?"

"You shot your secret lover and committed suicide," he said.

She tried to run.

Zolner bounded after her and caught her easily and threw her out the window he had opened.

Isaac Bell heard a woman shriek.

She was in the crowd on the dock gawking at his boat, and she was pointing a rigid arm up at the hotel. Bell saw a figure in the air beside the building, a woman streaming long black hair as she plummeted past the windows. Others were screaming before she landed on a third-floor balcony with a thud Bell could hear at the end of the dock. She bounced off a railing onto the veranda roof, tumbled the final two floors in a flurry of arms and legs, and flopped on the sand.

The wooden dock shook as thirty people ran to see the body.

Bell watched from the boat. A top-floor window was open, ten stories off the ground, seven above the balcony where the body first struck. No human being could have survived that fall.

"She came out backwards," said a male voice from the water.

Bell looked down at a skiff with a big motor that had just tied up behind his transom. A middle-aged Floridian, browned and puckered by the powerful sun, was squinting up at him.

"You saw?"

"Yup. I just happened to be looking up at that moment and out she came. Backwards."

"You should tell the police," said Bell.

"Well, the police and I are not on speaking terms."

"If you have evidence of foul play, you should report it."

"There's no law against falling backwards. Anyway, I don't have time to talk to the cops. It's you I come talking to."

"About what?"

"My thousand dollars that I hear you're paying to find that big black boat."

34

Three days in Florida had convinced Isaac Bell that Miami was a boomtown of braggarts, boosters, and liars.

At least the fellow holding his hand up for the reward money was not among the majority of citizens who were new arrivals selling tales about imaginary pasts. His weathered face, canvas hat, ragged shirt, and his over-powered little skiff signified a lifelong fisherman and crabber who had a new career running Bimini whisky up the Florida rivers and bayous that he knew as well as the Darbees and Tobins knew New York Harbor.

"Did you see it?" asked Bell.

"Yup."

"What does it look like?"

"It's black."

"What else?"

"It's big."

"So far, you haven't said a thing I didn't

tell that crowd of folks on the dock."

"It's faster than greased lightning."

"That's a safe guess, since I told everyone I want to race it in this one."

"It's got a big old searchlight on front. Almost as big as yours."

"Searchlights tend to go on this kind of boat. Does it have another one in back like mine?"

"Nope," he said, and Bell got interested. "What else?"

"Got a lot of motors."

"How many?"

"Couldn't quite tell. I knew it was three, but there could be another one. Like a spare, maybe. There's something back there that could be a motor."

"What's your name?" asked Bell.

"Why you want to know?"

"I like to know the name of a fellow I hand a thousand dollars to. If it comes to that."

"What's my name?" He cast a wary eye at the hotel, where cops were shoving through the crowd around the fallen body. "You can call me Captain."

"Tell me more, Captain."

"At night, she shoots fire in the sky."

"So does this one. Straight-piped Libertys. Where did you see it?"

"I answered a lot of questions, mister. But I don't see no money."

Bell leaned over the transom and stared him in the face. "You'll see the money when I see the boat."

Captain said, "He came by last night, and the night before that. You want to see him tonight?"

Three nights, *Black Bird* had set out for Bimini to buy a load of rye; three nights, she had captured other rumrunners instead before she was halfway there. Tonight she wouldn't even leave the bay. Tonight she was going to war.

With Zolner at her helm and her engines muffled, she backed out of her hiding place between two of the dozens of five-masted lumber schooners that thrust their bowsprits over Biscayne Boulevard. The Comintern had purchased the ships, which were identical to the dozens that moored there, to use as floating liquor warehouses.

Paralleling the beach along the boulevard, slicing a quiet two miles through the dark, *Black Bird* motored south. She passed the McAllister Hotel, marked by a lighted sign on its roof, and turned into the narrow mouth of the Miami River.

■ ■ ■ ■

Isaac Bell was thinking that "Captain" had sent him on a wild-goose chase.

He and Dashwood and Tobin had been waiting for hours in a hot, muggy, mosquito-infested freight-yard slip a quarter mile from the mouth of the river. Captain had led them here in his boat. After Bell had backed *Marion* into the slip, he had sent the rum-runner to the safety of the hotel dock — clutching a fifty-dollar down payment on his finder's fee — in the likely event of gunplay.

There was occasional traffic on the river, even this late, an intermittent parade of fishing boats, small freighters, and cabin cruisers with singing drunks. Some of the freight boats were steamers, others were sailing schooners propelled in the narrow channel by auxiliary motors. The auxiliaries kept playing tricks on ears cocked for the muted rumble of *Black Bird*'s engines.

Then, all of a sudden, Bell heard her coming. No auxiliary motor could make such a noise. It was neither loud nor sharp but, like a threat of barely contained violence, the sound of suppressed strength that could be loosed any second.

"That's her," whispered Tobin. He was a few feet ahead of him on the foredeck, manning one of the Lewis guns. Dashwood was on the stern, fifty feet behind him, manning the other. Bell was in the cockpit, his boots resting lightly on the electric starters, one hand on the searchlight switches, the other on the horizontal bar that bridged all four throttles.

"Tell me when you see her," Bell told Tobin, who had a better view down the river from his perch on the foredeck. Happily, the boat traffic had stopped for the moment.

She was moving very slowly.

Captain had claimed that he had seen her pass this slip. He had speculated she would hide in a boathouse on the new Seybold Canal, which served a development of homes where the owners moored steam yachts. He had not claimed to have seen her turn off the river into the canal, and, in fact, she could be heading for one of the factories or freight depots or warehouses that shared the banks of the little river with residences, hotels, boatyards, and houseboats.

Until Bell heard her muffled Libertys, he had not fully believed Captain for the simple reason that a river only four miles long that ended in a swamp was a risky place to hide. Once in, there was no getting out, other than by railcar, and loading a boat onto a railcar was far too slow a process to escape a chase.

"Here he is," whispered Tobin.

A long shadow glided by, fifty feet from their boat's bow, faintly silhouetted by factory lights across the river. Bell waited until it had cleared the freight slip and moved a hundred yards farther upstream. It wasn't likely it could outrun the Van Dorn boat, and, even if it could, it couldn't go far.

Bell stepped on his starters. He had warmed the Libertys every thirty minutes. All four fired up at once. He shoved all props forward and the boat shot from the slip. He turned his wheel hard over, swinging her upriver, and switched on the forward searchlight.

If Isaac Bell had any doubts that Marat Zolner was Prince André, they vanished when he saw *Black Bird*'s helmsman look over his shoulder into the glare. Bell recognized the lean, handsome face, the elegant stance he remembered gliding over the Club Deluxe dance floor, and the reptilian grace of movement he had first seen on the roof of Roosevelt Hospital the night that Marat Zolner shot Johann Kozlov.

Bell's boat covered the yards between

them in a flash.

He was pulling alongside before *Black Bird* unmuffled her engines. Suddenly, the black boat was thundering, leaping ahead on a boiling wake.

Ed Tobin shouted over the roar of their own engines, "I can't shoot!"

Bell saw why. Ahead, on both sides of the narrow river, were the red and green and white lights of small boats. Fishermen were standing in them, dragging nets. Behind them on one shore was a white-shingled hotel, and lining the opposite shore was a row of houseboats. The powerful Lewis gun would chew them to pieces and kill anyone with the bad luck to meet a stray bullet.

"Hold your fire."

The black boat was pulling ahead.

Bell poured on the gas.

The black boat left the fishing boats in its wake.

The channel ahead was clear.

"Fire!"

Ed Tobin triggered a burst of shells. He stopped firing almost instantly.

"Look out, Isaac!"

Bell was already jerking his throttles back.

"Hold on, Dash!" he shouted over his shoulder. "It's a trap!"

35

The fishing boats were racing to shore, hauling lines out of the water, dragging something across the channel.

Marion struck before Isaac Bell could disengage his propellers.

Bell braced for a timber-jarring crash and hoped the reinforced bow would take it. Surprisingly, the express cruiser slowed without collision and seemed to hang midchannel. Instead of a crash in the bow, he heard several loud bangs deep within the boat. His engines screamed, revving wildly, and he realized that Zolner's men had strung a heavy cargo net across the channel. Its thick strands had fouled his churning propellers. Blades sheared and driveshafts snapped.

The Van Dorn boat was trapped in the middle of the river.

"Thompsons!" Dashwood called coolly. "Get down!"

The night exploded with red jets of fire and flying lead.

Their searchlight went black in a burst of hot glass.

Thank the Lord for armor plate, thought Isaac Bell. And bless Lynch & Harding. She carried two thousand gallons of explosively flammable gasoline, but the speedboat builders had snugged her fuel tanks under the sole, out of the range of bullets storming past.

Their Lewis guns were still useless. Behind the Thompson submachine guns strafing them from both sides of the river were homes with thin wooden walls. Bell yanked from its sheath a .30-06 bolt-action Springfield rifle he had stowed for such a contingency.

Tobin had one in his machine-gun nest.

Dashwood had one in his.

The Thompsons' muzzle fire made excellent targets, particularly as the two-handled submachine guns were designed to be clutched snug to the torso. Bell fired. A gunman tumbled into the river.

Tobin fired and missed.

Dashwood made up for it, firing twice and dropping two.

The three Van Dorns whirled in unison to shoot the submachine gunners on the opposite bank. Before they could trigger their weapons, the shooting stopped.

Isaac Bell saw why in an instant.

The black boat was coming back.

It stormed downriver, Lewis gun pumping bullets with a continuous rumble. The rapid fire starred Bell's windshield and clanged off the armor. By now, he knew what to expect of Marat Zolner. He stood up and aimed his rifle. A man on the bow of the speeding boat was about to throw a grenade. James Dashwood shot it out of his hand and it exploded behind the boat.

A second grenade sailed through the air. Isaac Bell and Ed Tobin fired together, and the grenade dropped into the river. *Black Bird* raced past the Van Dorn boat at fifty knots, thundering toward Biscayne Bay.

"Close," said Tobin.

"Not close enough," said Bell, watching the red glare of her exhaust disappear behind a bend in the river. He called to a fisherman, venturing out in his rowboat. "Shooting's over, friend. Would fifty bucks get us a lift ashore?"

"A hundred."

"It's yours."

On shore, Tobin went looking for a tugboat to tow them to a boatyard for repairs. Bell and Dashwood scoured the riverbank. The ambushers had taken their wounded with them. Bell retrieved a Thompson submachine gun they had dropped. Dashwood found a full box of German stick grenades.

"I don't suppose our 'Captain' friend is waiting at the dock for the rest of his reward."

Bell said, "Zolner is counterpunching. Question is, where's he going to hit us next?"

Asa Somers had been in love many times. He had fallen head over heels for Mae Marsh in *Intolerance* and returned to the movie house again and again. Mary Pickford was next, in *Little Lord Fauntleroy,* and then Mabel Normand. And of course he fell in love regularly with girls he saw on streetcars until they jumped off at their stops. But never until now with a real live girl.

And Fräulein Grandzau was a real live girl. She was beautiful beyond description, wore wonderful-smelling perfume, and had a way of looking him right in the face when she talked to him. Her eyes were blue, a slatey shade, like the ocean on a sunny afternoon. And she was very kind. She showed him how to use a knife and fork in the European style, and she would touch her beautiful lips just lightly with her finger to remind him to close his mouth when he chewed so he would look the part of an important man in the liquor traffic. She even took him shopping — Mr. Van Dorn was paying — because even an apprentice detective masquerading as a clerk had to look as if he belonged in Nassau in a panama hat and a white suit almost like Isaac Bell's.

They ate in wonderful hotels because that's where the bootleggers ate.

Liquor dealers had to be where they could run into people who might buy their consignments like detectives had to be where they were likeliest to hear the latest about a big tanker full of grain alcohol that for some reason hadn't shown up yet. And detectives investigating a Comintern agent's girlfriend had to dress like people she would talk to.

Earlier that evening, they had eaten dinner on Miss Fern Hawley's yacht, which was bigger than the old CG-9, with much better food. There was plenty of laughing and kidding around with Miss Hawley, who was really a looker, too.

Somers listened carefully to how Fräulein Grandzau used small talk like a wedge.

"When I was in New York, Fern, I kept hearing an expression. Why is the ladies' lavatory called the powder room?"

461

Fern laughed. "Girls didn't go to saloons before Prohibition. Now we go to speakeasies, so they had to add places for ladies to go and they called them powder rooms. To powder their noses? Speaking of which, excuse me, I'll be right back."

Fern was gone a long while and when she returned she ended the party all of a sudden, apologizing she had a headache. The yacht's tender dropped them at the dock. But instead of calling it a night, Fräulein Grandzau had decided they would stop for a drink in a rough bar on Bay Street where she said she hoped to meet a buyer.

So far, no buyer had appeared. Somers didn't mind. He could sit at a table across from her for the rest of his life and not mind. She drank — drinking a lot less than she pretended to, he noticed — and put him to the test to guess, in a low voice, what was the business of the other patrons. What did this one do? What did that one do? What about the guy passed out in the corner? Not that one. The guy with two guns, a revolver peeking out of his waistband and some other weapon bulging under his coat.

"Bodyguard?"

"Who is he guarding?"

"Maybe it's his night off," ventured Somers.

"Maybe."

"He's fast asleep."

"Are you sure?"

"He hasn't moved since we came in. And the bottle on his table is almost empty."

"I agree," she said. "He's sleeping. What do you suppose he carries in his shoulder holster? Automatic or revolver?"

Somers eyed the bulge. "Revolver."

"Automatic," she said. She looked around for another test.

Two big guys came in, bought a bottle at the bar, and sat down at a table facing theirs. Fräulein Grandzau's German accent, which ordinarily Somers could barely detect, got a little stronger. He heard a *v* in the word "want."

"Asa," she said very quietly. "I vant you to do exactly what I tell you. Do you understand me?"

"Yes, ma'am."

"Do you see where I am looking at the floor?"

"Yes, ma'am. Right next to your chair."

"I want you to stand up on that spot and lean over, close to me, as if you mean to kiss me."

"Yes, ma'am."

"Now!"

He stood up and leaned close. Her perfume was intoxicating. She reached a hand behind the back of his head, curled her fingers into his hair, and pulled him almost to her lips. "Asa?" she whispered.

"Yes, ma'am?" His mouth was dry, his heart hammering his ribs.

"Did the Coast Guard teach you how to cock an automatic pistol?"

36

Dazed by Pauline Grandzau's perfume and dumbfounded by her question, Asa Somers asked, "Why, ma'am?"

"Do you know how to cock that gun?" A whisper. Fierce.

"Yes."

"I want you to go to the drunk. Take the automatic from his shoulder holster and cock it and bring it to me."

"Wh— ?"

"My hand is not strong enough to pull the slide, and my own gun is not heavy enough to stop those two . . . Don't look at them!"

Somers glanced at the sleeping drunk. "When?"

"When the shooting starts."

"Wh— ?"

"Now!" She tipped the table on its side so the thick wooden top was facing the two big men like a shield. She kicked her leg high.

Her dress flew open. As Somers dived toward the drunk, he glimpsed her snow-white thigh encircled in black lace. He saw a tiny pistol in a half holster, which she drew and cocked in a blur of motion. The shooting started before he reached the drunk, two quick shots like snapped sticks and a sullen *Boom!* back from a heavier gun.

The gunshots sent everyone in the place diving for the floor and woke up the drunk, who slapped groggily at Somers's hand. She was right about it being a big automatic — a Colt Navy M1911. Somers jerked the slide, chambering a round. Then he grabbed the revolver before the drunk could and leaped back to Fräulein Grandzau, who by then had fired two more shots. One of the men was down on the floor with a pistol half fallen from his fingers. The other was charging them with a gun in one hand, a knife in the other, blood on his shirt, and murder in his eyes.

Fräulein Grandzau took the automatic in both her tiny hands. She fired once.

The .45 slug knocked the man's legs out from under him and he went down with a crash.

She turned to Asa, her eyes oddly detached, as if she had left the room earlier.

"Good job, Asa. Now ve *auf Wiedersehen*

466

before the police."

Everyone else in the bar had scattered or was still hugging the floor. She led him onto a veranda and down rickety stairs into an alley, back onto Bay Street, past the liquor row of shacks and stables converted to warehouses that were receiving crates and barrels even at night, and onto Frederick Street.

"Who were they?" asked Asa.

"Two Russians who wanted to kill us."

"How did you know they were Russians?"

"I know Russians."

Ahead, at last, was their Lucerne Hotel.

"Is it O.K. if I hang on to this?" Somers asked. He opened his coat where he had slipped the drunk's revolver into his waistband.

"Yes," she said. "You earned it. Go get some sleep. I have to cable Isaac."

"No you don't."

Asa Somers pointed toward the patio. Isaac Bell was standing in the door, a grim-faced specter in white. Detective Dashwood was across the lobby, one hand inside his coat, and Detective Ed Tobin, the tough Gang Squad guy with the lopsided face, was on the landing up the stairs with a hand inside his coat.

Fräulein Grandzau said, "Go to sleep,

Asa. We'll see you in the morning."

"We chartered a flying boat," said Isaac Bell, "thinking Zolner might attack here."

"They just tried."

Bell looked at her sharply. "Are you O.K.?"

Pauline shrugged. "Alive. Thanks to young Asa."

Bell asked what had happened. Pauline told him. When she was done, she was shaking and blinking back tears. Bell slung an arm around her shoulders and walked her into the bar.

"Let me buy you a legal drink."

The sky over Nassau that a lifetime at sea had told Captain Novicki could be trouble had not lied, although the blow it had forecast had taken longer to shape up than he expected. He had sailed his wooden schooner through the Windward Passage and into the Caribbean without a change in the weather. Then, quite suddenly — due east of Port-au-Prince, west of Guantánamo Bay — the glass started dropping faster than a man overboard. Silky cirrus clouds thickened. He had to decide whether to change course for Cuba and run for shelter in Guantánamo Bay or chance continuing to

Jamaica.

The wind rose.

He ordered his topsails in, and reefs in his foresail and mainsail, and soon reefed again. A few hours later, he had her running under bare poles, fore and main furled, with only a storm jib and a rag of staysail for steerage. Whatever was brewing was going to barrel straight through the Windward Passage. So much for Guantánamo. It was Kingston or bust.

The falling barometer, the rising wind veering north, and the steepening seas warned that South Florida and The Bahamas were in for a drubbing. But an aching pain in an old break in his left foot, courtesy of a sawbones who'd swigged Bushmills Irish Whiskey while he set it, threatened a more ominous possibility.

"If this doesn't grow into a hurricane," he told his mate, "my name's not Novicki."

The mate, a grizzled Jamaican even older than he was, thought it would veer northwest along the Cuban coast and into the Gulf of Mexico.

"She could," said Novicki. "But if she recurves northeast, look out New York, Long Island, and Rum Row."

Isaac Bell swam across Nassau Harbour.

Employing an Australian crawl, he lifted his face from the warm water periodically to navigate by the cream-colored funnel that jutted above the mahogany wheelhouse of the steam yacht *Maya*. Alongside the enormous white hull, he hauled himself onto a tender and climbed the gangway rigged to the side. He stopped at the teak rail on the main deck and called out, "Permission to come aboard?"

Stewards swarmed.

Fern Hawley herself appeared.

She gave his swim trunks a piercing look and his broad shoulders a warm smile.

"Mr. Bell. You have more scars than most men I meet."

"I tend to bump into doors and slip in the bath. May I come aboard?"

She snapped her fingers. A steward handed her a thick Turkish towel. She tossed it to Bell and led him to a suite of canvas chairs under a gaily striped awning. "To what do I owe the pleasure of this visit? Or were you just swimming by and stopped to catch your breath?"

Bell got right to it. "I'm curious about your friend Prince André."

"As a detective?" she asked. "Or a banker?"

"I beg your pardon?"

"I looked into your background. You're of the Boston Bells. Louisburg Square. American States Bank."

"My father is a banker. I am a detective. Have you seen Prince André recently?"

"Not since New York. I believe it was the night we met at Club Deluxe."

He decided to throw the dice on Pauline's and Marion's belief that Fern Hawley was disappointed in Zolner. If they were wrong, he would find himself back in the water.

"I could swear I saw you with him in Detroit."

She hesitated. Then her smirk faded and a faint smile softened her face. "I hope," she said, softly, "that I won't have to call my lawyers."

Bell couched his answer very carefully.

"I mispoke slightly. I did not mean *with* him, I meant *near* him."

He was bending the truth only slightly. For while he was reasonably sure he had seen her in the Pierce-Arrow limousine at Sam Rosenthal's send-off, he had not seen her in it when it sped away, firing at the police. Nor had he seen Zolner's gunmen get into it. But by mentioning lawyers, she had all but admitted she had been there.

Fern acknowledged as much, saying, "Now you're the one taking a chance."

471

"How so?"

"Shielding a criminal."

"I did not see you commit the crime. *Before* the crime, I saw a young woman whose sense of adventure may have caused her to fall in with the wrong crowd . . ."

"You're very generous, Mr. Bell. I am not that young."

"You met 'Prince André' in Paris?"

"At a victory parade," Fern said. "A Lancashire Regiment marching up the Champs-Élysées. I couldn't believe my eyes. They were midgets. None taller than five feet. Prince André told me why. They were poorly paid coal miners. They belonged to a race of men who hadn't had a decent meal in a hundred years. I realized — for the first time — the difference between rich and poor. Between capitalists and proletariat. Between owners and workers." She touched Bell's arm confidingly. "I'd never even called them workers before. I called them workmen. Or, as my father referred to them, 'hands.' Never people."

"Prince André sounds unusually broad-minded for a Russian aristocrat. If there were more like him, they wouldn't have had a revolution."

"He can be sensitive."

"Do you know what he's up to now?"

"Business interests, I gather."

"Did he ever ask you to invest in his interests?"

"No. Why do you ask?"

"It's a cliché of our times. The impoverished European aristocrat courts the wealthy American heiress."

"Not this heiress. All he asked was to take him to Storms."

"Storms?"

"Storms & Storms. One of my father's brokers." She laughed. "It was so funny. Stormy old Storms was quaking, terrified that André wanted to borrow money. He knew the cliché. When it was just the opposite."

"What was opposite?"

"André gave him oodles to invest."

Bell looked up at the sky. A scrim of cloud was spreading from the south. It had reddened the horizon at dawn. Now it seemed thicker . . . Cloud the issue, Joe Van Dorn taught apprentices. Throw them off with two more questions after you hit pay dirt.

"Would you have lunch with me at my hotel?"

"Let's stay on the boat," said Fern. "The chef has lobsters. Not our proper New England lobsters — they have no claws — but if we share a third, we won't miss claws."

"I wish we could," said Bell, "but I have to send a cable."

"About Prince André?"

"No. But there was something else I wanted to ask about him. I was wondering how a refugee survives suddenly losing . . . all this . . . comfort, I guess, that privileged people like you and I take for granted." He gestured at her yacht, the gleaming brightwork, the polished brass, the attentive stewards. "That Prince André *took* for granted. What do you suppose is his greatest strength?"

"He's an optimist."

Three Van Dorn detectives — Adler, Kliegman, and Marcum, dressed like auditors in vested suits, bowler hats, and wire-rimmed glasses, and carrying green eyeshades in their bulging briefcases — paused before entering the Wall Street brokerage house of Storms & Storms to observe the Morgan Building, where the cops had found Detective Warren's gold badge. Other than some shrapnel gouges in the marble wall, there was no sign of the unsolved bombing.

They addressed their old friend as if he were alive. "Hang on a moment longer, Harry, we're going to get some back."

■ ■ ■ ■

The blue-uniformed guard at the front door ushered them in with a respectful bow.

Senior partner Newtown Storms's secretary was less easily impressed.

"Whom do you gentlemen represent?"

"Adler, Kliegman & Marcum," said Adler.

"I'm not familiar with your firm."

"We are auditors. Our clients include the Enforcement Division of the Internal Revenue Service."

"What business do you have with Mr. Storms?"

"Income tax evasion."

"Mr. Storms has paid his taxes."

"A client of his has not."

That got them into Storms's office. The patrician stockbroker kept them standing in front of his rosewood desk while he fingered their business cards, which were so freshly printed, Adler could smell the ink.

"Let me set you straight, gentlemen. I am not a government official. It is not my job to collect income taxes."

Adler asked, "Is it your job to help your clients evade taxes?"

"Of course not. It is my job to help my clients *minimize* their taxes."

Kliegman spoke up. "Minimizing. A slippery slope to the depths of evasion."

"Particularly," Adler said, "when enormous transactions are made with cash."

"Cash is honest," Storms shot back. "Cash deters excessive spending. People think twice when they have to count it out on the barrelhead instead of blithely scribbling a check in the hopes their banker covers their overdraft. Cash backed by gold. That's my motto."

The three detectives stood silent as bronze statues.

Storms asked, "Are you inquiring about a particular client of mine? Or are you just fishing?"

"Prince André."

That got them invitations to sit down. Storms looked considerably less sure of himself. When his voice tube whistled, he jerked off the cap and growled, "Do not disturb me."

"How rich is he?" Adler asked bluntly.

"Prince André is a wealthy man. He was wealthy before the market took off like a Roman candle, and he is wealthier now. And I assure you that, come next April 15, he will pay his fair taxes on his earnings in the market."

"We have no doubt," said Adler.

"Then why are you here?"

"Cash, Mr. Storms. Our old reliable friend cash. Backed by gold."

The mild-mannered Adler suddenly had a steel gleam in his eye, and steel in his voice. "Cash can come from untaxed gains. Even illegal gains. Does he have private accounts or does he represent a corporation?"

Storms looked a little surprised by the question, and Adler feared he had misstepped. It turned out he hadn't. Storms said, "Both actually. He has some corporate entities that maintain some accounts. And he also trusts us with the privilege of managing his personal holdings."

"Numerous accounts of cash?"

Storms sprang to his feet. "I have spoken far too freely about private matters, don't you think?"

"We think that a government prosecutor might wonder whether that cash was invested with you to hide all trace of ill-gotten gains."

"I don't like your implication, sir."

Adler quoted from his dictionary: "Concealing the origins of money obtained illegally by passing it through a complex sequence of banking transfers or commercial transactions is a crime."

Kliegman quoted from his: "To transfer

funds of dubious or illegal origin to a foreign country, and then later recover them from what seem to be clean sources, is a crime."

Adler added, "To help a criminal hide cash is to become an accomplice in the crime of tax evasion."

Detective Marcum had yet to speak. He had a deep voice that rumbled like a chain-drive "Bull Dog" truck. "To gain by not paying taxes is tax evasion, whether the original gain is legal or illegal."

"No one has ever been prosecuted for that," Storms protested.

"Yet," said Marcum.

"Would you like to be the first?"

Newtown Storms said, staunchly, "An American citizen would be violating his Fifth Amendment rights against self-incrimination if he admitted to illegal gains on his tax return."

"Would you like to spend years in appeal, waiting for the Supreme Court to eventually rule on that dubious interpretation of our constitution?"

"Mr. Storms, we're not asking for your money. We are asking you to betray a crook."

" 'Crook' is not a word that applies to the gentlemen classes my firm serves."

"What if we told you he was a Bolshevik?"

Storms laughed. "Next, you'll tell me President Harding wants America to join the League of Nations. And Marcus Garvey is signing on with the Ku Klux Klan."

"What if it were true that Prince André is a Bolshevik?"

"How can he be a Bolshevik? The revolutionaries kicked him out of his country and seized his estates."

"What if Prince André is a Bolshevik?"

"If it were true, Prince André would be a traitor to his class, and I would tell you everything you want to know."

The wind was rising in Nassau, shivering flags and slapping halyards, when Isaac Bell returned to the steam yacht *Maya*. Fern Hawley received him in the main salon, which had been designed in the old Art Nouveau mode by the Tiffany Company. It was a breathtaking sight, thought Bell, that would force anyone questioning the pleasures of wealth to change his tune.

"Why, Mr. Bell, where are your swim trunks?"

"I hired a launch. There's a mean chop on the harbor. Besides, it's getting dark and I'm told sharks dine at night."

"I'd have sent you a tender," said Fern. "Would you like a drink?"

Bell said that he thought a drink would be a wonderful idea.

"Daiquiris or Scotch?"

"Scotch."

"We're in luck. I have the real McCoy. Haig & Haig."

They touched glasses. She said, "I'm glad to see you again. Lunch was over too soon."

"I have not been one hundred percent honest with you," Bell replied.

Fern gave him a big smile. "Is it too much to hope that you lied when you told me you were always faithful to your wife?"

"I lied when I said I was not sending a cable about Prince André."

"That much I figured out on my own. What's up, Mr. Bell . . . I should call you Isaac, for gosh sake. I am going to call you Isaac. What's up, Isaac?"

"Prince André is a traitor."

Fern Hawley looked mystified. "A traitor to what? Russia? Russia is no more. Not his Russia."

"He is a traitor to your cause."

"I don't understand."

"Fern, let's stop kidding each other. Prince André's name is Marat Zolner."

"I know him as Prince André."

"Marat Zolner is a bootlegger."

"So are half the enterprising businessmen

480

in America."

"Bootlegging is a masquerade. Marat Zolner is a Comintern agent conspiring against America."

"He can't be a traitor to America. He's not American — or are you suggesting that I am the traitor? Traitoress?"

Isaac Bell did not smile back at her.

"Did Marat Zolner set the Wall Street bomb?"

"No."

"So you *do* know Prince André as Marat Zolner."

Fern answered tartly. "Spare me the battle of wits, Isaac. It's obvious you know a lot."

Bell's reply was a cold, "How do you know he didn't set that bomb?"

"Because Yuri did."

"Who is Yuri?"

"Yuri Antipov. A Comintern agent sent by Moscow to ride herd on Marat. Marat did not want to bomb Wall Street. So Yuri did it."

"Did you know he was going to explode a bomb on a crowded street?"

"*No!* They didn't tell me such things. I only learned afterward."

"Where is Yuri?"

"He died in the explosion."

"Along with forty innocents."

481

She hung her head. "They don't think the way we do. They've experienced terrible things we haven't."

"Those forty have."

"Moscow made Yuri a 'hero of the revolution.' Not Marat. He didn't do it."

"Why do you say Zolner didn't do it? Just because he wasn't killed in the blast?"

"Marat would never make such a mistake. He's too meticulous. Yuri was impetuous. He would blunder ahead. He couldn't help himself."

Bell looked at her and she looked away. He said, "Could Zolner have made a 'mistake,' deliberately?"

"Why?"

"To get rid of his watchdog."

"No." She shook her head. "No. Absolutely not."

"You say no, but you're thinking that it is possible that he killed Yuri, aren't you?"

She was silent a long moment, then said in a bleak and empty voice. "Yuri was my friend."

"He was a murderer," said Isaac Bell. "Forty times over."

"I didn't know he was going to do it."

Bell made no effort to hide his disgust. "Whether you are a traitor, or a foolish young woman who — as I said *generously,* earlier — fell in with the 'wrong crowd,' will depend on your next move."

"Betray him?"

"I will make it easy for you."

"How?"

"I just told you. He's already betrayed you. And your workers' cause."

"How?"

"You introduced him to Newtown Storms. Storms invests the enormous sums of cash that Marat Zolner earns bootlegging. Do you deny that he uses the money Storms makes in the stock market to finance his Comintern attack on our country?"

Fern Hawley returned Bell's wintery gaze in silence.

"I am asking you privately," said Bell. He had thought on this all afternoon. He had much bigger fish to fry than one confused spoiled brat. "Confidentially, Fern. Between you and me. All alone on your yacht in the middle of a harbor of a remote British colony."

"Why are you protecting me?" she asked in a small voice.

"Two reasons. One, I truly do believe that you fell in with the wrong crowd."

"What makes you believe that? You don't know me."

"A character reference from a colleague

whose judgment I trust."

"Who?"

"Pauline."

"She's yours?"

"She's Van Dorn's."

Fern covered her face. "Oh, do I feel like a fool."

"You aren't the first. Pauline is the sharpest detective you will ever meet. She sees a possibility of something worthwhile in you, and what Pauline sees is good enough for me."

"What is the second reason?"

"The second reason is far more important. You can give me Marat Zolner. Which is why I ask you about the Stormses' investments financing the Comintern attack."

Fern smirked the smirk that said she knew more than Bell did. "Actually, most of it comes straight from the bootlegging. Storms hasn't made him as much as he hoped."

"Oh yes he has," said Bell. "Storms is good at what he does, and the market has been kind."

"That's not what Marat said."

"That's because Marat siphons off most of his stock earnings. He has secret, personal accounts with Storms & Storms. He stashed money in London and Paris and Berlin and Switzerland. He has made himself a very wealthy Bolshevik."

Fern Hawley flushed. She took a deep breath. "Do you remember I told you he's an optimist? That's the least of it. He is a brilliant, natural-born liar. That dirty son of a —"

"I was hoping you would say that," said Isaac Bell.

37

With his muted engines turning just enough revolutions to make headway through the deepening chop, Marat Zolner kept *Maya* between him and the town as he eased *Black Bird* alongside the big yacht in the dead of the night. He tossed a canvas-wrapped grappling hook over the teak rail, pulled himself up, and went to Fern's cabin.

She was rubbing her beautiful face with a night cream and saw him in the mirror.

"Look what the cat dragged in."

"Sadly, the cat has only a moment. What did you tell Isaac Bell?"

"No more than I had to to make him go away."

"What did he ask?"

"He asked about the tanker. He knew the Comintern bought it. I confirmed that to keep him from asking more questions."

"Did you tell him where it is?"

"No. That was the point of answering his

previous question."

"You're good at this."

"I was taught by a master . . . What are you doing here, Marat?"

Zolner gave her a strange smile. For as long as she had known him, she could rarely tell what he was really thinking. He looked sad, but she couldn't swear to it, even when he asked, "Is the bank open tonight?"

Fern Hawley hoped that she was not a fool to wish that somehow what Isaac Bell had told her was not true. She opened her arms, saying, "All night."

It turned out to be a short night, and, afterward, he looked even sadder, she thought.

"What is it?"

"Isaac Bell has beaten me."

"How?"

"Detroit's exploded. They're killing each other like rats in a sewer. And I can't control New York without being on top of it. And now, thanks to Isaac Bell, I can't get money from Storms. But I will tell you this: Isaac Bell will wish he had died when I go home a hero."

"Russia?"

"You will come with me."

"Do you really want me, Marat?"

"Of course I want you. Now I need your help. Bell has put out a general alarm for my arrest."

"How can he do that?"

"The Van Dorns have the ear of the Department of Justice and every police chief on the East Coast. I can't take a train. I can't land in a flying boat. I can't board a liner."

"What will you do?"

"I'm going to New York."

"You just said there's nothing for you in New York."

"Comrades will hide me on a ship."

"How will you get there?"

"Black Bird."

"It's over a thousand miles."

"Twelve hundred."

"But you could find a ship in Havana. Or San Juan. Or Port-au-Prince."

"I have business to finish in New York."

"What business?"

"You don't need to know."

"Marat, how can I trust you if you won't trust me?"

"It's something Yuri and I were doing."

"Shall I meet you there?"

"No."

"Why?"

"It is something you would not understand. Meet me in Rotterdam. We'll go home heroes."

38

At breakfast in the Hotel Lucerne, nervous guests were discussing the storm. Gale warnings were flying from the stone fort that overlooked the harbor, and the morning newspaper quoted radio transmissions from Havana: Hurricane winds were sweeping Cuba, fashionable resorts were flooded.

"Brace yourself, Isaac," Pauline whispered. "She's back."

Fern Hawley rushed in, wild-eyed and windblown. She looked like she had not slept.

A brisk nod from Bell caused Ed Tobin and Asa Somers to excuse themselves from the table. Fern sat across from him and Pauline. "Marat came to me last night."

"Where is he?"

"He's on his way to Russia. He wants me to come with him."

"Where is he now?"

"He left in the night. For New York. To

meet a ship that will smuggle him back to Europe."

"He'll never make it. I've got trains and ports covered."

"He's going on *Black Bird.*"

"By motorboat? It's twelve hundred miles."

"That's what I said. It doesn't make sense. He could escape faster and more easily by running to Havana, or Port-au-Prince, or San Juan. Even Bermuda's closer than New York. But he told me he's finishing something he started with Yuri. But I think it's something else. He could have a lot of cash hidden."

"Then to Russia?" asked Pauline.

"That's what he said. Through Rotterdam. He said that you'd be sorry, Isaac, when he went home a hero."

"A hero of the revolution?" said Bell.

"He said you'll wish you were dead."

Pauline asked, "Why are you telling us this now?"

"Because I think he's up to something terrible."

Bell said, "You told me earlier that you didn't know where the alcohol tanker is. Do you?"

"Yes. It's anchored off Eleuthera. We stopped there on the way down. My captain will have the exact position in his log."

"Why didn't you tell me?"

"I gave you everything, Isaac. I wanted to keep something for myself."

Before Bell could answer, he felt Pauline's knee firmly against his, warning *Don't speak, let Fern do it.* And, indeed, Fern did speak. "I thought he kept the tanker at Eleuthera to do a stretching operation. But he could stretch in Nassau. Or up on Rum Row. So I wondered, was he hiding it for some reason?" She shrugged. "Maybe he was waiting for the price to rise."

Bell exchanged glances with Pauline. Why sail a shipload of pure alcohol all the way from Bremerhaven, then abandon it on a remote island? Pauline ventured, "Marat could sail it home to Russia. Or trade the cargo for another ship."

"He kept saying he's got business in New York."

"Or perhaps sail it to Rum Row and 'taxi' himself to the ship he's leaving on."

"Your guess is as good as mine," said Fern. "Except he kept saying he has business in New York."

James Dashwood walked in. He was pale and his hands were shaking. Bell had heard him coughing all night.

"Dash," said Bell. "Find a sawbones and

492

hunker down here."

"Where are you going?"

"That tanker makes me nervous. Pauline, you and I and Ed and Asa are going to Eleuthera." He waved for Tobin to come back. "How are we on gas, Ed?"

"Full tanks."

"Can we handle this weather?"

"Seventy feet long, four props, and eighteen hundred horsepower? I should think so."

"Better rig the cockpit tarpaulin and the motor shrouds."

"Already done."

"We'll need food and water in case we have to hole up for a few days."

Fern said, "There's a run on the shops. Come out to my yacht. I'll give you food and water."

"Women," Ed Tobin growled, helping Pauline with a heavy canvas bag. "Why can't they travel light?"

"Because we pack things men forget."

"Hope you don't get seasick. It's going to be a mess out there."

"I've never been seasick on the *Aquitania.*"

They headed across the windswept harbor on one engine.

Fern's captain had steam up. *Maya's*

493

decks were cleared, the awnings stowed. Stewards and deckhands formed a human chain to pass food and water out their pilot door, across their tender, and into the Van Dorn cruiser rafted alongside.

Bell went up to the mahogany wheelhouse while Tobin and Asa lashed canvas over two of the idle engines to keep spray out of the straight pipes. Fern's captain was an affable Connecticut Yankee. He showed Bell on his chart where he had seen the *Sandra T. Congdon* four days ago. Tiny Harbour Island was on the windward side of Eleuthera, the big island along the east side of Grand Bahama Bank.

"The tanker's heavily laden, drawing too much to enter the lagoon. She anchored on the windward side, inside the Harbour Island reef."

"Will she move for the storm?"

"She'll put to sea if it swings east." The captain glanced up at Fort Fincastle, where triangular red pennants flew. "But still only a gale warning. I just heard from a captain on the radiotelegraph that the storm is veering west across Cuba, while you'll be heading east." He nodded approvingly at *Marion*'s long, sleek hull. "It'll be rough, but it's only sixty miles, and your boat's got a seakindly bow and plenty of power. If the storm changes course, you'll have to hole up in Dunmore Town or Governor's Harbour. Of course, the truly prudent thing would be to ride it out right here in Nassau."

"Where are you going, Captain?"

"Bermuda."

Fern intercepted Bell as he was about to go down the gangway.

"Can I come with you?"

"Sorry. Van Dorn policy: We don't bring friends to gunfights."

Fern smiled. "Does that mean I'm a friend?"

"Only as long as you behave yourself."

"Isaac, what am I going to do? You've destroyed everything I believed in. Not you. He. I suspected, but you gave me proof, and it is terrible."

Bell was anxious to clear the harbor. With any luck, he would trap Zolner on his tanker in two or three hours. "If you want to believe in something, try this: Prohibition is killing the country. Why don't you join up with the society women trying to repeal it? Joe Van Dorn's wife is leading them."

"I have an aunt who's formed a committee. But I'm not ready to hang out with a bunch of frumpy old ladies."

Tobin started another engine. Bell raised

his voice to be heard.

"If you were to 'hang out' with Dorothy Van Dorn, you would have to get used to men looking over your shoulder to catch a glimpse of her. She's only a few years older than you are, stylish as Paris, and a dazzling beauty."

"Sounds like you've fallen for her, Isaac."

"Dorothy could make a good friend. I'll introduce you."

"I'll give you a piece of information in return." She stepped close to whisper in his ear. "Your 'colleague' is in love with you. Pauline never mentioned your name when we talked, of course, but now it's clear."

"I'm working on that," said Bell.

"Ready, Mr. Bell?" called Tobin.

"One second . . . Fern, you told me that Zolner did not want to bomb Wall Street. But you also told me that you didn't know about the plan in time to stop it."

"I didn't. Marat told me afterward, after Yuri died."

"Why didn't he want to bomb Wall Street?"

"He had bigger plans. Bombs would distract from the bootlegging plan."

"Good luck, Fern. Safe passage to Bermuda." Bell shook her hand, dodged her kiss, and ran down the gangway.

"Cast off."

The Van Dorn express cruiser *Marion* was ten miles up the Northeast Providence Channel, with Nassau and New Providence Island twenty minutes in her wake, when James Dashwood saw the gale-warning flag lowered from Fort Fincastle. A red flag with a black square in its center took its place.

Dashwood hurried to the cable office to warn Isaac Bell that a hurricane was approaching The Bahamas. But, as he had feared, remote Harbour Island had neither cable nor radiotelegraph. His friends might as well have been on the far side of the moon.

39

"Boss man, he go to Rum Row."

The Harbour Islanders who had been rolling gasoline barrels off a sailboat onto the Dunmore Town dock had stopped work to catch *Marion*'s mooring lines when the big cruiser rumbled into the harbor.

The tiny town occupied a low, narrow spit of land between the lagoon and ocean. Offshore, Atlantic combers pounded the fringing reef. But the sheltered waters inside the reef, where Bell had hoped to see the tanker looming above the shingled cottages, held not a single ship.

Marat Zolner had chosen well. The tiny shipbuilding harbor was both remote and cut off from the world. A four-masted schooner was under construction on shipyard ways, and the British Union Jack flew above a modest wood-frame government building, next to which ground had been broken to build another. But there was no radio tower, which made Dunmore Town not only remote but as cut off from the world as it had been in pirate times.

The *Sandra T. Congdon* had weighed anchor two days earlier, the islanders said.

Bell looked at Tobin and shook his head. "Making twelve knots, he's halfway to New York."

The sky was heavily clouded. They'd left the rain behind, and the forecast of the hurricane moving west over Cuba seemed to hold. But, Ed Tobin grumbled, wind gusts were swinging south of east, and the Dunmore Town residents had pulled small boats out of the water.

"Did you see a big black speedboat about the size of this one?"

"No, mon."

"The tanker could have hoisted it on deck," said Tobin.

"No, he'd have to catch up at sea," said Bell, "if the tanker left two days ago."

"Black boat last week," an islander ventured.

Made sense, thought Bell. Even in wind and roiled seas, *Marion* had covered the sixty miles from Nassau in less than three hours. Zolner would have found this an ideal place to hide *Black Bird,* too. He could have zipped in and out with the boat.

He shook his head again. "Last time we almost caught the black boat, Zolner blew up his boathouse."

"Maybe we're lucky he moved the ship. If he left it, he would blow it up like his boathouse."

"Going home a hero of the revolution," said Pauline.

"But first finish Yuri's job? What job?"

Bell smelled tobacco burning. The dock-workers had hunkered down behind the gasoline barrels to share a smoke.

"Douse that cigarette! You'll blow my boat to kingdom come!"

The smoker took a last drag, passed it to his friend, who inhaled another. A third man grabbed a quick puff and flicked the butt in the water.

The man Bell was talking to chuckled. "Just like de boss man. Every day he always say, 'No smoke by ship. Big explosion.'"

Isaac Bell plunged his hand in his pocket and pulled out his bankroll. Twelve tons of pure alcohol would make a very big explosion. "I want that gasoline."

Tobin said, "We've got plenty in the tanks, Mr. Bell. It'll only weigh us down."

"We'll burn it soon enough. It's twelve hundred miles to New York."

■ ■ ■ ■

They had stowed the last barrel they could fit, and Bell had tipped the dockworkers lavishly, when a church bell began to toll. The islanders' smiles faded at the urgent clamor. Their eyes shot to the government building. The Union Jack was descending the flagpole. A red flag with yellow stripes jumped up in its place.

"What's that?" asked Bell.

"Red flag with black square say hurricane."

"I know that. What do those yellow stripes mean?"

"Hurricane come straight here."

Marion thundered through South Bar Passage. The tide was strong, the ocean swell steep and destructive in the narrow cut and breaking on the sandbar. Bell aimed at what looked deepest and drove her through in a welter of foam and headed for the open sea.

Beyond the reef, the seas were big but orderly. He set a course north and was glad to see that *Marion* could maintain forty knots without straining. His crew, he could see, were apprehensive, and he tried to raise their spirits.

"Between a cashiered Coastie, a Staten Island pirate, and a yachtsman, we ought to be able to find Cape Hatteras Light. From there, it'll be an easy run up the coast."

"How far is Cape Hatteras?" asked Pauline.

Bell shrugged. "Less than eight hundred miles." He showed her the chart. "We'll steer a course just west of north."

Pauline's brow furrowed as she studied the chart in the murky light that penetrated the windshield and the isinglass side curtains. "It appears we have to get around Abaco, first."

"We should see Hope Town Light in a couple of hours," said Bell.

"If we can make forty knots in these seas, we'll take a full day and night to Cape Hatteras."

"We're burning a lot of gas at forty," said Tobin.

"There's a hurricane chasing behind," said Bell. "I want room between it and us."

Spray drummed on the cockpit tarp. The seas continued to mount and the wind rose. Every few minutes, the boat plowed into a wave markedly bigger than the rest and slowed dramatically.

Bell ordered a watch schedule in which each would steer for two hours, the limit before they lost focus and concentration. Asa brewed coffee in the galley tucked under the foredeck, then helped Pauline steer when it was her turn. Tobin passed around sandwiches of foie gras that Fern's chef had contributed. In the dark, the compass cast a red glow on faces growing weary of the constant motion and the ceaseless thunder of the Libertys.

Bell caught catnaps, sitting near the helm, but only when Tobin was steering.

He awakened with cold water dripping on his face. The tarpaulin was soaked and it was beginning to leak. He rescued the chart, which was getting wet. The boat was laboring. Reluctantly, Bell cut their speed to thirty-five knots — still a phenomenal pace for any vessel in any seas — and reduced it again in a few hours to thirty knots as the waves grew taller and chaotic.

He decided that, at that rate, they could stop the forward Liberty to conserve it. Asa wrestled on canvas as soon as the pipes cooled. Soon after, they stopped the sternmost motor, as the boat would make her speed on two having burned off the weight of the extra gasoline.

The wind, which had blown from the south and then gradually east, backed suddenly north. Bell pictured the storm whirling, its counterclockwise winds moving sharply to the east as if it had crossed their wake and was heading toward Bermuda.

This was good news if it was traveling away from them rather than overtaking them but bad news if the powerful north wind set up counter- and crosscurrents. Worse, it suggested a storm that was growing in diameter, flinging ever-more-powerful winds hundreds of miles from its eye.

"Getting bad," Tobin said quietly when they exchanged tricks at the wheel.

"She's a big boat," said Bell.

Ed's lopsided, scarred face formed a tired grin. "I never met a captain who didn't love his vessel."

They were twenty-three hours beyond The Bahamas when the western horizon, which looked darker than a coal mine, began to cast an intermittent glow. Bell steered toward it and in a few miles it appeared to be the pulsing beam of a distant lighthouse.

"Cape Hatteras?"

Pauline pored over the chart, careful not to tear the wet paper.

"How is it blinking?" she asked.

Bell timed the flashes. "Fifteen seconds."

"Cape Hatteras flashes every seven and a half seconds."

"What flashes fifteen?"

"Cape May, New Jersey?"

"We could not have gotten that far north already."

"To the south of Hatteras is Cape Lookout. Fifteen seconds."

"Ed, check the sailing directions. How bright is that light?"

"In these clouds? Less than twelve."

"Too close."

Bell powered away from the coast and steered east of north. Three hours later, they spotted the seven-and-a-half-second flash of Cape Hatteras.

"I read that Hatteras is called the Graveyard of the Atlantic," said Asa Somers. "Ships run aground by the thousands."

Pauline said, "Thank you for that information."

One of the Liberty motors coughed and quit.

Moments later, the second fell silent.

40

The boat lost way in an instant and turned her flank to the seas, which rolled her mercilessly.

Tobin and Somers ripped the shrouds off the reserve motors, and Isaac Bell pulled his chokes and hit the starters. One ground with the anemic wheeze of a weak battery. The other churned its motor over and over, but it wouldn't fire.

The stern drifted around into the wind. A gust filled the cockpit tarp, lifted it like a kite, and blew it off. Rain and spray drenched the cockpit. Bell tried the starter again, hoping there was enough juice left in the battery. The motor fired, coughed, died, and caught again, cylinder by cylinder, until it was hitting on all twelve. As the propeller dug in and the cruiser got under way again, he steered back on their northerly course. Pauline and Somers dragged the tarp back over the cockpit and tied it down. Tobin jumped electricity to the dead battery with Mueller clips. Bell coaxed a second engine to life.

He was concerned that the heavy spray would drown them, so he engaged the mufflers, shunting the exhaust into underwater ports and effectively sealing the manifolds from the vertical pipes. But protection was bought at the cost of power, and their speed dropped. With the engines muted, they could hear the full roar of wind and tumbling seas, which grew louder as the day wore on.

Pauline took the helm, with Asa watching over her. Bell and Tobin went to work on the engines that had quit. Water in the gas seemed to be the cause. Spray could have entered as they pumped from the barrels purchased at Harbour Island. Or one of the barrels could have been contaminated. They jettisoned the contents of the day tank that fed those engines and pumped in fresh gas from their main tanks.

Both engines started. They shut them down again and shrouded their pipes to keep them in reserve. Bell feared they'd be needed soon enough. The two engines currently pushing the boat were exhausting blue smoke, and their valves were clattering like a bowling alley. They clattered through the night, and when one of the engines began to sound as if it were approaching the end, Bell switched them both off after starting the reserves.

Bell was on watch hours past dawn the next morning, driving through heavy squalls, with Pauline huddled against him fast asleep and Tobin and Asa sleeping under the foredeck, when he heard a rumble like thunder. A flash to his left could be the lightning that caused it. Fifteen seconds later, it flashed again, and then again in another fifteen, and he saw a white flashing pinprick of light.

Cape May Light could be seen up to twenty-four nautical miles. But not in these conditions. To see the light from the low boat through the wind-whipped rain, they had to be almost on top of it. What he had thought was thunder might be surf pounding land. Then he saw enormous waves breaking on a sandbar. He could feel them gathering behind him, lifting the boat to drive them onto the beach. He swung the wheel, hit his throttles, and fled the shore.

Fighting to maintain twenty knots, he ran east for an hour, then swung north again. Two hours passed. Tobin was at the helm. Bell saw a steady white light that did not blink.

"Absecon Light," Pauline read.

"Atlantic City," said Tobin. "Getting close, Mr. Bell. Barnegat next."

Asa Somers spotted the red-and-white painted Barnegat Lighthouse itself, and again the cruiser peeled away from the shore. Two hours later, limping on one engine, holding the other that was still running in reserve, they saw the squalls race away and suddenly found themselves in sunlight on a patch of riled blue sea completely surrounded by heavy banks of cloud.

"What is going on?" asked Tobin, turning on his heel. "It's like a miniature eye of a miniature hurricane."

"Any idea where we are?" asked Bell.

"None."

Pauline dragged her heavy canvas bag out of the foredeck cubby and handed it to Tobin.

"What's this?"

"What you forgot to pack. A sextant and a *Nautical Almanac.* It's noon. I recall Isaac knows how to use it. He can shoot the sun and tell us where we are."

Bell said, "You drive, Ed. Keep her as steady as you can. On the jump. This won't last."

Indeed, the cloud banks were closing quickly around the strange clear patch. Bell swung the sextant to the sky and lowered the mirrored image of the sun to the horizon. From the scale, he called the angle to Pauline. She noted the time and ran her finger down the columns pertaining to the Greenwich mean angle. Asa held the chart.

"Approximately twenty miles from New York," said Pauline. "Steer three hundred ten degrees to Ambrose Light."

"Who taught you how to do that?" Tobin asked her.

"The captain of the *Aquitania.*"

Clouds and mist closed in abruptly. The visibility dropped to a quarter mile, then increased, then dropped again as squalls blew through fitfully. With twelve miles to go, they spotted a dismasted schooner. The storm-battered ship was tossing at anchor while its crew cut away ruined rigging. A bedsheet flapped from its bowsprit. An advertisement was painted on it in red:

CC

$55 CASE

"Rum Row," said Isaac Bell.

They sped past island schooners and rusty steamers battened down for the storm.

"Look at that," said Asa. "There's some lunatic driving a taxi."

"The price of booze goes up in bad weather," Tobin explained. "They'll get rich if they don't drown."

A fresh squall hit, riding a cold wind, and they were suddenly alone again on a seemingly empty sea. The squalls passed, and they could see for two or three miles that they were still alone except for a single big ship on a course similar to theirs, angling toward New York. They overtook it quickly.

"That's her," said Pauline.

"Are you sure?"

"Of course I'm sure. I saw her in Bremerhaven."

41

The tanker *Sandra T. Congdon* had a tall funnel in back, a sturdy white wheelhouse forward of center, and a straight bow.

"What's that on the bow?"

"A three-inch gun," said Pauline. "Left over from the war."

Bell studied it in the binoculars. "Not that left over. They've got a heap of ammunition all ready to shoot. Pity the Harbor Squad that runs into them. Ed, keep us behind their house."

Tobin altered course, as they caught up with the tanker, so that its wheelhouse blocked the deck gun's line of fire.

"What are those guys on top doing?" asked Asa.

Bell focused his glasses on a wood-and-canvas flying bridge constructed on top of the wheelhouse.

"Unlimbering a Lewis gun," he said. "Get your heads down."

Machine-gun bullets screeched overhead and frothed the water. Tobin cut in the reserve engine and hit his throttles. A minute later, they were a half mile behind the tanker, beyond effective range of its machine gun.

Isaac Bell broke into an icy smile.

"Look who's here . . . I'll take the helm, Ed."

Black Bird slid out from behind the tanker and sped at them, hurling spray.

Bell fired orders. "Pauline, down! Asa, foredeck gun! Tobin, stern!"

The two boats raced at each other at a combined velocity of one hundred miles an hour. Ed Tobin fired a long burst from the forward Lewis gun. *Black Bird* shot back. But a black boat proved a much better target than one painted as gray as rain.

Geysers of bullet-pocked water splashed around *Marion.*

Lead banged into *Black Bird*'s armor and crazed her windshield. Her gunner was blown from his weapon and pinwheeled backwards into the sea.

Another leaped to his place.

Less than fifty yards separated the speeding boats, and the new gunner could not have missed even if the Van Dorn boat had been invisible. Bell felt the slugs rattling off the armor plate. The man fired again. Bullets cut the air inches above his head. The boats hurtled past each other, missing by inches.

Asa Somers triggered the stern Lewis, raking *Black Bird*'s cockpit. All three men in it fell to the sole. Only one regained his feet: Marat Zolner.

Bell saw him twirl his helm and ram his throttles in a single swift motion. But nothing happened. The black boat did not answer her helm. Nor did she speed away, but fell back in the seas, barely drifting ahead.

"Good shooting, Asa!"

The young apprentice had blasted Zolner's controls to pieces.

Zolner jumped from the cockpit to the Lewis gun, ripped off the ammunition drum, and banged a full one into place. He tracked the Van Dorn boat, which was circling for the kill, and fired a burst.

Isaac Bell saw what appeared to be tracer bullets, trailing blue smoke. But when Zolner got the range, which he did on his third burst, raking *Marion* just ahead of the engines, smoke curled from the bullet holes. Marat Zolner was firing World War balloon-busting incendiary ammunition. Each phosphorus bullet laced the Van Dorn hull with flame, and the boat was suddenly on fire.

Pauline Grandzau dived for the nearest extinguisher, ripped it from its clamp, pumped up pressure, and sprayed pyrene on the flames. She sprayed until the brass container was empty and scrambled across the deck for another.

"Help her, Asa!" Bell shouted. "Ed, put out the fire! I'll get Zolner."

Bell stood up so he could see over the bullet-scarred windshield.

He steered into a tight turn that careened the boat half on her side. When he was facing *Black Bird,* he shoved his throttles wide open. Blue smoke streaked. Zolner had reloaded with incendiaries.

Bell zigzagged, rapid turns hard left, hard right. He cut the distance from two hundred yards to one hundred, to fifty. Marat Zolner stopped firing, his face a startled mask of disbelief at the sight of the burning cruiser flying at him.

"Ramming!" Bell warned his people. "Hold tight!"

Bell aimed for the softest target just ahead of the engines. The Van Dorn boat struck *Black Bird* dead center and cut the Comintern boat in half. Bell saw Zolner thrown from the Lewis gun into the water. Then he was past, drawing back his throttles.

He saw Marat Zolner swimming hard toward the tanker.

"*Ed! Asa!* Pick him up, right side."

Marion swooped alongside Zolner.

Tobin leaned over to grab him.

"Look out, Ed!"

Bell saw Zolner turn over onto his back to deliver a vicious thrust with a short dagger. The blade plunged into Tobin's forearm. Blood fountained. The detective swung his fist and pitched forward and started to slide over the gunnel. Asa Somers grabbed him, hauled him back into the boat, and wrapped his belt around Tobin's arm.

A Lewis gun opened up with a rapid *Boom! Boom! Boom!* Ricochets shrieked, splinters flew. The *Sandra T. Congdon* was raking them with machine-gun fire from the flying bridge.

Bell poured on the gas and peeled away. Zolner kept swimming toward the tanker. Bell ventured closer, but the gunner laid down deadly fire from the vantage of his high mount. Another rain squall tore between them. Bell drove into it, using it as cover to get closer. But when the rain lifted, the machine gun started churning bullets, even as a lifeboat approached Zolner. Any hope Bell had that the man was injured was dashed when the Comintern agent scrambled aboard like a monkey.

The rain fell hard. The tanker disappeared. Thick mist gathered.

"We'll never him see in this," gasped Tobin as Somers fought to stop the bleeding. "Where's he going?"

"Where he's been going all along," said Isaac Bell. "Wall Street."

Yuri Antipov had bombed a symbol of capitalism. Marat Zolner would burn its heart out with an alcohol-fueled fireball. And the Comintern would welcome the hero who incinerated New York's Financial District the length of Wall Street from the East River to Trinity Church.

Bell stepped on the starter. The third engine fired back to life.

The battered *Marion* roared for New York Harbor at fifty knots.

She carried them between the arms of Sandy Hook and Rockaway Beach and up the Lower Bay in ten minutes, through the Narrows and across the Upper Bay in another seven. The third motor died at the Battery. The second in the East River under the Brooklyn Bridge.

Peering through a scrim of sheet rain, Bell spotted the tall hangars of the Loening factory and, just past it, the 31st Street Air Service Terminal. His last engine coughed, running out of gas. Fifty yards from the dock, it died. In the sudden silence, Bell disengaged the propeller to reduce drag, and she drifted close enough for Asa to loop a line around a bollard.

Bell pulled the Thompson submachine gun from a locker. "Pauline, get Ed to Bellevue. Asa, grab that box."

"Where'd you get hand grenades?"

"Miami River. Come on!"

They ran to the Loening factory on the river's edge. The mechanics had floated the Flying Yachts into the hangars, out of the wind. Bell climbed onto his and threw off the lines. "On the jump, boys. Open those doors and start my engine."

"You can't take off in this weather!" the foreman shouted.

"My mother died when I was a boy. I've gotten by without one since. *Start my engine!*"

42

Bell battled high waves taking off from the East River and ferocious gusts in the air as his flying boat climbed toward the Williamsburg Bridge. He steered between its towers, whose tops were lost in cloud, and aimed for the lowest dip in its suspension cables. He cleared them by inches. The horizon vanished in the rain.

He kept track of the horizon with a new Sperry instrument that combined a turn indicator and an inclinometer. But it was no help avoiding the Manhattan and Brooklyn bridges, much less the skyscrapers of Wall Street, and he flew blind, relying on his compass, Tank watch, and memory.

Asa Somers couldn't stop grinning. He had never been in an airplane before.

When the Flying Yacht finally broke from the murk that enshrouded the port, Bell saw that he had already flown past the Narrows. The Lower Bay spread below him, dotted with ships. He ignored the vessels he saw at anchor. They were riding out the storm, huddled along the Brooklyn, Staten Island, and Jersey shores. Marat Zolner's tanker would be moving, steaming up the Ambrose Channel on a relentless course toward Manhattan Island.

Bell flew the length of the channel. It was empty of ships. Had he guessed wrong? Had Zolner simply turned around and fled to Europe? When he saw Ambrose Lightship tossed violently on the storm-churned ocean, he circled back. But in the entire outer harbor he saw only one moving vessel braving the storm. Nearing the Narrows, it was, incredibly, a little rumrunner stacked with crates of whisky and sheeted in spray as it pitched and rolled.

Asa tapped Bell's arm. He was scanning the water ahead through the binoculars. Above the Narrows, already into the Upper Bay, less than six miles from the Battery at the tip of Manhattan, a tanker was plowing toward the city. The Flying Yacht raced after it, and Bell soon recognized the *Sandra T. Congdon* by the tall funnel soaring from the back of her hull, her sturdy wheelhouse forward of center, her straight bow, and her graceful fantail stern. The cannon on her foredeck cinched it. Closer, he saw her crew frantically rowing away in the lifeboat. She was, indeed, a floating firebomb.

"Asa. Lash those grenades together in bundles of four."

"Are we going to bomb him?"

"*You* are going to bomb those cannon shells on the foredeck. I'm going to fly the plane. See that knob on the end of the stick? That's the detonator. Pull that knob when I tell you and drop it over the side fast as you can."

He banked into a tight circle, straightened up behind the ship, and descended. The flying boat caught up quickly. Asa stood up in the cockpit so he could reach over the side windows. Bell soared fifty feet above the stack and over the wheelhouse, his Blériot wheel in constant motion as he tried to counteract the buffeting wind.

"Now!"

Thirty feet over the foredeck, they couldn't miss. The bundled stick grenades landed on the cannon. They bounced onto the stacked cannon shells. But before they detonated, they skittered away and exploded with a harmless flash on the steel deck.

Bell circled for another try.

Zolner was ready with his Lewis gun. As Bell caught up with the tanker again, he flew into streaks of blue smoke. Incendiary bullets tore through his wing. Each left a trail of fire. Flames wrapped the wing.

"Seat belt, Asa, we have to land."

"How can we stop him if we land?"

"Watch me."

The wind, Bell thought, was blowing behind the ship, in line with her course up the channel, which would not make a dicey maneuver any easier. But slowing the plane by landing into the wind was not an option. Fanned by the slipstream, the fire enveloped the entire wing and tumbled into the passenger cabin directly behind the cockpit. He had no choice but to come down fast and hard.

Old Donald Darbee stopped his oyster boat in the middle of his hurricane whisky run to see what happened next. He and little Robin had noticed the tanker proceeding up the channel when no one in his right mind but a rumrunner was out. Then the tanker's crew lowered a boat and rowed away. But the ship kept going. Then Isaac Bell's airplane, which he recognized because it was identical to the Newport Flying Service planes but didn't have that name written on it, swooped out of the storm and dropped a bomb on the tanker.

That didn't do a thing to it. Then the

tanker shot blue tracer bullets at Bell. And now Bell's plane was falling out of the sky with its wings on fire.

"When he hits the water," he told Robin, "we'll pick up the pieces."

"He won't hit the water," said the little girl. "He'll hit the ship."

Sharp-eyed Robin was right. Bell's plane was flying behind the ship, catching up at forty knots to the tanker's twelve. At the last second, it dodged the funnel and smacked down on the middle of the ship, slid along the flat deck between the funnel and the house in a shower of sparks, and banged to a stop against a ventilator.

"That can't have done Mr. Bell any good," Darbee said to Robin. "Might as well head home."

"Let's wait," said Robin.

"What for?"

"It isn't over."

"Out!"

Bell grabbed the Thompson .45 in one hand and Asa with the other. He half helped, half threw the boy over the side, hooked a bundle of stick grenades on his belt, and jumped down beside him. "Run before it blows."

"It will blow up the ship."

"That's what I'm hoping."

They ran toward the house and took cover around the front of it.

Bell's flying boat exploded. Wings, tail, floats, most of the passenger cabin, and the burning fuel tank flew into the wind and fell in the harbor. The few parts still smoldering on the steel deck were drenched by the rain. The ship, which was pounding ahead at twelve knots, and its flammable cargo, seemed immune. Bell had one hope left.

He drew his Browning pistol and shoved it into Asa's hand. "Stay here. Take this. Shoot anybody who tries to follow me."

Detonating the three-inch shells stacked around the cannon would blow the bow off the ship and stop her dead. He had failed to do it from the safety of the air. Here on the ship, the trick would be to do it without blowing himself up, too. Bell ran toward the cannon on the foredeck. Could he throw a grenade accurately enough to detonate the shells yet from far enough to escape with his life? He was reaching for one on his belt when he heard a shot behind him.

Bell whirled around. Asa had fallen to the deck.

A shadow swooped out of the rain like a giant bird. In the corner of his vision Bell saw a wet rope glistening. He saw Marat Zolner's face — lips drawn with effort, eyes eerily calm. He saw a rubber-soled boot. The boot was flying at his face. Bell slewed aside. It slammed into his chest, knocked the Thompson out of his hands, and threw him halfway across the ship.

Bell tucked his shoulder, rolled, and sprang to his feet in a fighting crouch.

He was amazed to see the tall, lithe Russian so near, he could almost touch him.

Zolner was holding the rope. It was tied to the front rail on top of the wheelhouse, and Bell saw that he had jumped from the back to swing three stories to the deck.

"Simple physics, Bell. What are you doing on my ship?"

"Arresting a hero."

"You've spoken with Fern." Zolner let go of the rope.

Isaac Bell attacked, throwing lightning jabs and a hard left hook. He landed all three punches. Zolner shrugged them off. Bell threw two more with the same lack of effect. The man was so fast, it was like punching quicksilver.

Bell had twenty pounds on him, a huge advantage. He used it, wading in, punching hard. Ducking and weaving with incredible speed, Zolner pulled a long-handled blackjack from a back pocket and swung it. The blow was remarkable for its power and its accuracy, and Isaac Bell realized, as pain blazed through his elbow, that Zolner had hit him exactly where he intended to. His arm hung limply, coursing like fire, useless.

Zolner smiled. "That should even things up." He shifted the blackjack from one hand to the other, left to right, right to left, fast as a juggler. The weapon was a blur and suddenly, in a burst of synchronized movement, it jumped at Bell's face.

43

The blackjack whistled through the air. It came from Bell's left and Bell could not lift his left arm high enough to block the bone-crushing blow. He struggled to raise it anyway. Otherwise, he hardly moved.

The blackjack grazed his nose.

Bell had moved just enough to let the blackjack pass and draw Zolner's arm across his torso. He concentrated one hundred seventy-five pounds of bone and muscle to crash a low right cross straight into Zolner's rib cage. His reward was a soft crack of bone and a gasp.

The Comintern agent staggered.

Bell moved to finish him off.

Zolner was too fast and too strong. The body blow should have doubled him up. But before Bell could retract his right fist and cock it for another blow, Zolner charged with sudden fury, kicking, punching, swinging his blackjack. Another strike against

Bell's elbow took his breath away. They grappled. Zolner broke loose.

Bell swiped blood out of his eyes, vaguely aware that the blackjack had torn his brow. He felt as if the tanker's deck was shaking under his feet.

Zolner circled. Hunched, favoring his side, he said, "None of this would have happened if your precious boss hadn't blundered into a bullet."

"*Three* bullets." Bell went straight at him.

Zolner sidestepped and jerked his thumb in the direction where Asa had fallen on the deck. "Is your vengeance worth it? The boy is dead. Your boss is crippled. And I'll go home a hero."

Bell stopped in his tracks.

He's outfoxed me at nearly every turn, he thought. He's outfoxing me now, but I don't know how. Bell knew he was not thinking clearly. He was exhausted after two days in the storm. His arm was on fire. Something was going on that he didn't understand.

Suddenly, it struck Bell why the deck was shaking.

The tall detective smiled. "The tanker is moving. You've got a man in the engine room and a helmsman steering. And I'm along for the ride because you told Fern you'll make me sorry."

"The boy is dead," Zolner repeated.

Bell looked toward Asa, sprawled where he had left him at the back of the wheelhouse. He glanced over his shoulder at the deck cannon. Then he swept the foredeck with probing eyes.

"You're a brilliant liar. But I heard only one shot from my gun. Asa shot at you and missed you. You slugged him as you swung past. And now you are stalling me while your fireship steams on."

Bell turned as if to run to Asa. Zolner whirled to intercept him.

Bell spun the other way, darted across the ship, and scooped up the Thompson that Zolner had kicked out of his hands. By force of will, he closed his left hand around the forward grip, braced it against his body, and pulled the trigger. The recoil whipped it out of his weakened hand. All but the first bullet sprayed into the sky. The first struck its target.

Bell dived for cover.

A three-inch cannon shell exploded like thunder. A second detonated, and they all went off with a force that bucked the ship from end to end and lifted him five feet off the deck and dropped him like a sack of coal. He scrambled to his feet and ran for Asa. Zolner got there ahead of him. Bell pegged a wild shot that passed close to Zolner's head. Zolner ducked. Bell slammed him out of his way, heaved Asa Somers over his right shoulder, ran to the side of the ship, and jumped.

He seemed to fall forever before they splashed into the water.

It closed over his head. He kicked as hard as he could to push the boy to the surface. Asa struggled. The cold water had revived him.

"Swim!" Bell roared at him. "Swim!" And the apprentice obeyed.

The hull was rushing past. Explosion after explosion shook the ship.

Jagged chunks of wood, steel rails, and burning canvas rained into the water around them. Ash fell like snow, oil splashed. Bell kicked his feet and paddled with his one good arm. The ship was past them now, drawing away, still hurtling toward the city. It disappeared into the murk of rain and fog. Bell thought all was lost. But just when it seemed that nothing could stop the fireship from steaming to Wall Street, a column of fire evaporated the rain and fog. Roaring from the ruptured hold, pluming into the sky, the fiercely burning alcohol blazed stark light on the Comintern's tanker. It was sinking alone in the middle of the bay.

Isaac Bell saw Marat Zolner climbing a ladder up the back of the wheelhouse, racing the fires. He reached the flying bridge and stood for a long moment, a graceful shadow against the flames.

The wind bent the pillar of fire. An explosion blew the ship's bow apart. Water rushed in and she settled rapidly to the bottom of the channel, disappearing except for the top of her tall funnel and a cloud of steam.

"Wow!" said Asa. He had a huge bruise over his eye.

"Think you can swim to shore?"

Brooklyn seemed closest. Bell tried an abbreviated backstroke with one arm. Before they got a hundred yards, a little boat with a big engine pulled alongside, and Isaac Bell looked up into the wrinkled face of Ed Tobin's uncle Donny Darbee.

"I was coming by with a load of oysters," he said. "Thought you could use a lift."

"In return for which," said Bell, "you want me to talk your so-called oysters past the cops."

"That was Robin's idea. She thinks we'll get top dollar in Manhattan."

A taxi pulled up to the St. Regis Hotel.

Isaac Bell stepped out, soaking wet, his mustache singed, his face and hair glazed

531

with ash and salt and grease and blood. Asa Somers staggered after him in dripping rags.

The doorman waved them away. Burly house detectives blocked the steps.

"Buzz my wife," said Bell. "Tell her I'm coming up."

"Wife? Who's your wife?"

"Mrs. Isaac Bell."

"It's Himself!"

The house detectives escorted them solicitously to the elevator. Bell stopped dead when he saw a newspaper.

MAMMOTH HURRICANE PUMMELS SEABOARD
NEW YORK SPARED WHEN STORM SHIFTS
EAST
STEAM YACHT FOUNDERS OFF BERMUDA
HEIRESS FEARED DROWNED

Bad luck? Or divine retribution? It seemed, Bell thought, harsh punishment for falling in with the wrong crowd.

"Poor Fern," said Asa. "She was so nice."

"I'm not sure Fern would like to be remembered as 'nice.' "

"Fräulein Grandzau liked her."

"So did I," said Bell. "I've always liked characters."

Bell led Asa down the carpeted hall to

Marion's door.

He was suddenly aware that every bone and muscle ached. His left arm throbbed like a burning stick. He could feel the sea pounding, as if he had never left the boat, and could hear the Libertys roaring in his ears.

"Almost home, Asa."

He squared his shoulders and knocked.

A peephole opened. A beautiful sea-coral-green eye peered through it and grew wide.

Bell grinned. "Joe sent me."

Marion flung open the door. "You're all right!"

"Tip-top."

She threw her arms around him.

"Look out, you'll get dirty."

"I don't care . . . Who's this? . . . Oh, you must be the brave Asa who saved Joe. Come in. Come in, both of you."

Pauline was behind her, bright and perfumed in a thick terry robe.

"Asa, are you all right?"

Asa swayed and caught himself on the doorknob. "Yes, ma'am. Tip-top."

"Go take a bath." She pointed down the hall. "There's a robe on the hook."

Joseph Van Dorn was waiting in a wicker wheelchair. Dorothy stood beside him, her eyes at peace.

"You look like hell," he greeted Bell in a strong voice.

"You look better," said Bell. "Much improved."

"Hospital sprung me. That's something." Van Dorn hauled himself to his feet, steadied himself on the arm of the wheelchair, and reached for Bell's hand. "Well done, Isaac. Well done. I don't know how to thank you."

"Wait until you get the bill for my airplane."

"Airplane?"

"And you'll want a new bow and motors for the agency express cruiser. Don't worry, you can afford it. Texas Walt is raking it in hand over fist out in Detroit."

"He's still in business?"

"At least until we get the Coast Guard contract back."

Bell turned to Pauline. "Is Ed O.K.?"

"Ed's fine. They stitched him up. It was a vein, not an artery . . . Isaac, I must speak with you."

"What's up?"

"Marion has given me a wonderful idea."

Bell glanced at Marion. "She's good at them."

"I want to take young Asa for my apprentice."

"To Germany?"

"With his parents' permission, of course."

"I believe he's an orphan."

"All the better. So am I. Isaac, make it so."

The chief investigator of the Van Dorn Detective Agency turned to its founder.

Van Dorn said, "Your call."

Bell locked eyes with Pauline and shared a private smile. "Based on how your apprentice handled a machine gun this afternoon, you might consider allowing him to carry a small pistol."

"All in good time," said Pauline. "Thank you, Isaac. And thank you, Marion."

Van Dorn eased himself back down into his wheelchair and rolled toward the door. "We're shoving off. Dorothy wants me home in bed."

They agreed to talk in the morning. "Afternoon," Marion corrected them. "Late afternoon."

A freshly scrubbed Asa Somers appeared in a bathrobe with Band-Aids plastered on his brow. Pauline spoke quietly to him and they headed out the door.

"Alone at last," said Marion. "Is your arm all right? You're favoring it."

"Just a little sore. Where are they going in

bathrobes?"

"I got them a room upstairs."

"One room?"

"The hotel's packed because of the storm. It has twin beds, I think," she added briskly. "They'll work it out."

"Good idea."

"Now, what about you?" Marion asked. "What would you like?"

"I could use a drink."

Marion said, "I'll join you."

"And a hot bath."

"I'll join you."

ABOUT THE AUTHORS

Clive Cussler is the author or coauthor of more than fifty previous books in five best-selling series, including Dirk Pitt®, NUMA® Files, Oregon Files, Isaac Bell, and Fargo. His most recent *New York Times*–bestselling novels are *The Storm, The Tombs,* and *Poseidon's Arrow.* His nonfiction works include *Built for Adventure: The Classic Automobiles of Clive Cussler and Dirk Pitt,* plus *The Sea Hunters* and *The Sea Hunters II*; these describe the true adventures of the real NUMA, which, led by Cussler, searches for lost ships of historic significance. With his crew of volunteers, Cussler has discovered more than sixty ships, including the long-lost Confederate ship *Hunley*. He lives in Arizona.

Justin Scott's novels include *The Shipkiller* and *Normandie Triangle*; the Ben Abbott detective series; and modern sea thrillers published under the pen name Paul Garrison. The coauthor with Clive Cussler of five previous Isaac Bell novels, he lives in Connecticut.